DISSECTION OF A MURDER

JO MURRAY

DISSECTION OF A MURDER

MACMILLAN

First published 2026 by Macmillan
an imprint of Pan Macmillan
The Smithson, 6 Briset Street, London EC1M 5NR
EU representative: Macmillan Publishers Ireland Ltd, 1st Floor,
The Liffey Trust Centre, 117–126 Sheriff Street Upper,
Dublin 1 D01 YC43
Associated companies throughout the world

ISBN 978-1-0350-7268-2 HB
ISBN 978-1-0350-7269-9 TPB

Copyright © Jo Murray 2026

The right of Jo Murray to be identified as the
author of this work has been asserted in accordance
with the Copyright, Designs and Patents Act 1988.

All rights reserved. No part of this publication may be reproduced,
stored in a retrieval system, or transmitted, in any form, or by any means
(including, without limitation, electronic, mechanical, photocopying, recording
or otherwise) without the prior written permission of the publisher.

Pan Macmillan does not have any control over, or any responsibility for,
any author or third-party websites (including, without limitation, URLs,
emails and QR codes) referred to in or on this book.

1 3 5 7 9 8 6 4 2

A CIP catalogue record for this book is available from the British Library.

Typeset in Goudy Std by Palimpsest Book Production Ltd, Falkirk, Stirlingshire
Printed and bound in the UK using 100% Renewable Electricity
by CPI Group (UK) Ltd

This book is sold subject to the condition that it shall not, by way of
trade or otherwise, be lent, hired out, or otherwise circulated without
the publisher's prior consent in any form of binding or cover other than
that in which it is published and without a similar condition including this
condition being imposed on the subsequent purchaser. The publisher does not
authorize the use or reproduction of any part of this book in any manner
for the purpose of training artificial intelligence technologies or systems.
The publisher expressly reserves this book from the Text and Data Mining
exception in accordance with Article 4(3) of the European Union
Digital Single Market Directive 2019/790.

Visit **www.panmacmillan.com** to read more about
all our books and to buy them.

For Lynette

Murder
The offence of murder is committed when a person of sound mind and discretion unlawfully kills any reasonable creature in being under the King's Peace with intent to kill or cause grievous bodily harm.

The Jury
A jury is made up of twelve people who are chosen at random to hear evidence and decide if the accused is guilty or not guilty. The prosecution must prove the defendant has committed the offence beyond reasonable doubt; a defendant does not have to prove his or her innocence. A defendant is innocent until proven guilty. Upon hearing all the evidence in a case, the jury retires to consider its verdict. A defendant may usually only be found guilty or not guilty (acquitted) when all twelve jurors unanimously agree.

Following a prolonged period of deliberation, a judge may accept a majority verdict. When this happens, combinations of 11–1 or 10–2 are acceptable.

Solicitors
Solicitors provide legal advice in different areas of law. They represent clients in the lower criminal courts and hire ('instruct') barristers for serious cases. Solicitors prepare paperwork, gather evidence, and assist the barrister.

Barristers

Barristers are specialist legal advisers and courtroom advocates. They advise clients on the strengths and weaknesses of their case and represent them in court. Some barristers act on behalf of the Crown Prosecution Service (CPS). They wear wigs and robes.

Most barristers practise from a set of chambers; this building is their professional home. Because they are self-employed, a barrister might prosecute in a case defended by a colleague from the same chambers.

The bridge between law school and practice is called 'pupillage': a twelve-month training period within chambers where a student ('pupil') is assigned to a mentor ('pupil supervisor', previously known as 'pupilmaster'). King's Counsel (KC) or 'silks' are elite barristers appointed by the King.

All barristers are subject to the Bar Standards Board Code of Conduct, a regulatory body that imposes the highest standards of ethics upon all advocates. Integrity, honesty, and confidentiality are at the foundation of every honourable barrister.

This is how the criminal trial system works in England and Wales.

But not always . . .

Prologue

The Accused

WHAT IS JUSTICE? That's the question I've asked myself, repeatedly, over the past eight days.

Is it following the law to the letter? Or is it ensuring *real* justice is carried out, even if it means slightly bending the rules? Most people never need to think about it.

Would I class myself as a rebel? Yes, I suppose I would. A rulebreaker? No.

I know which rules I can twist without getting caught. But it's only ever been for the greater good. Selling this concept to a jury, however, is another matter. What they need to see isn't necessarily the 'truth', but whatever *appears* just. You think those are the same things, don't you? They're not. Especially in this case.

I know from experience that if jury members turn around to look at you when they enter the courtroom to deliver their verdict, you're about to be acquitted. If they don't, they're going to find you guilty.

It makes sense, I suppose. You wouldn't want to look directly into the eyes of someone you're about to send to prison.

A killer.

I've studied them all, sitting in the jury box to my left. Seven men and five women. Together, twelve ordinary members of society will decide my fate, having listened to the gruesome evidence that has stained the air of Court 1 with its squeaky spring benches and windowless walls.

It's a modern courtroom, not like the old ones you see on TV. I imagine it was designed to feel spacious, going by the abnormally high ceilings and soft grey panelling, but, at the end of the day, it's still a room where people are forced to pay for their sins under the glare of fluorescent strip lights.

The prosecutor stands to address the jury for what will be his closing speech. He's one of those aggressive lawyer types – cocky, full of himself. Brash and arrogant. He kept me in the witness box for an entire day during cross-examination and acted as if he'd already won. There was no doubt in his mind that the evidence he placed before the jury was strong enough to convict me. He stood, leaning against the bench, arms folded as he fired questions like a machine gun. The temptation to punch someone in the face has never been stronger. I couldn't do that, though. I couldn't show any signs of anger whatsoever because, to the ordinary people watching, aggression would indicate I'm a murderer.

My barrister is the prosecutor's opposite. She is quiet but firm, clever with her tactics and cool under pressure. Personable. I've a feeling the jurors have warmed to her. I hope they have.

'Ladies and gentlemen,' the prosecutor says in a patronizing tone, gripping the lectern for additional gravitas. 'You've now heard all the evidence in this case, and it is time for you to reach your verdict. The defendant before you is accused of murdering Anton Smythe, a fifty-six-year-old Crown Court judge. It is alleged that on Friday, 6 September 2024, he was killed by the defendant after suffering a fatal blow to the head.'

'Now,' he goes on, adopting the sinister tone he's used

throughout this spectacle. 'This trial has not been conducted free of drama. You will recall the defendant's evidence was "colourful", to say the least.'

Sitting in the dock, my eyes flick towards the jury. The man in the front row, who barely looks old enough to vote – I've named him 'Young Hannibal Lecter' – raises his eyebrows in a way he obviously wants me to see. 'Sad Susan' – who seems about to burst into tears any second – glances over to see my reaction. She looks very stressed. *I know how you feel, love.* I don't move an inch – it's not like I can smile at her.

'If this trial has taught you anything, ladies and gentlemen, it's that not everything is as it seems. One thing you *can* be sure of, however, is that this defendant is not trustworthy. The Crown rejects the preposterous tale offered by the accused. It is one of a fantasist. One of a liar. One of a killer. And in due course, I will invite you to return a guilty verdict.'

I remain silent as he bangs the nails even further into my coffin. While he runs through the evidence against me, I watch the jurors stare at him intently. The judge's eyes scan the packed courtroom. Each day has been busier than the last. They're all waiting to see: guilty or not guilty?

In a case like this, a jury starts not with a presumption of innocence, as they should, but with a presumption of guilt. The evidence against me is damning. The plan was always to sow a tiny seed of doubt in their heads, then water it and watch it grow.

Twelve jurors. Even if the majority are against me, all we have to do is plant enough doubt in at least three of their heads and they can't convict me.

Three. That's it.

Did it work? I'll find out soon enough.

The official nature of everything, rehashed and retold in this clinical setting, unsettles me as I sit imprisoned within the dock at the back of the courtroom.

As the prosecutor outlines the main pieces of evidence that ended Anton Smythe's life – which have led to my ruin – snapshots of that night flash through my head like a strobe light.

I see his body lying on the floor; you wouldn't have even known he was hours from death if it weren't for the delicate yet fatal trickle of blood coming out of his nose.

I knew then that everything would change. That I'd end up here.

My eyes scanned the room that night – 'the crime scene' – knowing every inch of it would be investigated. I'd been in the system long enough to know this was the calm before the storm. Everything I did from that second onwards would be scrutinized. Next time I saw the injuries, they would be in photos, only everything would look brighter because of the flash from the scenes-of-crime officer's camera. Rulers would be placed next to inanimate objects and take on names like 'the murder weapon'.

I thought I'd been so careful.

My downfall was the phone.

But what if all the evidence points towards you and it was more complicated than it seems? Are we just to accept you're either the victim or the killer and there's nothing in between?

That is not real justice.

The prosecution can tell whatever story they want, but I know what really happened. Don't get me wrong – it all got completely out of hand. When I think about the lies I've told, the people I've involved, the lives I've destroyed, I despise myself. But a life sentence for this wouldn't be justice.

I killed him, yes. But it wasn't my fault. I had to do it.

I never had a choice.

Part One

The Arrest

A jury consists of twelve persons chosen
to decide who has the better lawyer.

Robert Frost

I

Leila

Monday, 9 September 2024
126 days before trial

THE PARTY HAS already started by the time I arrive back at chambers.

Well, I say party; 'sombre gathering' is a more accurate description, given the circumstances of the last seventy-two hours. I don't understand why he didn't cancel it. Then again, coming together in times of crisis is something the Bar is incredibly good at.

Besides, Chester Vernon would never allow the murder of a Crown Court judge to come between him and a good drink.

The sound of low-volume chatter spills out of the chambers lounge into the corridor. It's because of Chester – our illustrious, wildly eccentric, wine-loving head of chambers – that we're known for boozy bashes. Any day ending in a 'y' has been used as a reason to party in the past. Today, though, is his fifty-ninth birthday. To have your absence noted would be professional suicide, and he's not the kind of man you want to make an enemy of. While not technically our 'boss' – barristers are self-employed – he is our elected, professional leader. What he says, goes. Every set of chambers has one.

'Chambers' is a fancy word for 'offices', but you're not allowed to call it that. Just another part of the tradition that comes with this job. I did actually call it an office once, during pupillage, and heads turned. I never did it again.

I scurry into one of the conference rooms. Well, as quickly as you *can* scurry while pulling a wheely suitcase behind you that contains a wig, robes, and a load of heavy books. Even after all these years, it still gets caught on chairs, tables, and, on one unfortunate occasion, a condom display in Boots.

'Leila!'

Poking my head out of the door, I see Chester beckoning me towards the lounge in the arrogant way a mafia boss might summon a waiter. God, I can't be bothered with this tonight. I won't be allowed to leave until I've had at least three glasses of wine. My icy blonde hair hangs down my back, untamed and wet from the rain. After five hours under a horsehair wig, it's not looking slick. The last thing I want to do is parade myself in front of some of the most important people in the legal profession like a kind of bedraggled peacock.

'Five minutes, Chester!' I yell back, furious with myself. I should have gone straight home.

No sooner do I close the door than it's thrown wide open again. I can tell by the way it's done that it's Jim, our senior clerk. He's always in a rush to get somewhere. Jim runs at least four marathons a year and is in his late fifties but looks younger because all he eats is fruit and lean meats – and he likes to tell you about it.

'Been waiting for you to get back. You going in?' he asks, nodding towards the lounge. In his hand he's clutching a thin brief, held together by pink tape.

Jim is responsible for getting cases in and distributing them to the barristers he thinks will be the best fit. Maintaining good relationships with clerks is vital if you want a healthy career. Thankfully, I get on with mine.

'Not really in the mood,' I tell him. After a long day in court defending a man accused of sexually assaulting his daughter, I have a banging headache.

'Great result today.' He smiles, alluding to the acquittal I secured for my client. 'Already had the solicitor on, singing your praises.'

'Really?'

'Said you were hypnotic to watch.'

'Hypnotic?' I repeat, delighted. 'I've never been called that before.'

Jim knows how excited I am to hear this. It's been so difficult to carve out a name for myself.

'And . . .' he says, pausing for dramatic effect, leaning against the oak bookshelves that spread across the wall, 'you've received a quote in the Legal 500.'

'Oh my god. Are you joking?' I squeal, before immediately clawing it back and composing myself.

Jim loves it when one of his barristers makes it into the Legal 500. It's a professional guide for clients that ranks sets of chambers. If you impress the right people, they single you out with a glitzy quote that can do wonders for your career. At thirty-six years old, this is a long time coming, given I've been a criminal barrister for thirteen years.

'What does it say?' I ask, urgently.

Peeling a neon pink sticker from the brief in his hand, he peers through the glasses perched on the end of his nose. His short, silver-white hair sticks up at peculiar angles.

> 'Leila Reynolds executes intuitive style and is an exceptional jury advocate. She approaches cases with a forensic eye and has a very clever way of interpreting evidence. Future bright star and KC in the making.'

It feels surreal, hearing those words describe me. Being professionally recognized is so important and this is the highest form of it.

'Who nominated me?'

He knows why I'm asking.

'I don't know,' he replies, fiddling with an elastic band from his trouser pocket.

'Can you find out?'

'I can try, but it's not always possible,' he says sternly, letting me know he will not be taking my request any further. 'This is fantastic news, Leila. Take it for what it is. The opportunities it'll send your way. You're an exceptional advocate – I'm hearing great things. Someone has obviously recognized that.'

He normally calls me Miss Reynolds, only ever calls me Leila when he's gone into 'dad mode', which I never really mind. Despite the fact that Jim is a clerk, I have more in common with him than the other barristers. We both come from working-class backgrounds around Newcastle. He has a thick Geordie accent, similar to mine. I've been advised to 'water it down' over the years, but I refuse to get rid of it. I'm fiercely proud of my roots and have always found clients and jurors relate to me more than my privileged colleagues because of it.

'You're right.' I smile at him. 'I'm grateful.'

'Anyway, I've got a new brief for you. Came in an hour ago. Client was very specific that he wanted you and nobody else.'

He holds the brief out towards me, and I take it.

IN THE CROWN COURT AT NEWCASTLE
R v Millman.

That's all it says on the front. When you've represented as many people as I have, most of the names blend together. Some spark recognition, but you can't connect them to a face. Others, you don't forget.

Like this one.

'Are you going to bloody look at it, or what?' Jim asks. I pop the bow on the ribbon and open the brief. A chill radiates through my body when I see the full name.

Both of them. On the *same* indictment.

I read the instructions from the solicitor:

PARTICULARS OF OFFENCE:

On Friday, 6 September 2024, JACK MILLMAN allegedly murdered ANTON SMYTHE. He gave a NO-COMMENT interview and appeared at Durham Magistrates' Court on Monday, 9 September for a first hearing. Proceedings will be transferred to Newcastle Crown Court and counsel is instructed to defend hereafter.

There's hardly anything to the brief, but there wouldn't be at this stage. It's flimsy, fewer than ten pages.

The murder of His Honour Judge Smythe on Friday night sent shockwaves through the legal community. News spread on Saturday afternoon after his wife told close friends, and information like that doesn't remain secret for long.

At first, people speculated it must have been a tragic 'wrong place, wrong time' type of incident, but as more details emerged, it seemed increasingly unlikely.

'Leila?'

I realize I'm staring at the paper and that my heart rate has increased. I'm used to the adrenalin that comes with the job, but this is on another level.

'You want me to *lead* a murder trial?' I ask. The words sound ridiculous coming out of my mouth. I feel embarrassed saying them. 'I can't. I'm not a KC. I've never gone near a murder before. I'll have to return it. I'm not doing it.'

'Don't freak out,' Jim says, calmly, as if he were talking to a toddler who's just realized they were riding a bike without stabilizers.

'I can't just defend a murder trial. And not *this* one! The murder of a judge! If it goes wrong, I'll look completely incompetent, and I've no chance of winning. Why do I have to do it?'

'Because Jack Millman specifically asked for you to represent him. Cab-rank rule, Miss Reynolds – if a client wants you to represent them, you can't turn them down unless you're not qualified for the case. I've spoken to Chester; he thinks you are.'

'Does he?' I frown but am secretly delighted Chester believes I can pull off something like this.

'I understand why you're worried,' Jim says in his 'dad voice'. 'The last time you represented him was . . . problematic.'

As understatements go, it's a big one. I represented Jack Millman five years ago for assault, and that case made me question everything – the law, the system, whether I should even do this any more.

'But you're more experienced now,' he goes on. 'And you must have done something right because he wants you again. I thought you'd be pleased. Big, juicy case. Something like this will throw you into the legal stratosphere. You heard the quote: "future KC". You could be, after this.'

'It'll be messy,' I tell him. 'I can feel it.'

'Well, he also "doesn't trust barristers" apparently, just to add that to the mix.'

'Sounds like him.' I sigh. 'Who's the solicitor?'

'Jessops. Davina called me about it this afternoon. She's content for you to defend.'

This, in itself, is a red flag.

Jessop Solicitors is the biggest firm in Durham. Run by solicitor husband-and-wife team David and Davina Jessop; they get all the big, dubious cases, and always advise their clients to answer no comment in interview. If you're represented by them, there's always more to the story.

'OK, so which barrister is prosecuting it?'

He attempts to phrase something several times before coming out with 'That's the other tiny little thing I need to mention.'

I know exactly what he's going to say.

'Tell me this is a joke, Jim.'

He doesn't reply. He screws up his face, pretending to be sorry, but – make no mistake – he's relishing the drama.

'Jim,' I say, perching on the edge of the desk and pushing my fingers hard into my temples. 'Please don't tell me my first murder trial is going to be prosecuted by Julian. He taught me everything I know.'

Not Julian, *please* not Julian. My pupilmaster, the best barrister in chambers, the one who trained me, nurtured me. The most feared prosecutor on our circuit.

And my husband.

2

Leila

I'VE ALWAYS BEEN able to spot him in a crowd, ever since my first day as a pupil thirteen years ago. I was a fresh-faced twenty-three-year-old who knew everything about the law and nothing about life. Julian Kesler showed me how to merge the two. When Innovation Chambers in Durham offered me pupillage straight out of law school, I immediately went to their website and looked up my pupilmaster, as they used to be called. They've since been renamed the less archaic and BDSM-sounding 'pupil supervisor', but I can't ditch the habit of using it.

I remember the excitement I felt, hearing he was going to be my guide over the next twelve months. Pupillage is the intense practical training period you must complete before becoming a qualified barrister, when you're assigned to work closely with a senior member of chambers during the first six months. In the second six months, you're given your own clients, but your pupilmaster shapes you into the barrister you become. The bond you form is long-lasting and special.

I spent hours searching the internet for information about Julian Kesler. I wanted to know everything about him; this was the man who would teach me how to be a brilliant advocate, construct crushing cross-examinations, deliver the most persuasive closing speeches.

Julian showed me how to do it all.

He's talking in hushed tones to a couple of other barristers in the corner of the attic lounge. Rain lashes down the sloped windows behind him. Like most buildings in Durham, ours is beautifully old and we're lucky to call it our professional home.

I cross the room towards him. 'Can I have a word?' I whisper. It's unusual to see him loitering in the corner at an event like this. Julian more often roams around the floor, making himself known to people.

He doesn't answer, just subtly excuses himself in the very classy, elegant manner he inhabits, which I've come to recognize over the years. Even after a full day in court, he retains the handsome features that have given him so many privileges: groomed dark hair with the slightest wild kink and silver streak shining through. Large eyes, the colour of dark ale. He has this ability to make you feel you're the only person in the room. He follows me away from the throng.

'You're panicking already, aren't you? You're doing the eye thing.'

Julian always says that my left eye does this weird twitchy thing when I'm really stressed out.

'Of course I'm panicking!'

I fully appreciate that from this moment on, Julian and I are professional opponents. I really ought to be holding my cards closer to my chest in terms of how nervous I feel, but this situation has gripped me by the throat. I can't breathe.

'Just think of it as any other case,' he says, taking a sip of his warm wine. 'But against me.'

'That's the problem. You've got a good eleven years' more experience. And you're King's Counsel. What if I mess up?'

He slides his hand around my waist, giving it a little squeeze. 'You'll be fantastic. This is your chance to shine.'

'Fine for you to say. You've got the easier job. Who's ever acquitted of murder?'

'There you go. Less pressure.' He smiles, giving me a casual, reassuring wink. Now that he's King's Counsel, he really only does murder cases – he could do them in his sleep and still win. 'When they called to ask if I'd prosecute, I obviously jumped at the chance.'

'You knew I was defending when they offered it to you, and you still said yes?'

'I'd have been mad to pass it up. Such a prominent case. It'll elevate both of our careers, not to mention the national recognition.'

I understand the logic behind it, but this case will be challenging enough. The nation casting its glare isn't something I really want.

'I'm surprised they allowed it, given our relationship,' I tell him, more out of defiance than anything else. I'm annoyed he took on the case, but I'm not surprised. Julian would have been the Crown Prosecution Service's first choice. He is fierce, strong, and fearless as far as advocates go, and his conviction rate is very high. The fact he's prosecuting against his former pupil *and* younger wife will have everyone in the CPS rubbing their hands with glee. They'll see it as a clear win, and if I'm being honest with myself, Julian will see it that way, too.

As will everyone else.

'They made it very clear that, providing we act professionally and impartially, and have open and honest communication, there's no reason why we can't be opponents. I mean, it wouldn't be the first time a husband and wife have gone up against each other in court. You're not suggesting I should have turned it down, are you?'

'Of course not!' I lie. 'It's just – this is a big deal for me, and

I want to do a good job.' I know how naive I must sound. I suddenly feel like a pupil again, walking into chambers every day desperate to impress everyone, particularly him.

'Have you read the papers yet?' he enquires.

'No, I haven't had the chance . . .'

'Looks pretty damning at this early stage. Don't think he's got a defence, so it probably won't even be a trial. I imagine an early guilty plea. You're worrying over nothing.'

After Julian hands me a glass of wine to calm me down, I try to act normal and chat with members of chambers, but all I can think of is the case. Colleagues insist on coming over to 'congratulate' me on securing 'the brief of a lifetime', saying Julian and I will be 'fighting it out to the death', as if we're starring in a Marvel film.

'Well done, Britney!' slurs Nigel, a high-functioning alcoholic who still somehow manages to run a very successful criminal practice. 'Britney' is my chambers nickname and was given to me in my first week. Everybody gets one. The men are assigned names pertaining to a variation of their surname; Julian's is simply 'Kes'. Ridiculous. It's different for women; we tend to be named after someone we vaguely resemble. When I joined chambers, I had long, blonde hair that contrasted with my big, brown eyes, so I was initiated as 'Britney Spears'. The only people who don't call me this are Jim, Julian, and Chester.

People crowd around Julian and me, clamouring for the tiniest morsel of inside info. As always, there are even some veiled suggestions that I got the case because of him.

'Wow! Very unusual for someone so *junior* to receive such a case. Unheard of. You must have made the right connections!' says Ophelia (aka 'Legally Brunette'), daughter of a High Court judge, who scraped a pass at law school and clearly doesn't understand what nepotism – or irony – is.

I know what they're getting at. It's the same thing they're always getting at – that I only get good cases because of my husband. Because when you marry a KC, that gives you a leg-up. You're suddenly 'someone'.

'Got to hand it to him,' Simon bellows, thinking I can't hear, clutching a glass of red wine like his life depends on it. 'Kes has played this one well. Get his younger, inexperienced wife to defend the trial of the decade. Guaranteed a win!'

Roars of laughter follow.

Brilliant.

I've always been surprised by the brutality of Bar humour. Barristers don't hold back. You need a thick skin and absolutely cannot complain, otherwise you'll be seen as weak and told to lighten up.

I consider butting in and saying, 'I was asked for *specifically*,' but I don't. It wouldn't make a difference. They don't want the truth; they want gossip and drama. They thrive on it.

You need to know how to play the game.

I landed the case they all want. The murder of a judge is career-defining. They don't think I deserve it. So, the only way to win the game now is to prove them wrong.

Somehow.

'Apparently, he was killed at the defendant's flat, which is *above* the club . . .'

'Who's the accused, anyway?'

'A doorman at Temptation. It happened late Friday night, it seems.'

'What the hell was Anton doing *there?*'

Julian and I glance at each other from opposite sides of the room as the gossip swells. He rolls his eyes and distracts himself by chatting with a group of colleagues. Neither of us should be hearing this.

But I'm not surprised they're asking questions. The place where he was killed – sorry, *allegedly killed* – is a place you wouldn't expect someone like Anton Smythe to be, yet it's exactly the kind of place you'd expect him to be.

Temptation is an elite men's club in the centre of Durham. Members only, and there's a rigorous vetting process to become one. Very few people are allowed access to the venue, so it's shrouded in mystery. Owned by millionaire Edward Sorrington, it may profess to be a decadent, luxurious venue, but the reality is it's dripping in illegal activity. A haven for dirty deals, high-class prostitutes, drugs, and money-laundering, it almost always involves the most respected people in our community, ones with teams of expensive lawyers making sure the news never gets published.

The only reason I know so much about Temptation is because of the case I did years ago when I defended – guess who?

Jack Millman.

'It'll be something to do with a pretty young girl, I'm sure . . .' Phoebe ('Shieldsy', because the men say she reminds them of Brooke Shields) says, much to the dismay of everyone listening. 'Oh, come on! We all know he had a wandering eye.'

No one responds. Instead, they gaze down at the floor, refusing to engage. But we are all thinking it.

His Honour Judge Anton Smythe must have been in his late fifties. But he was attractive, as far as older men go. He had a confident, charismatic air about him, as most male members of the judiciary do. The years had been kind to him, and he retained his good looks; intense dark eyes and a full head of silver hair. Very old-school, dapper.

It became a running joke that young female pupils could get away with anything when they were in HHJ Smythe's court, while their male counterparts would be pulled up for making the same mistake. There have been all kinds of rumours about him over the years – taking young female members of the Bar out to lunch, sitting on sofas in intimate pubs with young women.

I remind myself I shouldn't be listening to speculation, so I make my way over to the drinks table to get a glass of Coke. I don't want to be drunk tonight.

Standing beside the table, looking very out of place, is Demi, Chester's wife. There's a significant age gap between them; at thirty, Demi looks young enough to be his daughter.

'Hi, Demi, how have you been? It's been a while!'

'Leila!' she exclaims, looking like I've scared her half to death. She raises a hand to her chest in an animated way, communicating that I appeared out of nowhere. 'Congratulations! I hear you're defending the case everyone's talking about.'

Her beautifully highlighted, swishy hair hangs delicately down her back, stopping inches above her minuscule waist. As always, she's immaculately dressed. In her chic not-casual-but-not-too-dressed-up ensemble – camel wide-leg trousers and silk cream shirt – she could have stepped straight out of *Vogue*.

'I'm not sure it's a congratulatory matter, but thank you.' I attempt a half-arsed smile. 'Did you know him? Anton? I'm aware he was friends with Chester.'

'No, I didn't,' she says, shaking her head and attempting to walk away.

'Didn't you holiday with them a few years ago in France?'

'Oh, that,' she says, nodding, before taking a sip of wine. 'Yes. I didn't spend much time with him, though. How awful for his family. Will the defendant be pleading guilty? Not guilty? Might the trial "crack"? Sorry, I don't know all this legal jargon!'

She frowns and narrows her eyes when she says all this, as if she doesn't understand, but it feels insincere. Like she's trying too hard to come across as dumb. Her voice is sing-song in that way posh debutantes are. I don't think she's ever had a job in her life.

'I'm afraid I can't discuss that.' I smile at her.

'Oh, of course!' she gushes, nodding quickly and flicking her hair over her shoulder. 'Absolutely. Well, good luck! It's hard enough being a "trial widow" at the best of times, let alone when you're doing one with your own husband. When Chester is doing a murder trial, I barely see him, and he's so grouchy . . .'

'I'm not worried.' I laugh. 'In fact, we're going away this weekend for Julian's birthday. Barkenfield Lodge. Supposed to be beautiful.'

'What did you get him for his birthday? These barristers are so bloody hard to buy for. What do you get the man who has everything? I bought Chester an Omega watch last year and he said, "What the hell do I need another watch for?"' she says, barely pausing for breath. 'I love his fiery temper. It makes me laugh *so* much!'

'I've bought Julian an antique chess set. I've been teaching him how to play recently,' I tell her.

'Never had you down as a chess player, Leila,' she says, attempting to hide her shock. 'You're a woman of many talents!'

'Well, don't tell him I said this, but I just like to beat him at something.' I laugh again. 'That man does not like losing.'

'I can imagine! Anyway, lovely speaking to you!' She flashes her perfectly aligned teeth in a smile. 'I must find Chester.'

People in the tightly packed room move out of the way when they see Demi coming. She's like Moses parting the Red Sea. Men fall over themselves to accommodate the goddess she is. Women are fascinated by her energy, and it's not hard to see why – there's something captivating about her.

I remember the first time I met Demi; it must have been five years ago at a chambers function. Nobody could believe it when

Chester waltzed in with this breathtakingly beautiful blonde by his side. None of us thought it would last. He enjoyed the divorced single life too much. Two years later we all attended their wedding. They're still together, much to our surprise.

I've always found her elusive. She's one of those people who doesn't talk about herself, always switching the conversation back to you. You could be chatting to her all night and by the end of it still know nothing more about her.

She's an enigma. But men love that, don't they? Some women do it deliberately.

I watch her as she glides through the room, holding a glass of wine in her right hand, smiling, greeting everyone like the obedient, perfect wife of the host she is.

But the longer I watch, the more I notice it.

She speaks to everyone except my husband, the prosecutor in the case she just asked me about. I like watching people. It's part of the job, I suppose. You become very attuned to the behaviour of others. Being a barrister turns you into an amateur psychologist.

Often, it's the tiniest details that reveal the greatest secrets.

3

Witness X

Rule #1
Don't Get Caught

I'VE GOT MYSELF into trouble.
    Not the kind I'm used to, but *real* trouble.
If he finds out, I'm finished.
How did I allow it to get this far?
Play the game, bend the rules. Break them if you want. But never get caught. That's what he taught me.
Saturday was torture, having to pretend everything was OK, constantly refreshing social media outlets for news – any kind of news – until it appeared.

> **Man, 32, arrested on suspicion of murdering criminal judge**
>
> A man has been arrested on suspicion of murdering fifty-six-year-old Anton Smythe in Durham. Police said the thirty-two-year-old suspect was held in the central Durham area at around 11.30 p.m. on Friday night and is now in custody.

The last seven months have been a roller coaster of lies, risk, and *him*. Fast and hot. It was always going to explode at some point, but some hopeful part of me thought maybe this would be different.

How could I have been so stupid?

What's that saying: 'If you play with matches, you get burned'? Right now, the flames are licking at my skin, blazing up my body. Already, I can smell charred flesh.

My head is filled with the sound of laughter, that ugly high-pitched laugh that always made me feel small. He's saying the same thing over and over again.

'Did I not teach you *anything*? Rule #1: Don't Get Caught.'

I'd never broken the rules before. They're part of my DNA. He made sure they'd live in me like a poison, corroding me from the inside. Twelve toxic laws I've built my entire life around. He said they would keep me safe. Protect me. But now? Those lawyers are going to trawl through the last seven months of his life, and they'll find me imprinted all over it. I've made myself vulnerable.

I should have listened to him.

Nobody thinks, even when they're doing things they shouldn't, that their actions are going to be exposed in a court of law.

I can't let this happen. I'll do anything to keep my name out of the trial.

Anything.

Do you know what the worst part about all this is? The timing. You couldn't make it up. I was almost free of her. And now, after all this time, I need her help.

Only she can save him now.

4

Leila

121 days before trial

JULIAN AND I have agreed to put the Millman case to the back of our minds for what will probably be the last weekend in a long time, so we can enjoy our night away at Barkenfield Lodge for his birthday. It's a quirky place I found in Northumberland with beautiful, rustic cabins to stay in. It looks almost Swedish, but I'm luxuriating in the atmosphere. The timing couldn't be better for this getaway, given we have the first hearing in the murder trial on Monday. The stress is starting to build.

We arrive on Saturday morning, as the sun breaks through the defiant dark clouds hovering in the crisp autumn sky. As we park up on the gravel, a tall, raven-haired woman wearing a Barbour jacket and what can only be described as an 'outdoorsy posh hat' with an electric-blue feather in the side comes out to greet us. After he gets out of the car, Julian runs around to open my door for me.

'Mr and Mrs Kesler?' the woman asks in a voice that sounds like Joanna Lumley's. 'I'm Imogen. Follow me and I'll take you to your cabin.'

The breeze has that September feeling about it. Julian takes my hand as we follow Imogen past secluded huts that are tastefully and artistically placed against the stunning countryside.

The website promised 'dramatic, woodland views' and it doesn't disappoint. Each oak cabin is designed to blend in with the surrounding environment (something about bringing the outside in), so there are log fires, sunken baths, curiously angled architecture, and entire walls of glass in each one.

Imogen speaks to Julian the whole time and hoots with laughter every time he says something. She's been in his company less than three minutes.

'Everything you need is here,' she says, grinning from ear to ear. '*Please* don't hesitate to call reception if you require anything else. It can feel isolated at night, but for many of our guests, that's the attraction.'

'We'll be sure to make the most of it, Imogen,' Julian says, flashing her one of his dashing smiles.

This is what happens when women talk to Julian. His charm infects them like a virus. This is partly why he's such a good jury advocate: female jurors are transfixed by him, and he knows it.

I remember feeling such a sense of elation when we first got together; I was the one he had chosen. There were many before me. Julian had been divorced for two years when I joined chambers, and he was well into his casual dating stage by then. He'd tell me all about his latest disaster date over coffee, and I used to laugh at how this man was so academically intelligent but clueless when it came to the opposite sex. His love life was a carousel of women who idolized him and were boring and clingy.

I often wondered if he'd make a move on me in that year of pupillage, but nothing ever happened. Not even when we went for post-work drinks. We'd end up in a champagne bar in Durham, the one with a rooftop terrace overlooking the river, and in so many moments against the violet sky and tastefully placed fairy lights, I'd be desperate for him to kiss me.

He never did.

It would have been highly frowned upon and a breach of ethical code if he had, given concerns about abuse of power, despite pupillage not being at all like a teacher–student relationship. Once the twelve-month pupillage period is over, dating is no longer taboo, since everyone is self-employed. But we didn't get together for another five years; he was in and out of casual relationships and I was busy at work. Fate threw us together at the right time, I suppose.

We always went away for weekends in the beginning. We didn't want to risk being seen, not because we were doing anything wrong – we were both single – but he was my former pupilmaster and the gossip would have made it feel cheap. It would have been labelled the 'pupilmaster shags his former pupil, tale as old as time' trope. But we weren't the first to do it and won't be the last. It wasn't until we knew the relationship was sustainable, after about three months, that we went public. Julian made me feel intelligent and seen. And it went beyond our mutual love of the law: we both enjoyed travelling, we took pleasure in the same music and hated the same films. Being around him was my favourite place to be.

We hardly ever get an opportunity to slow down and recharge. Despite living in Durham, which is a beautiful city, it's rare that we manage to spend quality time together; there's always a case to prepare, an urgent document to draft, a closing speech to write. Even the air feels fresher here, and we make the most of it by exploring the surroundings all afternoon.

After getting changed, we go to the restaurant for an early dinner. We leave at twilight, to a dusky sky, and walk back to our cabin and light the firepit. Wrapping the huge tartan blanket around me on the outdoor sofa, I look at my husband. In the firelight his chiselled face could be that of a film star.

We open a bottle of Châteauneuf-du-Pape as a birthday treat.

It's Julian's favourite wine, which we drank at our wedding, a full-bodied, smoky, plum-coloured red, but at £150 a bottle it's reserved for exceptionally special occasions.

'Let's have a toast. To you on your birthday.'

'For surviving another year because I'm so old?' He laughs.

'I don't care about your age, you know that,' I tell him, placing my hand on his arm. 'Besides, you're the sexiest older man I know.'

He scoffs, 'You may be biased. I still can't believe you're eleven years younger than me.' He takes a large gulp from his glass and slumps down into the sofa.

'It says a lot, then, that you've bagged such a hot, youthful wife,' I laugh.

'Well, if I achieve nothing else, at least I have that.' He smiles. 'And on that note, a toast to your Legal 500 quote.'

I feel my face light up and I raise my glass of wine.

'Max did me a massive favour with that one,' he adds.

'Max?' I frown, confused.

'He put the quote in. Max Westwick. We went to Oxford together. He owed me a favour. I helped him out with a legal thing a few years back.'

Of course it wasn't real. I knew it, deep down. How naive of me to think it might have been authentic. I always try to be very aware of what my face is doing – Julian taught me that a poker face is one of your greatest weapons – but sometimes, the mask drops.

'What?' he asks. 'What is it?'

'Nothing. I just wondered if, you know, I might have earned that quote myself. I have been doing some great trials lately.'

He tilts his head and gazes at me in a way that makes me feel embarrassed and stupid.

'Do you know how hard it is to get into the Legal 500? Some

silks don't manage it. Took me twenty years. I've done you a massive favour.'

'Yes, of course. Obviously. I am grateful,' I gush, forcing a smile onto my wounded face. 'I just worry that . . .'

'Not this again.' He sighs.

'What again?'

'Look,' he says. 'You're married to someone more senior. With that comes perks. Embrace them. This profession is hard enough.'

'People already think I'm only getting the cases I am because I married you.'

'Is that true?' he shoots straight back at me, his eyebrows raised.

'No!'

'Prove it then. Show them that's not the case.'

'How am I supposed to do that when I'm getting all these perks? They hate me for it.'

'You'll have to win this trial, then, won't you?'

It's a light-hearted comment, but the challenge is there. Julian and I are competitive at the best of times. Going against each other in this trial is going to get tough.

'Perhaps I will,' I say, confidently. 'I mean, if Jack Millman asked for me specifically, he obviously thinks I'm up to the job.'

'Bet he fancies you, that's why!' Julian remarks, knocking back another large mouthful of wine.

'A bit reductive, Julian.' I sigh. 'I'm not biting.'

'I can see you want to, though,' he says, smirking and poking his finger into my ribs.

'Stop winding me up!'

We both burst out laughing, which resets the mood. A twisted sense of humour is essential in this job – it's the only way to stay sane. When the air falls silent between us, I catch him gazing at me.

'What?' I ask.

'I was just thinking about your first day with me as a pupil. Within a few hours, I knew you'd be something special.'

'Oh, stop it.'

'I did. I know talent when I see it. You were different from the other pupils we'd had previously. You had something electric about you.'

'That was imposter syndrome, Julian.'

'You know what I mean. Everyone else we had in before you was generic. The same indistinguishable, privileged minds, but with different faces. Then you burst through the doors. You had grit about you. Even then, you were fearless.'

'Well, that's what growing up in poverty around drug dealers does for you.'

'I mean it,' he says. 'You're different from the others. It's your strength.'

It's not often Julian gets sentimental. He reaches his arm out towards me; I lean in and cuddle up against his warm body. I feel his hand slip into my hair.

'It'll be OK, you know. This trial. It won't come between us,' he says, softly. 'I know you're worried about it. I understand.'

'I am. You're the first person I'd want to ask if I had a question, but now you're the one person I can't talk to.'

'You can talk to me about anything, Leila. You know that. I hope you'll continue to learn from me until the day I hang up my wig. That's how the relationship works.'

'Exactly. How am I supposed to go up against you in court?'

'Do your best. Remember everything I taught you.'

He bends his head down to mine and kisses me. He's trying to calm my nerves, but I feel as if I'm standing at the bottom of Mount Everest.

'What's he like?' Julian asks, against the sound of the fire crackling. Sparks fly and I watch as they dance about against the night sky. I've always been mesmerized by fire.

'Who?'

'Millman. What's he like? He obviously asked for you to represent him for a reason.'

'Besides my looks, you mean?'

His mouth curls up into a smile as he, too, gazes into the flames.

'We can't talk about the case,' I say.

'We're not talking about the case. I'm just asking you what he's like as a person. Since you've represented him before.'

'Yes, but that was years ago.' I feel immediately defensive, and my body stiffens. 'Sorry, Julian. I just don't think we should be talking about this.'

'Do you seriously think I'd ever say or do anything that would compromise you professionally?'

'Of course not.'

'This is how big cases work. Do you think silks dance around each other saying, "Well, I simply can't discuss this"? Of course we don't. It's give and take. We can talk about elements of the case, just not confidential information.'

'I don't know, Julian. It feels a bit, you know . . .'

'Leila, this happens all the time. It's better for clients. Everything would take ten times longer otherwise. Especially with us being under the same roof – it'll be much easier. We can help each other out. There's nothing illegal about it. Trust me, I've been doing this a long time.'

He says this softly, convincingly, as if he really is trying to guide me through this. I've never done a murder before, but I have seen silks having intense 'chats' in the robing room. Even at this early stage, I know I'll need all the help I can get with this case. It's looking grim already, and I haven't even had sight of forensic evidence yet.

But, as Julian's pupil, I'm also aware of the games he's capable of playing. I've seen them first hand. He taught me most of them. This is different, though. I may be Julian's wife, but I am his pupil first and foremost. He would not screw over his own pupil.

Besides, what choice do I have? I don't want to be the naive barrister who doesn't seem to know what she's doing. Julian is my pupilmaster. He's got me this far. I'm as good as I am because of him.

I sigh. 'Usual story. He was abandoned as a baby by his parents, who were drug users, brought up in care, and has been in and out of prison ever since. Doesn't trust anyone, has a very cynical view of the world. A lone wolf. Like most people who had a traumatic childhood, he's a survivor, a fighter. I wouldn't have thought he's the kind of person to kill someone. He's not like that.'

'Did you not last defend him for a violent assault?' he asks, cynically.

'Yes, but he was set up.'

Julian shoots me one of the looks he delivers in court when a witness gives an answer so unworthy of belief, it makes everyone in the courtroom want to die on the spot.

'Well, I look forward to seeing how he scrubs up at trial,' he says, and he means it. He's curious. 'He's going up against it, isn't he? Respectable judge, very well liked. Anton was known for being fair.'

I'm not entirely in agreement with Julian's assessment of Judge Smythe, but that's obviously how the prosecution is going to portray him.

'The jury didn't know Anton, though,' I remind him. 'But they will want to know why a judge was at a criminal's flat on a Friday night. There's a story there, and that's your Achilles heel.'

Julian likes clear motives and obvious evidence. He hates having to think outside the box.

'How do you think he'll perform under cross-examination?' he asks.

'I think that's definitely crossing the line now.' I laugh, playfully patting his leg to let him know I'm done with this conversation. I'll cooperate with Julian as much as I can, but my loyalty is ultimately to my client.

By 10 p.m. the fire is losing power and we go inside. The temperature has significantly dropped, and Julian is at the boozy stage where he's starting to pull at my clothes.

The cabin is dimly lit by small lamps. I remember Imogen saying you can close the blinds on the glass wall, so as Julian is finding a way into my black Zara jumpsuit, I try working out how to close them to give us some privacy. A knock at the door suddenly interrupts his seduction. Wriggling out of his embrace, I open the door.

'Sorry to bother you. I'm from reception,' says a young man who must be in his early twenties. His floppy, blond hair and steely blue eyes pop against his black T-shirt and trousers. He's holding a black gift box. 'This is for you.'

'Who's it from?'

'It was a request via our website,' he says, handing the box to me. 'They didn't leave a name.'

'A mystery gift!'

'Someone's got an admirer,' the man says with a cheeky smile, turning around and walking back down the stone path.

'I should be so lucky!' I shout back to him.

I take the box over to Julian, who is standing at the window, looking outside.

'Who was that?' he asks, knitting his brows together.

'Just someone from reception. Brought a fancy gift.'

'Leila, he looked about twelve!'

I look at him, confused. 'What?'

'Flirting with a child? Really?'

'He was *not* twelve. And I wasn't flirting!' I tell him, defending myself. 'Besides, you know from personal experience I can't flirt to save my life. Don't you remember our first date, when I got so nervous I delivered a twenty-minute speech about how underrated the *Scream* franchise is?'

'I don't think I could ever forget that.' He laughs as I open the box in front of him.

Inside is another bottle of Châteauneuf-du-Pape.

'Someone obviously likes you,' I comment, opening the card and reminding myself how much each bottle costs. He picks it up and blinks at the vanilla-cream label on the blood-red bottle.

'What does this mean?' I ask, holding out a small, pristine, white card with black printed letters.

Hell is empty and all the devils are here. Happy Birthday, J.

'Shakespeare?' he guesses, screwing his face up. '*Tempest*, isn't it? Very funny, Lei.'

'I didn't send this,' I tell him.

He stares blankly at me for a few seconds.

'I . . . I don't get it, then. I didn't tell anyone where we were going specifically. Who did you tell?'

'Nobody, really.'

'What do you mean, "nobody, really"? I want to know who sent this,' he says, his voice laced with annoyance.

'I mentioned it to one or two people at Chester's party.' I shrug. 'Maybe Chester sent it as a joke.'

'Who exactly did you tell?' he demands again. This time,

there's something in his voice I don't like. He stares at me with wide eyes, waiting for an answer. His jaw flickers, a sign he's clenching his teeth, which he only does when he's angry. Julian is the kind of person who would rather die than let anyone know something's bothered him. He used to tell me the best advocates were unshakeable and never allowed anyone to see past the titanium exterior they presented to the world.

This has bothered him.

'I can't remember exactly who I told. I'm sure it's just meant to be a joke.'

He takes a small step back; it's as if he catches himself in mid-frenzy and composes himself.

'I'm sorry,' he says, alongside a mild attempt at a laugh. 'I just can't stand cryptic things like this. We have to be so careful, with me prosecuting such dangerous criminals.'

'I'm sure it's nothing like that. I can't imagine many criminals go around quoting Shakespeare. You know what people at the Bar are like,' I tell him. 'And obviously this is from someone who knows you well. Take it for what it is. A gift with a stupid note.'

'You're right.' He nods, kissing me on my forehead. The lustful flames present minutes ago are now very much extinguished. 'I'm knackered. All that fresh air, food, and wine has worn me out!'

'Let's go to bed.' I smile as he picks up his mobile phone and heads to the bathroom with it, closing the door.

Turning to look out of the window, I place my hand on the enormous, chilled sheet of glass and stare out into the dark, black abyss. I'm acutely aware, in this moment, that anyone could be out there, looking in. Watching us.

In the darkness, miles from anywhere, and despite my reassurances to Julian, that note sounds nothing like a joke.

5

Leila

119 days before trial

JACK MILLMAN IS a thirty-two-year-old male from Hexham, in Northumberland.

As I told Julian, he went into the care system as a baby and has lived in more foster homes than he remembers. He became a regular in the youth courts once he'd reached the age of ten, the age of criminal responsibility in England and Wales. He also got in with the wrong crowd, which set in motion the revolving door of offending he was caught in.

It was only a matter of time before the violence started. All that pent-up rage and anger had to go somewhere. A boy let down by the system, abandoned. His experience in the justice system merely confirmed everything he felt about himself. A young man with no hope, no help, and nothing much to live for.

He is the reason I do this job, to be the person finally fighting in their corner.

The security guard walks Jack to the conference room in the cells of Newcastle Crown Court and ushers him in before slamming the door on his way out. Jack doesn't immediately look at me or his solicitor, Davina, but he's changed since I last represented him. He's bulked up in terms of muscle, and his hair is longer. Wilder.

He sits on the black plastic chair at the brown table, both of which are nailed to the floor. He doesn't slouch. His hands, handcuffed together at the wrists, rest gently on the table. The metal from the cuffs clangs against the cheap plastic top.

Jack's outward appearance is that of a bouncer. He clearly goes to the gym every day. Or used to. Even through his tracksuit top you can see where the material clings to the muscles in his arms. He's tall, around six foot two. Already, my lawyer mind is thinking about how this will affect his defence. What match was fifty-six-year-old Anton for a strong, thirty-two-year-old doorman?

The tattoos on his forearms peek out from the cuffs of his sweatshirt and burst out onto his hands. Another climbs past the neckband and up to his jaw. The more traditional jurors won't like these. They'll assume he's a thug, and first impressions count.

Despite all this, behind the tattoos and the muscles, Jack seems like a little boy. One who was never given a break in life. He looks as if he's carrying the weight of the world on his shoulders.

Some clients are awful. The ones who couldn't care less about the hours, blood, sweat, and literal tears you put into their case. The sleep you lose over them. Getting up at 4 a.m. to write their closing speeches so it's ready by 10.30 a.m. sharp. You'll secure an acquittal and, in turn, their liberty, and they'll stroll out of court without so much as a thank you.

Jack isn't like that.

'We really have to stop meeting like this, Miss Reynolds. People are gonna start thinking I'm some kind of common criminal,' he says, with the faintest hint of a smile. His black, cheekbone-length hair is messy and unstyled around his face, which hasn't been shaved for days. 'Somewhere a bit classier next time? Nando's?'

I can't resist smiling.

'Clearly you missed me too much,' I joke back, but then follow what I said with a steely look. This is serious. I open the brief in front of me.

'How are you, Jack?'

The bravado melts away. He swallows hard and looks down at the table before answering. I struggle to drag my eyes away from his handcuffed hands. I can't imagine how awful it must be, being restrained like that.

'All right, considering. I wouldn't say I'm doing well, but I suppose I'm coping.'

'Good. I'm here to do the best I can, Jack. I need you to know that,' I reply, faffing around with my papers so we don't descend into any kind of sentimentality. I acquainted myself with his antecedent history before the conference and it was a depressing read: burglary, theft, drugs, violence. But nothing in the last five years, not since I last represented him. He's really tried to turn things around, by the looks of things.

'I know you've been here before, but I'm going to set out how this works, so we're all clear.' I smile at him. 'You won't enter a plea today; we're just setting a timetable. You've instructed me to represent you, and I will assess all of the prosecution's evidence. Based on that and what you say about the offence you're charged with, I will advise you on whether to plead guilty or not guilty.'

'I'm not guilty,' he interrupts, calmly.

My eyes flit towards Davina, his solicitor, for a second; she doesn't take her eyes off Jack.

'It's not a decision to make now,' I reiterate. 'We'll discuss it in due course.'

'My plea won't change. I'm going not guilty.'

Ninety-nine per cent of clients say they intend to plead not guilty at the first hearing, but it's my duty to set out what the situation is from a defence point of view at the outset.

'Jack, when you called the police at 11.07 p.m., you said, "Judge Smythe from Durham Crown Court is dying in my flat." When the operator asked what happened, you replied, "I've been here all night. He's seriously hurt." You then gave a no-comment interview.'

He nods, not taking his eyes off mine.

'I don't suppose you know where your phone is, do you? Mobile phones can offer a real insight into your life and be helpful in these cases. It's very unusual that it wasn't at your apartment.'

'I don't know where it is, and it's not gonna turn up anytime soon,' he says, shaking his head.

I stare at him, waiting for him to continue.

'It was stolen, a few hours before the incident.'

I notice his carefully worded language. *The incident.*

'Where and when did you last have it?'

'In the club. I was working, moving around a lot. It's difficult to say when it went missing. I only realized when I needed to call 999.'

'How are you so sure it was stolen and not lost?'

'There are things on there that could be dangerous if they got into the wrong hands. It's either in my pocket or in my flat. It was stolen.'

Davina remains silent, despite this revelation – she knows that to probe too deeply now would be dangerous; he'll tell us when he's ready – but I have no doubt he's just said what he did deliberately.

'Can you share with us what was on your phone?'

'Nope,' he replies in a clipped tone.

'Look, Jack, I appreciate there are perhaps sensitive matters behind this case, but if I'm being honest, unless you have a convincing defence,' I go on, 'it's not looking good.'

'We'd better start thinking of some good defences, then,' he says, raising his eyebrows.

This was a problem in our last case. He doesn't behave in a way that indicates that he's aware of how much trouble he's in until it's too late. It's inappropriate, but his natural charisma allows him to pull it off. I hope it'll work in his favour in front of a jury.

'Jack,' I say, seriously, 'this isn't like the other times you've been in court. You're charged with murder.'

'They can prove I did it, then,' he says, shrugging his shoulders. 'That's how it works, right? Innocent until proven guilty beyond reasonable doubt. If you think I'm making this in any way easier for them by giving them an inch so they can take a mile, you're dead wrong.'

There's a firmness in his voice now I didn't see last time, a stubbornness.

'Jack, you've already given them enough ammunition to prosecute and likely convict you. If I were prosecuting, I'd be feeling confident right now,' I tell him, honestly. 'You were found at the scene, admitted you were there all night, and you failed to give an explanation for anything in interview. It won't look good to a jury.'

'You'll get your answers, but not until the trial.'

I look at Davina, but she is still watching Jack. She's been silent throughout, sizing him up. Until now.

'Let me get this straight,' she asserts in a calm, Geordie lilt that sounds mildly menacing. 'You want us to let you swan into the witness box in a murder trial, with no idea of what you're going to say?'

'Pretty much, yeah.'

'Can you believe this?' Davina laughs, turning back to me.

'Jack,' I intervene, 'I can't put forward a defence if you don't talk to us, which makes it difficult to convince a jury you're not guilty. All I'll be able to do is test the Crown's evidence and throw doubt on its credibility. It's high risk.'

'It's bloody suicide!' Davina butts in. 'Jack, you have no idea if what you're going to say even amounts to a real defence. You could play right into the prosecution's hands. We are here to advise you. You're playing with your life here.'

'It's my call,' Jack says, unswerving. 'If I wanted lawyers who played it safe, I'd have gone elsewhere. But I need someone with a backbone, someone who isn't afraid to take a risk.'

Of course. This is our unfinished business. My opportunity to make things right.

At law school, it was drummed into us that nothing is more important than fighting fearlessly for your client. You must go above and beyond to explore all avenues, seek out the best defence, pursue anything that could secure an acquittal.

The other thing that was stressed, perhaps even more so, was the importance of following your client's instructions. You can do nothing without the consent or permission of your client. You may not run a defence without consulting them first. You cannot raise any significant submission without their support. They are very much running the show.

That message, now, is loud and clear.

'Who's prosecuting?' Jack asks, leaning back into the cheap, plastic chair.

I take a deep breath before telling him. It's not the best news to give a client.

'I need to speak with you about that. It's Julian Kesler, KC.' I pause. 'My husband.'

He gives a little laugh and looks down, as if to compose himself before bringing his eyes up again to meet mine.

'Are you joking?'

'I'm not. Because we're both self-employed, we are permitted to be on opposing sides of a case and will adhere to the highest standards of confidentiality, impartiality, and integrity, as dictated by the Codes of Conduct. But you're entitled to sack me and instruct other counsel if you'd like.'

'Is he any good?' he asks.

'Very,' I tell him, honestly.

'Is he better than you?'

'He's very experienced. I'm just being transparent with you.'

'Miss Reynolds doesn't miss a trick, Jack. You can rest assured you are in the safest hands,' Davina interjects.

Jack shifts towards Davina. 'I know. I don't like lawyers. Never have. Even though our last trial didn't go the way we wanted it to, Miss Reynolds is the only person out of everyone who's ever represented me who didn't treat me like I'm stupid.' He angles his shoulders back towards me. 'You know what happened last time. I need you to prevent me from falling into another trap.'

Davina's eyes shift between us. Her job in client conferences is to note down what is said for future reference. I see that her pen was set down minutes ago. She's not been recording this conversation. And that is also, I presume, why he asked for Davina.

'I won't let that happen again, Jack,' I say. 'You have my word. But this strategy will be difficult, procedurally, I mean. Please reconsider.'

'I can't, Miss Reynolds,' he says, sternly. 'If I were to talk, then—'

He cuts himself off before looking away, shaking his head and taking a deep breath. I give him a second to recalibrate.

'This situation, this case. What . . . happened,' he tells us. Jesus, he can barely bring himself to say it. 'It goes high up.

Much higher up than me. I'd have to expose people, put myself at risk. People would get hurt. That's all I'm prepared to say – for now.'

My head turns towards Davina to see what she makes of this. Her face gives nothing away, but it's clear she'll be concerned about Jack's attitude going forward.

'Who are you protecting?' I ask him.

'No comment,' he says, shaking his head.

Jack stands up in court to confirm his name and date of birth, then sits back down, dwarfed by the huge sheets of glass that surround the dock in Court 1. You can feel movement in the air from shuffling journalists. I vaguely recognize Anton's wife and his son in the public gallery. She still looks in shock – emotionless and distant, her thin frame hidden by a big, black coat with a fur collar. Her shoulder-length black and silver hair pulled back in a way that would look chic in different circumstances. Their eighteen-year-old son, Quinn, sits next to her, wearing a black suit and tie. He keeps his head down the whole time; the hearing is obviously too much for him.

My nerves ignite the second Julian glides through the doors of the court in the way KCs do. The professional gap between us flashes like a beacon. We may be sitting at opposite ends of the same long, wooden bench at the front of the court, but the differences in our professional dress mark us as unequal. As King's Counsel, he has earned the right to wear a silk robe, not one made of wool, like mine. His is lighter and has a more free-flowing movement to it; the one draped around my shoulders is heavy and cumbersome.

Silks are elite advocates, appointed by the King. And they make sure everyone knows it.

The hearing lasts only seven minutes and is uneventful. The defendant will enter his formal plea to the charge in just under one month's time. No application for bail.

I leave court with a sense of dread closing in on me, like fog on a cold winter morning. I feel I'm being tested and failing at the first hurdle in this impossible race. What are you supposed to do when you can't fight fearlessly because your client won't talk? How can I put the best defence together with limited instructions? I feel that I'm going against everything I was taught as a barrister.

But, as Jack insinuated – cleverly, many times throughout his conference – I don't really have a choice.

I owe him.

6

Leila

117 days before trial

Durham Crown Court is over two hundred years old. It's well known that His Honour Judge Smythe had wanted to be the Recorder of Durham for many years before finally landing the job. It's the most senior judicial position at that court centre. I recall seeing him many times up on the bench where he would dispense justice to those who had shown little regard for it.

Court 1 is the venue for his professional memorial service. I debated whether to come, but it felt like the right thing to do. The room fills up shortly before 9.30 a.m. on Wednesday morning, in advance of the day's hearings.

I'm not a fan of the old courtrooms; they're cramped, and you never know where to sit. Lots of dark wood, draughts, and there's rarely enough room to lay out all your papers. They're also unpleasantly hot in summer. Walking into one of them, wearing the wig and robes, you feel you're in a Dickensian novel, and someone's about to be handed the death sentence for stealing a loaf of bread.

Barristers, solicitors, and court staff pile in. There's barely any space, so people sit and stand shoulder-to-shoulder. The public gallery at the back of the courtroom is packed with people who need to be seen to be in attendance.

Julian and I manage to squeeze through as subtly as we can. Julian moves towards the front of the court, but I hang back, preferring to stand unobtrusively at the side.

Everyone from the legal community in Durham is here. Chester is down at the front, and I watch as a glamorous blonde woman in a black suit and pale-blue shirt taps him on the shoulder. He turns around, smiles, and kisses her on the cheek. It's a bit too close to her mouth, for a few seconds too long. As he pulls away from her, his eyes flick towards Julian, who stands beside them. A smirk appears on Chester's face.

He can't help himself.

A loud knock echoes throughout the courtroom, indicating the judiciary are about to enter. The hum quietens and everybody stands, facing the bench that rises above us at the front. Entering from the right, several Crown Court judges, all dressed in their black and violet robes with red sashes called tippets, sit in red leather chairs in front of the ornate, cream, panelled wall. Behind them hangs the Royal Coat of Arms present in every courtroom in England and Wales. On it the motto, *dieu et mon droit*, 'God and my right'. It is this we bow to when entering or leaving a courtroom to show respect for the King's justice.

Each of the judges speaks about Anton and his long legal career; twenty-eight years as a barrister, seven of those years as Queen's Counsel before spending the last five years of his life as a Crown Court judge. He was 'a juggernaut of legal intelligence' and always 'three steps ahead of any counsel who appeared in front of him'. One goes on to say Anton was 'a guiding light in our judicial circle, a searcher of truth', that he had an 'impeccable moral compass'.

It's difficult to listen to. A swirl of nausea rises in my gut. I take a deep breath. Wrapping my robes around myself, I look down at the floor.

I shouldn't be here. It was a mistake to come, maybe even inappropriate in the circumstances, given my current role to defend his alleged killer.

I consider sneaking out, but the court is so full, I'd draw too much attention, and how would that look? The barrister defending the man accused of murdering Judge Smythe couldn't even be bothered to stay for his whole memorial service. *How disrespectful*.

They go on to talk about the cases he did over the years, how he was a 'formidable head of chambers' and 'outstanding silk'.

'But above all,' HHJ Harvey says, 'he was a family man. He lived for his loving wife, Sarah, and their son, Quinn. When he wasn't on the bench or with his family, he loved being on the golf course. On a personal level, Anton was a colleague who always gave immaculate advice, even if it was seasoned with a rather blunt delivery.'

Muffled laughs bounce around the courtroom. He *was* known for calling a spade a spade.

'But he was a wonderful judge. A wonderful friend. Justice will be served.'

'Hear! Hear!' everyone bellows, and while that last line isn't directly targeted at me, it might as well have been.

Thankfully, it's a short service. People start leaving the room as soon as it's finished, but not fast enough for my liking. I need some fresh air.

'If you were expecting people to be nice to you today, you were always going to be disappointed,' a male voice says in my ear.

I turn around to see Keiran Fox. He was Anton's pupil years ago. I've always got on with him – he's a decent guy, about ten years older than me. I used to do cases against him before he left the Bar a few years ago to teach student barristers full-time in Newcastle.

'Honestly, I didn't know if I should come or not. I figured I'd be called insensitive either way.'

'Leila,' he says, shaking his head, 'we all know how this works. It's not as if you get a choice in who you represent. Don't feel bad about it. That said, I hope you lose.'

I smile. Of course he does. I get it.

People outside this profession rarely understand the bond between pupil and pupilmaster. For the first six months of pupillage you can spend up to ten hours a day with them: watching them in court, travelling long distances with them by car, having lunch with them, researching for them, attending social functions with them. Nobody knows you better professionally than your pupilmaster. It's why their validation is so priceless.

'We spoke only the day before,' Keiran says. 'We went out for lunch. He was talking about his ambitions to become a High Court judge. He'd have been great at that – can you imagine? I mean, don't get me wrong – he was one of the last old-school judges, had no time for people who weren't dedicated. But he was a great man.'

Judges like Anton used to be the norm, but they're a rare breed now. Judges who take the view that since their superiors made life hell for them when they were starting out, they should do the same for baby barristers. Most pupils hate it, but not me – that approach felt familiar. It made me a better lawyer.

Made everything feel earned.

'I'm so sorry. I really am,' I murmur. What else can you say when someone has lost a person close to them? 'How's the job in Newcastle going?'

'It's very rewarding and, sorry to say this, has great working hours, salary, pension, paid annual leave, and job security. Don't know why I didn't do it sooner. Jealous?'

'No, because I still get the thrill of tax-bill anxiety every year. You're missing out on that.'

He laughs. 'I know people think I've sold out, but it works for me. Anton hated it – he was always trying to talk me into coming back to the Bar.'

'I'm sure he was happy for you,' I tell him, reaching out and placing my hand on his arm.

I know this isn't true, but it's what he needs to hear. The fact is, Anton was unsupportive of Keiran's professional choice to leave the Bar, and he didn't hide it, even going so far as to call his ex-pupil a 'bloody waste of time'.

'I hope so. He was a great mentor, despite the rough edges.' I smile at him.

'Leila . . .' a soft northern female accent interrupts us. 'How are you?'

The blonde woman who was hugging Chester now stands beside us. She is Sienna Fox, married to Keiran Fox.

And Julian's ex-wife.

She's about ten years older than me, around the same age as Julian, but doesn't look it. She obviously has either a personal trainer or a very hefty gym membership because she looks incredible. Even in her trouser suit, you can tell she's toned and lifts weights in hideously expensive leggings. She's also plainly mastered the Dyson hair wrap, going by the honey-coloured locks that bounce around her shoulders. I feel decidedly unglamorous standing next to her in my wig and robes.

'I'm well, thank you, Sienna. You?'

Our conversations are always civil and polite. Why wouldn't they be? Our paths have never crossed, and her marriage to Julian was over before I entered the picture – it's just awkward. She had an entire existence with the person I'm now married to, and I know nothing about it.

Nothing.

Whenever I see Sienna in public, I catch myself staring at her and thinking: *Is he the same person now as he was around you? At what point did you start to hate each other and why? Does he ever think of you when we have sex?*

'Busy,' Sienna says. She's a partner in one of the oldest leading criminal solicitor firms in Durham. They're very well respected, and so is she. 'You are, too, by the looks of things.'

'Yes,' I say, through a forced smile. 'Speaking of which, I'm on in Court 2 at 10.30, so I'd better get going.'

'Are you ready, darling?' Julian says to me in his charming voice, the one he reserves for when he wants other people to notice him. He slides his arm around my waist in what some would describe as a territorial move. 'Sienna. Keiran.'

Neither of them says anything. Sienna takes the subtlest intake of breath and turns away from both of us. Keiran just stares at Julian. The scene makes me uncomfortable.

'Keiran, I'm very sorry for your loss,' he says in an unusual display of sympathy for a man I know he despises. An excruciating silence simmers between the four of us. This is precisely what Julian is known for in court – making his witnesses uneasy and then delivering a blow out of nowhere.

'As a pupilmaster myself, I understand the bond that develops.'

'We call it "pupil supervisor" now. Though I guess some people's relationships with their pupils are much *closer* than others,' Keiran says to Julian, his eyes turning towards me.

He shouldn't have said that. The suggestion that our relationship is rooted in any kind of impropriety is something Julian is fiercely sensitive about. He pauses for a few seconds, allowing the insult to evaporate in the air and thus lose any power it might have had.

'*I understand* the bond that develops,' he goes on, as if Keiran hadn't said anything at all. 'And I have to say, one of the most important things as a pupil supervisor is feeling immensely proud of your pupil's achievements, just as I do with Leila. I can't imagine a more tragic situation than the feeling that your pupil never reached their full potential. I mean, I wouldn't necessarily use the word *disappointment*, but . . .'

It's harsh, even for him.

'Fuck you, Julian!' Keiran says, in a way that's so aggressive Sienna places her hand on his arm to calm him down.

'Don't!' she whispers to her husband. People around us start looking over, while Julian displays a shocked face, knowing full well he's the reason for the outburst.

'It's not the time or the place for this,' I say, quietly. Sienna pulls Keiran away as I steer Julian outside and into one of the adjoining conference rooms.

'What the hell was that?' I ask him, closing the door.

'I'm sorry.'

'It's pathetic, Julian!'

'He made the comment first.'

'Seriously?' I ask, astonished. 'Your defence is "*he started it*"? You're a forty-seven-year-old barrister, for god's sake!'

He sits down on one of the chairs, throwing his wig onto the table.

'Why do you still get like this around her?'

'Like what?'

'Angry. She still has such an effect on you.'

'You know what she did,' he says, looking at me. 'What *they* did.'

After being married for three years, Sienna moved out and told Julian it was over. A few months later, she got together with Keiran and people put two and two together. Julian concluded they'd had an affair and he made sure everyone knew. She never denied it.

'Whatever happened is in the past,' I tell him, perching on the edge of the table in front of him.

'I know it is, but she can't resist rubbing it in my face. Did you see her practically throwing herself at Chester in there, and in front of her husband, too? She doesn't change.'

'If anything, it was Chester being overly flirty in that way he is sometimes. Also, I hardly think greeting someone is "throwing yourself" at them. She's known Chester for years! You're being paranoid.'

Now, *Chester* would do it to piss him off, but that's not the point.

'Don't be naive, Leila,' he says in a serious tone. 'I've told you what she's like.'

'I just don't know why you care.'

'I don't. I suppose I worry it could happen again with you.'

'That's absolutely not going to happen,' I tell him. 'You can be a right stubborn pain sometimes, but you know I'd never cheat on you. Not after what you've been through.'

He smiles at me, and I lean forward to kiss him. It lingers long enough to reset the mood.

'I don't deserve you,' he whispers as his eyes meet mine, the tips of our noses touching.

'You don't.' I smile, softly. 'But at least you know it.'

This trial is going to test our marriage in so many ways. The case will be career-defining, life-changing. Things are changing already.

I have to be ready for it. *We* have to be ready for it.

7

Leila

111 days before trial

ONE OF THE things I love most about this job is getting outside the courtroom and using my platform to help young, aspiring barristers – especially women – enter the profession. I started a legal blog back when I was at law school, hoping to give a realistic account of what it was like to study at Cambridge. *Chats at the Bar* gradually became a hit among law students, but those followers had already been successful, to a certain extent. I wanted to do more, ignite a spark in those who were surrounded by people who threw cold water on their ambitions, much like I had at their age.

So, this evening I'm lecturing at Mountcross Academy, a local secondary school and sixth-form college on the outskirts of Durham. We've opened it up to students sixteen and over, in addition to the public. Advertising it on Insta to my 32,750 followers felt like a real achievement, and all 180 tickets sold out within a few days. I asked that the proceeds go to the National Society for the Prevention of Cruelty to Children.

I walk into the modern theatre-style building to rapturous applause, following a brief introduction by the headteacher. The bright white stage lights dazzle me; the only people I can see are those in the first few rows. I've dashed straight from work to make the 6.30 p.m. start. My hair, neatly tied into a ponytail this morning, now sags at the back of my neck, and stray hairs jump about my face. I'm also pretty sure my eyeliner isn't where I put it ten hours ago.

'Good evening, everyone!' I speak into the microphone. 'Thank you for inviting me to your wonderful school. It's an honour to be here.'

I tell them my name is Leila Kesler by marriage, but because female barristers are always referred to by their maiden name, I am professionally known as Miss Reynolds.

We dive straight into the Q&A. This is how I like to run these talks; the floor is theirs to ask whatever they like.

'What made you want to become a criminal barrister?' enquires a girl in the front row.

It's always the first question, and my answer is always the same.

'I actually had no clue what I wanted to do with my life until I was about sixteen,' I answer, truthfully. 'Around that time, I met a barrister through *my* school and was fascinated by his job. He spoke with such passion about criminal law, running trials, cross-examining defendants. I knew then that it was what I wanted to do. Meeting that person changed my life.'

'I love that, Leila!' Rachel, our host and headteacher, says into the microphone. 'Never underestimate how influential the right person can be. OK, next question . . .'

She moves to a girl in the second row.

'Is it realistic for people like us, who don't go to a private school or come from wealthy backgrounds, to get into criminal law? My parents say I've got my head in the clouds.'

Rage starts to gather in my body.

Nothing makes me angrier than a parent dampening a child's desire to do well for themselves.

'Fuck that,' I say calmly into the microphone. It has the intended effect. Gasps and giggles rebound around the room. 'You're all smart, driven, intelligent young people. You can do anything you want. Prove them wrong.

'I went to a school just like this one, and I had nobody in my corner, either. You'll be told it's not for you, that it's impossible, you're wasting your time. Ignore them. You need to be your own champion. That's OK. I believe in you. I believe in all of you.'

'Leila, off the back of that, do you think you've been disadvantaged in any way because of your working-class roots?' Rachel asks.

'Absolutely not!' I shoot back. 'Your background is an asset, not a flaw. I didn't have money or contacts, but I had grit, steel, and determination – just like you.'

The room bursts into applause.

'Leila!' another girl shouts. 'What changes do you think need to be made post-#MeToo?'

It's a change of topic, but I was expecting it to come up tonight.

'The #MeToo movement has given all of us a platform and the courage to call out and extinguish latent sexism in this profession. I've seen women having to put up with leery male solicitors, or being told, "I'll send this brief to someone else if you don't comply." Women feeling that the only way they'll succeed in this career is because of how they look, or who they're willing to sleep with. No more. We *must* stick together. We are worth more than that.'

People whoop and clap in agreement. To see a new generation of potential lawyers talking openly about preparing themselves to tackle this makes me think change really is possible.

When the noise dies down, Rachel moves to a girl at the

very back of the auditorium. I can't see her at all. I can only hear her voice.

'Could I just ask, off the back of the #MeToo stuff, which is all very empowering and current, et cetera,' she says. Condescension dances on the surface of her voice. 'Are you saying that girls should *never* consider performing sexual favours in this profession even if it would *significantly* advance their career?'

It's an odd thing to say, particularly in today's climate, and it's loaded with a tone I don't like.

'You'd be gaining success via the back door. So, no.'

'Wouldn't you?' she asks, surprised. The room is silent.

'No.'

'Were you ever tempted?' she challenges. 'When you were younger, especially coming from such a *disadvantaged* background?'

I pause, aware that I have hundreds of eyes on me, and I don't like what she's insinuating. The heat from the stage lights is starting to make me sweat.

'I wasn't,' I reply, firmly.

'Your husband is King's Counsel, isn't he, Leila?'

The host sees where this is going and takes the microphone away from the girl asking the question. Or is it a woman? She sounded older than a teenager. And there was a familiarity in her voice I couldn't place.

'We only have time for one question each, I'm afraid!' Rachel says, moving on, and I'm grateful for her tact. As the next girl asks her question, I smile, but my mind is reeling. Who would ask a confrontational question like that?

The Q&A lasts for another hour. At the end, some attendees approach the stage and ask for selfies, which I don't mind. It's good publicity for *Chats at the Bar*.

It's dark when I leave, just past 8 p.m. My car is at the far side of the car park, dimly lit by one tall lamp-post at the other end. There's a car parked next to mine and a few others scattered around, but most have gone. I wish I'd parked closer to the entrance.

My pace quickens as I approach my car. Reaching into my handbag, I fumble for the keys and press the button to unlock the door so I can get straight in. As the reverse lights flash, a hooded figure is illuminated at the rear. The person jumps slightly, then turns sharply to walk away.

'Hey!' I shout out, instinctively.

The figure doesn't stop, moving further into the dark.

A feeling of dread settles around me. *Why was someone by my car?*

Something is off. And my instincts are very rarely wrong.

8

Leila

110 days before trial

The downside of doing talks and events is that you have to post where you'll be. If someone doesn't like you, or you have an ex-client who wants access to you, it tells them exactly where you are.

After checking my car thoroughly, I drove home and decided not to tell Julian. I can't even be sure the person was doing anything to my car. Nothing was damaged or taken, and he'd tell me we don't have any proof, which is true. Besides, if I raise any kind of official alarm about being followed or watched, all kinds of red alerts would be enacted, which would cause far too much drama.

One of my colleagues tried a dangerous case a couple of years back and became the target of a terrifying intimidation campaign courtesy of the wider gang network. It began with him being followed home from court, then progressed to threatening mail sent to chambers. It wasn't until a petrol bomb was posted through the letterbox of his family home that he finally took it seriously.

This profession comes with risk, one we take on when we step through the door of a criminal court. You are prosecuting and defending dangerous people. For my colleague, the petrol bomb meant police presence outside his house, enhanced connection to 999, a visit from the Ministry of Defence to make his house more secure – which included CCTV in every room – and police escorts for him and his wife everywhere they went.

I don't want any of that. The last thing I need is people whispering about how I'm some terrified, incompetent girl, and that this case is too big for me.

I don't have time to dwell on it the next day, as I'm in court until mid-afternoon. Finishing earlier than expected, I head back over to chambers. I really need to do some Millman case prep before evidence from the prosecution is served. As I reach the old stone steps of our building, I see Chester coming out.

'Miss Reynolds,' he smiles, tipping his head ever so slightly in a bid to appear gentlemanly. Chester Vernon is one of those older men who's big on chivalry and manners. I've seen him make a dash from one end of the robing room to the other just to hold a door open for a woman struggling under the weight of all the books she was carrying.

'Fancy a quick one?' he asks in a tone that would get him immediately disbarred by the Bar Standards Board. 'I was just about to head home, but I'm much more interested in hearing all about this case you're doing with your frightful husband.'

He's acting more animated than usual, and his eyes have a glaze about them. I catch the distinct smell of booze when he speaks, so I gather he's been for a long, liquid lunch, which used to be very common at the Bar 'back in the day before things went woke'. What's likely happened is everyone else has gone home and he's looking for an excuse to stay out.

The more inquisitive part of me wonders why. With a wife like Demi – half his age, looking like a model – shouldn't he be running home?

I'd usually say no to a drink when I've got a huge case, but there's something I wouldn't mind talking to him about if the topic arises, so I decide to go. 'Just one. I mean it, Chester. One, then I'm going home.'

After I've dumped all my gear in chambers, we head to a nearby bar. It's just after 3 p.m., so there's barely anyone here. Chester orders a large glass of red wine, and I ask for a small white, which he predictably promotes to a large to match his.

We choose a sofa in the corner, but not so close to the window where we could be seen. We have nothing to hide, but the Bar is a vicious place for gossip, and people can get the wrong idea. I ensure there's a decent amount of space between us so there's no ambiguity.

He places himself comfortably in the corner of the sofa, swinging one arm along the back of it. His immaculately tailored black suit – no waistcoat, which immediately marks him out as being a KC in the robing room – makes him look stylish and distinguished, even at his age. His dark grey hair is slicked back, culminating in small curls at the nape of his neck. White streaks at either side of his head give him the appearance of a Harry Potter villain. Slicked-back hair is a must for King's Counsel; it adds to the mystique.

'So, Leila,' he bellows, 'I hear you made an impression at some school last night? Demi saw it on the Instagram.'

'*The*' Instagram.

'Yes, it was a talk I did off the back of the blog I do.'

'Is this the "no flirting allowed" blog?'

I give him a playful stare, letting him know his outdated views are inappropriate. 'Chester, times have moved on.'

'Doesn't sound any fun to me,' he puffs, rolling his eyes and reaching for his wine.

He's a bit of a relic, but Chester was my biggest champion when I applied to chambers. He was on my seven-panel interview for pupillage and asked questions that gave me an opportunity to shine. I think he liked my spirit and confidence and was probably vocal in convincing the others to give me a shot. I'll always be grateful to him for that.

'How are you feeling about the Millman case?'

'Ready for the challenge but also terrified,' I confess.

'What are you afraid of?'

'I really want to use this opportunity to show people I'm up to it, but it feels like I'm doomed either way. If I lose, I'll look incompetent. If I win, I'm worried what might happen to my marriage. I'm not sure Julian could handle it if I won. Imagine the hit his ego would take. A woman. A non-KC. His *wife*.'

Chester is probably the only person I can admit this to.

'You're up against it. Really up against it, here. Not only with the case, but with him. He's a dirty player.'

Chester and Julian can't stand each other. Never have. It's a tangible dislike whenever they're in the same room. Chester would love to kick Julian out of chambers, but his professional fees are huge and because we all pay a percentage of them into chambers, he brings a lot of money in. 'Incompatible personalities' isn't a good enough reason to send him packing.

'Oh, come on, he's not *that* bad,' I protest, even though we both know he *is* – that's why he's so good at what he does. 'He was my pupilmaster, remember? I know all of his tricks. Seriously, though, do you have to wind him up at every opportunity?'

'I don't know what you mean,' he says innocently, taking a sip of his drink with the slightest hint of a smirk on his face.

'I saw you at the memorial. Sienna.'

He delivers questionable side-eye my way, like a toddler being told off for stealing a biscuit.

'Look, I care for Sienna. She's a bloody good woman and a loyal solicitor. She sends me decent cases,' he explains, attempting to justify his actions. I'm not buying it. 'OK, fine. I'll stop. Just watch yourself. Julian's cocky and I loathe cocky. He'll do whatever it takes to win.'

'So will I,' I whisper menacingly with a wink.

'That's my girl!' He laughs, raising his drink to mine. The music in the bar is turned up a notch as we sip from our oversized glasses.

'Leila, I hope you know you can come to me for help or guidance. I'm always here, professionally or personally,' he says, reaching out and very gently placing his hand on the top of my leg. His fingers curl around, ever so slightly, to the inside of my thigh.

I look at him with a cold stare. He quickly removes his hand and runs it through his silver hair. He crossed a line, and he knows it. I should rant and rave at him right now about how he's overstepped the mark, but I don't.

I consider it for a few seconds. It's the right thing to do.

But.

I really need to ask him something. And I can't do that if I launch a tirade of feminism at him. And he's my head of chambers; he could make life very difficult for me if he wanted to. Chester is known for being a great ally if you're on his good side – and lethal if you're not.

Something deep inside is still niggling away at me after seeing the way Demi acted at Chester's birthday party a couple of weeks back.

'Sorry . . . sorry . . . I shouldn't have done that . . . I suppose I just . . .' he mumbles. 'I don't know what I was thinking. I just . . . I've a lot going on at the moment. Sorry.'

'It's *fine*,' I say, despising myself. Just last night, I was empowering students not to stand for this shit, and now here I am, planning on using what just happened to my advantage. If I need information from him, now's the time to get it. It's a classic cross-examination technique.

'Forget it, Chester,' I say, dismissively, moving even further away from him. 'How are things with you, anyway? How's Demi? She looked beautiful at your party.'

'What?' he says, distracted, leaning back into the sofa. 'I tell you what, Leila, I'm not doing this again.'

'Doing what?' I ask, forcing a huge gulp of wine down my throat.

'Marriage.'

'What do you mean?' I try not to ask too quickly.

'I think she's having an affair.'

I knew something was going on. I *knew* it.

'What? Demi? No.'

'Was. Is. I'm not sure. But something's up.'

'What makes you think that?'

'Well, firstly, I'm not as oblivious as she thinks I am. Secondly, I've been there and done that, haven't I? I know the signs. Serves me right, I suppose.'

Chester had just split up with his first wife when I joined chambers. He had the look of a broken man, one who had ultimately messed up and lost everything: his wife, his home, his life. Risked it all for the thrill of another woman. It's not difficult to see how he managed it. Even now, he oozes charisma and charm.

It took him a couple of years to get over what happened. I rarely saw him around chambers during that time. Apparently, he didn't like coming in, being around people. I think he drank a lot. After that, he became a bit of a cliché; bought a fast car, a city apartment overlooking the river. Every Friday night he'd be surrounded by young women in champagne bars – no expense spared.

'I'm fifty-nine years old, Leila, and what have I got to show for myself? On the way to two failed marriages and a kid who won't speak to me.'

Honestly, he's an intelligent man. How can he not see that actions have consequences? And yet, for some stupid reason, I feel sorry for the idiot.

'It's never too late, you know. To make things good with Elise.'

Everyone in chambers knows Chester's daughter hasn't spoken to him since he cheated on her mother. I think he maintains a strained relationship with his son, but the daughter wants nothing to do with him.

'She made her views about me clear a long time ago. It is very much too late.'

There's a sadness and fragility to him as he says this.

'So, what are you going to do about Demi?' I ask, attempting to drag him out of his melancholy.

'She's been so erratic these last few months. Distant. Going out at weird times, not saying where. She's unpredictable. It's like she can't stand to be near me.'

'Maybe it's not an affair. Perhaps it's something else. Maybe she's just stalking people and then killing them,' I say, deadpan. He throws his head back and laughs, which sets me off, too.

'Do you have any idea who it might be?' I ask.

'No. Not yet,' he says, calmly. But the emphasis on 'yet' is intended to convey he will soon enough. 'She's not the sharpest tool in the shed. She'll trip up at some point, and I'm watching her like a hawk now. But I'll tell you something, I won't be made a fool of, Leila.'

Now that, I believe.

9

Witness X

Rule #2
Become Someone's Addiction

Nothing quite hits a man like the first woman he has an affair with.

You want to make him crave you in a way he'll remember, even when you're long gone.

Be elusive. Be enigmatic. Be whatever you need to be. Just ensure you intoxicate him. It's easier than you think. Men are basic creatures.

Be who they want you to be. Don't be yourself. Men want a fantasy. Something they can reach out and almost touch but never have. Look available but never *be* available.

Don't give too much away about yourself. Allow him to fill in the gaps. It doesn't matter if he's wrong. After a conversation, make sure you know a lot about him, but he knows barely anything about you. Wrap yourself up in mystery, one he will want to solve. He never will, of course, because the plot twist is that it's all fake. The version of you he knows doesn't exist, and that's why it's so alluring. He will never figure you out.

If you can get a man to fall in love with this version of you, he'll be in your pocket for ever, or however long you need him for.

'Men are fucking pigs,' Dad used to tell me, not sensing the irony in what he was saying. 'You're nothing but a piece of meat to them. They'll never want *you*. If you want to survive around them, you need to learn how to manipulate them. Play them at their own game.'

I didn't even know what that word meant back then. Manipulate. Dad explained it was 'having control', which sounded good to me. But I was only a kid – how could I have control over adults?

'I'm going to show you something you'll never forget,' he said, one overcast Sunday in October. He drove me to some kind of club that only had men in it, and by the time we got there, I had started to feel weird because of the drinks he'd given me before we left the house. As the doors swung open, clouds of cigarette smoke hit me in the face. Men turned to look at me, a girl young enough to be their daughter. And he was right. I looked older because of the dress and lipstick I was wearing. I felt older. I sensed their eyes all over my body and I used it, toyed with it after that until I became an expert.

I learned that men love the thrill of pursuit. If an attractive female bulldozes into their boring life and reignites that youthful sensation of lust – and makes them feel desired in the process – they will do anything for you. I revelled in the attention they lavished upon me and, as I got older, I weaponized it. Every woman should have a man completely wrapped around her finger. You never know when you might need him.

'Remember,' Dad whispered into my ear, each time he saw their eyes land on my adolescent flesh, 'always make sure you have control. Never, ever beg. Use them, but don't fall for them. I'm the only man you can trust. Don't forget that.'

It never occurred to me he was the one man I shouldn't be trusting.

I quickly realized that my sense of worth and lovability was tied to how manipulative I could prove I was around men. So, I got very good at it.

It was the only time I ever saw him proud of me.

The first man I had complete control over was Declan, when I was nineteen. He was a rugby type, ripped and unbelievably handsome. Kind and affectionate. Funny.

It was blissful in the beginning, when I showed him a fake version of myself because – as Dad said – he'd never want the *real* me. Instead, I showed him the kind of girl I so desperately wanted to be. But as time wore on, I began to push boundaries. I was constantly testing his dedication to the relationship, creating drama where there was none because this lovely, normal relationship was more than I deserved. It felt abnormal and unfamiliar. It scared me at times, seeing how dreadfully I treated him, but I didn't care. The anger and self-loathing I felt for myself was overwhelming, but I couldn't stop it. I didn't know where it came from.

That relationship turned me into a monster. I became obsessed with having power over him, ensuring he was continually idolizing me, prepared to drop his plans to be with me. On the afternoon he went through my phone and found I'd been cheating on him, I sat and watched him – a fourteen-stone rugby player – sob into a pillow because I had broken his heart.

I despised myself for it.

But at the same time, I felt incredible because *I'd* caused that destruction, and finally had proof of my ability to control someone – just as Dad had always wanted.

And now, all these years later, I've done exactly the same thing. Only this time, the stakes are higher. Because if my husband finds out I've had an affair, he won't just cry about it.

He'll kill me.

10

Leila

102 days before trial

My conversation with Chester last week in the bar left me stewing for more reasons than I'd like.

After brushing off the hand-on-knee situation, I was filled with guilt and disappointment at myself. How am I supposed to set an example if I can't uphold basic feminism?

But that was the least of my worries when I left the bar that afternoon.

The gut feeling I'd had about Demi had only intensified. I've always been an intuitive person. Hypervigilant. It's what makes me a good lawyer. It always starts with a gut feeling that something isn't quite right. You know how, sometimes, when you walk into a room, you can sense something has changed? Even if it's a small detail, like a picture has been taken down off the wall? Nobody else has noticed, but you do.

It's like that.

That's how I feel about Demi.

I have a conference with Davina in chambers this morning. We fill the enormous table in Conference Room 3 with files and papers that have been sent to us by the prosecution.

By my husband.

It is against this evidence that I will advise Jack what his defence should be, if he has one, and whether he should plead guilty or not guilty.

Jim arranged for a tray of coffee and pastries to be sent in for Davina. Solicitors usually only get biscuits, but none of us will forget the (only) time she was subjected to this and proceeded to march down to the clerks' room to complain. There was a veiled threat of refusing to send further work to chambers if 'our firm is worth no more than a standard Marks and Spencer biscuit selection'.

Davina is a force of nature. I was terrified of her when I first started. Always immaculate, she wears her platinum hair in the same high, slick bun every day, and even wears a hairnet to keep it secure. I mean, this woman has her life together. A heavy, blunt fringe sits just above her brows. She is known for her bold look – orange lipstick, smoky black eyeliner – and is an influential person within legal circles, so I'm keen to impress her in this trial. Do a good job for someone like Davina and you'll never be out of work.

'So, what do you think his defence is going to be?' she asks, draining the caramel latte she brought in from Starbucks. Within seconds, she's pouring another coffee from the French press Jim supplied. 'Because it sounds to me like he's intending to plead very not guilty.'

'What are you thinking? Self-defence?'

'It's the only defence he can advance, surely?'

'What's Anton's motive for attacking Jack, though?' I ask her. 'You wouldn't place them both together. It's just so . . . peculiar.'

'Yes. What was Anton doing there in the first place? That's what will make people think there's more to this than meets the eye.'

'I agree,' I confirm, nodding my head. 'And going by what Jack said, there already is.'

'Perhaps that's the one thing we have going for us. No motive.'

'Well, if I know anything about my husband, he'll find one,' I say with a hint of anxiety in my voice. 'The jury will speculate all kinds of reasons why Anton was visiting a doorman on a Friday night. Drugs? Was he gay? The prosecution will paint Anton as a friend of the people, but you and I know he was often controversial. He carried outdated views and routinely upset people. And he liked women.'

'Yes, I noticed nothing was said about *that* at his memorial,' Davina interrupts.

Typical of Davina to point this out.

'What's your relationship with Jack?' I ask Davina. 'Have you dealt with him before?'

'Nope. But I'm aware of him. You know me, Leila, everyone's on my radar, but I was surprised he wanted us for this.'

'Surprised? Why?'

'You know we have a very particular way of doing things at Jessops. It's not for everyone and it's not for the weak. It's strategic. We go in hard and make the prosecution prove everything. No-comment interview. "It wasn't me. I wasn't there. If I was there, prove I did it." We don't make it easy for them. It comes with risks. Sometimes it pays off, and sometimes it doesn't. We don't pussyfoot around clients – we tell it like it is. They are loyal to us, and we are loyal to them.'

As summaries go, she's putting it lightly. Davina and her (equally dodgy) solicitor husband blur the line that separates lawyers and criminals. When people go to them, they don't just get a criminal lawyer, they get a *criminal* lawyer.

They will do anything to secure an acquittal, even if it's not by the book, and are funded by all the big-time criminals.

'Why is he doing this? The riddles, the cryptic clues?' she

says. 'I sensed some friction when he mentioned the last time you represented him. Anything I need to be aware of?'

I place my pen down on the table. It still stings to talk about it. 'I advised him – entirely properly – on how to proceed with that case but it backfired. He was convicted, labelled a grass and went to prison.'

'So, what's changed now? No offence, but I'm surprised he instructed you again.'

'He knows I'll run the trial however he wants. No defence statement. No idea what he's going to say in evidence. It's a disaster waiting to happen, but he knows I won't stop it. I owe him.'

'If he makes us work out what happened, I guess he technically hasn't grassed anyone up?'

'Exactly.'

'And it has the added bonus of clawing his reputation back, by the look of things. The criminal network talks. Whoever he's protecting – and it sounds like they're high up – they remain safe. That'll get out. He's smart, this one.'

This is why Jack chose Davina as his lawyer. Damage limitation. He knows that as long as he doesn't speak, Davina will make sure the criminal underground hears about it. Whether he's acquitted and gets out or goes to prison, his reputation as a snitch will at least be gone.

'I wonder if I should have a conference with him alone, see if he'll talk.'

'Alone?' I ask, confused. 'Why?'

'I think he'd be more likely to talk to me if you weren't there.'

'Why do you think that?'

'I think clients like Jack – they're removed from the likes of you. They see the wig and robes and there's an air of distrust. They trust me because I'm more on their level. He might open up to me. I'd relay everything back to you, obviously.'

Setting aside the fact that I'm not remotely convinced Davina would tell me everything Jack said in a secret conference of this type, I'm insulted she's portrayed me as being stuffy and out of touch with my client.

'I don't think it's necessary.'

'Leila . . .'

Why is she pushing this? What's the urgency to be alone with him? Especially after the conversation we've just had.

'No,' I say, firmly. 'I think it's best we see him together.'

A silence hangs in the air. I don't want the conference to get off to a bad start, but I need to be definite with her about this.

'So, where do you want to begin? The post-mortem?' Davina asks, abruptly. 'Pretty grim reading.'

'Cause of death – subdural haematoma. Bleeding to the brain as a result of blunt force trauma. Died a few hours after arriving at the hospital,' I confirm. 'He was hit over the head with a blunt weapon, something heavy by the looks of things.'

'It's this,' she answers, picking up a photo of a kettlebell, surrounded by markers to demonstrate how big it is.

'What weight is it?'

'10 kg. Pathologist claims it's consistent with the injury.'

'That's bad for us if he's going to go down the self-defence route. The kettlebell was found at the scene, effectively acting as a doorstop in the bedroom. No attempt to hide it and no prints, is that right?'

'Yes. Odd, isn't it?'

I lean back in my chair, staring at this photo of a black and electric-blue kettlebell.

'Very. Is there any indication where it was kept before that?'

'Nothing in the file.'

'Can you make enquiries, Davina? It's a bit of a reach, I know. But if anyone can do it, you can.'

Picking up her pen, she writes frantically in her notebook.

'Whatever happened that night, he appears to have intended to cause serious harm,' she observes. 'I can't imagine that being classed as reasonable force for self-defence. If you look at the arresting officer's statement, PC Walker confirms Jack displayed superficial injuries on his face and neck when the police arrived at the scene. Look at the photos.'

We shuffle through the papers and find the photos taken at the police station following Jack's arrest. As per the statement, redness has formed around Jack's right eye and the middle of his neck. His hair is wild, unstyled. He's wearing a white T-shirt, although it's inside out and back to front. The label sticks out from the collar, visible below his chin. There's also a large, wet, brown stain down the front.

'Yes,' I tell her, 'but, as you say, even if there was a scuffle for whatever reason, it doesn't justify Jack picking up a heavy weight and cracking Anton over the head with it. It's disproportionate.'

'Having said that, Anton's prints have been found on a small kitchen knife,' Davina points out. 'It was on the kitchen floor. Might give us a run at self-defence?'

'Given Anton's dead, the Crown will say it was him who picked up the knife in self-defence. Jack didn't have any injuries from it. Not a scratch. Besides, we need to be careful running that in front of a jury – you've seen Jack. Would they seriously believe he'd fear an out-of-shape near-pensioner holding a small knife? Jack is built like the lead in a Magic Mike show, for god's sake.'

It's hard, shooting every point down, but we need to be realistic. I've seen how jurors react to these kinds of defences. We need to be smarter than this.

'What about other forensics?' she asks. 'What have they found?'

'A lot,' I answer, nodding my head. 'Fibres from the clothes Anton was wearing were found on Jack's T-shirt and jeans, suggesting a struggle. But they also went through the room with a fine-tooth comb and found some other stuff, too.'

'Like what?'

'Jack's fresh semen on the sofa.'

The room goes quiet for a few moments. The question is clear on Davina's face – is this relevant in any way? It's difficult when you're examining crime scenes because something that appears normal could either be totally irrelevant or essential information. It's often only experience that allows you to determine between the two.

'I'm not sure where to place this piece of information yet. But there are also seven different strands of hair,' I go on. 'Ranging in lengths but likely female, they were found in the living room where Anton's body was. There were also six different sets of prints on various items in the same room: five glasses from the club and a lighter. The police can't find a match to any of them.'

'Good for us, though?' she says, optimistically. 'Shows the apartment wasn't only used by Jack? That there could have been other people there?'

'It depends on what his defence is.'

'What about CCTV at the club?' she asks.

'None.'

'I thought so.' Davina nods. She wouldn't be surprised by this. She's the kind of lawyer who advises people to get rid of CCTV for this exact reason. 'What about the bar downstairs?'

Temptation is located on the first and second floors of a Grade II listed building. It is linked by one door to the ground floor – a bar called Innocence, which is owned by Eddie Sorrington too. Members also have their own secret entrance to Temptation from the outside. It's not advertised.

'Same. No CCTV anywhere. It's a place people go to not be seen. They know there's no CCTV there or leading up to Jack's apartment upstairs. That's why they go. To become invisible.'

'I'm concerned what the jury will make of his phone, Leila,' Davina says, changing lanes, looking at me. 'Or, lack of it.'

'Me too,' I agree with her. 'A phone that goes missing the day you're accused of murder isn't a great start, is it? We'll have to see what the phone company records bring back, but the prosecution will have a field day with that side of things. It looks bad.'

'Drugs?'

'Maybe,' I reply, mulling over her suggestion. 'But I don't think it's as simple as that.'

'Why?'

'Just a feeling.'

Davina smiles but doesn't respond.

'I'm really not happy about him jumping into the witness box at trial to lay out his version of events without telling us what he's going to say first, Leila. It makes me edgy. This isn't how I do things.'

'I know, but it's how he wants to run it, and we can't force him to talk. Then again, how are we supposed to prepare a defence out of thin air?'

'All cases have weak spots,' Davina says, reaching for a croissant. 'We'll just have to find one.'

Two hours later my head is banging. Needing fresh air, I nip out to buy lunch. The crushing weight of expectation and stress that comes with this case bears down on me so heavily now I feel suffocated by it. I'm going to humiliate myself publicly and get Jack convicted at the same time.

What I really want to do is ask Julian for help. *Am I doing this bit right? How would you approach this?* But I can't do any of that because, right now, he's my opponent.

Waiting in the never-ending line to get served, I reach for my phone for the first time since I left chambers. I have a new private message on my *Chats at the Bar* Instagram account. It was sent seven minutes ago.

> @JustAnotherDumbBlonde
>
> Very much enjoyed your talk at Mountcross Academy. Particularly entertaining to hear you talk about your terribly sad childhood *eye roll* You must have forgotten about the top boarding school you attended. Excellent advice about how we shouldn't encourage sexual inappropriateness with people at work . . . just a shame you can't follow it yourself. If this is how you distort your own truth, I worry for Jack Millman.

II

Leila

Friday, 8 February 2019
Durham Crown Court
Five years earlier

THERE IS SOMETHING in legal circles known as a 'hospital pass', which is a case nobody else wants. It's often a case that's unwanted because it's going to be tied up in legal argument all day, or the witnesses are going to be a nightmare (if they turn up at all). Sometimes, it's because the case is at a court at the other end of the country. They're usually given to junior barristers because they're less likely to kick up a fuss.

Jim called me at 8.32 a.m. *this morning* with the immortal and now familiar words.

'Miss Reynolds, I'm aware you've booked to be out of court today, but I have a plea and trial preparation hearing I need returning, and you're the only barrister available.'

I couldn't say no, even though Julian and I had planned to set off for our trip to the Lake District. He'd booked a cottage for the weekend, and we were meant to be leaving in thirty minutes.

'No problem, Jim,' I said, as Julian violently shook his head in my direction. As a barrister, you become used to this at the junior end. Julian would be allowed to turn it down as he's more senior, but I'm not yet at a point in my career where I'm able to do so.

'Thank you, Miss Reynolds! I'll get it on early so you and Mr Kesler can be off as soon as possible. He's spoken of nothing else all week.'

Cute. It's been a hectic twelve months, what with getting married and Julian taking silk. We try and grab these moments away when we can. It's not easy trying to coordinate diaries, especially when this kind of thing happens.

'I appreciate that. What's the name of the defendant?'

'Millman. Jack Millman.'

I dash into chambers to pick up the brief before heading to court. I need to become acquainted with it quickly so I can advise Mr Millman as to whether he should plead guilty or not guilty at his hearing today. He's charged with Section 20 inflicting grievous bodily harm, the less serious of the two GBH offences. Mr Millman works the door security at the Temptation Club in Durham (dodgy in itself) and it's alleged he assaulted the complainant – a man called Tony Flanagan – by delivering a punch to the jaw that forced him to stumble backwards and fall into a glass table, which cut his body to bits.

It doesn't take long to understand why nobody wanted this case. Tony Flanagan is well known within the criminal network. He's also the rival of Eddie Sorrington, who owns the Temptation Club.

It's going to be a knotty case.

I call out for Mr Millman on the concourse, and a man with short, jet-black hair and striking blue eyes stands and walks towards me. Unlike most of my clients, he's formally dressed. A navy-blue suit and white shirt rest smartly on his broad frame.

'Are you Miss Reynolds?' he asks, offering his hand for me to shake.

'I am, yes.' I nod, surprised by his politeness. I take his hand and meet his eye. I always think you can tell a lot about a man by his handshake. 'I'm your barrister today. Sorry, but your solicitor is tied up with another case at the moment. Let's have a chat before we go in.'

I take him into a conference room beside court and get straight to it. I've seen from his antecedent history he's familiar with the system but doesn't have anything for violence since he was fifteen. Now, at twenty-seven years old, this allegation seems quite out of character.

'You gave a no-comment interview upon arrest so, as far as the prosecution are concerned, they have no idea what your version of events is. I've read the notes from your solicitor, which details what you told them in conference – namely, that your reason for assaulting Mr Flanagan was because you found him in a room attempting to sexually assault a young woman called Mia Woods, who is twenty-two?'

'Correct,' he confirms, sitting opposite me across the table. The case papers are spread out between us.

'And she works at Temptation as a hostess.'

'Yes.'

'Your solicitor says Miss Woods is prepared to give evidence in court to confirm this?'

'She is, yes.'

I pause for a moment to check the papers. Something isn't sitting well with me.

'Mr Millman, did you have a solicitor in your police interview?'

'Yeah, he advised me to go no comment. He said because of who it was, he didn't think it would go anywhere.'

'What do you mean?'

'Tony Flanagan doesn't want unnecessary coppers in his life. Or, at least, that's what we thought.'

'He doesn't get on with Eddie, does he?'

'Nah. They've been rivals for years. That's what this is all about. He wouldn't be pursuing it otherwise.'

I'm aware of Flanagan. He's a dangerous man. Notorious. Jack's solicitor was right to advise him not to say anything in interview, but it's going to cause issues now.

'Mr Millman, from what I've seen and heard, you should plead not guilty to this offence. Your defence should be that you were defending another from harm.'

'Yeah, I'm good with that.' He's soft spoken for a man of his build.

'You'll have the opportunity to tell the jury what happened when you give evidence if you plead not guilty.'

'Well, I *am* not guilty,' he tells me, firmly. 'If I hadn't got Flanagan off her, Christ knows what he would have done.'

There's sincerity in his voice. I believe him.

'Let's hope she turns up at court and says just that.'

His piercing eyes drill into mine.

'You don't think she will, do you?'

I lean back in my chair and cross my legs. My robes drop to the floor.

'Do you? Honestly?' I ask him straight, to his surprise. His eyes don't move from mine. 'Your defence hinges on her. Flanagan knows who she is. He's a dangerous man. It will be difficult to show a jury you're not guilty if, for whatever reason, your main witness doesn't show up.'

This man in front of me has no idea of the legal dilemma I face, because this is not a normal case. It never is when influential people are involved. I have two choices and both carry pros, cons, and an element of risk.

I can cooperate with the prosecution and serve them a defence statement that sets out everything Mr Millman has told me regarding his defence. This could help him in the long run, as they might find and disclose evidence to corroborate his version. The disadvantage is that the prosecution will know exactly what he's going to say at trial, and given the people involved, Flanagan might ensure the vital witness in this case goes missing.

Or I could take the more maverick approach and not serve a defence statement at all. The prosecution will have no clue what Jack is going to say and so won't be able to sabotage anything. But the jury will be told they can draw an adverse inference from this when they come to determine his guilt.

It's difficult, weighing these kinds of decisions, when it's someone's liberty at stake.

'Who will represent me at trial?' he asks, leaning back in his chair, mirroring me.

'It'll probably be me now, if you're content with that?'

'Yeah.' He smiles, the dimples in his cheeks revealing themselves for the first time. 'You've got your wits about you. And you're more on my level than the other one.'

'Your level?' I frown.

'You know.' He shrugs. 'Not stuck up.'

'I take that as a huge compliment,' I laugh, gathering all the case papers from the table. 'Come on, then. Let's hope your witness isn't given an incentive to stay away.'

Julian taught me you should always serve a defence statement; it's never worth the uncertainty not to. He's right. It's the safer option, even if there is still risk attached to it. At least that way, you can't be criticized, whereas you will be questioned on your decision not to serve one.

Always better to be safe than sorry when you're dealing with a human life.

As I enter court, I mentally drown out the voice inside my head screaming that it's the wrong decision. I'm doing what my pupilmaster taught me and he is always right.

At least, I hope he is.

12

Witness X

Rule #3
Knowledge Is Power

'THE REASON CON artists get away with everything they do is because they're good at finding people's weaknesses.'

He'd know.

My dad was charming and charismatic. Men wanted to be his friend and women wanted to sleep with him. None of this had anything to do with his status in society; most of the people he manipulated knew nothing about him or what he did for a living. But he always seemed to know what people wanted, what they needed to hear. Dad was an *incredible* listener. He studied people and wore different masks depending on who he spoke to. A chameleon. I was the only one who saw the real him.

'The only way to protect yourself from people is to gather information to hurt them with later on. If you don't do this, they'll strike first.'

Everybody has an emotional wound, he'd tell me, and once people know what that weakness is, they can use it to destroy you.

Or you can use it to destroy them.

Take Jack, for example. He wouldn't have done what he did

if he had protected his weaknesses a bit better. Then there's Anton – his weakness was more complicated. More conflicted. He paid the ultimate price for it in the end.

Neither would have ended up where they are now if they'd been more guarded. More careful.

I honestly walk away from some men and women – people I've met at parties for all of fifteen minutes, airing their childhood trauma – and think, 'Do you know how easy it would be for someone to hurt you?' What do they expect, if they make themselves vulnerable to strangers?

That's the key: once people start talking to someone who is willing to listen, they'll reveal anything. We all want to be heard, even if we give away our own secrets. Beware people accusing you of something; it's very likely they're doing it themselves. Projection is powerful.

Dad used to ask me to give him obscure challenges: get personal, financial, or childhood details from strangers, and he always managed it. He found out their imaginary friends as a kid, bank account details – he even once got a woman to give him £600 in the space of twenty minutes. It was a sport to him. And Dad was right. Everyone has a wound, even me.

Especially me.

How I managed to reach adulthood without becoming an alcoholic, a drug addict, or killing myself was purely down to my determination to be nothing like him in the end.

That has always been my biggest fear.

And so, when someone or something threatens what I've worked so hard for, I cannot look the other way. Because I escaped that life, that wretched life drenched in constant fear. It's the smaller, subtler things I'm now fiercely protective of, like feeling safe when I turn the light off before I go to sleep. The knowledge that my bedroom door won't be opened in the middle of the night. Recognizing that my body is my own and I now get a say in who touches it.

The things I had to do to get here, you'd be horrified to know. I learned the tools I needed to escape, and I used them.

Find the weaknesses in people and then exploit them. That's where your power is.

13
Leila

101 days before trial

I'VE BEEN STARING at the message from @JustAnotherDumb Blonde for the last twenty-four hours. The lawyer in me keeps asking the same questions: *Who are they? What do they want? What do they know?*

Most of the message can be explained away. Harmless. But the other stuff . . . that's complicated. More dangerous. It could cause a lot of damage. I'm very aware a Google search could unearth what they're referring to in seconds, if they knew what to look for.

The 'sexual inappropriateness' is obviously referring to Chester, which means someone's been watching me. I'm sickened, thinking of it.

I look like a hypocrite.

I need to find out who @JustAnotherDumbBlonde is. It 'sounds' like a woman. But when I click on her profile, she has no followers, and the only account she follows is mine. She hasn't posted any photos, which means one thing: this account has been set up explicitly to troll me, and I need to find out why.

Every Friday at 7.30 p.m. I visit my mother-in-law. It's an odd set-up, but she's seventy-eight years old and in the very early stages of dementia. I've always liked Audrey; she's a no-nonsense, well-spoken woman who still lives in the house where she raised Julian. It's a massive Victorian, semi-detached property in one of the leafy suburbs that's way too big for her, but she refuses to move 'until they carry her out of it in a box'.

Balancing two bags of fish and chips in one hand and a bouquet of vibrant candy-pink roses in the other, I open the front door without any resistance, which means she's left the lock off the latch again. I shudder at the thought of anyone having free access to this house. I had two extra locks and a chain placed on the door last week and told Audrey she must lock the door at all times for her own safety. I, more than anyone, know how dangerous it is for a vulnerable woman to be alone, especially in the winter, but she still lives in the 1960s, when people left their doors wide open all night.

'Just me, Audrey!' I shout, my voice echoing in the hallway against the sound of Classic FM which creeps out of the dining room. This property would look beautiful if renovated: light and airy. But it's been kept the same for decades, all yellowing flock wallpaper and swirly garish carpets.

She's sitting in her chair by the window in the lounge. Heating on full blast. A salmon-pink dress with a formal collar hangs off her frail body. She wears a sparkly silver brooch above her collarbone. Audrey does not do casual.

'There's no need to bloody shout. Who else is it going to be on a Friday night at this time?' she says, wide-eyed. Her immaculately coiffed white hair curls neatly around her wrinkled face. Audrey is the kind of woman who wears a full face of make-up even when she's not leaving the house. She's been like this for as long as I've known her. It's become harsher in recent times, though; her classic ruby-red lipstick could have been applied by a child. The baby-blue eyeshadow she used to wear so subtly, so elegantly, is now pulled all the way up to her eyebrows.

'I didn't want to scare you,' I tell her, closing the long, green, velour curtains, glimpsing my reflection in the large sash windows. It makes me uneasy; someone could be looking in and you wouldn't see them. 'And you really shouldn't leave your door off the latch. Anyone could walk in.'

'What a vulgar thing to say!' she replies in a voice that suggests I've uttered the most ridiculous thing, despite the fact that I, myself, have just demonstrated the very point I'm making. 'Who on earth would want to bother an old woman?'

'You'd be surprised,' I tell her, throwing off my long puffer coat.

'Not everyone is a murderer or a psychopath, you know. Leave your work in the courtroom. And go and lay my supper out, I'm starving.'

Audrey used to have an active social life. It's tailed off in the last six months because she's become quite forgetful, and it's taken real organization to keep her connected to the local community. She won't hear of getting any help in, so I came up with the idea of bringing her supper on Fridays, as a way of making sure she's OK. The routine anchors her in reality, and she doesn't see it as – god forbid – *help*.

Because Audrey is very proper, we eat in the dining room off a Royal Doulton dining set, with freshly brewed tea out of a teapot. The dining room overlooks the garden, which is starting to overgrow as autumn takes residence. I should call the gardener to sort it out. Audrey has an old record player in here, and she makes me play her crackly old vinyl when we eat. Today, I play Gerry and the Pacemakers, 'You'll Never Walk Alone'. It makes me smile.

'I always used to take Julian for fish and chips on a Friday, you know,' she tells me. 'When he was very little. To Whitley Bay.'

She tells me this story every week, and every week, I pretend I haven't heard it before. I was the one to notice it, initially. How she'd repeat things or forget details and names more than I'd consider to be normal. I told Julian but his response was that she's just 'getting older'. He struggled to accept it. His father died when he was just six, so his mother was the only person in his life for a long time.

'He always used to complain, Julian,' she goes on. 'The chips are too soggy, the chips are too hot. There was never any pleasing that boy. Is he coming tonight?'

She asks every week, and every week the answer is the same.

'He can't make it today, Audrey. Working on a big case, but he'll be around soon. Stuck with me, I'm afraid!'

A vague, lost smile settles on her face. Her eyes hop around the room and settle on a framed photo on the wall. It's a picture of our wedding day. Lake Garda in the late afternoon sun. We look so happy and in love. I was super-blonde back then and only recently have started to go darker; I have had caramel and mocha lowlights put in ahead of winter.

The wedding was an intimate ceremony. I didn't want the full shebang, so it was just the two of us and a witness off the street. Julian and I spent the following two weeks exploring Italy and it was beautiful. The photo almost looks out of place, surrounded by landscapes in dark wooden frames.

'What was her name again?' Audrey asks, looking up at the wedding photo.

'That's me, Leila.'

'I knew the other one wouldn't last,' she says, taking a sip out of her teacup.

It's difficult having conversations with Audrey these days. She switches between topics so quickly, it's challenging to keep up.

'The wife. What *was* her name again?' she goes on. 'Samantha . . . Sarah . . .'

She's talking about Julian's ex-wife.

'Sienna.'

'That's the one,' she says. 'Wasn't keen on their wedding. December, it was. Freezing cold. I don't remember going to your wedding.'

'No, Audrey, we didn't have any guests.'

'I didn't see your parents there. Have I met your parents?'

'No, Audrey,' I say, softly. 'You haven't.'

Audrey has always been a bit of a mother-figure to me. Before the memory started to go, we used to watch musicals when they came to Newcastle. She used to look so glamorous for a night at the theatre. She'd flounce in, dripping in sparkly jewellery and a fabulous dress.

'Does he know you're hiding something from him?'

It takes me a second to register what she's said. The cup of tea I'm about to take a drink out of brushes against my bottom lip, before being carefully placed back on the table.

'What?' I ask, smiling.

'I know what it is,' she whispers, staring right at me. Sometimes when you look at Audrey, she appears to be a million miles away, but right now, she seems completely lucid. Every word coming out of her mouth is said with intent. 'You can trust me; I won't tell him. But I know your dirty secret.'

I do a little laugh to mask the awkwardness.

'I'm not hiding anything, Audrey—'

'Yes, you are,' she interrupts. 'You can't fool me. I see everything.'

Pressure builds inside my chest, like a stormy sky just before the thunder starts. I'm suddenly very aware of my heart, which feels about to break free from my ribcage.

She doesn't know. How could she possibly know?

'Your hair,' she says, deadpan. 'You're not naturally as blonde as you are in that photo. I know you dye it. I won't tell him. Our secret.'

I stare at her, allowing my body to return to its normal state.

'You've got me there!' I laugh, as my body regulates back to a calmer state.

She winks and goes back to eating her food, talking about an old lunchbox she saw on *Antiques Roadshow*.

After supper, I do a bit of clearing up around the house. We pay for a cleaner to come once a week, but I always do a quick tidy.

'Can you pick up a new jigsaw for us to do?' she asks.

'Of course. I'll bring a new one next Friday.'

'Why aren't you coming on Tuesday?' she asks, confused.

'I always come on Friday. I bring you fish and chips, bring you some flowers, we do some jigsaws, then I leave around 10-ish. That's our routine.'

She stares at me, allowing the words I've said to chew over in her mind.

'Have you always done that?'

She's getting worse. I nod my head, placing my hand on hers.

'I have, yes.'

'Are you sure?' she asks, frowning. 'I'm sure you never used to . . .'

I hate leaving her like this.

'Yes, Audrey. I've done this for a while now.'

She looks into my eyes, trying to find the truth. They dart around, not fully settling on anything. She looks lost.

'I'm sure you're right, darling!' She smiles. 'See you Friday!'

As I tidy, I do a quick sweep of the house, just to make sure everything is in order.

The landing creaks as I walk past every room. The house has four bedrooms, three of which are unused. They all look undisturbed, the same every week. It's charming in a classic, old-fashioned way.

Take the small, front bedroom, for example. Opening the bedroom door, I press the light switch, which illuminates the entire room in a dazzling yellow glow. It resembles a movie set from the 1960s. The double bed is neatly made, draped in a floral bedspread. The mahogany wardrobe in the corner shows no signs of being disturbed. A vintage dressing table hosts a large mirror, with all kinds of trinkets and ornaments carefully placed on the shiny surface.

So many valuables. So many cherished memories. It makes me feel sick to think anyone could simply walk into this house uninvited. She needs to start locking that door.

14

Leila

10.23 p.m.

JULIAN ARRIVES HOME not long after me. The smell of whisky follows him around. He pours himself another one after throwing his suit jacket on the armchair, something he only ever does when he's incredibly stressed out. Slumping onto the sofa opposite me, he removes his tie while flicking through his phone.

'Good night?' I ask, in an attempt to drag him out of the weird state he's in. He doesn't reply, clearly preoccupied with whatever – or whoever – he's dealing with. This is the hazard of being married to a barrister. It's not a nine-to-five job. There's always an email to deal with, some evidence to review.

'Julian? Did you have a good night?'

He shoots me a surprised look, as if he's only just realized I'm here.

'What? Oh, yes, darling.'

'Who was out?'

'Usual crowd.'

'Where did you go?'

'Advocacy skills 101?' He laughs. This is an inside joke between us. It's difficult not to appear to be cross-examining someone when you're asking questions. 'Just had a few in the Elvet.'

'I've been to see your mum.'

'How is she?' he asks, tapping on his phone without looking up.

'She's getting worse every week, Julian. I think you should go and see her. She was asking about you again.'

He throws his phone down beside him on the sofa and puts his feet up on the coffee table.

'It's hard seeing her like that. She's not the woman I remember. I appreciate you going over there, but you don't have to.'

Walking over, I sit next to him and swing my legs over his knees. Putting his phone away in his trouser pocket, he slides his hands over my legs.

'I just want to help her,' I tell him.

'But you've got your own life. You should be out on a Friday night with your friends, not staying in and playing backgammon with my mother! Why don't you tell her you're busy from now on?'

'I couldn't do that,' I tell him. 'I'd feel bad lying to her, and she looks forward to me going.'

'Well, I'll pay for some help to go in.'

'Please don't. She'd hate that. But it'd make her day if you popped by,' I tell him softly, slipping my hand into his hair, which finally raises a smile from him.

'OK,' he whispers. 'I'll call by in the morning after my round of golf.'

I remember the first time I watched Julian properly perform in court. On week two of my pupillage, Julian prosecuted a rape case. The trial was fascinating. I had, of course, completed many mini-pupillages – when you spend a week with a criminal barrister, usually observing a trial – but this was different. I was *inside* it this time. Immersed.

I looked on in awe as he delivered his closing speech to the jury. There is something hypnotic about witnessing high-quality advocacy in a courtroom. Anyone who says delivering a closing speech is a skill is wrong; it's an art. It's been said barristers are actors without Equity cards, and that's true.

The courtroom is your stage, your robes are your costume, and the jury is your audience. How successful you are isn't necessarily based on what evidence is presented – it's all about your performance.

I cringe thinking back to the innocent baby barrister I was when I joined chambers; the 'law school way' I'd prepare sentences or skeleton arguments. Julian would make me stand in his office, with ten minutes' preparation time to simulate real life, and prepare a plea in mitigation for a case he'd be doing for real later that morning. He'd sit behind his desk, lean back in his chair, head cocked to the side with his arms folded, and I'd panic, wondering if what was coming out of my mouth made any sense. His eyes locked onto me and didn't move; he wanted to see if I could handle the pressure of a courtroom. Would I stand up to intimidation? I was convinced he could see my heart pounding in my chest. He'd then rip my submission apart. He was utterly brutal. I hated him for it.

But I loved it, too. It made me a better advocate.

My whole professional life, I've wanted to be as good as him.

But I'm not stupid. There's no doubt whatsoever that he sees me as an easy victory in this case.

'Darling,' he says, stroking my leg, 'just a little thing about the plea hearing next week. I'm assuming since I haven't received anything from the defence it's going to be a guilty plea to murder?'

I remember what Julian told me on our weekend away, that this is how big trials are run. It's not as if we're discussing intimate details of the case. I'm not breaching client confidentiality; I'm just giving him a heads-up.

'No,' I tell him assertively. 'I expect a not-guilty plea.'

'Oh! Right. OK.' He muses for a few moments. 'Has he actually said that? Are those your instructions?'

'He isn't saying anything at all.'

'I see. So, you won't be serving a defence statement, then?'

The defence statement is the most important document in any criminal defence. It sets out exactly what defence you'll be relying on at trial. Perhaps most importantly, it triggers disclosure from the prosecution; if they have any evidence to support your defence, they have to give it to you.

'I don't see how I can in the circumstances.'

'No, of course. Yes. Obviously.'

I watch as he drums his fingers on the sofa in a rhythmic way. It's subtle, but it's something he does when he's anxious. I first noticed it when I was his pupil; he did it when jurors entered court to deliver a verdict, and a pattern emerged. People talk with their actions.

Julian despises 'defence ambushes' in trials. He likes to be prepared and know what defendants are going to say before he starts cross-examining them. Without a defence statement, he can't do that.

'I'll keep you updated,' I tell him formally. Julian taught me murder is the same as any other trial, the only difference being that someone has died, so the stakes are higher. But essentially, the process is the same. I need to have faith in my own ability.

'Certainly. Just planning ahead. Thanks for letting me know. I really thought this was going to be a straightforward guilty plea to murder, but it sounds like we'll be having a trial?'

'Probably. It makes no sense, though. There's no motive.'

'I'll find one,' he says, tapping me on the leg and signalling he wants to get up.

I have no doubt he will.

Later in bed, Julian faces the opposite way to me, no attempt to connect. I remain awake for a while, overthinking everything.

Just as I'm dozing off, I see a light shining into the bedroom that appears to be coming from the back garden. It takes me a few seconds to work out it's the security light. Not unusual – next door's cat usually sets it off.

A few minutes go by, and the light is still on.

Julian is fast asleep, so I can't ask him to go, and I'm far too cosy in bed to check for myself, so I pick up my phone and tap the security app to look at the CCTV we have covering the back garden to confirm there's nobody there.

But someone *is* there.

On the black-and-white image, someone wearing a big, black coat and black woollen hat is peering through my patio doors in the middle of the night.

Frozen to the spot, I quickly glance at the time. It's 12.23 a.m.

'Julian! There's someone trying to break in!' I whisper frantically, shaking him awake. He barely registers what I've said, and I don't know what possesses me to do it, but with my eyes on the screen, I jump out of bed to see this person for myself.

Switching every light on upstairs to let them know I am very much awake, I watch them quickly look up before turning around and running down the side of the house. Rushing to the front bedroom, I see nothing of where they went until, about ten seconds later, what looks like a red Mini zooms down the otherwise quiet road.

A Mini? That's not a thug's car?

When I drag Julian out of bed, he's more concerned that I've interrupted his sleep than anything else. He thinks it's an opportunistic thief looking for an open window on a Friday night. He stops me from calling the police, saying we'd be wasting their time because what can we offer them by way of identification?

I didn't get a good look at the person's face, and we don't have a registration for the car. I can't even prove it *was* their car. I go back over the CCTV and that reveals nothing, either – their coat, or perhaps a scarf, goes right up to their nose, and the camera is positioned high up on the wall, so it only captures the person from above.

There's something about the fact that someone was here, at our home, that makes everything feel dangerous. Closer. More threatening. The questioning at my event, the figure loitering by my car, the social media message – all those things happened, arguably, at a distance. But this? This is a step too far. This is my safe place. By coming here, this person has confirmed what I'd already started to suspect.

Someone is out to get me.

15

Witness X

Rule #4
Let People Underestimate You

Dolly Parton once said, 'It costs a lot of money to look this cheap,' and it always reminds me of Dad. People underestimated him, too. It was one of his more strategic traits.

Most people want to be seen as intelligent, culturally elevated human beings, edging as close to the top of the social hierarchy as possible. Not Dad. He curated his public personality to be seen as the joker, the philandering fool, the life of the party, the one you can't take seriously.

Nobody ever suspects the nice, stupid person of anything.

He liked it when people underestimated him. You saw it in his eyes – they lit up when he got the opportunity to surprise people. Or, rather, humiliate them. He lived for it. He was never a man who demanded respect from people he met; he preferred to lurk in the shadows and wait for an opportunity to strike. Like a snake.

He was the complete opposite to my mother. Even from a young age, I could never work out why she and my dad were together. She was always drunk, screaming and shouting right up in his face. She scared me. Dad had always been quieter than Mum. When I was really young, I thought that meant he was kinder and safer. I didn't understand he was even more dangerous than her.

The problem with allowing people to underestimate you is that they can get quite nasty about it. Everything in life comes with a cost.

It was at one of Declan's family parties that his dad cornered me. It was early on in the relationship and I was still enjoying the newness of it.

His dad was a quiet, intellectual type. Never said much, but you could tell he took everything in. It was out of character for him to spark up a conversation with me away from everyone else; I knew something bad was coming.

'This won't last,' he said, glancing around the room, smiling like a raging sociopath so as not to arouse suspicion. 'He's drawn to the excitement of a girl like you. I understand it, I do. But you're short term. And you can drop this ditzy, nice girl act – I don't buy it.'

I was caught off guard.

'I care for your son a lot,' I replied, hoping he couldn't sense the panic in my voice.

'No, you don't,' he said, finally turning to look at me. 'Cheap, common little slags like you don't care for boys like my son. You see them as toys. You use them and spit them out when you're done.'

This man was a sensible accountant; small in height, skinny. He wore rimless glasses that made him look like a kind little grandad. Part of me was incensed; the other, toxic part of me was impressed.

Because he was right.

That's the thing about pretending to be something you're not: you have to be prepared for someone to see right through it. You can't fool everybody. And, when someone comes along holding a big, shiny mirror up to your behaviour, you must be ready to face the grotesque, distorted monster staring back at you.

Then, you have two choices.

Either you can decide to be a better person and prove them wrong, or you can do exactly what they predicted, and be the manipulative slut they already think you are.

I've never, ever forgotten what he said to me that night or how I felt when he said it.

The shame. The guilt. The self-loathing. The crushing sense of humiliation and exposure.

The only other time I've experienced those emotions with the same level of intensity was the night Anton Smythe died.

16

Leila

98 days before trial

'I've just had to ward off three journalists harassing me about you,' Davina says, throwing a large bundle of files down onto the table in the robing room. To a casual observer, I'm calm and cool, sipping the dregs of the filtered coffee I bought from the cafe and leaning back in my chair, my legs crossed, as the heavy black robes I wear fall elegantly to the floor. My pristine white collarette, which sits snugly around my neck, stands out against my favourite black, fitted trouser suit. It's my power suit, the one I wear for special cases. Something about the cut makes me feel confident.

But I am not confident. It's all an act.

'What do you mean, "harassing you about me"?' I ask, placing the white cup down onto its saucer. A faint lipstick mark kisses the rim.

'They know you're married to the prosecutor,' she says. 'It gives an already juicy case extra frisson.'

I roll my eyes and start gathering my stuff. I knew this would happen. It isn't a big deal; married barristers come up against each other frequently in this job and the press know it, but they will make it out to be an issue here because of the nature of the case. They will pit us against each other, and it could eclipse the case itself. It's also likely to draw unnecessary attention to us. That's Julian's territory – I'm not a fan of being under the microscope. All it will do is highlight my inexperience. If a juror sees it, it could influence their verdict.

'Right, well, that sounds like something I'll worry about tomorrow,' I say, standing up. 'Let's enter the lion's den, shall we?'

We're the first case on in Court 1 of Newcastle Crown Court in front of His Honour Judge Byson. Jack Millman will formally enter his plea to the charge of murder.

Julian stands outside court, talking to some police officers. His confidence oozes out of every pore. I do a cursory nod as I walk by, aware people will be watching. I want to appear professional.

We drove separately to chambers this morning; it didn't feel right to arrive together. It was a weird atmosphere in the house as we both got ready for work. Usually, we chat about the day ahead and I sing along to whatever is on the radio. Not today. We shuffled around each other, barely saying anything as we prepared for war. We've had a challenging weekend. Julian kept getting angry every time I mentioned the intruder at the house on Friday night. I finally told him about the incident with the car and mentioned the other weird things happening, including the message on social media. His response was to simply 'turn it off'. He said I should remain vigilant but not be overly concerned, claiming that these things happen sometimes, and it's easy to think they're related but that we shouldn't jump to conclusions. He conceded it's natural to be paranoid when involved with a case like this, but I need to remain focused on the trial and not let these things affect my judgement. He is, of course, right. The only thing to do is put it all to the back of my head for now. I've got more important things to worry about.

As we approach the door of the court, a middle-aged man with neat, combed-back greying hair and a trimmed beard walks towards us. Next to him is a woman who looks as if she might be his age, but her face doesn't match the rest of her. Her blonde hair is in a slick, low ponytail, contrasting the sharp, fitted black dress she wears with patent black stilettos. Her immaculate cream Louis Vuitton handbag sits obediently beside her leg.

'How is he holding up, Davina?' the man asks.

'Sorry, who . . . ?' I ask, pretending to be confused, even though I know exactly who he is. The biggest crime boss in the north-east.

'Miss Reynolds, this is Eddie Sorrington and his wife, Daniella. Eddie owns Temptation,' Davina says, to which they smile and shake hands with me. 'Eddie and Daniella are good friends with Jack. I think it was you who got him the job at the club, wasn't it, Eddie?'

'Yeah, after he came out of prison. He needed a break, especially after . . . you know . . . so I gave him a job. Was it you who dealt with him for all that back in 2019?'

'Yes, it was.'

'Hmm.' He nods, making eye contact with me. 'I'm sure you'll do him justice this time around. He had a bit of a rough ride after that. Upset a lot of people. I'm sure you can imagine.'

Yes, I know.

'He's a hard worker,' he goes on. 'Very loyal to those who stand by him. He always does the right thing.'

'Does he?' I ask.

'Always. I took him in and gave him chances when nobody else would. Got him out of the system doing odd jobs for me. We liked having him around, didn't we, Daniella? He was like a brother to . . .'

Something changes in his demeanour. The steely exterior drops and the glamorous wife – who has served as a prop until now – discreetly reaches for his hand.

'We suffered a bereavement a while ago,' Daniella says, robotic in tone. Her mouth is the only part of her that moves when she tells us this. She exhales slowly, as if it hurts physically to push the words out of her mouth.

'I'm sorry to hear that,' I tell them both, but don't enquire further. I always think you can tell when grief is raw and needs to be handled with care.

'Please look after him, Miss Reynolds. Jack is a good man,' Eddie says. His voice breaks a little bit. He swallows hard to compose himself.

'We really appreciate you coming to support Jack,' I tell him. 'We'll let him know you're here.'

The public gallery is packed. Journalists fill the jury box, a common sight for short hearings where there's significant public interest and a jury isn't yet required. The air is thick with tension.

Two loud knocks echo through the courtroom, indicating the judge is about to appear. My heart starts galloping. I hear the blood in my body pumping in waves. His Honour Judge Byson appears on the bench to a cry of 'All rise!' and that's it. We're off.

A jangle of keys is heard coming from the back of the court and the door from the cells to the dock opens. Everyone turns to look.

Jack walks through the door, momentarily shocked by the eyes fixated on him. He freezes, like a deer caught in headlights. Giving him the subtlest of smiles, I attempt to get him to focus on me. He catches my eye and doesn't let go until he sits down behind the monolithic bulletproof panes of glass in the dock. The usual housekeeping matters are addressed before the formal indictment is read by the clerk. Asking Jack to stand, he holds up a piece of paper and reads the charge aloud.

'Jack Millman, you are charged with murder, pursuant to common law. The particulars of the offence are that on Friday, 6 September 2024 you murdered Anton Smythe. Do you plead guilty or not guilty?'

I turn around to look at him, as does everyone else in the courtroom. The silence chokes us all as we wait for his answer.

'Not guilty.'

'Please sit down,' the clerk instructs. Whispers echo around the courtroom.

My husband jumps to his feet to address the judge. His mission for a conviction begins now.

'Your Honour, the Crown has not had sight of a defence statement,' he remarks in his court voice. It's slightly different from the one he uses at home: more clipped, posher. Louder. It's also laced with annoyance. 'Despite repeated attempts to contact Miss Reynolds about this over the past week, no document has been forthcoming.'

Oh. I see. Like that, is it? Right.

Julian knew I wouldn't be serving a defence statement because I told him, so why is he trying to make me look incompetent in front of the judge?

'Miss Reynolds, why on earth has a defence statement not been served? Are you aware this is a murder trial?' Judge Byson asks, waiting for answers I don't have.

I rise to address the court, irritated by both my husband's unnecessarily aggressive stance and the patronizing tone of the judge, who speaks to me now as if I'm a teenage girl.

'As matters currently stand, Your Honour, I am not in a

position to properly draft one. I have made my learned friend aware of this.'

That is barrister code for: my client refuses to tell me what happened, aka 'I'm stuffed'.

'I see,' the judge responds, turning his gaze towards Jack in the dock. 'Is your client aware that failing to serve a document setting out what defence he proposes to rely upon will prompt an adverse inference direction to a jury in the event of a trial?'

'I have made him aware of this, Your Honour. Of course.'

'Well, let me remind him,' HHJ Byson booms, staring at Jack. 'Mr Millman, if you do not speak to your barrister and tell her what your defence is, she is unable to put that in a document called a defence statement. This document is very important, as it is given to the prosecution, so they are aware of what you're going to say in the event of a trial. If they know what your defence is going to be, they have a duty to look through the evidence and disclose anything that may assist your case. Do you understand?'

'Yes,' he says, clearly and politely.

'It is also important to make you aware that failing to provide a defence case statement can trigger the jury to draw an "adverse inference" in your case. That means that, if you suddenly put forward a defence at trial without giving notice of it in this document, the judge will direct the jury to take that as an indication of your guilt.'

'I'm aware of this,' Jack replies, confidently. I continue facing forward, but the disdain and contempt felt for Jack by everyone in this room is too powerful to ignore. They all knew Anton as one of their own. Now, this young, cocky man accused of killing him refuses to say anything about it.

'We've identified a mutually convenient date for trial, Your Honour,' Julian helpfully advises the court. 'Monday, 13 January.'

'Very well. It will require a High Court judge owing to its sensitive nature. Miss Reynolds, I'm aware this is a frightfully challenging case, but please endeavour to have more open communication via the proper channels with prosecuting counsel in future so that court time is not wasted, and everybody is on the same page.'

I want to answer back and tell him Julian knew I wouldn't be serving a defence statement but, of course, I don't. Instead, I bow, politely, and vow to have it out with him when the time is right. I'm not making a show of myself in front of everyone.

Afterwards, I go down to see Jack in the cells with Davina before they take him back to prison. His foot taps uncontrollably on the floor and his hands repeatedly rub over his chin. I guess things just got very real.

'So, we're having a trial, then,' I declare.

'Well, I'm not guilty of murder, so . . . yes, we are.'

'Look, Jack, I'm going to give it to you straight: we have a well-respected, upper-class judge who's dead, and a doorman with a criminal past charged with his murder.'

'But it wasn't . . .' he starts saying, before cutting himself off. I watch as he begins to inhale more quickly, then hyperventilate. 'This has gone too far. Murder. I'm charged with *murder!*'

The reality of the situation has set in, and it's hard to watch. I've seen it happen before; charges like 'murder' are simply words until you appear in court and your liberty is suddenly in the hands of someone else. He bangs his fists on the table; the handcuffs clank against the surface. Security peers through the glass window into the conference room, ready to dive in. I raise my hand, letting him know I have everything under control.

'Hey, Jack. Look at me,' I say, calmly. His head remains lowered, covered by his hands. 'It's going to be OK. You're not guilty.'

I quickly look at Davina, who is taking in the whole scene.

She's already unhappy with Jack's decision to stay quiet until trial, and this won't inspire confidence. Her worst nightmare is a client who crumbles at the first sign of stress.

'Nobody is going to believe me. You heard the judge. Who's going to believe me over what they think Anton was like?'

'It'll be difficult,' I say, placing my hand out in front of him on the table to calm him down.

'He wasn't as squeaky clean as they all think he was, you know.'

'What do you mean by that?' I ask, quietly, my eyes quickly flicking to Davina, who is perched on the edge of her seat.

'Everyone's making such a big deal of my phone going missing. What about *his* phone? Have you searched through that? Because *that's* where you'll find your answers to this.'

'Unfortunately, Jack, we won't get access to that because we haven't prepared a defence statement setting out what your defence is. If we do that, the prosecution is compelled to give us any evidence that may assist our defence. If we don't, we get nothing.'

He leans back in the chair.

'I can't,' he says, shaking his head.

'Why? Why can't you do that?'

'I'm not a grass.'

'Jack, this is your life. Your liberty is at stake. You need to think of yourself.'

He shakes his head again.

'So, what's the plan? Prison for the rest of your life? Doesn't sound like a great alternative,' I point out, exasperated.

'Look, if you want to put a defence together,' he says, 'you'll have to figure it out yourself.'

'Elaborate, please,' Davina demands. She doesn't attempt to hide the impatience in her voice.

He shifts towards her. 'I'm not going to tell you what happened that night. I can't. But the answers you need are right in front of you. Where was I the day of the murder? Look at what was happening elsewhere.'

The security guard knocks on the door, signalling they need to take Jack back to the van. As he pushes his chair back, it drags along the floor, sending an ear-shattering noise through the room. Before he reaches the door, he turns to look at me.

'One last thing, Miss Reynolds,' he says. 'Don't trust anyone. That's what you told me last time, remember?'

17

Jack

Tuesday, 6 August 2019
Durham Crown Court
Five years earlier

'Four years?' I say again, as if repeating it will change the outcome. 'That's the longest sentence I've ever had.'

I can't go to prison for that long. An image of my foster mam flashes through my head as I sit on the edge of the plastic chair, my hands together in front of my mouth as if I'm praying. I can't help but think of the disappointment she'd feel if she was still here. It was bad enough I was in prison when she died, unable to say a final goodbye. I've never forgiven myself for that. She warned me not to do it, but I was adamant I'd give her a good send-off when the time came. That's the only good thing about terminal cancer: you can at least plan your funeral. They're expensive, though, so I needed to get some money in, and quick.

I'd planned to sell coke and pills, just for a few weeks. It was pure bad luck I was caught. Even though the judge took circumstances into account, he still locked me up. Some posh prick who didn't have the slightest clue what it was like to lose the only person you've ever loved.

Now here I am again, only a few years later, this time for a longer stint and charged with an even more serious offence. She'd be thoroughly ashamed of me.

'I am so, so sorry,' my barrister, Miss Reynolds, says. 'This shouldn't have happened.'

'Can we appeal it?'

'No,' she says quietly, but firmly.

'But it didn't happen like that.'

'I know, Mr Millman. But a jury has heard all the evidence and found you guilty.'

'They didn't believe me, in other words.'

Taking a deep breath, she reaches for her wig, pulls it off and slings in onto the table. Her blonde hair sticks up everywhere. I've never seen her without it on before.

'I think it was very difficult for them to piece your evidence together without hearing from your main defence witness. Because she didn't turn up.'

'Well, we know *why* she didn't turn up, don't we?' I say. 'She was obviously paid off by Tony Flanagan.'

'It was unfortunate that the victim in this case happened to be a connected crime boss who would have had the resources and influence to do that,' she says, choosing her words carefully. She's clever. I've come to like her over the course of this trial.

'How did the jury not see through his lies, though? Playing the whole Mr Nice Guy. That's what I don't understand. I've met some shady characters in my time, but he is the worst.'

'It happens all the time,' she says, abruptly. 'I see it every day. There are people in this world who are very good liars, and there are others who are easily deceived. Get those people together and you have a dangerous situation. You can make them believe anything. Flanagan painted himself as a victim, a harmless customer of Temptation one Saturday night just having a good time. And you – the angry doorman who worked for his rival with an axe to grind – assaulted him viciously.'

'I'm finished after this,' I tell her, shaking my head. 'Word will get around I've pissed off one of the biggest criminal names in the area. It's a small world. It's probably safer for me to stay in prison.'

'You've been sentenced to four years. You'll be out in two if you demonstrate good behaviour. What's done is done. People have short memories. Keep a low profile when you get out and with luck I won't see you again.'

She smiles at me in a way that makes me feel that everything is going to be OK, which is mad, given I'm about to go back to prison.

'Thanks, Miss Reynolds.'

'I really do wish you the best, Mr Millman,' she says. 'I'll certainly miss your dark humour.'

We both laugh, and I make a pathetic attempt to lighten the mood by making a dry comment, forcing her to write it down in her barrister notebook. It's been a running joke during this trial that she writes down absolutely everything I say.

'Thanks for believing me, Miss Reynolds. Not many people do.'

'I'm sorry I couldn't do better. I really am. You're not a bad person, Jack.'

'I put myself here. Whether I was trying to defend someone or not, I have to take responsibility for that.'

Picking her wig up off the table, she stands and goes to walk out. Her heels click on the floor, then stop.

'Our mistake was letting the prosecution know what your defence was going to be,' she says, without turning around.

'What?'

'Speaking off-record here,' she says, quietly, now turning to face me. 'Flanagan would have done *everything* in his power to cover this up. You're right – there's no way he would have allowed that woman to give evidence. She's probably either received a huge sum of money to keep quiet or has been threatened.'

'You're saying I never had a chance?'

'There's always a chance,' she says, shaking her head, 'but it should have been left to the jury. We shouldn't have served a defence statement. That way the prosecution would have had absolutely no notice of anything you were going to say at trial. You can't sabotage what you don't know is coming. We gave Flanagan all the information he needed to derail your defence. The trick is to say nothing until trial. Especially when high-profile people are involved. I see that now.'

'But didn't the judge say that would be bad for my case? That there are inferences the jury can make if I leave my defence until then? You're not supposed to ambush them, are you?'

'Yes, and that's why I didn't go down that route. But every member on that jury is human. They can be manipulated into thinking exactly what you want them to . . . if you've got a good enough barrister.'

'Manipulated?' I repeat back to her. I don't think she's aware she used that word.

'Persuaded . . .' she says, correcting herself. 'It is jurors – not the prosecution, not the judge – who are the keyholders to your liberty. Remember that next time.'

'Trust me, there won't be a next time. Not after this.'

She smiles and reaches for the door handle.

'I have to admit,' I say, 'I didn't have you down as that kind of lawyer.'

'What do you mean?'

'It's hard to think of you doing anything that isn't by the book.'

She thinks for a few seconds, seeming to consider what to say. 'You'd be surprised.'

Her guard drops when she says it. She's not the same Miss Reynolds I've been with over the past few days. It's someone else, someone more vulnerable, more complicated. Someone with a story.

'Any last words of advice before they lock me up and throw away the key?'

'Yes, actually.' She nods. 'Don't trust anyone. Especially lawyers.'

18

Leila

80 days before trial

I can't catch a break at the moment. All I want to do is work on the trial, now I know for sure Jack is pleading not guilty, but people keep insisting on giving me unrelated tasks.

Often when you're defending, you suspect your client is guilty, but it is not your function to make that judgement. It is our job, as barristers, to present the evidence before a jury; they determine guilt or innocence.

But with this case, I just *know* Jack is innocent, and I can't let him down again. I need to dedicate everything I have to this case, and I have to win. I don't have time for distractions.

However, Roger, the head of the pupillage committee, has decided that as part of our initiative to draw in 'the best of the best', we must make an appearance at the annual autumn law fair held at Durham University. And when I say 'we', he means me.

'We need to appeal to the youngsters, and you're good at all that, aren't you, Britney?' he said to me in his wildly aristocratic voice, fanning his hand around in a bid to demonstrate how beneath him this entire concept was. I had been immersed in drafting a document in the library at the time.

'Well, not really . . .'

'Yes, you are. What about that blog thing you do? The feminist one?'

'What about it?' I said, suspiciously, peering up at him.

'I think you should go and be our representative. Take some chambers swag. Set up a stall. Be charismatic!'

Easy as that.

It's the last thing I want to be doing on a Friday morning, but as directed, I take a box full of pens, sticky notes, stress balls(!) and tote bags, all emblazoned with our chambers name, and head down to the university. For good measure, our chambers manager also picked up loads of sweets to dish out, so I'm sorted.

At least, I thought I was.

Upon arrival, I realize I've been given the wrong time, and it starts an hour earlier than I was told. Other chambers and solicitor firms are pretty much set up when I walk into the grand hall, and I'm told it's a case of find anywhere that's left. I loathe looking unprepared and *of course* the only space left is directly opposite Sienna Fox.

It's not ideal to look flustered in front of your husband's ex-wife.

She has obviously arrived early because not only is her stand immaculately tidy with pens already lined up like little stationery soldiers, but she is chilling with a cup of coffee and gently pacing in front of her stand with nothing else to do but admire it.

'Need a hand with anything, Leila?' she shouts over to me, as I throw everything down before glancing at the clock. It's 9.52 a.m. The fair opens in eight minutes.

'No, thank you,' I yell back, hoping I don't sound unhinged.

As I rush about, getting everything ready, I can't help but feel an internal anger over the fact I've been asked to do this at all. Julian would never be asked to do it, nor would any of the men in chambers. They're always asked to undertake the 'important' jobs, sitting on the finance or accommodation committee; the places where big decisions are made. The women in chambers are always on things like the marketing committee – not that there's anything wrong with marketing, but it's seen as less important.

Just like this fair. I look around the room and it's full of women. The men are all at court doing Very Important Cases. They aren't lining up pens and handing out swizzle sticks.

As the clock hits 10 a.m., students start pouring in through the doors. Wide-eyed law students, eager to learn and impress, just as I was at their age. I smile and attempt to look welcoming. None of them understands what this job really entails. It's impossible to know until you start. Some will make it, most won't. But one thing is for certain: the reality of this profession is not the same as the expectation.

It fills up quickly. A few of the students recognize me from *Chats at the Bar* and take selfies. I gush about chambers and the sweets go down well. Mercifully, the time goes quickly.

Just after 11.30 a.m., I'm starting to wish I'd brought a chair to sit on, when a takeaway cup appears in front of my face.

'Thought you could use one of these,' Sienna says, holding it out to me. Her hair is tied up in a bouncy ponytail. She wears a tight, black pencil skirt and pink shirt with obscenely high black heels. Sienna is the kind of woman you see when you're a teenager and want to be when you're 'old' (i.e. in your thirties).

'Oh, you didn't need to do that . . .'

'It's OK! These things can be tedious. Important to stay refuelled. Latte all right?'

'Erm, yes, thank you,' I say, taking a sip. I don't face her. I continue to look around the large room, which is packed full of students. The sound of chattering is amplified to the point where it's too loud to speak at a normal volume.

'You know, you don't have to be so wary of me,' she says, in an attempt to get me to turn around. 'I mean, I understand why you might be, but it's unnecessary.'

'It's just a bit weird, if I'm being honest,' I say, finally looking at her.

'Because of Julian?'

'Yes, obviously.'

'That was a very long time ago, Leila . . .'

'I just don't understand why you're being like this.'

'Like what?'

'Just . . . all friendly.'

'I see. Is this because I'm the only solicitor to say openly that most barristers are up their own arses?' she remarks playfully.

I don't say anything. If she wants something from me, she'll have to spell it out.

'OK,' she says, as if I've caught her out. 'I just thought you might need a friend. I mean, we're not so dissimilar, you and me. We're both women from working-class backgrounds and, hell, it's hard being in this profession with that behind you.'

I frown at her. I've seen Sienna around court for years and not once has she tried to be chummy with me, so why now? Why all of a sudden?

'Where is this coming from, Sienna?' I ask her.

She thinks for a few moments, turning away before answering.

'Being married to Julian and then going up against him in court, in *this* murder . . . that's challenging. I'm here if you need anything.'

I study her as she talks. She chooses her words carefully, like any lawyer would. If Julian knew she was saying this, he'd be furious.

'Thank you, but I'll be fine.'

She smiles; she knows I'm not going to take her up on the offer.

'Of course! Well, you know where I am. Good to see you.'

She places her hand on my arm briefly before she leaves, and I watch as she walks back to her stall. There's so much about this woman I don't know. Everything I do know about her I've been told by Julian. The way she acts towards me does not align with that.

One of them isn't giving me the full story.

The temperature in the room begins to rise with the number of people in it. It's one of the old buildings with enormous gold-framed portraits of men on the walls. A crystal chandelier hangs from the ceiling. All I can think about is how much work I have to do.

'Miss Reynolds?'

The voice catches me off guard.

'Mrs Sorrington?'

She looks different from when I saw her at court at Jack's plea hearing. More alert, less zombified. She's wearing a poppy-red fitted dress that contrasts with her platinum, poker-straight hair.

'I thought it was you. Call me Daniella, please!' she says.

'What are you doing here? Are you looking around the law fair?'

'No! We sponsor various student events at the university. I have a stall over there.' She points towards the corner of the room where there's a gaudy banner with the words 'Electric Dreams' printed in hot pink. 'The girls love the free beauty treatments. I have a salon not far from here, we give out freebies at this sort of thing. Nice for them when they're working so hard.'

'That's lovely.'

'Listen,' she says in her soft Geordie accent. 'I just wanted to nip over and say I'm sorry I wasn't quite myself at Jack's hearing. I've been having a really difficult time lately.'

'I'm very sorry to hear that, but there's no need to apologize.'

'It's been a tough couple of months, you see,' she says in a lowered tone, barely a whisper. 'We lost our son and, well, it's put a lot of strain on the family. Eddie has been so distant since it happened, he's like a different person. It's been horrific, to tell you the truth. What with that, and now all this happening with Jack, it's a lot to deal with, you know?'

'Absolutely. I mean, I can't imagine, but please, don't feel you need to make an excuse.'

'I know people look at us, at me, and think we have a perfect life – the house, the holidays, the money. But nobody really knows what goes on behind those four walls, do they?'

'No, they don't.'

She's right. So many people are envious of others when, in reality, their lives are less than perfect.

'Take care of our Jack, won't you, Miss Reynolds? He's so very dear to me. I mean, he's special to both of us,' she corrects herself, 'Eddie and me. He always has been. He'd never, ever harm anyone like that. You have to believe me.'

'I'll do all I can. I promise.'

As she walks away, she sees Sienna at the stall opposite and turns towards me again.

'Didn't she used to be married to your husband?' she whispers, discreetly.

I nod, subtly.

'I'd watch her, if I were you. She hasn't taken her eyes off you the whole time I've been here.'

A quick glance over to Sienna shows her talking to a couple of students. She clocks me looking over at her and smiles. Daniella saunters back to her stall in the corner, which, by the way, is surrounded by young women. Refreshers and Haribo can't compete with a fresh set of nails, it would seem.

I watch Sienna at her stand for a few minutes. She's very good with people, both male and female, and reads them well. She knows when to turn it down or crank it up, depending on who she's with. She subtly matches the energy of whoever she's talking to. As a result, people fall under her spell. Clever. She reminds me of my husband.

Yet there's something off about her which I can't quite place. She's either a bad actress or a very good liar.

19

Witness X

Rule #5
Be a Good Liar

You can't learn how to become a good liar; it's something you're either talented at or not.

When I was a kid, I used to tell outrageous lies. It came naturally to me, as Dad recognized, even when I was young. He sent me to the front door whenever someone knocked because it would always be for him, and he never wanted to see them.

The worst ones were the men who turned up in suits or black puffer jackets asking to see him. Dad always told me to think of something to tell them – anything – but under no circumstances to ever let them into the house. Something about how, if I did, I'd get him into a lot of trouble and they'd take away our furniture, including the TV. He was terrible with money and spent it as soon as he had it. January was a month in which I learned to stay out of his way and keep quiet. I knew it had something to do with 'tax' but never understood what it was, just that he never had enough money for it at the beginning of the year, which predictably resulted in him drinking more heavily and things being thrown about the house. More often than not, that would include me.

I'd give the men at the door a different story each time: you've just missed him, he's popped out to see a friend, he's at work. But then my stories got wilder and more unbelievable. 'He's had to go to hospital because he was up all night sick, and then the ambulance came and took him away. So, my auntie came up from Sheffield to look after me, but she brought her dog and he ran out of the back, so she's had to go and get him, so it's just me here at the moment . . .'

I don't even have an auntie.

I enjoyed the mechanics of lies and deconstructing their different flavours and textures. I knew the difference between a 'harmless' lie and a 'serious' lie. The lies I told to other people were always to protect us, like the men at the door.

The lies Dad told me to tell were presented as secrets, a shiny, wrapped-up, exciting version of a story. They had a different kind of taste, a darker colour. But I still told them.

The lies he told me, about what we were doing, were the worst of all. He said it was normal as a child – *his* child – and I believed him.

I became so skilled at lying, even I wasn't sure what was real any more. And, what I noticed was, the bigger the lie, the more people appeared to believe it. As if nobody would possibly make up something like that, so it must be true.

But – and this part is crucial – you must always anchor your lies in truth. You need an exceptional memory to remember what you say to people, and that is much harder if you make everything up. If the lies are woven carefully enough with the truth, it's virtually impossible for anyone to separate them.

The problem with such intricate, complex lies is that if the person being lied to ever finds out, the hurt they feel is immeasurable. The consequences irreparable.

I remember the day when all Dad's lies fell away. The moment I discovered the truth for myself. That Dad hadn't just taught me to lie to others, he had been lying to me all along. Nothing was the same after that.

For so long, I believed that I was special. I loved him and he loved me.

I was fifteen years old. Kallie Dawson invited me around to her house during the summer. She had moved over here from Australia – something to do with her dad's job. Dad told me there was no way I could go, but at fifteen I was starting to think for myself a bit more. I told Kallie I could come for tea but not stay over.

Her parents were the nicest people I'd ever met. They kept asking if I wanted more food and they bought us sweet treats for after. Neither of them drank alcohol when I was there.

Her brothers were eighteen, seventeen, and twelve. I watched as they shared silly little in-jokes, teasing the oldest one about how he looked like Hugh Hefner, walking around the garden in his dressing gown wearing sunglasses. Kallie's mum made a comment about the age gap – how she couldn't believe Hugh was allowed to get away with dating women who were young enough to be his daughter.

'Some of them are teenagers!' she told her son, who had regretted coming outside in his robe by this point. 'It's disgusting.'

'Poor girls,' Kallie's dad said, shaking his head.

The house felt safe. Kallie was safe. And I realized that I was not. That my dad and his view of the world – of girls, of me – was not 'normal'. That Kallie's dad did not feel the same.

That was the moment I woke up.

Some things need to lie dormant until you are strong enough to face them.

Things were going to change.

But I knew I wasn't ready, that I needed to be careful and plan. And so, for a while, I existed in two worlds: my cruel reality and a fictional, safer world in my head.

I kept this fantasy going until I was strong enough to escape it. It was then that I promised myself I was going to get everything I wanted.

Perfect husband, perfect house, perfect career. Perfect *everything*.

The life Leila Reynolds has.

Smug, fake bitch.

20

Leila

70 days before trial

SINCE THE PLEA hearing, the Crown has been serving us evidence as they receive it, including evidence from Jack's phone. Well, I say Jack's phone: they're extremely limited in what they can extract, given they don't have the handset. What they do have, however, are the records taken from his mobile phone provider outlining the date and time of every call he made and every text message he sent since the beginning of the year.

'Davina, have you seen the phone evidence?' I ask, perching my own mobile phone between my chin and shoulder, my eyes skimming over what's been placed in front of me.

'Yes, just looking at it now. I think there's a lot more to this than we thought, don't you?'

'As I suspected. Can we meet?'

'Yes. I also have something for you.'

'Jesus. Is it good or bad?'

'I'll leave that up to you. Boat Club, 5 p.m.'

She hangs up without saying goodbye.

It's quiet for a Monday evening. The Boat Club is situated on the river with cinematic views of Durham Cathedral. It's dark outside by 5 p.m.; the cathedral is lit up and looks spectacular. We sit in the corner of the restaurant, in a curved booth for extra privacy. It also means I can see who comes in and out. These last few weeks have made me paranoid.

'Thought you should see this,' Davina says bluntly, slamming a newspaper down in front of me.

It's a full-page article in the local rag about the trial. The headline is 'HUB AND WIFE TEAM IN JUDGE KILLER TRIAL'. My heart sinks. It's the last thing I need. There's barely anything about the actual murder; the majority is about me and Julian.

What really pisses me off is that they make me sound like a naive sixth-form law student. Julian, of course, is described as a distinguished silk with many victories to his name. They've pulled up our photos from the chambers website. Julian looks exactly like a barrister in his, sophisticated and suave. My long blonde hair falls over my shoulders in mine; I wish I'd had the sense to tie it back. I look young and unprofessional next to him.

'I suppose I had to expect it.' I sigh.

'Ignore it. Nest of vipers, the lot of them.'

'All it does is highlight how underqualified I am to be doing this case,' I tell her. 'I don't need it being broadcast even louder than it already is.'

'You're not underqualified. You're right where you need to be.' She smiles. I don't know what it is about Davina; even though she can be scary at times, she's also quite caring, if you catch her in the right mood.

We set to the task at hand, ordering drinks before we get started.

'The kettlebell,' she says, dramatically, the second the waiter leaves our table after pouring us each a huge glass of wine. 'Get this . . . it's always used as a doorstop for the bedroom door, which means Jack removed it from there and then put it straight back.'

My eyes don't leave Davina's.

'Who uses something as a weapon, then puts it straight back? No attempt to dispose of or hide it?'

'I know,' she interrupts. 'These aren't the actions of, well . . .'

'An experienced criminal?'

'Quite.'

'What evidence have you got?'

'For about two months prior to the incident, Jack had been weight training with an eighteen-year-old lad called Kit Gordon, who works at Innocence. He used to go up to the apartment before his shifts, and Jack would show him how to bulk up with exercises. For Kit's birthday, Jack bought him the kettlebell, which he kept at the apartment. They used it in their sessions.'

'Why the doorstop, though?' I enquire.

'It was apparently a running joke that Jack considered it a "woman's weight" – way too light for him – so the only use he had for it in his flat was—'

'A doorstop? Good work, Davina!' I grin at her. 'And have you seen Jack's phone evidence that's come through?'

'Yep. Who was he messaging incessantly for seven months?' Davina asks. 'Given how shady he's being, I'm going to take a wild guess and say that's the person he's protecting in all this.'

'Agreed,' I confirm, nodding.

'The communication begins on Tuesday, 6 February 2024 at 7.57 p.m., and over the course of seven months, there are 1,284 text messages. No phone calls to that number at all. Only texts.'

'It's a burner phone,' I say. 'We checked and it's not registered anywhere.'

'But look at the times of the texts – most of them are late evening or past midnight. Selling drugs?'

'Or an affair with a married woman.'

Davina's eyebrows jump as she reaches for her glass of Sauvignon Blanc.

'But it's what happens after Anton is killed that intrigues me the most. The cell site analysis is quite revealing.'

Cell site analysis is an absolute gem in criminal cases. Every time your mobile phone passes a transmitter, it sends information to your mobile phone provider, who collates that data and determines where you are. Providing your phone is switched on, you're trackable. You don't need to have the physical device to analyse it, and you can comb through months of data.

'Have you seen what happens to his phone?' I continue. 'Cell site analysis traces it to Temptation in the centre of Durham at 10.41 p.m. The signal is then terminated; the phone is presumably switched off or the battery dies. Now, Jack calls 999 from the club landline at 11.07 p.m. and he's arrested shortly after. When the mobile phone signal is received again, at 11.27 p.m. – forty-six minutes later – it's moved, and look at its location.'

'Pickford?' The relevance of this information balances on the tip of her tongue. She recognizes it, but doesn't know where it's from, so I tell her.

'Pickford is twelve miles away from the centre of Durham. It also happens to be the tiny, remote village where Anton Smythe lived. Not only that . . . the cell site placed the phone signal within five metres of Anton Smythe's drive. So, basically, just outside his house.'

Davina's eyes widen and she takes a deep breath. You can almost see the cogs whirring inside her head, wondering how to piece everything together.

'I'm assuming you don't think it's a coincidence?'

'You know I don't believe in such things,' I reply.

'It gets weirder by the minute. The prosecution must be going wild with this information.'

'Oh, I know. They'll have gone through that area with a fine-tooth comb trying to find it. It's all fields and countryside over there, so I imagine it's been dumped.'

'Didn't Jack say his phone was stolen on the day of the murder?' Davina asks.

'He did, but it's far too . . . convenient that it ends up close to the victim's home, if it was randomly stolen and has nothing to do with the crime.'

'The other question it throws into light is how did the phone get turned on in Pickford at the time the cell analysis states, when we know for certain Jack was already in police custody by then? Where else does the cell site place his phone during the day of the murder? Does that help us determine his location? He did say the key to this was finding out where he was that day.'

'His phone was at his apartment all day. Doesn't mean he was,' I remind her. 'Jack's clever. He's been in and out of the system since he was a kid. He knows all the tricks in the book. If he's up to something – or going to see someone he shouldn't be connected to – he knows better than to take his phone with him.'

'But there's always CCTV. He's not completely invisible from being tracked,' Davina says, correctly.

'No, he's not. Don't you see? The person who took the phone the night of the murder must have known they'd be tracked, which is why they turned it off.'

'You think someone else was there that night,' Davina states.

'A good criminal does his homework and is always prepared. They're meticulous. That's how they get away with it.'

'So we need to think like a criminal, find the phone and whoever took it.' Davina smiles.

'Yes. In fact, organize a site visit. It might help us gain some clarity, see the events of that night in a clearer way.'

'I'll get it sorted,' she barks, picking up her diary to add it to the million other jobs I've given her over the past week.

Finally, we have a tiny glimmer of something to grab onto.

'You really think he's innocent, don't you?' she says.

Davina is a very functional, practical person. She holds her cards very close to her chest, so I'm slightly thrown by her asking this now.

'I do,' I tell her, openly and truthfully. 'Don't you?'

'Who knows?' She shrugs. 'I don't have the time to contemplate whether my clients are telling the truth or not. I do my job the best I can, go home and forget about them. And so should you.'

'It's difficult when you've seen an innocent person suffer an injustice and you get a second chance to put it right. That's what we have here. This case is more than just a job for me.'

She goes to say something, just as her own phone starts ringing, which she answers. I can tell it's a phone call about Jack by the way she frowns in that intense way she does sometimes.

'Mmm-hmm . . . right . . . yes . . . Christ. OK. I'll let them know. Well, it's not ideal. Yes. Fine.'

'What is it?' I ask the second she hangs up.

She takes a gulp of her wine before delivering the news, which I can tell is going to be bad.

'We've just received more details about the offence Jack was sent to prison for in 2014. He was charged with supplying drugs and his barrister submitted that he ought to be spared prison, because his foster mother had just been diagnosed with an aggressive form of lung cancer and was not expected to last more than a few months. He asked for one last chance so he could spend her remaining months with her, as he'd never get over allowing her to die on her own.'

'I don't like where this is going.'

'The judge rejected his submissions and sent Jack straight to prison.'

'Who was the judge?' It's a rhetorical question, but I ask it anyway.

'His Honour Judge Anton Smythe.'

I steal a long, sharp breath.

'Well, I guess Julian just found his motive for murder.'

21

Leila

60 days before trial

'She's jealous of you, Leila. I wouldn't trust anything she says.'

I told Julian about Sienna cosying up to me at the law fair. I was interested to hear his take on it, although I knew it wouldn't be positive.

'Why would she be jealous?' I ask him, leaning into the doorway to our dressing room at home. 'You split up years ago and, no offence, but she left you.'

He stops what he's doing. Julian likes to select what he's wearing for court the night before and had been reaching up for a suit before pausing to turn around. This was Julian's house, originally. He lived here with Sienna but bought her out when they divorced. I wasn't sure about it, initially, moving into their old marital home. I felt I'd be a diluted version of her. I did suggest to Julian we buy a more modern property when we married, but he almost vomited at the mention of a new-build and wouldn't hear any further discussion about it.

'She obviously realized what a mistake she made,' he says, with deep satisfaction running through his voice. 'I mean, look at who she ended up with. Bloody Keiran Fox. He's hardly a catch, is he? Couldn't hack it at the Bar, so went to teach instead.'

'There's nothing wrong with teaching, Julian.'

'No, but he obviously didn't have what it takes for this job. That's the measure of the man.'

'I got the impression it was a lifestyle choice rather than him not being able to handle it.'

'Well, whatever it was, it's a waste of everything he worked for.'

'It's just very weird that she's started being like this.'

'Look, simply stay away from her,' he snaps. 'I don't know why she's intent on doing this now, but she's very two-faced. She fools a lot of people, and trust me, I know what that's like.'

Julian gets touchy whenever I mention Sienna. I know when to leave it.

A few days later, I'm walking back to chambers at lunchtime, clutching my sandwich and luminous green smoothie from Pret. I'm trying to be healthy at the moment.

'Leila!' Chester calls out from somewhere. I turn to see him standing in the reception area. Late autumn sun streams through the large sash windows and scatters a warm, golden glow everywhere. Our building is old – I believe from the Georgian period – and this would have been the drawing room. He stands beside an imposing fireplace; the blue, pink, and white patterned tiles pop against the black surround. An oversized vase of lilies sits on the coffee table.

I fell in love with Innovation Chambers the moment I stepped foot in it. Each set of chambers has its own personality in terms of ethos, building, barristers, and speciality. Some sets are strict and straitlaced, others are non-stop party chambers. Some are downright corrupt. This one felt right to me: legal excellence laced with strong, eccentric personalities, not afraid to be different.

Speaking of eccentric personalities, I smile and walk over to say hi to Chester. He glances around at the reception desk to see if anyone's there.

'I wanted to apologize again for my behaviour in the bar,' he says, quietly, having avoided me around chambers since it happened. 'Your reaction was entirely appropriate.'

The giddy, excitable look Chester had in his eyes that day is absent. He is now sober and has likely thought about the incident and reflected on it. He will be embarrassed, and rightly so. But I'm not going to punish him for it. People make mistakes.

'Chester, how long have we known each other?' I whisper. 'It's forgotten. Don't worry about it.'

The smile he gives me is one of relief. He's obviously got some stuff going on; the last thing he needs is me threatening to make life harder for him over this.

'How are you getting on with your "issue" at home?'

He looks at me quizzically, frowning in a way that suggests he has no idea what I'm talking about.

'You mean the wife?' he asks, with a significant raise of the eyebrows. 'All quiet. Nothing since. Probably my paranoia or a symptom of my old age.'

'Seriously?' I laugh. 'You're one of the sharpest minds I know, Chester, don't give me that.'

'Back to normal,' he says, quietly, shaking his head. 'I think I must have just imagined it. Everything is tickety-boo.'

I don't believe it, and he doesn't either. But it's easier for him to believe the lie because it's more tolerable than confronting the reality and having his life blow up.

'Speak of the devil . . .' he says, and I turn to see Demi skipping up the steps outside chambers. Within seconds she makes a majestic entrance into the reception area. Her long, camel coat swishes around her, with a personality of its own. She clutches a shiny, black Balenciaga handbag, which complements her tall, black boots. Dark brown sunglasses sit on her head as her honey-coloured hair cascades around her shoulders.

'Leila! Hi!'

'Hi, Demi, nice to see you,' I remark, catching a glimpse of the short, fitted dress she's wearing underneath the coat. It's no wonder Chester is willing to overlook her scurrilous activities. 'Are you going out for lunch?'

'Yes,' Chester tells me. 'We're meeting Tom. We haven't seen him for a while.'

I smile at Chester. I know seeing his son will mean a lot to him.

'Darling,' Chester says to Demi, laying a hand on the small of her back. 'I've just remembered I need to have a quick word with Edward. Give me two minutes.'

He dashes off, leaving the two of us alone.

'Hope the case is going well,' she says politely, glancing at my lunch to see what I've bought.

'Yes, really well, thank you.'

Just as I'm wondering whether to excuse myself or take this opportunity to dig under the surface a bit, she beats me to it.

'I wanted to ask, Leila, what did your birthday card mean?'

Her tone has changed. She's not playing the dutiful wife now. She's asking with purpose. I'm thrown for a second.

'Sorry, what?'

'Your birthday card to Chester. It's still on his desk. I saw it when I was in his study the other week.'

'Oh, just a silly joke!' I laugh, suddenly catching on to what she means. 'We both love the classics, and we always put a quote in each other's birthday cards every year. Nerdy, really.'

'*Fas est et ab hoste doceri*. "It is right to be taught even by an enemy"? What's that supposed to mean?'

Demi is never this direct, and I've never seen the non-giggly, non-daddy's-girl version of her before. I'm also thrown by the Latin coming out of her mouth.

'Chester is always giving me savage, sage pieces of advice. You know, how to survive at the Bar and all that. I thought it was funny. Didn't know you read Latin, Demi.'

'I went to boarding school. It was compulsory. I'm surprised *you* do. Chess *extraordinaire* and now Latin scholar. Be careful, Leila, people will start to question your working-class background.'

I say nothing. She wants a reaction, and she isn't going to get one.

'I'm kidding!' She laughs.

I deliver the kind of smile you reserve for people you despise.

'I need to get back to work, Demi. Gorgeous to see you.'

I convince Julian to go for a quick walk with me after lunch just to get a bit of fresh air. Being inside court and chambers all day can feel claustrophobic. I'm also mindful of the fact we're spending less time together at home, so it's a good opportunity to reconnect. We grab a couple of coffees from the deli around the corner.

'I was talking to Demi earlier,' I tell him, as we saunter along the nearby cobbled streets. 'She came into chambers to meet Chester. She's very odd.'

'In what way? What did she say?'

'There's just something off about her. About their marriage. They were going to meet Chester's son, Tom. Not the daughter – I assume she still wants nothing to do with him. Have you ever met her?'

'Elise? A few times.'

'What's she like?'

'She used to come into chambers and wait for her dad. She was always in trouble at school. Mature. Older than her years.'

I frown. 'Older than her years?'

He sighs.

'She'd come in when she was sixteen or so and be, how can I phrase this, sexually suggestive around male members of chambers. It was . . . problematic. It seemed that she did it to get a reaction out of her father. They didn't get on. And when she found out about the affair it turned very ugly, very quickly.'

'Who did he have an affair with?'

'No idea.' He shrugs. 'It was all very hush-hush, but it spread like wildfire. I think it was someone important, though. Possibly a judge. Certainly someone already married with a powerful husband.'

'Why do you think that?'

'He went to enormous lengths to ensure nobody found out who she was. She had some kind of hold on him. He obviously had more to lose by revealing who she was than never speaking to his own daughter again. Some men do stupid things in the name of love. Or lust.'

'But why hasn't Elise told anyone, if she didn't get on with him?'

'I don't know. That's the part that doesn't make sense. She just walked out of his life and disappeared.'

How horrible.

'But you know what Chester is like. He thinks with his dick,' Julian says with a little more vigour than the situation calls for. 'Pretty women are his weakness. He'll never learn. What do you expect if you cheat on your wife?'

His views on this topic are black and white, always have been. Infidelity is punishable by hell, which explains his feelings towards Sienna.

After a stroll through the winding streets surrounding Durham Cathedral, we head back to chambers for a steady afternoon of work. Sitting down at my desk, I see a notification on my *Chats at the Bar* account. It's from her: @JustAnotherDumbBlonde.

I know it's a threat from the preview. I sit down, promising myself I won't panic, that they're just words and that nothing bad has happened since the last one. They're empty threats, that's all. Designed to scare me.

But it's more chilling than I imagined. It isn't just about me. It's about the trial.

> **Feeling the pressure yet? You are, aren't you? Is he really ready to face questions about why a judge went to visit a criminal at 10.30 p.m. on a Friday night? I hope you're as good as your client hopes you are, for both your sakes.**

Nothing about this case has been reported in the press, yet this person knows what time Anton arrived at Jack's flat.

How is that possible? Who the hell is sending these? Are they connected to the case? They can't be. How much do they know?

If there's someone out there who knows anything about what really happened the night Anton was killed, I need to be aware of them before this trial begins.

22

Leila

46 days before trial

Julian continues to build the Crown's case against Jack, serving evidence upon which he proposes to rely to secure a conviction. The trial isn't until mid-January, but criminal trials are meticulous beasts with timelines and deadlines to be adhered to. Among all of this, I have to continue conducting other trials and cases knowing there's someone out there taunting me, playing with me.

They know something I don't.

It feels odd to address my husband in emails so formally, but this is how it must be done. I emailed him from the kitchen the other day, despite the fact that he was sitting in the next room. As November passes by and we sprint towards the final month of the year, freezing cold temperatures set in around the house in more ways than one. I've never been a fan of big, old houses – I find them overpowering. Too many cracks and draughts. I feel that I can't breathe sometimes. That sounds ungrateful, doesn't it?

Julian and I are conducting a site visit to the location where the murder was allegedly committed next week. But I can't stop thinking about what Jack said about Anton's phone and how that's where the answers are. Julian will have forensics on that by now and I wonder what he's found.

I've noticed we both get a bit spiky when new evidence lands; it's as if we're guarding our thoughts so the other can't read them. We go into separate rooms to review it, fearing the other could read our body language if we remained where we were.

We still eat dinner together, when we can. But it's becoming less frequent, a sign that this trial is pulling us apart, since our conversations inevitably – problematically – drift to issues surrounding the case.

'I assume you've seen the newspaper article? The one that painted me out to be some kind of novice lawyer?' I ask, as he's about to stuff some chorizo and roast pepper pasta into his mouth.

'I've seen it, yes.' He nods. 'There were some copies lying around the robing room.'

'So, everyone's read it, then.'

'This is just part and parcel of being in this kind of trial. People love theatrics. They're going with the David and Goliath angle to sell papers. Don't read anything into it.'

'Are you relying on the contents of Anton's phone to prove the Crown's case?' I ask, before I have time to think about the words leaving my mouth.

He looks up at me, studying my face for a few seconds. The same way he does to criminals he's cross-examining in the witness box.

'Nothing on there of interest,' he replies, continuing to eat his dinner.

'Can we see it, then?'

'Nice try,' he says, smiling.

'If it's unused material, just hand it over.'

'You haven't served a defence statement. Come on, Leila. You know the rules. This isn't a fishing expedition. What's wrong with you?'

Oh, *now* we're following the rules.

I need that phone.

'I'll tell you what,' he says, brightly, 'I'll do you a swap. I'll give you Anton's phone if you give me Jack's.'

I smile at him, sarcastically.

'I'm sure you've seen the cell site analysis and know where it was traced. Outside Anton's house,' I point out, monitoring his face for the tiniest shade of a reaction. He doesn't give anything away.

'Of course I have,' he replies, refusing to look at me and continuing to eat. 'It could be explained by various scenarios.'

He's hiding something.

'Obviously, you don't want that admitted as evidence,' I go on, undeterred. 'It complicates your case, doesn't it? Why would the defendant's phone end up outside the victim's house, twelve miles away, when Jack was already in police custody? How did it get there? Jack couldn't have been in two places at once. Who took it?'

I'm pushing it, I know. But I can tell this worries him by the way he slowly inhales and lifts his eyebrows. It's something I've seen him do in court, countless times, usually when an opponent presents him with a submission he doesn't like.

One that means he can no longer win.

'Look, Leila,' he says, sternly. He adopts this voice sometimes, like a father about to scold a child. He places his cutlery down onto his plate. 'I know you've been shafted with this one. But don't get carried away and let it ruin your credibility. Everyone is watching to see how this plays out. Stick to what's in front of you. Don't turn this into something it's not.'

'Julian, I have a duty to my client to explore all avenues. Don't you think it's odd his phone was switched on less than an hour after he allegedly killed someone in a different location, at a time when he was detained by the police? And that location happened to be the deceased's home? There's a missing link here. As far as we know, before that night they weren't personally known to each other. There's no way this is a coincidence. Are you that desperate for a conviction you can't even consider that someone took it and—'

'Wait,' he interrupts, urgently. 'Are you insinuating he wasn't alone when he committed the murder?'

'*Alleged* murder.'

He rolls his eyes at me in a dramatic manner.

'Yes, yes, *alleged*. Is that the angle you'll be coming from? I mean, are those the instructions from your client? Has he specifically said that?'

'Well, no.'

'Because, as I understand it, he hasn't given you any clear instructions regarding his defence, which is why you haven't served a defence statement.'

'Yes, but—'

'And you know to coach him or lead him in any way would be *completely* unethical,' he preaches. This is rich, coming from him.

'Really?' I snap. 'I must have missed that part after I skipped the entirety of law school. Don't patronize me, Julian. I was merely pointing out how odd it is that Jack's phone was found near Anton's house on the night he was killed.'

The room goes silent as he starts to eat again. I just want to have a professional conversation about this.

'It would make a lot of sense, though. If that were the case,' I offer.

'No, we'd have something else to hang it on and, at the moment, we have nothing. There are no forensics connecting any other person to Anton. Millman's DNA was all over him. There were limited fibres from unknown sources, but that's because Millman's flat was covered in multiple extracts that were unidentifiable. Christ knows how many people were in there or what goes on in that bloody club. The entire place is dripping in depravity. In any event, Millman told the police his phone was stolen hours before he was arrested. It's entirely possible that whoever took it either lived in the village or passed through it. It's not that remote.'

'Nonsense, Julian,' I scoff. 'It's unlike you to accept such a weak explanation. The only reason you are is because it works for you, and you don't want the inconvenience of considering the alternative. You want a nice, tidy conviction.'

Julian doesn't 'do' getting annoyed, or rather, he doesn't wear it on his face when he is. He stares at me now, processing what I've said. He won't argue with me – I know him too well. But he knows I'm right, and he'll hate that. His eyes don't leave mine. It's his way of reminding me he knows best.

That I'm not as good as him.

'The Crown will not be relying on Millman's phone as evidence against him, so if you want to tell the jury about it, you'll have to do it yourself. I'd highly recommend you have a credible, solid reason for doing so, though – otherwise it'll seem that your defence is all over the place. That's solid advice from your pupilmaster. Don't tell anyone I told you that.'

He flashes me a quick smile, letting me know it's OK between us, that there's no need for things to get nasty. I rest my knife and fork on the plate and slump back into my chair.

'I'm sorry. The stress of this is getting to me.'

'It's fine,' he says, 'I get it. But some cases are unwinnable, Lei. There's simply no solid evidence of anyone else being there. Suspicion is not enough. And besides, I'm sure Millman would be the first person to throw someone else under the bus if he could. You've been given the short straw here, but you can still come out of it with dignity. Just run through the motions and do the best you can with a shit brief.'

Never in my legal career have words tasted so sour. I have not been trained to *run through the motions*. Being a barrister means fighting fearlessly, going the extra mile, doing the best you can. The responsibility of defending a man accused of murder should always weigh heavily on your shoulders.

I think about how different things would have been for Jack if I had trusted my gut last time instead of trusting what Julian taught me. *He is not always right.*

'And, what about us?'

'What about us?' He frowns, reaching for his glass of wine.

'I don't like this atmosphere. You're barely at home, and when you are, sometimes it's like we're strangers. It doesn't help when you pull stunts like at the plea hearing, either.'

'What did I do?' he asks, bewildered by the accusation.

'You made out I didn't know what I was doing after we'd had a discussion about the defence statement. You *knew* I wasn't serving one, but you acted as if you didn't know in front of the judge. Why did you have to make it seem that I didn't know my job?'

'God, Leila,' he says, rolling his eyes. 'It's all for show! I have a duty to the CPS to kick up a fuss if a defence statement hasn't been served. You wouldn't want people to think I was going soft on you for being my wife, would you?'

'I have more to lose than you. People's opinions matter to me.'

'Lei, we're both preparing a murder trial,' he tells me, as if I didn't know. 'The *same* murder trial. I know you haven't done one before, but this is how it is. You simply don't have time to be getting hung up about things like this.'

We finish the meal in silence.

After dinner, Julian goes to the study to work while I catch up on emails. I also post on my Instagram page for *Chats at the Bar*. Even just half an hour away from this case is a relief.

I try to get an early night, so head up to bed around 9.30 p.m., but it never works like that, does it? I lie awake for hours, staring at the crack of light shining through the curtains from the streetlamp outside.

At 11.45 p.m., I realize I haven't connected my laptop to the charger, and I'll need it for work tomorrow, so I creep down the stairs to plug it in. Julian is on the phone in the kitchen, the door shut. It's late for a phone call, but that's the thing about our job – 'working hours' don't really apply. Shivering in the cold hallway in my thin pyjamas, I quickly make my way to the study.

And then I hear him say something that stops me in my tracks.

'I know it was you who sent the wine on my birthday. What the hell were you thinking?'

His voice is raised. He must think I'm asleep. I dare not move, mid-stride. Who is he talking to?

'You need to get over this and move on with your life. Why is it taking you so long to get this? Are you stupid?'

I stand, frozen to the spot, like an awkwardly positioned statue. All the air is trapped in my lungs. I'm certain he'll hear if I exhale.

'If anyone finds out, we're both finished. Do you understand?'

A cold chill reverberates through my body.

Without any warning, the kitchen door flies open, and Julian is standing in front of me. I don't know who looks more startled, me or him. His phone, the one he's just been yelling into, now sits quietly in his right hand. He discreetly attempts to slide it into his pocket.

'I, erm, just came downstairs to plug my laptop in,' I mumble, trying to look like I haven't been eavesdropping. 'Is everything OK?'

'Oh, yes.' He nods, trying to read me to see how much I know, how much I heard. 'Just dealing with the usual bloody incompetent solicitors. You know what they're like.'

'This late at night?'

'For the case tomorrow morning.'

Liar.

'You got it sorted?'

'Nothing for you to worry about,' he says, kissing my forehead and heading upstairs. 'I'll see you up there.'

Big, red alarm bells are going off in my head. I should have probed more, but I know Julian well; he's too clever for a head-on confrontation.

I'll have to watch every move he makes.

Grabbing my laptop from the sofa, I can't find the charger anywhere, so I look in Julian's wheely suitcase, as he always keeps one in there. Glancing through it, I notice a bundle of papers, the top of which says, 'Anton Smythe mobile telephone records 01/01/24–06/09/24' and underneath, lots of numbers and text messages highlighted in yellow.

All the information I need is right there in front of me, yet I'm not allowed to look. But then I remember the last time I represented Jack, how I played everything by the book and how it landed him a stint in prison.

I'm not making that mistake again. He deserves more, and so do I.

'Lei? Could you bring me up a glass of water while you're down there?'

Julian's voice slices through my indecision like a sharp knife.

'Yes, just plugging my laptop in.'

I grab the charger and close the suitcase. Walking out of the room, I switch off the light and close the door.

Your pupilmaster should be your biggest champion, your professional guardian – the one person who always has your back, no matter what. It's becoming increasingly obvious that I can no longer trust Julian as my teacher.

Or my husband.

23

Leila

40 days before trial

THE AFTERNOON OF the site visit is metal-grey and rainy. The Christmas decorations around Durham city centre lack the magical feel tourists have come to expect and instead look sad and lacklustre. Four days into December, I don't think I've ever felt less excited for this holiday.

Rain slashes down on the car windows as I drive through the old, narrow streets to our destination while Davina sips her Starbucks latte.

The building screams trouble. I don't know if it's the unmarked door to the second floor, which you wouldn't notice unless you were looking for it, or the sombre lighting coming from the Georgian windows upstairs, but it looks like the kind of place where sin is encouraged.

As we walk into Innocence, the bar below Temptation on the ground floor, we see Julian and Detective Chief Inspector Brady. Julian has worked with him before, and he's the kind of man who despises defendants who give no-comment interviews – people like Jack. A polite nod in their direction is the only acknowledgement required.

I want to see the full layout of the club, so we're taken upstairs via the 'public' route, which turns out to be not so public.

Next to the female toilets is a plain white door, which is the gateway to the club upstairs. Through it is a small vestibule that's always manned by security. Once you've been identified as a member, you're allowed access through the second door. The decor dramatically changes from clinical and white to violet uplighters. It's dark, but there are mirrors on the wall that reflect the light in such a way that makes it hard to gauge how big the space is. Like one of those frightening fairground rooms you can't figure your way out of.

'Is that a novelty entrance or something?' I ask.

'It's to allow people to enter without being seen,' DCI Brady says. He arrived on the scene shortly after Jack made the 999 call, which identified a criminal judge as the victim, and he's been leading the investigation ever since. 'They enter through Innocence, and it looks as if they're in there when they're actually upstairs.'

'So, to confirm, there's no CCTV anywhere in the entire building?' Davina asks.

'Nope,' DCI Brady replies, with no attempt to hide the disgust in his voice.

We follow him up a flight of stairs, and he gives a running commentary as he goes. There are rooms branching off the narrow landings.

'These are the boudoirs. Full on Friday and Saturday nights. Usually start filling up around 10.30 p.m. with the girls and customers.'

'What's that room?' I ask, walking past a door which is half open. In it is a desk and three computer monitors. The walls are stacked full of shelves and host A4 files. It is windowless. An overweight man dressed in a black T-shirt sits quietly at the desk. He briefly looks towards us, then turns away again.

'The office. We've checked it. Nobody saw anything,' DCI Brady confirms. 'Millman's flat is on the next floor up.'

We follow right behind him, up the final flight of stairs. As we do, I think about how Anton made this trip on a Friday night without being seen. How did he know where to go? This building is quite the labyrinth, and you'd have to know exactly where you were going to get to Jack's apartment.

The staircase to his flat is small and steep, at the top of the building. Even though it's a chilly day, the temperature rises as we ascend. The stairs groan and creak, announcing our arrival. We line up as DCI Brady clinks the keys and opens the door.

It's small and dark. There's a stillness to it that feels antithetic to what must have been the atmosphere that hot September night. It's obvious the windows haven't been opened in a long time. It has the kind of musty smell places have when they've been unoccupied for a while. The door opens straight into the main living space, a small lounge and kitchenette. A TV in the corner sits beneath the attic roof, which slopes towards the ground. The two-seater sofa in the middle of the room faces it, with its back to the kitchen. There's barely any room to swing a cat in here.

The walls are an off-white colour. The carpet, beige. A large movie poster of *Robin Hood: Prince of Thieves* is displayed on one of them, stuck up with Blu-tack. It's the one with Kevin Costner about to launch a flaming arrow from his bow. Apart from that, there's nothing else that personalizes the room.

'Odd choice of "art",' Julian scoffs.

'I quite liked that film,' I shoot back, feeling immediately defensive of my client.

There's an eerie feeling to this space. There is one door on the opposite side to the main one. It's closed.

'Am I allowed to go in, DCI Brady?'

The way he stares at me, I might have just asked if I can whip my clothes off.

'It's your site visit,' he says in a patronizing tone. 'You can do what you like.'

Men.

We break off into our separate teams: prosecution and defence. I hear Julian mumbling as I walk into the bedroom by myself. The door swings shut behind me. The room is gloomy and lifeless. A dripping sound leads me to the tiny attic en-suite bathroom. I grip the shiny silver cold tap and tighten it. The rain thumps onto the skylight inches above my head.

Walking back into the bedroom, I run my fingers along the edge of the stripped bed as I look around and think about Jack's life here and what happened that night. How everything changed in a split second and will never be the same again. How he's counting on me to piece all this together and show a jury he's not guilty.

I head back into the kitchen area, and the sound of the bedroom door slamming behind me again makes me jump.

The kettlebell.

'DCI Brady, can you confirm where exactly the kettlebell was when you came in here that night?'

He walks over to where I'm standing and opens the door I've just walked through. He pushes it open about halfway, then stops to look at me.

'There,' he points to the edge of the door. 'The kettlebell was on the floor.'

'Are you absolutely sure?'

DCI Brady isn't used to being questioned. He's been doing this for a long time and is a respected police officer. He takes a deep breath before answering.

'I'm sure, love.'

I pause, looking at him in the eye. *Love*.

'Thank you,' I say cheerily, delivering him one of my biggest smiles. I will not descend to his pettiness.

'No problem, Britney,' he says quietly, smirking. He shoots back off to the other side of the room where Julian is. How utterly disrespectful. You do *not* refer to a barrister by their first name, let alone a stupid nickname that has been forced upon them.

People always underestimate me in this job; I should be used to it by now. You prove yourself by your actions, not words. People like DCI Brady just make me even more determined to win this case.

But I need something big now to blast through the noise and allow everything to make sense for the jury.

Walking into the middle of the living area, I picture the scene that night. My most successful jury speeches are the ones that ask jurors to tap into their own emotions; if you had a split second to act, what would you do? What would they have done in this situation? I assess the room from the perspective of a killer to see if things click into place.

I think about the conversation I had with Julian about Chester, how he protected the woman he had an affair with. He had too much to lose by saying who she was, so he sacrificed his own reputation and shielded her from it. Only infatuation or an obligation to someone would convince you to do such a thing. It need not make sense to an outsider, only to them.

That's it.

'Davina!' I whisper, loudly, beckoning her over to the corner of the room. 'Jack is an experienced criminal – it's never made sense why he would kill someone with a heavy weapon and then put it back where he found it.'

'Yes, we've already established this.'

I glance over at Julian, who is pointing and gesturing towards the door.

'Remind us where Anton was when you came in?' I ask DCI Brady.

'Over here,' he says, taking us over to the kitchenette where the carpet meets the cheap lino floor. 'His head was over that side, facing the door. He'd been knocked flat out, just as I said in my statement.'

Anton was struck on the right side of his head, just above his temple. The blow was fatal. I know from experience how heavy these kettlebells can be, but they're easy to swing with enough room.

'Didn't the police statement say Jack's clothes were covered in Coke when they arrived?' I ask.

'Coke?' Davina frowns, looking confused.

'Cola,' I clarify, quickly. 'In the kitchen, on the floor?'

My eyes dart around the small kitchenette and I mentally place Jack and Anton in the space.

'That's why he isn't saying anything.'

'Why?'

'If there was a struggle between Jack and Anton in the kitchen, Jack wouldn't have had time to run to the bedroom, get the kettlebell, and whack him over the head with it.'

'He might have done if he felt threatened, for whatever reason.'

'They were in the kitchen. We know Anton picked up a knife at one point because his prints are on it. Even if Jack did run to get the kettlebell, it would have given Anton enough time to get out of the flat – the front door is right next to the kitchen. He was caught completely off guard. Literally didn't know what hit him.'

She looks at me, waiting for the light bulb, the eureka moment, the breakthrough.

'So, what are you saying?'

I smile at her. 'There was someone else here when Anton died. I don't think Jack did it.'

24

Witness X

Rule #6
Never Lose Your Cool

KIDS AT SCHOOL used to say they were scared of their fathers when they roared in their faces for doing something wrong. I was the opposite. My dad never, ever shouted at me. Showing anger would be showing weakness.

He was most frightening when he was quiet and calm. When he stared at you with those dark grey eyes and said nothing, because you knew what was coming. You always knew.

'Always be calm, even in the face of intense stress, and don't ever raise your voice. You must never surrender to anger, as it demonstrates a lack of control and allows others to think they've got the upper hand.'

Respond, don't react.

It was in the first wave of the Coronavirus lockdown that things started to go sideways, and I was reminded of Rule #6. I had seen flashes of the darker side of my husband previously, but had ignored them, pushed those moments aside in the hope they would go away, much as I did when I was a little girl around my dad.

The state-forced imprisonment within my own home with this person – my husband – meant I had no choice but to face that malevolence every single day.

But just as I'd been taught, I never lost my cool. Even though, on occasions, I allowed him to think I did, because that's what he needed to believe.

My husband only knows the version of me I've allowed him to see. The one I've created. It bears no resemblance to who I actually am. He doesn't know what's coming.

I had been looking for my escape for a while, and almost had it before that night. It's funny, really, because before Anton died, I was the absolute happiest I'd been for a very long time. In fact, I'm going to say it's the happiest I've ever been in my life. The seven months before he was killed were the only time I've felt real, proper love. Ironically, that's why it didn't go to plan. Why I made mistakes.

For the first time in my life, I'd stopped following the rules. Now Anton is dead, and I'm counting on Jack Millman to keep everyone in this sordid story safe.

25

Leila

40 days before trial

THE FIRST THING I do after arriving back at chambers from the site visit is look at the photographs taken by the scenes-of-crime officer the night of the murder. True enough, the kettlebell that caused the fatal blow to Anton Smythe's head is holding the door to the bedroom open as a doorstop. The jury will have full access to these photographs as exhibits in the case and will find the reinstatement of the weight back to its original position following the assault as peculiar. *Why not hide it? Why put it back in full view of the police?*

After a few hours running errands in the city centre, I swing by Sainsbury's on the way home to pick up ingredients for chicken risotto, one of Julian's favourite dinners. By the time he arrives home, he's knackered and walks straight to the fridge for a glass of wine. Loosening his tie, he exhales loudly before taking a drink.

'Everything OK?' I ask, stirring the risotto.

'Yes, it's just been a hell of a day.'

His phone starts ringing. Julian is the kind of person who jumps whenever his phone makes a noise – there's always something for him to deal with. But this time, he lets it ring.

'Aren't you going to get that?' I ask, nodding towards his trouser pocket as I continue stirring the pan.

'I've had solicitors wanting a piece of me all day. I just want time with you tonight.'

He's lying. Never in our entire courtship has Julian *not* answered a work call. Even on our honeymoon, he was speaking to solicitors and clerks from chambers about cases.

Is the caller the person he was speaking to that night in the kitchen?

'You're too good to me.' I smile, walking over and kissing him on the lips. He seems tense and distracted as he sits down at the breakfast bar. 'I thought the site visit went well.'

'Always good to get a feel for the places where crimes are carried out.'

'Absolutely. It helped to put some of the evidence into perspective, too. The kettlebell is intriguing.'

'How so?' he asks, quizzically.

'Think about how strong Jack is. I'm surprised Anton had much of a face left.'

'Where are you going with this?'

The invitation is there. The question is: do I accept it? I will not compromise my client, but I am interested to see how he reacts to the idea.

'I think someone else did it,' I tell him, dramatically. 'A woman.'

'Leila—'

'Have you considered that?' I interrupt.

'There's no evidence of it.'

'Doesn't mean it didn't happen.'

'You know as well as I do it's not going to go anywhere in court. No substantial evidence of it, and Millman would have surely mentioned it by now.'

'How do you know?'

'Leila,' he says, confidently. 'Stop this.'

We stare at each other for a few moments, and the air between us vibrates with tension. He knows he's got the professional edge on me, but he also knows I adopt a more maverick style that tends to work in my favour. It's one of the reasons I was given a tenancy in chambers. After pupillage, every member of chambers must vote on whether you'll be accepted as a 'tenant', aka permanent member. One thing members noted was my ability to think outside the box in court and 'take fearless and calculated risks'.

Perhaps my biggest risk of all was making a move on Julian all those years ago. It was after the annual Christmas dinner at Crestview Hall, a manor house in Northumberland. Everyone from chambers went to stay there for the weekend.

It wasn't planned – it just happened. The dress code was black tie, so Julian was wearing a tux, and I was in a floor-length, ruby-red, silk dress that had a slit up my right thigh. I could tell by the way he was looking at me all night that something had shifted for him. I went to his room a few minutes after he'd gone up. Bold, I know. He'd never seen this side of me before and had dragged me into his room the second he opened the door. It was urgent, passionate. Like we had waited all this time for it to happen.

Once we went public, I was attending dinner parties as Julian's date and spending weekends away with judges and high-ranking legal professionals. There was an awful lot of sailing involved and shortened versions of place names I had to learn if I wanted to fit in (Harrogate became 'Row-gate', for example). Solicitors started sending me better-quality work based on 'my new role'. I never questioned it. Perhaps I should have. That's how things work in this profession. Who you know takes precedence over what you know.

If I'm being honest, I think my relationship with Julian tamed me in many ways, on a professional level. Over time, the reckless streak that had brought me so much success dissipated, and I became more cautious, more apprehensive. I started questioning myself and my decisions, constantly wondering if my pupilmaster – and husband – would approve of them.

That ended the day Jack Millman was convicted of assaulting Tony Flanagan. I should have trusted my instinct. I promised myself I'd never make the same mistake again.

'Damn!' I sigh now, standing in front of the kitchen cupboard, moving jars around. 'I'm out of chicken stock. Could you do me a huge favour and nip to the shop to get some?'

'Can't you do without?'

'I can't make the dish without it,' I reply. 'Go on, it's less than ten minutes away.'

Rolling his eyes, he slides off the chair, grabs his keys, and heads out of the front door. The slam reverberates through the hallway, plunging the house into silence. I can hear myself breathe. Walking out of the kitchen, I pause in front of the study and listen for the car to leave the drive.

The study is Julian's man cave and where he prepares all his cases. I rarely go in, preferring to work in the dining room. We like having our separate spaces. He's started to lock the door in the last few weeks, given the sensitivity of the evidence stored there, and the fact I'm allowed nowhere near it. He's right about this, of course. Maintaining integrity throughout this trial is so important. It's the cornerstone of our profession.

He shouldn't have trusted me to honour that.

I am not losing this case.

After counting to sixty in my head, I quickly remove from my jeans pocket the shiny gold key I had cut earlier today. He didn't even know I had taken it from his keys at work. Walking to the study, I pop the key into the lock, twist, and open the door.

I've got six, seven minutes, tops.

His desk is scattered with documents, most of which I already have. Julian is messier than I am. I like order but he prefers chaos. Even though this desk looks like a bomb has hit it, he will know exactly where everything is. I need to be careful. He misses nothing. I attempt to search for what I need as delicately as I can without moving much, otherwise he'll know I've been in here.

As I pick up documents, I attempt to assess mentally things he's highlighted and annotated. What's the relevance of it? What has he noticed?

And then I see it. What I'm looking for.

It's the document I spied last time. A schedule of Anton Smythe's mobile phone activity and a list of phone numbers he's called and texted. But the real bonus with his phone is this: because the prosecution has access to his handset, they were also able to extract the content of his messages. Removing my phone, I start taking photographs.

The priority is taking photos of every page, which I do at speed. There are over thirty. My heart races with each click of the camera. The internal voice, telling me, *You really shouldn't be doing this*, screams on repeat. In these few seconds, I've undone over a decade's worth of immaculate and conscientious work.

I am now professionally dishonest.

I don't like how that sounds, but I can't take it back now.

Just as I reach the final few pages – the most crucial – dated 6 September 2024, I hear Julian's car pull up on the drive.

Shit.

I speed up, unsure of the quality of the photos, but I need to get this finished. Reaching the last page, I take a photo and return the document to where it was. Running out of the room, I lock the door and shove the key into my pocket.

When he walks into the kitchen, I'm standing at the stove, stirring the pan. My breathing is quick, irregular, and I'm sweating. I hope he doesn't come too close.

'Please don't make me go back if it's the wrong one,' Julian says, throwing a box of stock capsules onto the kitchen top.

'They're fine, thank you,' I respond in the best upbeat voice I can muster, opening a window to cool down.

For the rest of the night, I'm on edge. All I want to do is look at the evidence I now have in my possession. I try to wait until the morning so I can dissect it thoroughly, but in the end, I can't hold myself back.

After dinner, I tell Julian I'm going for a long bath and take my phone upstairs.

While the water is running, I lock the door, sit on the toilet with a towel wrapped around me and open my photographs. Zooming in, I skip straight to the day of the murder. No wonder Julian was keeping this quiet.

It appears Anton was calling and texting one number repeatedly. At 3.47 p.m. on the day of the murder, he texted that same number:

> No, not there. Diamond Lounge 6 p.m. Don't panic. Nobody knows.

But it's the last text message at 3.52 p.m. that makes me understand why Julian never wanted me to see this.

> This will be sorted by tonight. I'll make sure of it. I love you.

26

Leila

39 days before trial
12.21 p.m.

It becomes clear after a night of barely any sleep that I can't keep this kind of information to myself, so after thinking long and hard about it, I elect to tell Davina. Given her proclivity towards the less ethical side of lawyering, I'm hopeful I can speak to her in confidence.

After requesting an emergency conference with her just after midday, when I meet her in Starbucks she practically launches herself at me. She must have sensed there has been a development, for she is wearing one of her statement piece power suits with significant shoulder pads.

She barely flinched when I told her what I'd done. *This is why Jack instructed her in the first place.* It's a necessary means to an end.

'We need to find out whose number that is,' she confirms, picking up her enormous red cup. 'And fast. Clock is ticking. This is only the tip of the iceberg, I suspect.'

'What have we got ourselves into here, Davina?'

'Whatever it is, we can handle it,' she says, completely unperturbed. 'So, how do you want to do this?'

'We need to be careful. We can't do anything that alerts the prosecution to the fact we know about the texts.'

'But we need to know who he's messaging. I mean, what's he talking about, "Nobody knows"? Sounds shady to me, and relevant to the case.'

'Yes, but without any kind of defence being put forward, the prosecution won't disclose the messages – they don't know it's relevant to us.'

'There's only one way to know whose phone number it is,' she says. I already know where she's going with this. 'We'll have to call it.'

'Absolutely not,' I reply, sharply. 'Just seeing these texts is bad enough. Calling any of the numbers is interfering with potential prosecution witnesses. Not to mention the fact that it would leave a trail back to us, and if found out, I'd be disbarred.'

'Not necessarily.' She shrugs, casually. 'We don't have to disclose who we are. Think of it as a fact-finding prank call in pursuit of justice.'

The way she phrases it makes me think this isn't the first time Davina has done this. I let the knowledge relieve my guilt slightly. I'm not the only one at fault here.

'Even if we could call it, how would we do it? I'm not calling from my phone.'

'Use our work mobile! It's the one we use whenever we call clients. The call comes up as a withheld number. Do you think any of our punters would answer the phone if the firm's name popped up?'

Jack's face flashes into my head for a moment. The one from the last time I represented him, and he was about to be sent to prison. I can't see that again.

'What would we even say?' I ask.

'You're the barrister. Be creative!' she says, her words bathed in nonchalance. Tapping the number into the phone, the display says 'calling' and she hands it to me.

'No!' I whisper, through gritted teeth. I hear the ringtone before holding it up to my ear.

Feeling panicked, I scramble to think of something to say when someone answers.

It's a man.

'Hello?' the voice says after four rings. He's obviously somewhere outside. I hear traffic and beeping from a pedestrian crossing in the distance.

'Hi there,' I reply, looking at Davina. 'Erm, this is PC Windsor calling from Durham Police Station, central division. Is now a good time to chat?'

He doesn't reply immediately, and the sound of traffic in the background fills the space.

'Sorry, what's this about?'

'It's about an offence you've been implicated in.'

'What the . . . ?' he replies, confused. 'What offence? Who's implicated me in it? How do you have my number?'

He sounds young – in his twenties, possibly younger. When you cross-examine liars for a living you become skilled in reading people's voices, their tone, pitch, and timbre. His voice is sprinkled with a touch of panic and a dash of anger. Interesting.

'I'm afraid I can't tell you that. But it will be easier if you cooperate with us, David.'

'David?' he repeats back, puzzled. 'My name isn't David.'

'This isn't David Welby?'

'No! You've obviously been given incorrect information.'

There's relief in his voice.

'I'm really confused,' I tell him. 'Is your number 09734837271?'

'Yes, that's me.'

'I don't suppose you know a William Morrison? Fifty-four years old? Likes to sit and drink cans of Fosters all day in his garden and shout at people?'

'Never met him!' He laughs. 'I've got nothing to do with this!'

'That bloody swine!' I sigh, looking at Davina, who stares at me. 'He's been brought in for theft and implicated someone else. Gave me this number. I'm sorry to waste your time but obviously we have to chase these things up.'

'No problem,' he says. 'You had me panicked there!'

Hmm. Did I?

'Just for the record,' I go on, 'so I can sign this off, could I have your name? I'll need it to write up my notes and show my superior I've made this call and discounted it.'

'Sure,' he says. 'It's Quinn Smythe.'

'Quinn Smythe . . .' I repeat back to him, so Davina can grasp the enormity of this. Her mouth drops open in shock and her eyes widen like large saucers. 'Anton's son?' she mouths to me, in an exaggerated way, and I nod my head vigorously.

'Brilliant. Thanks, Quinn. Just writing that down,' I lie. 'Have a good day.'

I hand the phone back to Davina, and as much as I want to feel bad about what I've just done, I don't. Instead, I smile.

'I've got to hand it to you.' Davina grins. 'Top extraction skills.'

'Cross-examination technique.' I shrug. 'Make them panic, place them in a state of alert, bring them into safety, and most people will give you what you want.'

'So, what were Quinn and Anton hiding? It's obviously something important, and I'd say relevant, given the timing and urgency of the message.'

'I agree.' I nod.

'Which bar was it again?' she asks.

'Diamond Lounge. Think it's in town. The one on the river, with an outdoor terrace.'

She muses for a moment, squinting her eyes, staring at a corner of the room until a smile creeps onto her face.

'The good thing about this job is that you have friends in useful places,' she says, standing up. 'Come on. Are you bringing that coffee with you?'

'Where are we going?'

'To watch what happened when Anton met his son a few hours before he was killed.'

27

Leila

12.42 p.m.

To say this case is a baptism of fire would be an understatement. It's partly because of Davina, who is relentless in getting the best outcome for her clients by whatever means necessary. But now I'm also a willing party to this method.

I'm justifying my actions by telling myself that in doing this, I'm representing Jack more fairly. I mean, yes, if the Bar Standards Board found out what I'm doing I'd be hauled in front of a disciplinary panel and disbarred, but they won't find out, and all I've really done is broken into the prosecutor's office, looked at some confidential evidence, and potentially interfered with a witness.

Could have happened to anyone.

Diamond Lounge is one of those places where professional types go on a Friday night. The kind that plays non-distinct house music and everyone drinks either cool European beer out of bottles or cocktails out of fancy glasses, most of which have dry ice slithering out of them.

Davina leads the way. She marches in as if she owns the place which, given her background and dealings, wouldn't surprise me at all.

'Is Keany in?' she barks at a young man behind the bar, dressed in black.

'He's out back. Who's looking for him?'

'Tell him it's his lawyer.'

The lad shuffles quickly out of the bar area and disappears for a minute or so.

'Do you know everyone?'

'I'm well connected,' she says. 'I represented him about a year ago. Drugs possession. He works security.'

'I'm surprised he kept his job.'

'Where do you think he got the drugs from?'

Keany – a short, stocky fella with a buzzcut – comes out from a side door, looking terrified and shocked in equal measure.

'Davina? What you doin' 'ere?'

'We need a favour. Can we have a word in private?'

'Err, yeah. Come through the back,' he grunts, ushering us down a dark staircase to a poky basement office with no windows or ventilation.

'Now listen, Keany. This is strictly on the nod. We don't want you blabbing to people that we've been here. I assume you've had people in already looking at the CCTV in relation to Friday, 6 September – would I be right?'

He nods, reluctantly, saying nothing.

Bloody Julian. He's already seen what we're looking for. He's way ahead of us.

Keany searches for footage of that day; the cameras show different perspectives of the bar. I feel nervous, sick.

As the footage reaches 6 p.m., Keany allows it to play.

My eyes dart between the split screens, frantically searching for Anton or someone I know. Christ knows, I need something to put before a jury.

6.02 p.m. Nothing.

6.05 p.m. Nothing.

'Maybe he didn't go?' I whisper.

'Give it time,' Davina says.

At 6.06 p.m., a broad man wearing a brown tweed jacket and chinos walks through the main door to the bar. He doesn't look like the other customers around that time, who are all young, trendy types. His metallic silver hair is combed back away from his face. It's Anton. He orders a drink – looks like a Coke – and takes it to one of the tables near the window.

'There he is,' I say, pointing at the screen.

He looks anxious, distracted. Perching on the edge of a leather sofa, he fiddles with his hands and keeps leaning back, then forward. He can't settle.

Just then, a young guy walks over to him – dressed in black, just like all the other lads who work there – and starts talking to him. At first he seems to be making polite conversation, but after a minute or so, the young man sits down next to him. Something about the way they talk to each other makes me think there's more to it; it looks intense. The young man lowers his head, and Anton places his hand on the young man's back and speaks to him closely.

Davina and I look at each other, confused. This isn't what I expected to see at all. I lean closer to the monitor to get a better look. The angle of the camera is such that I can't see the young man's face. The quality isn't great.

'Who is it?' Davina asks.

'It's Quinn,' Keany says, from behind us. We turn around to look at him.

'What?'

'Quinn Smythe? He worked here for a while,' he says, casually.

'Quinn Smythe worked here?'

'Yeah.'

'Does he still work here?'

'Nah, he left to go to uni in September. I remember it because

Quinn's last shift was the night his dad died. He'd been bangin' on for weeks about movin' to Cambridge and all the *freshers* parties he'd be at. I *think* it was Cambridge. Might have been the other one. I dunno. One of the posh ones with the boats. Only worked 'ere over the summer. You know, had a rich family but had to get a "job" to prove to Mummy he was independent. Bad what happened to his dad, though.'

'Yes,' I say, not taking my eyes off him. 'What was he like when he worked here?'

'Typical posh lad. Confident, cocky. He was always crackin' on with the lasses. That's the only reason he liked workin' 'ere, to be honest. Went very weird before he left, though.'

'What do you mean?'

'It must have been about a week before he left. He went . . . quiet. You know, jumpy.'

'Jumpy? In what way?'

'He looked like shit, for a start. Like he hadn't been sleepin'. It was after a fella came in wanting to speak to him and he absolutely freaked out after. Started having a panic attack or something.'

'Did they have a fight?'

'Nah, nowt like that.' Keany laughs. 'This fella walked in and had a quiet word with Quinn and he just lost it. This bloke was being dead calm but Quinn went proper weird after. He was nearly cryin', sayin' he needed to take his break early. He wasn't the same after that.'

'Was this the man he was talking to on that occasion?' Davina asks, pointing to Anton on the screen.

'No. Not him! Much younger. Longish dark hair, tattoos, ripped.'

Davina and I glance at each other. As soon as we hear the description of this 'mystery man', it's clear we're both thinking the same thing. Davina gets her phone out and taps away before holding it up in front of Keany's face.

'Is this the man you're talking about?' she asks. It's the mugshot from the night Jack was arrested.

Keany takes one look at the screen, before giving his answer immediately.

'Yeah, that's him. Good-lookin' fella.'

'Do you know what they were talking about?' I ask him. 'Please, this is really important.'

'Sorry, no idea. But Quinn lost his mind over it, I know that much.'

I've only seen Quinn Smythe a handful of times. On each occasion, he's given off a confident, privileged vibe, but the last few times I've seen him, at Jack's court appearances, he's looked gaunt, scared.

'What business would Jack have with Anton's son a week before his death? It can't be connected to Anton getting killed, can it? Surely a coincidence?' Davina whispers to me.

'I don't believe in coincidences,' I tell her.

28

Leila

33 days before trial

There he was, just as Keany had said.

At 4.57 p.m. on Friday, 30 August, exactly one week before the murder, Jack strolled into Diamond Lounge and went straight up to Quinn Smythe to speak with him. Two things struck me while watching this footage: firstly, they appear to be having an intense discussion about something serious. This, in itself, raises questions. Jack is a prolific criminal, and Quinn is the high-achieving son of a Crown Court judge. They have no reason to be acquainted.

Secondly, Jack's phone is located at Temptation on the cell site analysis for that time of day, which means he either forgot to take it (and who forgets to take their phone anywhere?), or he deliberately left it for some reason.

Keany was right; Quinn responds negatively to Jack's presence. He appears agitated at first, running his hands through his hair, fidgeting with his face for a few minutes before completely losing it. Quinn gesticulates with his open hands, starts pointing at him and, at one point, reaches out to place his hand on Jack's arm, as if to plead with him. Jack calmly removes it. People in the bar start looking over.

We need to get to the bottom of this, so we organize a

conference with Jack, but have to wait until the following week to get clearance for a visit.

When we finally get to see him, Davina and I can barely wait to question Jack on what we have discovered. We're only a week away from everything shutting down for Christmas, and I want to do so with some feeling of confidence.

He walks calmly into the conference room, as if he isn't awaiting trial for murder, casually nodding to both of us. He's wearing matching light grey joggers and sweater. His wild hair is tied back into a messy, low ponytail-thing. Christ knows where he's got a hair-tie from in here. I worry about how he's treated in prison, but he's equally someone who deceives people with his looks.

To look at him, he's a beautiful man. Tall, toned, and athletic. You could easily mistake him, perhaps, for an actor or model on the street, the kind of man who would run the other way in a dangerous situation when, in fact, *he* is the danger. He has stolen, supplied drugs, and committed violence. Despite possessing a charming eloquence and calm manner, you wouldn't want to mess with him. This is what worries me about putting him in front of a jury.

'Quinn Smythe,' I say directly. 'We know you went to see him a week before the alleged murder. We know Anton went to see him a few hours before he died. What are your dealings with him?'

A small smile spreads across his face.

'Looks like I have a very switched-on legal team,' he says. 'Why don't you just go and ask him what you want to know?'

'He's the son of the man you're accused of murdering. Something tells me he isn't exactly going to be upfront about his involvement with you.'

'Too right there,' he says, leaning back in his chair and refusing to pull his eyes away from mine.

'So, what is it?' I ask. 'And why didn't you take your phone when you went to see him?'

'Didn't wanna lose it.' He shrugs. 'Phones have a terrible habit of going missing, you know.'

He's toying with us.

'Interesting how you went to such enormous lengths to keep it safe and then it mysteriously went missing at such a pivotal moment on the day you're accused of murder.'

Jack smiles and looks down at the floor for a second.

'It's a funny old world, isn't it?' he remarks. 'Unpredictable.'

'So, Quinn—'

'Look,' he interrupts, 'I don't know what you want me to say.'

'The truth would be a start.'

'I told you, I'm not a grass. Especially when it comes to a judge's son. The judge I'm accused of killing. Did you learn nothing from the last case you defended me for? Things and people have a habit of going missing when you're upfront about them, and I'm not prepared to put myself in that position again.'

'It's just me and Davina, Jack, you can trust us.'

'Never trust anyone, not even lawyers, *remember?*'

He spits out the last word. I inhale, deeply, to hide my frustration. This is getting ridiculous now.

'*You shouldn't have talked,*' he goes on, mocking me. '*You should have presented your case to the jury.* That's what you said, so that's what I'm doing.'

Davina looks at me out of the corner of her eye and I'm momentarily embarrassed. I don't know why – she's said far worse things to clients – but I dislike my words being exposed in this way.

'You're the barrister,' he continues. 'You put my case together.

You find the clues. You get the evidence and make them find me not guilty. That's your job.'

'I can't just magic an acquittal out of thin air.'

'Everything you need is right in front of you,' he says slowly. 'Like the CCTV you found.'

'You weren't alone that night, were you?'

He smiles, like a proud parent, and we stare at each other over the small table.

'No comment.' He sighs.

'For god's sake, Jack!' I shout at him. My shrill voice bounces off the stark walls of the tiny room. 'You need to take this seriously.'

I loathe the sound of my voice when I'm angry. I shouldn't be speaking to a client like this. I don't ever allow myself to get annoyed with people I'm representing. He goes quiet for a few moments. I think he's going to say something profound, something helpful.

But then he smiles to himself, in a way that suggests he might be about to laugh.

'What?' I snap at him. 'Something funny?'

'It's . . . nothing,' he says, shaking his head and lowering his gaze towards the floor.

'What?'

'It's just,' he says, looking up at me, 'you remind me of someone.'

Davina and I glance at each other.

'Who?'

His head lowers again, almost as if he regrets sharing a small part of himself.

'It doesn't matter.'

I give him a moment to breathe, to take stock. I don't know what's happening to me these days.

We all need to calm down.

'Is it true that barristers have to keep those blue books you write all your notes in for, like, years?' he says, breaking the silence.

I look at him and then Davina.

'We have to keep them for seven years. Why?'

'Does that mean you'll still have the one you used for my last case?'

'Yes.'

'Maybe you should go and have a read through that,' he says, before abruptly standing up and walking to the door. The security guard comes to collect him, and he's ushered out, leaving Davina and me in silence.

'Sounds like there might be something in your conference notes he wants us to see,' she says, like a shark who's sensed blood in the water.

29

Leila

26 days before trial

All barristers use traditional notebooks to prepare their cases in. Supplied by chambers, they're encased in a rich blue exterior, A4 size, and filled with lined paper. We're obligated to keep them for seven years once we're done with them, in case an appeal is raised. They're stored away in a locked room, and each barrister has their own section. As you might imagine, over the course of a year, they pile up.

Looking in the chambers online diary, I choose a time when Julian is listed to be in court to go and find it. The last thing I want is him asking what I'm doing.

Packed tightly together on the shelf in date order, the notebooks snooze quietly, side by side. My professional life's work, all right there. The defeats, but mostly successes. The closing speeches I've stayed up late to write, the plea in mitigations that meant the difference between someone getting a second chance or going to prison. The hard work, the determination, the sacrifice; all of it lies within these pages.

Running my finger over the thin spines, I pull a random one out to see the date. In the top right-hand corner, written in black ink, it says 'Leila Reynolds, 16.1.2019'. Too early. Jumping further along the line, I pull another; 7.7.19. Closer.

Leaping several books ahead, I yank out the next notebook. 4.8.2019.

This is the one.

The trial lasted only two days. The whole thing was a disaster. I could tell as soon as the jury were sworn in that we'd have a fight on our hands.

I've become skilled at reading jurors over the years; you become attuned to watching their body language and facial expressions, what and who they like. The jury is a rich, diverse tapestry of our social demographic, thrown together to judge one person accused of committing a crime. All from different backgrounds, with separate values, professions, and experience to bring a unique, nuanced angle of understanding to the case.

But you can always spot 'the ones'. The ones who hate your client from the start. The ones who stare at them. These jurors have likely never, ever come close to breaking the law. They do not question authority in any way and abhor those that do. They turn up for jury service in smart clothes and take their civic duty seriously, unlike the ones who shuffle in wearing joggers, yawning because 10.30 a.m. is far too early in the day to be up, and this entire trial is an inconvenience for them.

The jury in Jack's assault trial had far too many of the former type of juror for my liking.

You get trials like this occasionally, where everything that can go wrong does. When the main prosecution witness is a high-profile character, it's never going to be a fair run.

In the end, they painted Jack out to be not only a liar, but a snitch. His reputation was trashed. Grassing up someone like Tony Flanagan was suicide. And he was convicted anyway.

Marching back to the conference room where Davina sits waiting for me, I close the door, the blue book in my hand. She looks regal, sitting at the head of the huge oak table. She is surrounded by bookshelves; I briefly catch her gazing out of the window. Her eyes are immediately drawn to the book the second I enter the room.

Sitting next to her, I open the notebook and begin flicking through as she watches, in silence.

'Do you have any idea what you're looking for?' Davina asks, as I turn the pages.

'It would be something Jack knew I had written down. That would only be something he said in a conference I had with him.'

My eyes are drawn to the top of each page, looking for any headed '*Conf*'. We had quite a few throughout the course of the trial and I documented each one, thorough as I am. I record everything in trials – you never know when you'll need something.

'Anything?' she asks.

I shake my head, before something catches my eye.

At the bottom of one page, I see a sentence with several exclamation marks at the end. I'd never usually write something like that, but it's definitely my writing. As soon as I read it, I turn the book towards Davina.

'This is it!' I whisper.

> Client joked that the next time he commits a crime in Tempt, he'll do it in the only room with CCTV. Have advised against any further acts in the future!!!!

'Temptation has a room with a camera,' Davina breathes. Her eyes lock with mine. 'We need to see that footage.'

30

Leila

2.36 p.m.

T*HE IRONY WASN'T* lost on either of us: if the assault Jack was accused of had taken place in a different room, he would have been acquitted because he would have been able to prove he was defending another person. The camera would have captured it.

That footage could change the direction of the case. One thing I know about a jury is that they love evidence that's tangible. Something they can see or hear.

I haven't received any reference to the footage from the prosecution, which makes me believe they aren't aware of this camera. The fewer people who know about it the better.

We visit Temptation on the final working week in December. Davina and I face no resistance from the staff on our way up to the office. Saying we're Jack's legal team is enough. The door is open, the white sterile room a sharp contrast to the dark landing just outside.

The guy I saw last time is sitting at the desk.

'Afternoon,' I say. He doesn't look up. 'We need to talk to you about a delicate matter. It's about Jack Millman's criminal case. Can we come in?'

He turns to face us.

'Are you on your own or with your friends today?'

He presumably means the prosecution team we came with to the site visit.

'We're on our own.'

He nods his head ever so slightly, indicating we can enter.

'Close the door,' he says. It's a demand, not a request.

We stand beside him at the desk and he swings around on his chair to face us.

'I know there's a secret camera in Temptation,' I tell him.

He pauses. 'There are no cameras here.'

'I know there's a camera in here somewhere,' I interrupt. 'In one room, nowhere else. Don't ask me how I know, but I do. And I need to view the footage. For Jack.'

He resists for a moment, not knowing whether to concede or keep up the act.

'When from?' he says, eventually.

'That's the thing. I don't know.'

He looks at me as if I'm stupid.

'OK, let's start with Friday, 6 September, the day of the alleged murder. Can you get that for me?'

'Right now?'

'Yes, now. That's why I'm here. I'm trying to run a criminal defence, and we don't have much time.'

'Give me five minutes,' he says, fiddling about on a computer in the corner while we stand looking around the office.

'What room does this camera cover? Temptation has no CCTV inside or outside. You pride yourself on the fact.'

'This is the only camera,' he says. 'And it covers Boudoir 3.'

'What happens in Boudoir 3?' Davina asks.

'The usual stuff. Eddie set it up,' he confirms. 'He likes to watch.'

'Watch what?' I ask, unsure whether I want to know.

'What goes on in there.'

'What *does* go on in there?' Davina enquires. She's unable to hide the sound of disapproval in her question.

'Look, I just deal with security,' he shoots back at us, sounding really pissed off. 'Don't ask me what thrill he gets from watching fellas get sucked off by girls barely old enough to drink.'

'Always knew he was a weird one,' Davina whispers into my ear, which I choose to ignore. Now is not the time.

He taps away on a laptop for a few minutes as we wait patiently. There's an overpowering stench of salt and vinegar crisps in here. I begin to wonder if this man ever leaves the room.

'It's ready,' he says, passing us two sets of headphones before moving out of the chair. 'Use that to forward through or go back a day.'

We sit down and play the video.

The camera is positioned on the wall, higher than eye height but not on the ceiling. The 'boudoir' looks as awful as it sounds, with leather-looking sofas positioned around the room. There's a time and date stamp in the corner of the black-and-white image. The quality is poor, not helped by the dim lighting. I begin at midnight on the day of the alleged murder, and it starts to dawn on me that this could take a long time to go through. Time I simply don't have.

It's occupied by punters, seedy and sordid. Young girls walk in, leading the way. Glass of champagne in one hand, the hand of a man in the other. Even with the bad quality of the video you can see that their bodies are barely covered; long limbs stand out against the grainy darkness of the room. Within minutes, they're engaging in sexual acts. I fast forward without looking at Davina. We don't need to see this. It goes on until 4 a.m. It's empty as the time stamp races through the morning: 10 a.m., 11 a.m.

At 11.24 a.m. the door opens, and a man walks in. The camera is positioned in such a way that you can't see who's entering; you can only see who is in the middle of the room.

'This is the one place in the building we won't be heard by anyone,' the man says. 'Trust me, we're safe.'

The sound is slightly muffled, but I know his voice. As the man moves to the centre of the room, I recognize his dark hair and sleeve tattoos that I can just about make out against the white sleeveless top he's wearing.

It's Jack.

Behind him is a man who isn't in shot. All I can see are his legs; he's wearing black trousers and shoes. But I know one thing; Jack has led him here because he knows there's a camera in the room.

'Listen,' the other voice says. 'I can't stay long – I start work at 12. But I can't do it. I've thought about it – I really have – but I just can't.'

'You have to,' Jack interrupts.

'Come on, man! Do you understand what you're asking?' the other voice says. Even with the inadequate sound quality, I can tell it's laced with panic. 'My life will be over!'

'That's not my problem,' Jack says. 'It has to be today. I've given you enough time, longer than others would.'

'Please.'

'No. No excuses. It's going to get so much worse if you don't do it. Trust me.'

'You know, you're messing with the wrong person here. Do you even know what you're getting into with this? Who I am? Once this gets out—'

'Do you realize who *you're* messing with here? Because I don't think you do. I gave you until noon today. You've had a week and you know what will happen if you don't.'

'We're talking about killing someone!' the other man says. Davina's hand lands briefly on my arm. My eyes don't leave the screen. 'I'll go to prison for the rest of my life. I'm going to university *tomorrow*! Please . . . *please*!'

'You'll do it today.'

There's silence for a few moments.

'No,' he replies. 'I won't. I'm not messing my life up because of a stupid mistake. This will go away. I'll make sure it goes away.'

'There's a video,' Jack says, calmly.

The other man doesn't reply for a few moments.

'What?'

'I have a video,' Jack says. 'I filmed it.'

The room goes quiet.

'I don't believe you . . .'

'Yes, you do.'

'What kind of sick person are you?'

'Not so cocky now, are you?' Jack asks, making no attempt to hide the satisfaction in his voice.

'You filmed it? What's wrong with you?'

'You'll do it by the end of today, or I'll make sure everyone sees it.'

'Does blackmailing me make you feel powerful? Some kind of twisted revenge, hitting back at the system?'

'Do it, now. Today.'

'Screw you, Jack. And this video you claim to have, because I don't believe you.'

At that, he storms out of the room, closely followed by Jack.

The other guy remained out of view the entire time. I only heard his voice. It was one of those plummy posh-boy accents, from someone raised in a middle-upper-class environment. They have an annoying inflection at the end of sentences that drips with privilege.

But I've heard this particular voice before. I recognize its pitch and timbre, the rise and fall of his words. His speech, tinged with the same urgency it had over the phone.

The young man in the video is Quinn Smythe.

31

Witness X

Rule #7
Beware the Talented Student

Once you become good at something, you become a threat to others who have the same skill. But beware most of all the person to whom you impart all of your knowledge.

The student.

You want someone whose mind is in alignment with yours, but whose appetite for dominance will never exceed your own. Pick your pupil wisely. The last thing you need is your protégé becoming too powerful. It's a tricky balance to achieve. If a student becomes more skilled and successful than their mentor, things can turn ugly. It triggers all kinds of inferiority complexes. Things can get out of hand.

I heard her before I saw her.

Even though we were both only sixteen at the time, that husky voice made her sound like she smoked thirty fags a day. She spoke with the confidence that money affords you. Laughing loudly, the girls around her directed their adoring, magnetic attention her way. I had never seen her before, but I could tell she was the dangerous one, the rebel. She wore the same pristine uniform as the rest of us but somehow looked better in hers. The pencil skirt grazed the top of her knees, a good two inches higher than ours.

The top button on her white shirt gaped open, as her tie hung loosely around her neck. She wore two sets of studs in each ear; we were allowed one. The uniform code was applied strictly here. You expect that at a boarding school – the sanctions are tough – but this girl was prepared to bend the rules.

After eyeing one another up around school for a few weeks, we found ourselves gravitating towards each other. It was inevitable: we each saw a piece of ourselves in the other.

I spent a year beside her, observing her, before introducing her to the rules. I needed to ensure she would respect and use them wisely. They required emotional intelligence, impeccable timing, and restraint. They were powerful in the right hands, and dangerous in the wrong ones.

She knew how to play people in a way even I had not yet learned. I had become an expert at manipulating boys. I knew the kind of person I needed to be around each of them to secure their placement in my pocket: a nerd, a tease, a vixen, a coquette. It was transactional.

But she knew how to work the girls. Was a natural social climber. A keen sense of justice ran through her blood and people trusted her; she always made the right call, even if it pissed people off. She was skilled at being fake in a way that made it appear that she wasn't.

We could help each other.

A model student, she was patient and asked questions. She had an insatiable thirst for the dark knowledge that was being fed to her, and she lapped it up.

It wasn't until we applied to go to the same university that our behaviour soared to the next level. Suddenly, we possessed an even bigger world in which to create our chaos.

We revelled in causing as much destruction as we could, playing people against each other, covertly causing rifts within friend groups and fucking our way through hot, influential male students. Guys with girlfriends always had more value. The ultimate challenge. How long would it take for them to cave in and cheat? But they had to be under the illusion they initiated it. We never actually wanted them, of course – it was all just part of our game. We were attracted to their status, their unavailability.

Could we make them want us? Need us? Love us? Even for just a few weeks before moving on to the next?

It was a playground, a place for us to hone our skills before moving into the real world, where we set our sights on married men. The stakes were higher, and the thrills were, too. We collected broken marriage vows like sweets and became drunk on the power it gave us.

How irresistible. How intoxicating. How powerful.

How fucking pathetic.

But even this got boring after a while, and that's when it happened. My insatiable desire for self-destruction pushed me to a place where I'd never quite recover.

You can break down defining moments, the ones that become landmarks. The decision I made to start talking to her changed the trajectory of my life. Theoretically, we shouldn't have worked. She was not like me, but she was also very much like me.

We met at a time when I wore a veil of shame, and I observed the world through it. I hated *him*, but I hated myself more. I'd internalized the neglect and abuse I had suffered as a child for so long, I believed I had no value. That I was defective, worthless, dirty, and certainly not deserving of love.

I felt I should be punished for being so damaged – so broken – so I constantly put myself in situations where I could be. I would binge drink until I blacked out, all the sex I had was unprotected, I'd study so hard I'd only get four hours' sleep a night, I didn't eat well. I cheated on good people who loved me because what better way is there to prove to yourself that everything you believe is true?

I was a disgusting, terrible, vile person, and I enjoyed collecting proof of this. Dad knew it. Declan knew it, Declan's dad knew it. I knew it.

Self-destruction was the only way to distract myself from what he did to me, from the shame I couldn't help but feel. It was all I knew. The irony was that the only thing that made me feel better was attaining the thing my father had conditioned me to crave: power. Finding these little pockets of control, over people and situations, was the one way to anchor the rage I felt for myself. Meeting someone who felt the same was blissful, because it made me less alone, less . . . singular.

But I took it too far.

I once heard someone say that you meet people for a reason, and when that reason is fulfilled, the friendship will naturally end.

That may be true in most cases, but I can categorically say we should never have met. Some partnerships are too dangerous to exist. I told her all of my nasty little secrets, and she told me hers. It was the first time either of us had felt safe enough to share those parts of ourselves with anyone else.

We never imagined it would end as horribly as it did.

On paper, she had it all: the perfect family, the incredible house, rich, successful parents. But things are never quite as they seem, are they? School was her escape. She hated going home to her narcissistic bully of a father and emotionally distant mother.

Perhaps that's what drew us together. Trauma finds trauma. She had a complex, toxic relationship with her own father. Of course she did. That's what makes it so much worse, what I did.

I know she'll come for me one day, because I taught her the rules, and she isn't going to let me forget them.

I created a monster in her, just as my dad did with me.

Look how that turned out.

32

Leila

26 days before trial
3.58 p.m.

'It obviously won't be admissible in court because we can't prove it's Quinn. The prosecution would never allow it as evidence, and I'm not sure a judge would, either,' Davina says the second we get back into the car after leaving Temptation. 'Besides, what would our argument be? That Quinn murdered his own dad?'

We almost had something. I cannot believe Quinn isn't identifiable in the video. A judge would have to be satisfied that an expert could positively identify him from it, and I've done enough of these cases to know that isn't going to happen. As Davina points out, what would we even be saying? That Quinn killed his father? Without further evidence to support this, it could make our case even worse. We'd look desperate and unsympathetic in front of a jury. If you're going to make a claim like that, you need to have solid, indisputable evidence.

We need to tread lightly with this. 'The timeline adds up,' I say, rather unhelpfully.

'Why was Jack saying, "You'll do it by the end of today"? Surely, it's too much of a coincidence that Quinn's dad was killed hours later. Why won't Jack just tell us what happened? If Quinn is involved somehow, why not just say?' Davina fires these questions at me, and I barely have time to think.

'Because he fears he wouldn't get a fair trial. People would be paid off, and others would be protected. Look at Quinn – privately educated, perfect student, studying at Cambridge. Of course Jack isn't going to offer that information up before the trial. He's learned the hard way that all it would do is give people time to hide what they've done.'

I continue to drive, thinking of a way through this. I need to allow the jury to see that Quinn is hiding something without revealing what I've just seen. Reaching over to my phone, which is connected to the Bluetooth system, I call Julian. After a few rings, he picks up.

'Yes?' he says, in a clipped tone.

'What do you intend to do with Quinn Smythe?'

He doesn't answer immediately. I can almost hear him thinking.

'Anton's son? What do you mean?'

'We have reason to believe he was one of the last people to have contact with Anton before he died. Do you have a statement from him? Because we would like to see it, if so.'

He pauses for an unnecessary amount of time. I know what he's doing: he's wondering what information I have about Quinn and whether Jack has said anything.

'I'll get it over to you,' he says, hanging up, abruptly.

Davina executes a dramatic, audible sigh.

'Well, you've gone and dropped a bomb on this case now. I hope you're ready for the explosion when it comes.'

When I arrive back at chambers, I remember I agreed to do an interview piece with Serene Kirkbride, an influencer who showcases women in business. She has a huge following on Instagram and has asked to meet for a drink to discuss my journey to the Bar. I could really do without it, but she talked me into it by saying I would be the 'prime Christmas guest'. It was a coveted spot with her, so I couldn't say no.

I meet her at the Pacific Hotel bar in the city centre. She's drinking a glass of prosecco when I arrive, wearing a tasteful Christmas sweater that makes her look Scandinavian, but I'm sure she's from Wallasey or somewhere like that. Serene greets me with a double air-kiss and enormous smile. Some people don't look the same as their social media persona, but she does. Exquisite silver hair swishes around her perfectly made-up face, giving her the appearance of a mythical fairy. After declining a glass of 'fizz' on the basis I have work to do after, we settle down to chat.

'I've been so excited to meet you, Leila! I've followed your blog for some time. You're an intriguing character!'

'Am I?' I ask, puzzled.

'Yes! Beautiful, smart, sexy career . . .'

'I wouldn't call it sexy. I practically live in a seventeenth-century wig and robes.'

'It's glamorous, though. Surrounded by drama.'

And blood. And violence. And death.

'Yes, well, it's very hard work.'

'Oh, of course!' she says. 'Tell me, Leila, why do you think you have such a high success rate? You're in the Legal 500 as someone who "Executes intuitive style and is an exceptional jury advocate. Approaches cases with a forensic eye and has a very clever way of interpreting evidence. Future bright star and KC in the making". What's your secret?'

Just hearing that quote again makes my skin prickle. I should be beaming with pride, but knowing it was gained through a back door makes it feel meaningless. Even my own husband doesn't believe in me.

'Honestly, people are fascinated with human psychology, and how we make split-second choices during volatile moments,' I tell her.

She pauses in silence for a second, her pen frozen in anticipation above the pad she's writing on.

'That's it?'

'That's it.' I shrug. 'When you defend a trial, you usually start off with twelve people against your client. Guilty until proven innocent. No smoke without fire. The minute they walk into the courtroom, the second they look at the defendant and hear the charge laid out against them, they've already decided if he or she is guilty. So, you have to place doubt in their minds. The way to do that is to dig into the kind of person the defendant is: how did they end up in the dock? You have to make them human.'

'It must be more complicated than that.'

'Of course. You need evidence to back it up. The two go hand in hand. I've seen so many advocates preach about the technicalities of how to address a jury. They overcomplicate it,' I tell her, thinking of Julian and how I trusted his methods implicitly before what happened at Jack's last trial. Until I realized they didn't always work. 'You connect with a jury by observing human behaviour and presenting evidence in an easy, digestible way. A lot of it is instinctual.'

She hangs on my every word, as if I'm giving a TED talk.

'Incredible insight, Leila. And so humble. Our young legal followers, especially our women, will be thrilled.'

'Glad to be of some help.'

'Would it be OK if I asked some questions from our followers?'

'Please.' I smile, tapping my phone to see what time it is.

'Great. Kayla, a criminal pupil in London, has asked, "What's your top tip for preparing a defence trial?"'

'I'm giving away all my secrets here!' I laugh. 'The first thing I do is prepare as if I'm prosecuting. That way, I spot all the holes in the defence case I need to close. Simple but invaluable.'

'Clever!'

I shrug my shoulders and smile.

'Hit me with another question.'

'OK, this one is from Liza: "Hi Leila. Do you think it's important for barristers to have a close relationship with their head of chambers, and how important is professional integrity to you?"'

The smile I've adopted throughout the interview vanishes. This isn't a question from a law student.

It's from *her*. It must be.

'Great questions there. Can you explain exactly what a head of chambers is, Leila?'

'Of course,' I say, forcing the smile back onto my face. 'Barristers work from a set of offices – or chambers. The head of chambers is our leader and makes all final decisions that affect us.'

'So, things like which students to take on for – what's it called? Pupillage?'

'Yes. Sometimes the head of chambers is on the pupillage panel. But it's difficult to get in – you have to impress them first with an outstanding CV, then spend a week with them. If they think you're good enough, you get an interview.'

'Sounds intense!'

'It is. My head of chambers has been a tremendous supporter of mine since day one. It's important to have that from senior members. I applied to Innovation because of their reputation for upholding exceptionally high moral standards and integrity.

There is nothing more important to me than maintaining professional excellence.'

I watch as Serene scribbles this down in her notepad; the diamonds from the rings on her fingers sparkle in the light.

'Sorry, who asked that question?' I ask her.

'A girl called Liza.'

'No, I mean what's her username?'

'Yes, of course. Give me a second.' She fiddles about on her phone for a minute or so, not that I need her to. I know exactly what name she's going to give me.

'It was @JustAnotherDumbBlonde. She sounds switched on, doesn't she?'

It *is* her. Of course. It's been her all along.

It didn't quite click before: the girl asking weird questions at the lecture, the figure hanging around my car, the person at the house. The messages. Call it naivety or denial, but she's been gone such a long time, it's taken me a while to realize – or admit – she's back. This is about so much more than the case and my behaviour as a lawyer – this is about us, our past.

Now she's here, I know she won't be satisfied until she's destroyed me.

But why is she mentioning the trial? How is she connected to it? The thought sends me into a blind panic.

Calm down, Leila. She's just scoured the papers and is trying to scare you.

If she thinks she's going to re-enter my life after all these years and sabotage the most important moment of my professional career, she's wrong.

33

Leila

21 days before trial
11.41 a.m.

'Can I have a word, darling?' Julian says like a smiling assassin, poking his head around the door to the conference room I'm working in at chambers. He doesn't wait for an answer before striding in and standing over me. His white shirt – the one I ironed for him – looks immaculate against the salmon-pink tie hanging around his neck.

He's wearing his smug face, the one I've seen countless times before as his pupil. He'd tell me before we went into court that he was about to decimate his opponent with a piece of evidence that would shut the case down, and that I ought to watch their face when the penny dropped. I lean forward over my notebook so he can't see what I'm doing, which is a bit rich, given that I stole evidence. I'm immediately suspicious of him coming in to see me now on the final working day before we break for holiday; whatever he's about to give me he's purposefully left until now, knowing I won't be able to do much with it until we return in a couple of weeks. It's a tactic I've seen him deploy in the past.

My professional spikes shoot up, knowing something bad is coming.

'We're in possession of CCTV that traces Jack's final movements in the hours before the murder.'

There it is. I'm sure he'll have had this CCTV for at least a week. He hangs on to evidence and deliberately presents it at the last, or worst, possible opportunity. One of the 'tactics' he taught me as a pupil. Unbelievable.

'Alleged murder,' I rephrase through gritted teeth. He sighs, knowing I'm being pedantic.

'Thank you for this. I'll consider it over the Christmas break,' I say to him sarcastically. 'What does it show?'

'At 1.17 p.m. he leaves Temptation and goes to a beauty salon in West Sutton. He remains there for six minutes, then leaves.'

'That's it?'

'Wait until you see whose salon it is,' he says, with the faintest sign of a smirk, handing me the USB stick. 'The reason you didn't know about it before now is because it didn't show up on cell site analysis. He didn't take his phone. Odd, isn't it?'

'Not really,' I reply, upbeat, while knowing exactly how odd it is.

'Millman never takes his phone anywhere, does he? I wonder what he has on there that's so important.'

God, he can be so condescending. No wonder people don't like him on a professional level. I choose to ignore this side of him because he's my husband, but I've been seeing it more and more throughout this case, and I don't like it. As his pupil, I thought his arrogance made him smart; now, I'm cringing at how much of a dick he can be.

'Maybe he's just a private person.' I smile. 'Anything else?'

'Yes, actually,' he says, almost as an afterthought, walking round to the other side of the conference table. 'I'm sending you Quinn's statement, too. I got on that immediately. You'll see that he says Jack had been harassing him for several weeks prior to the murder. Anton was there on 6 September telling him to leave his son alone.'

Crap. There's Anton's motive for being at Jack's flat. And it's a strong one.

'Harassing Quinn Smythe?' I ask. My tone is abrupt, and I want him to know it. 'For what reason?'

I'm dying to ask him what evidence he has to back this up, but I want to keep my cards close to my chest.

'You know what bouncers are like at these clubs. They take an instant dislike to a posh lad who comes in. Then, they find out it's actually the son of the judge who sent them to prison. Couldn't make this up.'

The grin on his face is too much to bear.

'No, you *really* couldn't. And he volunteered all this to you, did he?' I ask, sceptically, because I know what's happened here. I've seen Julian do it before. He'll be in conference with a witness and come within an *inch* of coaching them, while staying just far away enough from the line that it couldn't be proven improper.

'In fact it was you asking about Quinn's statement the other day that made me think he had something to do with it. I couldn't figure out where the smoking gun was until you mentioned it. So . . . thank you.'

He allows this to linger in the air, like smoke in a filthy bar. He wants me to know I've led him to this conclusion, that it's because of my *inexperience* he's got the upper hand.

'We have CCTV of Anton visiting a distressed Quinn at work, hours before the murder,' he goes on. 'The timescale works. It fits.'

I use every ounce of strength I have to look unbothered and unbroken in front of him. He's revelling in what he's doing to me, like some kind of sadist.

'Well, in that case, take this as notice that I want you to call

Quinn Smythe as a prosecution witness, because I want to cross-examine him, under oath.'

'I don't have a problem with that. Cross-examine him all you want. He's got nothing to hide.'

He absolutely does, going by what I've seen on Temptation's secret camera.

'Anything else?' I smile.

'A matter of formality, obviously, but just confirming in the absence of a defence statement that Millman won't be giving evidence? I'm wondering when speeches will be.'

'Oh, he will be,' I reply, cheerily.

His eyes widen. He's shocked. I knew he would be.

'You're joking.'

'I'm not.'

'You're allowing your client, who hasn't given you any instructions throughout a murder trial, to give evidence?'

He pronounces each word slowly, as if English isn't my main language.

'Yes.'

'Do you have *any* idea what he's going to say?'

'No,' I say, casually. A part of me is enjoying this.

'Leila, I'm speaking as your pupilmaster now,' he says, placing his hands on the table opposite me to demonstrate how serious he is. 'Have you lost your fucking mind?'

'It's his call.' I shrug.

'If this goes the way I suspect it will, people will question why you allowed it. You do understand this? For your own sake, convince him not to get in the witness box.'

Scare tactics. Nice.

'Tell you what, Julian,' I say, raising my voice slightly. 'You concentrate on your case, and I'll concentrate on mine. OK?'

It's only when he leaves the room that I realize how clenched my jaw is. My chest feels tight, and I'm so angry I can hear the blood pumping into my brain. In the space of five minutes, Julian has completely derailed our case and insinuated I'm going to lose and be laughed at. With only hours to go before the entire legal profession shuts down for Christmas, there's nothing I can do until January, and by then, it'll only be a few days until the trial.

He's done this on purpose.

Just like Chester warned me, Julian will stop at nothing to win. I need to get to work.

34

Leila

11.55 a.m.

I GRAB THE USB memory stick and insert it into my laptop. The CCTV shows Jack leaving the Temptation car park in his car at 1.17 p.m. It's then captured by several other cameras on various roads in town, moving through traffic on the way to West Sutton. It pulls up outside a shopping parade at 1.32 p.m. and he steps out. He walks into one of the units, 'Electric Dreams'.

Hitting pause, I try to recall where I've heard that before. It takes me a few seconds before I recognize that it's Daniella's shop. Eddie Sorrington's wife. I remember it from the law fair when she was giving out free manicures.

I call Davina. She answers immediately.

'You need to get over here. We've got a problem.'

Fifteen minutes later, I'm driving us to the salon. We need to figure out what this is about before everything closes for Christmas. The fact Eddie Sorrington has potentially become relevant in this case is troubling.

As far as 'hard men' go, Sorrington's up there. There are figureheads at the top of every criminal network. The stupid ones make mistakes and get caught. The savvy ones recruit other people to do the slippery work for them. Eddie is the latter. The official line is that he's made his money from property investment, car sales, and a chain of beauty salons across Durham. Those of us who are more worldly know this couldn't possibly pay for the holidays to Dubai, the supercars, the huge houses, and the multiple kids in private schools. It's more likely funded through drugs and money-laundering. The police would love to get him, but, apart from some time for petty stuff when he was younger, he hasn't slipped up.

Yet.

'Jack is adamant he doesn't want to grass anyone up. What if the person he's trying to protect is Eddie? They're very close,' Davina says, no doubt concerned about the person who funds the majority of her clients' fees. This trip is making her edgy.

'We've got three weeks until the trial. I'm not prepared to stand in front of a jury with nothing to say.'

'It might not come to that.' She shrugs. 'There's still time. Anything could come to light between now and then.'

'This isn't a film, Davina. When have you ever seen that happen in real life?'

'I'm just saying, there's obviously more to this story, and it'll come out eventually. I do love a good plot twist.'

'I appreciate your enthusiasm, Davina, but in my professional experience, the ultimate plot twist is there *is* no twist. The answers are usually in front of you the whole time, and if you miss them, it's because you aren't looking properly. But the last-minute confessions, the hidden evidence found with seconds to spare – they're myths. A good lawyer should be able to spot them a mile off.'

'You're no fun at all.' She laughs.

'Sorry.' I smile. 'Now, are you coming in with me or not?'

Electric Dreams looks like a money-laundering front: cheap, neon sign outside, palm tree decals on the windows. A bell chimes on the door when we enter, alerting everyone in the nail salon that we've arrived. It's rammed with customers, presumably in the pre-Christmas rush, and 'Last Christmas' by Wham! blasts out at a volume that's too high for my liking.

Daniella walks over to us. The smell of acrylics is overpowering but strangely comforting. She smiles at me, delivering the faintest glimmer of recognition.

'I hope you're looking after our Jack, Miss Reynolds,' she says. There's still something about her glazed, not-fully-with-it look I can't work out. She also appears to have lost weight since the last time I saw her. The black jumper dress she's wearing hangs off her tiny frame. 'He's a good boy.'

'I didn't realize how well you knew him,' Davina says.

'Oh, well, you know, he's a very good family friend,' she explains. 'He's always around the house. If anything needs fixing, he's the man I call. Eddie is useless with stuff like that. Jack's always on hand when Eddie's away on business, if I need help with anything. There's just no way he's done this. Jack isn't a murderer. You need to make sure the jury sees that.'

'I'm doing my best.' I smile at her. 'Lovely shop. Had it long?'

'Six years. Eddie bought it for me. I've always loved beauty and fashion.'

Glancing around the salon, I see another neon sign on the wall, written in swirly writing. *Don't You Want Me, Baby?*

She catches me looking.

'It was Eddie's idea to get that. He's very hands-on with how he wants his places to look. I actually *was* a waitress in a cocktail bar when he met me. Cheesy, I know! First dance at our wedding.'

Davina instinctively pulls the kind of face you'd expect her to pull at a woman saying this, which prompts Daniella's face to redden.

'Oh, I know that sounds weird!' she says, laughing to hide her embarrassment. 'A song about . . . well . . .'

'A man controlling you?' Davina interrupts.

'I suppose. But it's not like that. I know he's forceful with certain people, but he's not like that with me. He's really done a lot for me.'

There's something about how she says this that I don't like. And by the look on Davina's face, she doesn't, either. Especially now that we know Eddie has a proclivity for watching women give blow jobs on a secret sex camera.

'How long have you been together?' I ask her.

'Twenty-two years in June.'

'Congratulations!'

'Yes, a long time. We have – sorry, *had* – three great kids. We married young. God knows where I would have ended up without him. I'm lucky to have the life I do!'

She's upbeat, a contrast to how she spoke to me at the law fair. I wonder if I caught her in a moment of vulnerability then. Is she performing for Davina?

Daniella is one of those women who looks polished from afar, but up close, the cracks show. Her face has obviously had enhancements by way of Botox and fillers, but her overall look is drawn and tired.

'Daniella, we wondered if we could ask you about the time Jack came in wanting to speak with your husband on 6 September.'

'On the day of the, erm . . .'

'The alleged murder, yes . . .'

'He spoke with Eddie, not me.'

'Do you still have the CCTV from that day?' I ask her. I'm pushing it a bit, but we need something to latch on to.

'Yes, of course.'

She leads us back through to the office and fiddles around with the computer before leaving us to it.

The time stamp says Friday, 6 September 2024, 1.32 p.m. Jack's phone records indicate he'd already called Eddie multiple times before he left the club.

The jury will wonder what was so urgent that he needed to speak to Eddie on the phone and then follow up in person.

The camera shows Jack walking into the salon and waiting at reception. He looks bothered; he can't stand still and is repeatedly dragging his hands through his hair. After about thirty seconds, Eddie walks from the back of the salon to the front. He appears to be in a rush, edging towards the door as Jack talks to him and gesticulates animatedly with his hands.

Eddie grows impatient and keeps looking at his watch. Jack attempts to guide him into the office – away from the body of the salon for privacy, it seems.

Then Daniella emerges from the office, and something changes.

Jack spots her standing in the doorway and stops. It's as if he has second thoughts about the entire thing. Moving away from Eddie, he walks backwards towards the door and grabs the handle, opening it. Eddie looks bewildered as Jack leaves.

By 1.38 p.m., he's gone.

35

Leila

3.21 p.m.

After dropping Davina back off at her firm in the city centre, I realize I don't want to be around Julian right now. His gloating earlier today made my skin crawl, and if that's the kind of behaviour I'm in for when the trial starts, I'll have to distance myself from him. It's intolerable.

Driving through the streets, I glance at all the Christmas trees in the windows and warm white lights decorating the houses. Crowds of schoolchildren wearing their best festive clothes – little girls in sparkly dresses and boys in smart shirts – walk down the road holding hands with their parents. The excitement of finishing school for Christmas shows on their faces as they skip along, not a care in the world.

Suddenly, I feel desperately alone. I'm not the kind of person who always needs someone by my side, but right now, everything is collapsing around me.

I decide to reroute to visit Audrey. There's something comforting about her house and being in her company.

As I approach, I notice there's a red car parked where I usually go. As a Victorian semi, space to park is tight on this road. I generally know everyone who has access to the house, but I don't know who this is. Dread settles over me as I wonder if it's anything to do with the messages I've been receiving.

No. She wouldn't be that obvious.

Parking a little further up, I get out of the car and walk towards the house. Just before I reach the path, the front door opens and a blonde woman wearing a long, grey coat comes out. She slams the door shut and begins walking down the path.

'Sienna?'

It's dark now, and she didn't expect to see me. She stops and makes the kind of noise women do when someone has sneaked up on them.

'Jesus Christ, Leila!' she says. 'You scared me!'

I pause for a second, trying to figure out how best to handle this.

'What are you doing here?'

'I'm sorry?' she replies with a hint of aggression in her voice.

'Why are you here?' I ask again.

'What? I'm not allowed to see a friend? I was related to Audrey for a time.'

'Well, you're not related any more,' I point out.

'That doesn't mean I don't still care about her. I always bring her a little something at Christmas. What's wrong with that?'

'You've been before?' I ask, raising my voice.

'Sorry, Leila, I don't understand the issue here.'

'Do you have any idea what Julian will do if he finds out?'

A huge smile appears on her face. She starts laughing.

'And how is he going to find out?' she asks. 'Are you going to tell him? Because he sure as hell isn't going to catch me here himself. Let me guess, last time he actually came to visit his mother was, what? A year ago?'

I stare down at the floor, because it's too embarrassing to look her in the face. She's right. It's been months since Julian last visited Audrey.

'Some things never change, Leila,' she tells me. 'People don't change.'

I take a deep breath and shake my head.

'They do, actually,' I say. 'People can change. They do it all the time.'

'Maybe.' She shrugs. 'But not people like him.'

The wind starts to whip up around us, and the sound of Christmas tunes whizzes by from nearby cars.

'Look, I like Audrey, and I enjoy coming to visit her,' she says. 'She appreciates the company. You come a lot?'

'Every week,' I tell her, wrapping my coat around myself to keep warm.

'She's got really bad. I was last here six months ago or so, and she's got much worse.'

'I know.'

'Still switched on, though. She's always been one of the few women who isn't scared of him. I admire her for that.'

I frown, seeking clarification of what she's implying.

'Scared?'

'I think you know what I mean,' she says, smiling softly. 'Here anytime, Leila.'

Sienna walks to her car, her heels clicking on the path, and I wonder how she became this way. What was her marriage to Julian like? What really happened? I'd love to know. Or maybe I wouldn't. I watch her drive off and decide I won't be telling Julian about this.

Audrey's house is stiflingly hot. Predictably, she's had the heating on all day.

'Come in, dear!' she sings. 'Aren't I lucky? Two visitors in one day! Just had Samantha here. Lovely girl. I'm sure she used to know Julian.'

I smile, allowing her to chat as I make cups of tea for the pair of us. Bringing them into the living room, we sit down on the sofa and she throws a blanket over me so I don't 'freeze to death'. Her cheeks are posy pink with too much blusher, and she wears a baby-blue knit with a pearl brooch on her left collarbone. Her hand shakes slightly as she lifts the cup to her mouth, so I allow mine to hover beneath in case she drops it.

'For god's sake, Leila!' she cries out. 'I'm not an invalid!'

I ask about her day, and she tells me a fantastical tale about how she went to Knaresborough on the bus and then to the market to buy some groceries. It's not true, but she believes it is, and that's enough. I nod along and ask questions, and she gives the most imaginative answers.

But what Sienna said is on my mind and curiosity gets the better of me. I ask her, not knowing what she will say.

'Audrey, what do you think of Julian?'

'Julian?' she ponders, in her little crackly voice. She smiles in that way she does, seeming to have gone into her own little world. She could be anywhere, gazing off into the distance. It was unfair of me to ask – she may not even remember who he is. I lean over to grab my cup of tea, but she reaches for my hand, takes it like a mother would in both of hers. They're so frail – the blue veins pop through her skin, making it appear tracing-paper thin.

Her eyes look directly into mine.

'You can't trust him, you know,' she says, very quietly. 'That's why he doesn't come to see me. He hates women who can see through him. He's threatened by it. That's why he doesn't like you.'

Normally when Audrey says something unusual or bizarre, I correct her. Not today.

She says it with such clarity, such precision, that right now, I believe every word she says.

36

Witness X

Rule #8
Be Patient

So many people underestimate the beauty and importance of silence. A pause, executed at the right time, can be very powerful. Everyone is in such a rush these days.

I blame social media. Everything is so instant and available now.

And nobody cares about the proper execution of revenge any more.

It's not difficult. Opportunities will present themselves if you really want to hurt a person. You don't even have to go looking for them. This is where people mess up: they become impatient and force the situation.

It may take weeks, months, or even years, but believe me, if someone has it coming, your opportunity to end them will appear. All you have to do is be patient and seize the opportunity when it arises.

In my case, it came at 1.46 a.m. one cold Saturday morning. I thought it would make things better. It did in some ways, but not in others.

Sometimes, of course, the best revenge is no revenge at all. To simply move on and live many happy, successful years, knowing you're better than the person who wronged you. It takes a colossal amount of character to rise above. Not many people have it in them.

Declan did. After I shattered his heart into a thousand pieces, he left the next day without so much as a word. No more contact. No drama. Nothing.

Imagine having that much restraint. That much dignity. He simply disappeared, like a ghost.

His silence hurt more than any number of verbal insults could have. That action said, *I am better off without you. I do not need you.* I wanted him to beg for us to work through it.

He didn't. *His life improved without me in it.* Is there any crueller revenge?

I search for him on Instagram sometimes in particularly potent moments of self-loathing, for who I am, for who I could have been.

He's aged well. In each of his photos, he's surrounded by his pretty, brunette wife and three beautiful children. Declan is a family man; I always knew he would be. His life consists of splashing around the pool with his little blonde-haired daughter on his shoulders, date nights with his dewy-skinned wife, and team days away at corporate functions. He's always been well liked. Good for him, truly.

The best thing to happen to him was me breaking his heart. That's a tough pill to swallow.

I'm trying so hard to shed the skin of the person I was. I know she existed to survive what was happening around her, but I did not like her. I am ravaged with shame because of it, and I think I am a better person now. I try to be, anyway.

But her? Has she changed? I doubt it.

She learned from the best, after all.

37

Leila

20 days before trial

I NEVER ENJOYED CHRISTMAS as a kid. I was always so jealous hearing about all the nice things my friends got up to with their families. My parents would spend the majority of the day not speaking to each other, sitting in separate rooms of the house, so I'd watch films to distract myself from thinking about how much of a magical time everyone else was having.

The first Christmas Eve I spent without either of them was the best one I'd ever had. I went for a long walk on my own that lasted hours. I felt free. I moseyed into a church I'd never even been to before and attended a mass. As the carols bounced around the magnificent building, I thought about my parents and whether they would have enjoyed it.

I concluded that they wouldn't. They never found joy in anything.

Every year, Julian and I go out for Christmas Eve lunch and spend the rest of the day cosied up drinking champagne and eating expensive, overpriced food from posh delis. We got together shortly before Christmas, so our first one was spent in a loved-up state together doing just this, and the tradition continued thereafter.

We haven't booked anywhere this year. The official line is

it's down to us being too busy to sort anything out, but the real reason is we haven't been feeling connected lately. And when I say that, I mean I can't remember the last time we had a proper conversation about anything other than the case. I didn't tell him about Sienna – it would have been just another thing for him to complain about. We're working such erratic hours, we've even started sleeping separately. I like to work on my laptop in bed late at night; he wants to go straight to sleep. It makes sense that he sleeps in the spare room. But I can't ignore the siren going off, alerting me that this feels irreversible.

Audrey has gone to stay with her sister 'down south' for the week, so this morning I went to check on her house. Knowing Audrey, she's likely left the heating on full-blast for the entire duration. On the journey there, driving through the dull, foggy weather, I was constantly checking in the mirror to see if *she* was following me. What is she planning? I know she's planning something.

It'll be well timed, whatever it is. Designed to cause maximum damage. That's how she works.

I considered, for a second, whether I should speak to her father. If she's spiralling, he could potentially get through to her. That really would blow everything up, though, and no matter what has happened between us, it would be a step too far, bringing him into it.

But I can't risk her getting to Julian. Or sabotaging this case. There's too much at stake.

When I arrive back home, Julian is dressed in a way that suggests he's off somewhere. Despite the fact it's late morning, all the lamps are on in the house because it's dark outside. The tree lights are lacking the twinkle seen in previous years. Light rain begins to patter at the windows; even the weather gods aren't feeling festive.

'Are you going out?' I ask him, confused. 'On Christmas Eve?'

'A few lawyers are meeting for a drink in town. Want to come?'

His tone suggests he's asking out of obligation rather than a genuine desire for me to join. He stands next to the table in the hallway, ready to shoot out of the door. I'm wearing joggers and a hoodie. He knows it would take me far too long to get ready. But I recognize what he's doing, ostracizing me professionally.

'Who meets up for drinks on Christmas Eve?' I enquire, part comedically, part pissed off.

'Well, the people I'm meeting, obviously.'

'People who are either single or divorced?'

He sighs, looking in the mirror and fingering his hair. He ignores my targeted attempt to provoke him.

'Are you coming or not?'

'Why have you arranged to do this today?' I ask, folding my arms. 'We always do something together.'

'Well, we haven't booked anything and, to be honest, it didn't feel as if you wanted to do anything this year,' he observes correctly, though it feels cutting to hear it said out loud.

'Why do you think that?' I ask him, defensively. Usually, we spend the Christmas break going for walks and pub lunches. I don't think that will be happening this year. It's only Christmas Eve and we're already leaving the house separately just to escape the unspoken, unbroken tension. It can't go on much longer.

'You haven't seemed yourself,' he remarks slowly, dramatically, in a way that suggests I'm a hysterical woman from the Victorian era and require a priest to bring me back to sanity. Of course *I'm* to blame for this.

'Suppose I'll see you later, then. Have fun.' I spit the words at him in the most sarcastic way possible.

He looks directly at me, saying nothing. Without responding, he walks towards the door, opens it, and leaves. There's something about the sound of a door slamming in a quiet house that is so devastating.

Tears surge and spill out uncontrollably. The feeling of being isolated in this way cuts through me like a knife. Is this part of his strategy? How is he happy to leave me on my own on Christmas Eve?

Well, I refuse to spend the rest of the day dragging myself around the house, so I get wrapped up and go for a long walk on my own in the rain, like something out of a nineties music video. Couples and families are everywhere, delighting in the magic of Christmas, while I slowly fall apart walking among them, my hands clasped pathetically around a paper cup of hot chocolate.

This case has changed my life in more ways than one. How naive of me to think life would carry on as usual. A year ago, I would have killed for this kind of opportunity, to prove myself in this professional capacity. Right now, all I want is to give the case to someone else. But then I wonder what Jack's Christmas Eve looks like in prison. And I know some things are more important.

I head back at twilight. I'm drenched from the rain, so I jump in a hot shower and use all of my expensive creams in an attempt to cheer myself up.

Julian returns just past 7 p.m. and I can smell the drink on him as soon as he stumbles into the living room where I've been eating all the nice food I bought for both of us. I've opened the champagne and started watching *Die Hard* (yes, it is a Christmas film). His presence irritates me, and I just want him to go away.

'This looks nice!' he has the audacity to say, clumsily attempting to grab the smoked salmon blinis from M&S.

'Didn't you eat while you were out?'

'No, I didn't want to ruin our classic Christmas Eve feast.'
'Bit late for that.'
He winces. 'What?'
'Nothing.'
'Leila, what on earth is the matter with you?' he snaps. 'You've been a nightmare for days.'
'Oh! Have I?'
'Yes, you have. Just tell me what the hell I've done. Look, I know you don't like Christmas. I know you didn't get on with your parents. But is that a good enough reason to ruin it for everyone else? For the last time, what is the matter with you?'

His voice is louder than normal.

'Nothing,' I repeat, through gritted teeth.

'There it is again. *Nothing*. Jesus Christ. Look, I don't want to fight,' he says, sitting down on the sofa next to me. 'What have you done today?'

The cheek of him, going out and leaving me on my own, then coming home, acting all concerned.

'What have I been doing today? Well, I've been working on that evidence,' I say, knowing it's going to provoke him. 'You know, the evidence you served deliberately late so I wouldn't be able to do anything about it until January.'

'There it is!' he shouts, slamming his hands down onto his knees. 'We got there in the end. That's why you're pissed off with me? Because of Quinn Smythe's statement? Over some CCTV evidence? Jesus Christ!'

He leans forward, rubbing his eyes with his hands. I know this is the wrong time to bring it up, but I'm so mad right now – I can't hold back any longer.

'Tell me, Julian, how could you fuck over your own pupil?'

Even as I'm saying it, I'm forced to recognize my own hypocrisy, knowing I've looked at his confidential evidence. But the difference is that he doesn't know about that. He has deliberately and knowingly screwed me over here and, worse, has seemed to enjoy it.

'Sorry, Leila.' He smiles, suddenly smug. 'This is how big, grown-up cases are won.'

Dick.

'Don't patronize me. There was no need to do it that way. You knew it would cause unnecessary stress.'

'Well, don't spoon feed me valuable information that will help the prosecution, then complain when it backfires on you!' he shouts, standing up to illustrate how *stupid* I've been. '*That's* what you're annoyed about here. You didn't realize what you'd done until it smacked you in the face.'

It's intended to be harsh, and it is. He knows it will hurt.

'Don't you see the damage you're creating? It's not just this case that's at stake here. This is testing our marriage.'

Even as the words leave my mouth, I know what I'm doing – I'm seeing how far I can push it. How far I can push *him*. I want to know *exactly* what means more to him. Is it me? Or is it winning? Because, I understand now, he can't have both.

I want him to say it.

Would he really be prepared to screw me over, his pupil, his *wife*, and end our marriage for a victory in court?

'Look, I'm not going to compromise my working practices for anyone. A win is a win. I'm sorry if you can't understand that.'

Win at all costs. That's his ethos. Even if that cost is his marriage. But there has to be a *tiny* part of him that thinks he might not win, and then he'll have lost the case and his wife. I think about what Audrey said. Is all of this because, beneath everything, he feels threatened by me?

'Are you afraid you'll lose? Is that why you're acting like a prick?'

He smiles as if I've said something funny, genuinely funny. And suddenly it's clear there is not one part of him that thinks he might lose.

'No.'

'Why not? You always used to say to me no case is 100 per cent winnable.'

He sighs, loudly, in the way men do when they're about to deliver bad news.

'Don't take this the wrong way, Lei. You're my wife, my pupil, and of course I want the best for you, but you can't win this. Whether I served this evidence weeks ago, now, or the day of trial – it really doesn't matter. I'm only being honest with you. Don't beat yourself up over it.'

No shouting, no screaming. His most damaging blows are always quiet.

It dawns on me that his advice regarding Jack giving evidence – to convince him otherwise, to keep him out of the witness box – was genuine. Because he knows it will be a disaster, but also he knows he will win either way.

He turns and walks out of the room. His words float in the air and dance about my head, carefully selected to cling to my worries, my anxieties, my weaknesses.

And I start to believe him. That's how good an advocate he is. He's right: the timing of that evidence doesn't matter. He's still got the upper hand. Who am I to think I can win against someone with eleven years more experience? King's Counsel, for god's sake! This man, who taught me everything. I'm kidding myself. The power and confidence in his words, the way he delivers them – it's terrifying, thinking how a jury will react to him.

Maybe it's true that I will not, and do not, stand a chance.

As far as Christmas Days go, it's bleak. Julian gives me a pretty, but overpriced Tiffany bracelet, and we go for lunch at a local restaurant. We stick to non-work chat, but it feels forced, stale. Neither of us can forget what was said last night and the only thing to cleanse the air now is going to be the end of the trial itself. This case hangs over our heads like a dark thundercloud, gathering electricity, waiting to unleash hell in a matter of weeks.

I'm relieved to get home and settle down in front of the TV. At about 8 p.m., our phones buzz at the same time and I momentarily panic, wondering if it's something to do with *her*. But it's not.

It's a message in our chambers WhatsApp group from Chester.

> Never thought I'd be saying this again, but guess who's about to become a father for the third time? Demi said she'll do all the nappies providing I fund the 'Insta Nursery', whatever the hell that is. Baby Vernon due May 2025!

Attached to the message is a scan photo of a baby. I read it and immediately look at Julian. He has no reaction whatsoever and puts his phone straight back down again.

'What do you think about this, then?' I ask, surprised.

'Good for them, I suppose.'

'You can't honestly see Chester running around after a toddler? At his age?'

'None of our business, is it?'

And then the possibility of it hits me. I pause, while my head scrambles to work things out.

'If the baby is due in May, that means it must have been conceived around . . . August-ish.'

He looks at me, puzzled.

'So?'

'Just something Chester said a while back, that's all.'

'What did he say?' Julian asks, turning to look at me.

'Oh, nothing. Just . . . you know what he's like.'

We continue watching TV, but my mind is running one hundred miles an hour. Chester's message has given me an idea, but more importantly, it's given me hope.

Julian was wrong.

If anyone's coming out of this a winner, it's going to be me.

38

Leila

3 days until trial

It's the Friday before the trial starts. The last working day to ensure everything is in order. We begin Monday morning, 10.30 a.m. sharp.

I've set up one of the conference rooms as a base, and Davina comes in when she can. The large table is taken up with folders, documents, photos, and empty Starbucks coffee cups. Jim brings me pastries from the bakery around the corner whenever he nips out, and I couldn't love him more for it. I'm mainlining coffee like there's no tomorrow and only eating things that require one hand to do so. I'm averaging around five hours' sleep a night. The classic pre-trial ritual.

When I finish, around 6 p.m., I'm grateful to go somewhere that isn't home or chambers. With everything going on, visiting Audrey's house on a Friday night has become my constant.

The external lights switch on as I walk up the driveway, signalling my arrival. The savage January wind wraps around my body and threatens never to let go. I pull the long puffer coat around myself as I make my way towards the house.

The door is unlocked again, and a wave of irritation rushes through me. Why have I bought extra locks for the door if she never uses them?

'Only me!' I yell, as music travels down the hall. Odd. It doesn't sound like her usual Classic FM.

Walking into the lounge, I see Audrey sitting in her window chair, looking unusually bright and cheery. Whenever I come to visit her, she has a drawn look about her – a result of being bored all week. But, today, she looks invigorated and has natural colour in her cheeks. She looks as if she's been brought back to life.

'You look well!' I tell her.

'I am well, darling! We've had lovely, blustery weather this week.'

'Yes, cold but sunny.'

'I love this time of year. It's made for long walks. Been lovely to get out.'

It takes me a second to register what she's said.

'You've been out?'

'Yes, dear!' She smiles. 'Oh, I've been all over. To the park, to the butcher's – got some lovely ribs. Really juicy.'

God, she's lost it now. Audrey hasn't gone out by herself for months.

'I brought you some fish and chips,' I say. 'I'll go and set the table.'

As I head down the hall towards the dining room as I have done hundreds of times before, I suddenly stop. Something feels off.

I pause, mid-stride, like a predator who's sensed a target.

Everything looks the same. It's not that.

It's the music.

Only when I listen to what it is does a chill slide down my spine.

The music is grainy and crackly, the way music used to sound in the 1960s. The quality is poor, yet the full drama of the song rips through the air. The deep, penetrating vocals sit alongside a waltz-like rhythm. It's a song about jealousy. A song about revenge. A song about betrayal.

'Delilah' by Tom Jones.

Delilah.

Poking my head around the doorframe, the rest of my body stiff, I stare into the room. Everything is as it should be, still, except for the old record player in the corner. I watch as the single turns around, the old needle propelling the music into the air.

As the song comes to a close, the arm returns to the beginning of the record and starts again. It's on repeat.

Running into the lounge, I startle Audrey with my insistence.

'Audrey, this is very important,' I say. 'Who put that music on?'

'Tom Jones. I saw him, you know, in 1965. Never had a thing for him. All the other women did, but—'

'How long has this music been playing?'

'What music?'

Jesus Christ.

'The music in the dining room. Can you hear it? It's playing "Delilah".'

'Oh! That? All bloody day. I don't know how to turn it off. Same song all the time. None of his other hits.'

This can't be happening.

'What time did it start, Audrey? Please think.'

'Erm . . . about 2 p.m., I think. Or it might have been 5 p.m.'

'Audrey, this is really important. Can you tell me who put that music on?'

'I think I put it on.'

I stare at her, willing, hoping she's right.

'Have you been on your own all day?'

'Well, I was with Leila earlier on . . .'

I close my eyes tightly in sheer desperation. My head spins, and my heart is racing. I want to shake the truth out of her.

'I'm Leila, Audrey,' I say, very slowly. 'Who's been here today? Can you remember?'

'Nobody's been here today, darling! What are you talking about?'

'Audrey, I need you to concentrate. I know this is confusing, but has *anyone else* been here today?'

The music continues, and it's like nails down a blackboard, torture in my ears. I can't wait any longer. Leaving Audrey to think about my question, I rush down the hallway and into the dining room. As I push the needle off the record, a scratchy screeching sound punctuates the abrupt end of the music. Standing in the quiet now, I can feel everything crashing around me.

I have to be calm. She can't have been here. How would she even know about Audrey? I'm running away with myself and getting paranoid. This would be a step too far. Audrey and I always listen to old music; she definitely put it on herself and forgot. But . . . '*Delilah*'.

It's a coincidence.

You don't believe in coincidences.

Just as I'm standing in the hallway, trying to cling to the last bit of sanity I have, my phone makes a tri-tone chime sound indicating I've got a message. Pulling it out of my pocket, I look at the locked phone screen to see it's from someone called *@DntMessWithMe*. I've had virtually no activity on my *Chats at the Bar* account for a few weeks, as I've been busy, so this takes me by surprise. It's not until I start reading the message that it becomes clear what's going on.

Enjoy your day trip to the salon before xmas? The secret trips to Temptation during the day? How about visiting your dear mother-in-law at Applethorpe Grove tonight? You're a very busy woman, aren't you? Watch your step or you'll get your throat cut.

OK, now I'm scared.

Aside from the obvious anger and fear pulsating through my body like water gushing out of a tap, my attention turns to the commentary on my location. Not only does this person know exactly where I've been, they know where I am *now*.

How? How do they know where I am?

I would have noticed someone following me.

It's as if they've been tracking me. How long has this been going on? Weeks? Months?

And then it hits me.

I dash outside to the car and switch on the torch feature on my phone. Shining the light under the arch of the two back wheels, I curl my fingers around each one to see if I can feel anything.

There it is. Behind the rear passenger wheel, a small, black device lifts off the arch and fits neatly into my hand. The reason someone was by my car after my lecture at Mountcross Academy.

I've come across tracking devices in cases I've worked on. You can buy the damned things off Amazon.

Whoever it is has been following me for months. What am I supposed to do? Why now? Could it possibly be someone else? Have I got two maniacs after me days before the biggest case of my life? Surely not. But how does everything fit together?

The trial starts in less than seventy-two hours.

What a mess.

Bursting into tears, I throw the tracker to the ground and plunge my face into my hands. Tears pour so fast and hard, it's pointless attempting to stop them.

I need a new plan. And there's only one man who can help.

I don't stop to think. Activating my phone, I scroll through my contact list until I find who I need.

'It's Leila,' I sob. 'I'm so, so sorry to call you on a Friday evening, but if you're at home, would it be OK if I came over?'

39

Witness X

Rule #9
Don't Stand Out

Do not stand out from the crowd. If you want to get ahead, you need to fit in and be like everyone else. Never underestimate the power of the tribe.

He always told me that people don't suspect those who blend into the background. That it's vital you never draw attention to yourself when executing other rules. They must be carried out discreetly.

However, there is an exception.

The only time it's acceptable to stand out from the crowd is if you do it for the right reasons.

Dad said people don't like cocky or brash; a big ego will never be liked or trusted. You must have 'something' about you that people will gravitate towards. Whether it's charisma, a unique fashion sense, or enough confidence to say what you think in an eloquent way without offending anyone. Whatever it is, people must admire it and want to possess that quality.

But you can only rely on this to stand out if you are both likeable and relatable. She was very good at this, just like dad was.

Blending into the background was never an option for her. She needed to shine.

And she used me to do it.

It happened so gradually, she thought I didn't notice. But I notice everything. I'd catch her paying close attention to what I wore, what I said, how I talked, even down to the way I walked. It became her personality.

I became her personality.

She morphed into a different person; her real self fused with a copycat version of me. That's when I suspected that she had a dark side even I had not yet seen. The thought scared me.

'You're the only real friend I've ever had,' she said to me the evening of our graduation.

'Don't be silly,' I laughed. 'You've got millions of friends.'

'No,' she replied, in a serious voice. She wanted me to understand. 'You get me. No one else does.'

I don't know if she was telling the truth, or if it was part of the deceit, but I've thought about those words a lot over the years. We shared our deepest, darkest secrets, and we promised never to tell anyone.

Likeable and relatable; I'm neither of those things.

But Leila Reynolds is.

I'm real and she's fake. Or is it the other way around? I don't think I even know any more.

I know what her colleagues would think if they knew the truth about her, and the mask is starting to slip.

It's going to be a horror show when it falls off.

40

Leila

62 hours before trial

THE LAST PLACE I expected to be the Friday night before my first (and probably last) murder trial is Chester's house. He resides in a small village just outside Durham, the kind of place King's Counsel live with their young wives who have nothing better to do than tart the house up and post pictures of it.

Many boozy summer evenings have been spent in Chester's 'garden' with the rest of chambers. He holds an annual Easter drinks do and the entire house – a three-hundred-year-old detached cottage set against the backdrop of many acres of land – looks spectacular.

Pulling up onto the gravel drive, I see his silver Porsche 911 Carrera, which looks even more impressive illuminated by the gentle external lighting on the house.

I check my face in the mirror before going in. All the crying has smudged my mascara. I look like something out of a slasher film.

'Lei!' he gasps, opening the front door. 'Come in. Let me get you a bloody drink.'

Ushering me through to the open-plan and newly renovated kitchen at the back of the house, he sprints to the fridge and drags out a bottle of white wine. Scanning my surroundings, I see just how much of an influence Demi has had on the place since I was last here a year ago. This isn't Chester's vibe at all. It's stark and sterile – bright white walls and monochrome styling. Heavy plops of rain begin thudding down on the skylights we're standing under before the heavens open. It sounds as if it's about to come through the roof.

'Have some of this, and tell me what's happened,' he says, pouring wine into the biggest glass I've ever seen.

'I can't, I'm driving.'

'Don't worry about that. I'll get you a taxi. Or Demi will drive you.'

'Yes, I guess she's not drinking for the foreseeable future.'

He looks at me through a classic side-eye, handing the glass over to me.

'Is it yours?' I ask, bluntly.

'I've no way of knowing for sure. I don't have any proof it's not.'

'Maybe you don't want to find any.'

'Maybe.' He nods. 'She said she waited so long to tell me because she didn't know if I'd be angry about it.'

'Really?' I say, walking over to a gallery wall of photographs. Each one is carefully placed and set within a thick, black frame. They're mainly of Chester and Demi: their wedding, them skiing, on a beach, on city breaks. Each one, a snapshot of their very childless life.

At the top, there's a photo of Chester standing with a young woman with jet-black hair cut into a sharp shoulder-length bob. Her facial features are defined: cat-like eyes and a plump mouth painted red. She wears a floor-length emerald-green dress, and Chester smiles with his arm around her.

'Do you ever see her? Elise?' I ask. I hear his footsteps on the floor as he walks and stands just behind me, close enough that I can smell the scent he's wearing.

'No.'

'Don't you think she'd want to know she's about to get a baby brother or sister?'

'I think that ship has sailed, Lei,' he replies, gently brushing his hand onto the back of my waist, ushering me to the sofa that faces enormous bi-folding doors leading out to the garden.

'Where *is* your radiant wife?' I enquire. 'I haven't yet had a chance to congratulate her.'

'She's out. Went to the cinema with a friend. She should be back soon,' he says, glancing at the clock. 'Aren't you going to tell me why you're here?'

'Chester, I can't do this.'

'What?'

'This case. I'm in way over my head.'

'Is that it?' he spurts out. 'Leila, you're probably the most talented junior advocate who isn't yet a silk on our circuit.'

'You're just saying that because—'

'Because what?' he interrupts. 'Because you think I fancy you?'

We both burst out laughing. I love his directness; it helps clear the air. We clink glasses, maintaining eye contact as we take a drink.

'He doesn't believe in me, you know. Julian. He thinks this is a clear run for him.'

'Of course he does. That's what he's like. Arrogant bastard.'

'Perhaps he's right.'

'Look, I've prosecuted and defended countless murder trials. And, let me tell you, most of them aren't won on the evidence. They're won on likeability and engagement. How you connect with the jury, how you present the case – you know all this. I've seen you in court. You're mesmerizing. Your strength is that people like you, they relate to you. He doesn't have that. He's got an attitude, and a jury will see through it.'

'He's more experienced than me.'

'So what? Let him underestimate you. That means nothing when you're as good as you are. You just need to believe it.'

'Do you really think so?' I whisper, placing a friendly hand on his arm. He goes to say something, but it's interrupted by the sound of keys rattling in the front door, followed by a slam.

Demi is back.

I instinctively shuffle further away from Chester on the sofa. I don't know why – it's not as if I was doing anything wrong.

'Oh! Hi, Leila!' she says, stopping momentarily in the doorway to the kitchen. I can tell, immediately, that she does not want me here. The last time I saw her was when she grilled me over the Latin card for Chester's birthday, and I wonder, briefly, whether Julian has ever seen that side of her. She removes her winter coat and glides her hands over a small, snatched baby bump swathed in a virginal white chunky knit. 'I didn't realize that was your car on the drive.'

'Yes, sorry, I just popped over to speak to Chester.'

'I hope everything is all right?' she asks, staring at the state of my face.

'It's just quite intense at the moment, what with the trial starting on Monday.'

'Yes, I can imagine.' She nods, attempting empathy.

'Congratulations on the baby! What marvellous news! You must be thrilled.'

'Yes, I'm very excited!' she replies, gazing down at her unborn child. 'Do you both mind if I make myself a sandwich? I'm starving and, well, baby needs food!'

'Go ahead, darling,' Chester replies, as I excuse myself to fix up my face.

Walking through the house to the loo, I'm reminded of just how much money these two have. It's ridiculous. As I pass the hallway window, something catches my eye. Something that wasn't on the drive when I came in.

A red Mini.

I think back to the night someone attempted to break into our house and how, minutes later, a red Mini whizzed down the road. I'm right about this. I know I am. I've got Chester on my side, and now I need to get what I really came for, because I sure as hell didn't come here for comforting words.

Spending a few minutes longer in the toilet than I would have done, I sit, thinking.

I need to get under Demi's skin.

One thing about her is she needs to portray herself as being the friendly, sweet type in front of her husband. She learned quickly that he's only prepared to finance her lifestyle if she plays a certain role.

She's an actress.

Let's see how she performs under pressure.

They're sitting together on the sofa when I walk back into the dining room. I can tell they're talking about me because the room is full of whispers.

'Sorry for hijacking your evening like this,' I say, quietly.

'Please don't apologize,' Demi says, curling her feet up onto the sofa and elegantly taking a bite from a chicken salad sandwich (on wholegrain bread, naturally). Her phone sits on the armrest next to her. 'I can't imagine the pressure you're under.'

'Look, if I tell you both something, can you please promise you won't tell Julian?'

'Yes, of course.' They both nod.

'I've been receiving threats. Varying in severity, but enough to be classed as criminal activity,' I tell them, beginning to cry.

'Jesus Christ!' Chester says. 'Why didn't you tell anyone?'

'I've been trying to be professional, run this trial, do all my other work,' I sob, as big tears run down my face. 'It's all got too much!'

'Where have these threats come from? Do you have them on record?'

'Yes, they're on Instagram. I'll show you,' I reply, picking up my handbag and rummaging through it. After a few seconds, I roll my eyes to the ceiling, pretend to take a steadying breath.

'What's wrong?'

'I was at my mother-in-law's house before I came here. I was so busy sorting her out that I've left my phone there.'

'I want to see them,' Chester says. 'Can't you email them to me? I don't know how bloody Instagram works.'

Of course he doesn't. Chester wouldn't understand an app if it hit him in the face.

'No.' I laugh tearily. 'You can only log into your account on a phone that also has the app.'

'Well, Demi's on there. Darling, give her your phone so she can show me these threats.'

Her body stiffens; I watch it happen. She's mid-chew with her food and does that thing where you wind your hand around a few times to let it be known you're about to say something. But it's obvious what's happening – she's stalling.

'Is now the best time to do it? Late on a Friday night? You can see how upset she is, Chester.'

'I'm not having one of my barristers being threatened and worrying about it the weekend before the biggest trial of her life.'

Picking her phone up, she activates it with the face recognition feature and fiddles about with something for an excessively long time before handing it to me.

'Thanks.' I smile. 'Won't be a minute.'

The phone is unlocked and completely open. Chester starts banging on about something I'm not listening to. It's just noise, meaningless conversation, a necessary soundtrack to this scene she will remember – and regret – for years to come.

I sit, casually, in the armchair under the skylight, as Demi stands up and walks to the kitchen island, trying to look interested in what Chester is saying, but it's pointless. She's handed her power over to me. I can imagine what must be going through her head. *How did she get me to do this?*

This is the first trick of cross-examination: you have something I need, and I'm going to make sure you give it to me.

She has already logged out of her Instagram account, likely fearful I'd go snooping in her messages. Wise move.

Unfortunately for her, she hasn't clocked that another powerful cross-examination technique is misdirection. People will fiercely protect something when you place a great deal of importance on it, leaving the jewel you really came for vulnerable.

Without any resistance whatsoever, I tap on the green WhatsApp icon, which opens her chats. There are eight listed, none I care about and none of which I came for. Pulling the screen down, I see archived chats and tap on that.

There it is. Just as I expected.

A chat with just a phone number, no name.

The profile picture is nothing, just a shadow. The chat preview reads:

Fine. I'll do it myself if I have to.

The two small, blue ticks on the left-hand side indicate it was a message sent by her and was read on 8 January, two days ago.

Tapping on the conversation to open it, I look up to see Demi talking to Chester, but not fully giving him her attention. She keeps glancing over; her eyes tell me she's on edge. There's something on this phone she doesn't want me to see. And I'm pretty sure I've found it.

I don't know what you want me to do about this.

Demi: Maybe be a man and face up to your responsibility?

Hardly in a position to do that. You're aware of my situation. What the hell do you expect me to do?

Demi: How can you turn around and be like this after everything? Did it mean nothing to you? Because it did to me.

Don't be dramatic. We had a good time but it can't continue. How do you expect me to be a father now? It's impossible and not something I want anyway.

Demi: How can you be so cold? Maybe people should know what the real you is like.

Don't do anything stupid, Demi. This is my life.

Demi: Fine. I'll do it myself if I have to.

My eyes flick between Demi and the phone screen, which not only reveals evidence of her infidelity, but also the fact that Chester is not the father of her unborn child. I could end their marriage here and now if I wanted.

But I don't.

Coming out of the app and closing everything down, I smile at her before handing the phone back.

'Thanks so much,' I say. 'I can't for the life of me remember my password. Must be the stress. I think I'm going to go home. I'm tired and need to get some rest before Monday.'

'Are you sure, Leila?' Chester asks, standing up and guiding me to the door. 'I want you to send me a copy of those threats as soon as you get home.'

'I will. Thank you . . . both.'

This is it. What I've been searching for all along. Who'd have thought the last missing piece of the puzzle – the thing that would get me out of this whole mess – would have landed in my lap so easily, in this way, here and now. I almost have to stop myself from laughing.

I was right about one thing: no plot twists here. The answer was in front of me. I just needed to find it.

41

Witness X

MY ENTIRE LIFE could be annihilated in forty-eight hours. Just two days until this trial begins. I know he will protect me; I trust him with my life. But the rest of them are unpredictable. Who knows what they'll dredge up?

It's crazy to think all of this started nearly a year ago. I should have known right then and there it would end badly.

It had snowed all day; crazy, fat flurries that dropped from the sky like large pieces of pure white lace. It was heavy enough to stick, at least a few inches thick by nightfall. The frost in the air bit my face as I left the house shortly before 8 p.m.

I didn't plan on going there, obviously. Why would I go *there* on a Friday night? Alone?

We'd had a row, so I stormed out of the house just to get away from him. I can't even remember why, now. All the arguments were the same anyway, the same issues yelled in different ways. I couldn't stand being in the house a second longer.

What took me there? Initially, I went into Durham city centre thinking I might bump into someone I knew. I can usually find someone on a Friday night to meet up with. I have lots of acquaintances. But I don't really 'do' friends. As soon as I parked the car, though, I realized I didn't want to talk to anyone. Not anyone I knew. I can't stand most of them. They're nothing like me.

It dawned on me that I was alone. Totally alone. That's the thing, pretending to be someone you're not, wearing a mask. It's a solitary existence.

But that night, I needed to pull it off.

I wanted to be somewhere I *knew* none of them would be.

Nobody I know would dare go near Innocence. Well, they would, but they certainly wouldn't be wanting to chat if they saw me.

It was busy when I arrived; full of young twenty-somethings in their tight bodycon dresses taking selfies and sipping pornstar Martinis.

When Jack and I locked eyes, I knew instantly something would happen between us. The attraction was magnetic. It was impossible not to notice the shape of his toned arms through the thin material of his black, long-sleeved shirt. Messy, dark hair framed his strikingly attractive face.

I'm not going to say, 'Oh! It was so unlike me!' because it wasn't. It was exactly the kind of thing I'd do. I didn't think about my husband for a second. He didn't deserve my guilt. After leading me through Temptation up to his flat, we enjoyed a glass of whisky before Jack pinned me up against the door and kissed me so passionately I felt we were destined to be lovers. He could tell I wanted it. Hard and hot.

That was it at first. Passion.

The problem with passion is that it's dangerous, unpredictable. People say it all the time, don't they? 'Follow your passion!' It's the worst thing you can do. You don't think rationally if you're acting out of lust.

I fell in love with him. The kind of love I'd pack up my entire life and run away for.

And maybe it would have ended that way, if not for that night.

The night everything went so horribly wrong.

Now here we are, a year later, Jack accused of murdering Anton Smythe.

What I do know is that this jury isn't going to hear what really happened that night. They'll get a different version, one they can tolerate, one that will make sense, one that will make Anton look better than he was. They will hear a version that is 'just'.

Not necessarily the truth.

When Anton went to Jack's apartment that night, the last person he expected to find was me. You see, I know his secret, the one that would have had him sacked as a judge if anyone found out. And that's why Jack is protecting me.

Sometimes, I wake up in the middle of the night and replay the entire thing in my head. I hear the thud of that kettlebell on his skull seconds before his body fell to the floor. I remember the desperation in his voice, the last words to leave his mouth. The ones he'd never want his family to know. His big secret. The one that had led him to Jack's flat in the first place.

But they can never know the truth.

Nobody can.

… Part Two

The Trial

Chicanery

Noun

1. Clever, dishonest talk or behaviour that is used to deceive people

2. A slick performance by a lawyer

42

Leila

R v Jack Millman
Day 1
10 a.m.

Flushing the vomit away, I start brushing my teeth and make a mental note not to attempt breakfast tomorrow. I've been awake since 4.36 a.m., going through the case in my head. I feel wired, dizzy, sick. Adrenalin has entered the chat. I put on my best fitted trouser suit. A high, black, stiletto heel. Liquid eyeliner with a respectable wing. Red lipstick.

I hear Julian shuffling around in the spare room. We're used to the practical choreography of it all now; he uses the bathroom while I'm in the kitchen, then we switch. We never pass on the stairs. The fact we even have a routine of this type demonstrates how far apart we've drifted. I leave the house at 7 a.m. just to get out of there.

After speeding away from Chester's house on Friday, I went home and collected my laptop and case papers, then took them all to Audrey's house and stayed the night. I locked all the doors to ensure there was no way of *her* getting back in. Protecting Audrey and her home is a priority. First thing on Saturday morning, I called a locksmith to come and make the house more secure, with a few added measures to give me peace of mind. I need to be able to focus on the trial.

A kaleidoscope of butterflies takes residence in my stomach as I pull my suitcase out of the car and drag it into court. I catch a few members of chambers on their way in, and they wish me good luck, in the professional sense, of course. But they want me to lose. After all, I'm defending the man accused of killing their friend and colleague.

The atmosphere in Newcastle Crown Court robing room is sombre. Weaving through the files and bags on the floor, I head towards the corner so I can robe away from everybody else. The volume drops once I enter. This is the only case people are talking about.

'Best of luck, Britney!' some of the men say, which sounds ludicrous in the context of this situation.

Putting my robes, collarette, and wig on today doesn't feel like court dress; it feels like armour. Standing in front of the full-length mirror, I take a quick breath and release it slowly. Here it is – the most important moment of my career.

Something to prove. Everything to lose.

Entering Court 1, I see Julian setting up the bench. As King's Counsel, he is allowed to use a lectern in court, whereas I am not. So, straight off the bat, that's the first thing that marks me out to the jury as inferior, in addition to the different robes. It immediately says, 'He is more senior to her.'

Walking straight past him, I go over to Davina, who is setting up our benches next to the jury box. This is a privilege you have when defending, which I love. There is nothing better than speaking directly to a jury, up close and personal.

'Day of reckoning, then?' Davina announces, dramatically.

'I suppose,' I reply, with a raised eyebrow. 'Shall we go and see him?'

I'm taken aback when Jack walks into the cells. In contrast to how he's looked the last few times I've seen him, he's now immaculately groomed and wearing a white shirt, with black trousers, a suit jacket, and a black tie. His hair, usually messy, has been tamed and teased into a side parting. It looks respectable but still retains a slight air of rebellion.

'You look great, Jack,' I tell him.

'Thanks.' He smiles. 'Eddie helped me out. Wanted me to make a good impression.'

'You do.'

'Have you thought of a decent defence for me yet?' he asks, the tiniest of smiles curling up his mouth.

Even now, on the morning of his murder trial, he's making jokes. It worries me.

'No,' I say, shaking my head. 'Just running with what you've disclosed in the police interview, which is absolutely nothing.'

'Let's trust the process, shall we?'

I catch Davina glaring at Jack, presumably trying to read him. She'll be hoping this confidence translates well in front of a jury.

'Are you sure there's nothing you want to tell me before it starts?'

'Nope.'

'For the record, I need to tell you again that whatever you say in evidence is going to be held against you because you're bringing it up late. The judge *will* direct the jury that they are allowed to hold an adverse inference against you.'

'I'm aware. You've said it enough times.'

'The prosecution barrister is going to try to annihilate you. I'm not saying that to scare you, but you need to be prepared.'

'Your husband?'

'Yes,' I answer. 'My husband.'

'Are you OK?'

Jack is the only person who has asked me, with any sincerity, how the case has affected me and my marriage. It catches me off guard and I take a sharp intake of breath.

'This case will hinge on many factors. The fact I'm married to the prosecutor will not be one of them. I—'

'Miss Reynolds? I have no regrets.'

Upstairs, people are taking their places in court. As per tradition for a murder trial, white shirts must be worn by the legal team. The public gallery is filled with journalists and Anton's family. Barristers have come in to watch, as have some solicitors, including Sienna. I even catch Demi sitting right at the back, as well as Eddie and Daniella Sorrington. People are treating this as a day out, it seems.

Presiding over this trial is Mrs Justice Brightman, a High Court judge from London with a reputation for being stern and exceptionally sharp. When you think of judges with this level of seniority, you imagine them to be old men, but she is a petite woman with a short, baby-blonde bob and gold-rimmed glasses. I'm grateful to have a woman presiding over the case, especially with Julian as my opponent.

At exactly 10.30 a.m., she walks onto the bench and Jack enters court.

After dealing with standard housekeeping matters, we agree a jury can be selected, and twelve people are brought forward to take the oath. It is always at this point that I like to study each one. What kind of person are you? Are you empathetic? Are you easily persuaded? Are you a leader or do you follow others? Are you kind? Are you strict? How would you react if a family member got into trouble? How do you treat your spouse?

You can get a good grasp of people just by watching them. I can always tell who the foreman is going to be. For me, this moment in the trial process is very important. Julian never even watches this part.

Our jury is made up of five men and seven women. Once they're sworn in, they're addressed directly by the judge, who informs them that the evidence upon which they will decide the case is the evidence that will be presented to them in court. All twelve jurors listen intently. Some glance fleetingly over at Jack, before drawing their eyes back to the judge. The responsibility bears down heavily on their shoulders by the time she's finished.

Next, Her Ladyship asks them to leave the courtroom so we can address a few other matters before the trial gets underway.

'Miss Reynolds,' the judge barks, 'it's my understanding that the Crown has requested to adduce a conviction dating back to 2019 against your client as bad character evidence. He was convicted of a s.20 assault inflicting grievous bodily harm?'

'Yes, My Lady.'

'You haven't resisted this application?'

'No, Your Ladyship.'

'Is your client aware that the circumstances of that offence will be made available to the jury? And they will be entitled to consider whether such an offence means he has a propensity to commit violent acts?'

'He is, Your Ladyship,' I reply, feeling all eyes on me straight away. 'In fact, Mr Millman is content for all of his previous convictions to be revealed to the jury.' An odd decision, but Jack 'wants his day in court'.

Christ.

The judge peers down her glasses at Jack, then directs her eyes back to me.

'Very well.' She nods. 'Bring them back in.'

The usher guides the jury back into court. As they take their seats, something in the air changes. Everyone sits up. My heart starts to race. This is it.

'Mr Kesler,' the judge says. 'Would you like to begin?'

43

Leila

R v Jack Millman
Day I
11.03 a.m.

I'VE WATCHED JULIAN give countless opening speeches over the years. Each one of them well-crafted and carefully curated. Hours of hard work go into preparing such things, and this one has the entire legal faculty watching.

He loves it, the drama and attention. As advocates of the court, we are expected to maintain exceptionally high standards throughout our professional life – never being swayed by outside influences, or allowing praise to affect our judgement.

Some adhere to this advice more than others.

'Ladies and gentlemen of the jury, this case concerns the brutal murder of a well-respected Crown Court judge. His name was Anton Smythe and he was a much-admired member of the judiciary before, we say, the defendant – Jack Millman – killed him in cold blood, one hot night in September last year.'

The prosecution is supposed to present the facts to a jury in an impartial manner, and this opening is anything but. I resist all temptation to roll my eyes, since the jury would see, and I don't want to get off on the wrong foot. At this stage of any trial, if you're defending, you're losing. Despite the prosecution's requirement to discharge the burden of proof, as in any criminal case, the reality is that defendants are usually guilty until proven innocent in the beginning, and it's for me to swing that around over the course of the trial. I don't want to get their backs up now by pulling faces.

I also don't want to object, although I would be technically permitted to do so. However, it is highly frowned upon to interrupt a KC in the middle of a speech and, no, the same courtesy would not be extended to me.

Criminal trials are like a game of chess, and he wants me to react. He wants – *needs* – the jury to see me as the bullish, hysterical, inexperienced female lawyer against the backdrop of his cool, suave, confident demeanour.

Chester was right: evidence doesn't win trials. Lawyers do. It's about likeability.

He stands to my right, speaking to the jury as I sit between them. I look straight ahead, displaying no emotion on my face. As a barrister should. One of the many things my pupilmaster taught me. One of the many things *he* taught me. Once my biggest supporter, my mentor, my ally . . . *my loyal husband.* Now we stand against each other.

'In order to find the defendant guilty, the prosecution does not need to prove that the defendant had any kind of grievance with the victim. We need not prove that the two were involved in any kind of dispute. We need not reveal a motive – we may never know what that was. All the Crown must prove throughout the course of this trial is that it was the defendant – and no one else – who killed Anton Smythe, and that when he did so, he intended to kill him or cause him serious harm. That is enough.'

He's going for high drama, just as I knew he would. I need to watch my temper.

The problem for him is that I know him well.

Too well.

I know all his dirty tactics, backdoor behaviours, his professional Achilles heels.

And his private ones.

If he thinks this trial is purely about securing a professional win, he's wrong.

44

Leila

R v Jack Millman
Day 1
11.29 a.m.

THE FIRST PROSECUTION witness is DCI Brady, the kind of man who always looks as if he never has to be anywhere. Whenever I've seen him throughout this investigation, including at the site visit, he has the appearance of someone who's just rolled out of bed. Even now, as he hauls himself into the witness box to give evidence in this trial, I wonder how he didn't think even to fasten his suit jacket. His belly is spilling out of his trousers.

I am not deceived, however, by his appearance. DCI Brady is a fierce detective. He leads the biggest investigations for a reason. Nothing gets past him. He is not good for us.

The jury scrutinizes the first witness as he takes the oath to tell the truth. Of course, they will trust everything he says because he is a police officer – and a senior one at that.

Julian walks him through the formalities first, but we all know what's coming.

'Could you please tell the jury what happened on the night of Friday, 6 September 2024?'

'Yes,' DCI Brady says, loudly, turning towards the jury. He is a pro at this. 'At 11.07 p.m., a 999 call was received from the landline at Temptation from the defendant informing the authorities that a man had been seriously hurt, and the identity of that man was His Honour Judge Smythe. I attended the scene at 11.23 p.m.'

'To confirm: the defendant himself reported this?'

'He did.'

'Would you usually attend the scene of an assault of this type?'

'No, I would not. I'd normally come on board to a murder investigation at a later stage. But I was called upon to do so in this case as a senior member of the judiciary had been seriously harmed.'

'Can you tell us what happened when you arrived, please?'

'We located the defendant on the second floor of the building. The door to his apartment was open and no force was required to gain entry.'

The defendant. Jack has been reduced to a thing, not worthy of a name. Cementing with the jury early on that he's worthless and, in turn, guilty.

'Can you describe the scene to us upon arrival?'

'The victim was in the lounge, lying on his back, being assisted by paramedics.'

'If I could stop you there, please. Dear members of the jury, if you would kindly turn to tab one in your jury bundle, you'll see a layout of the flat.'

A flurry of activity takes place within the jury box, as everyone scrambles to find the map. They feel part of this now, you can tell. He's locked them in. *We're in this together, ladies and gentlemen. Let's convict the bastard who killed this loving husband and father.*

'Does everyone have sight of that document now?' Julian asks the jury, flashing that dashing smile he reserves for occasions such as this. The women on the jury nod, and going by the look in their eyes, would be prepared to convict Jack right now based on virtually no evidence if it meant they could have just one night of uninhibited passion with my husband. He knows exactly what he's doing. It's not even lunchtime yet. 'DCI Brady, please explain the layout to us.'

'As you can see, it's a very small flat. The front door leads directly into an open living room–kitchenette area. Just off the main room is one bedroom, which contains an en-suite bathroom. It's almost like a studio.'

'Can you tell us where the victim was when you found him?'

'Yes. He was on the floor, with his head nearest to the front door, about five feet away. His feet were in the kitchen.'

'So, he was effectively half in the lounge, half in the kitchen area?'

'That's correct.'

'Where was the defendant?'

'He was sitting on the edge of the sofa, waiting for us,' he confirms in a hard, Geordie accent. His hands are clasped together in front of him. It's a serious, dominant stance.

'How far away from the victim was he?'

'Maybe six feet?'

'And the defendant was making no attempt to help the victim?'

'My Lady,' I interrupt, 'counsel is leading the witness.'

The judge glances at Julian before turning her eyes back to me.

'Mr Kesler, would you like to rephrase the question?'

Julian pauses. I know what he's thinking. He *hates* being interrupted when he's questioning a witness.

'DCI Brady, what was the defendant doing when you walked in?' Julian asks the question now in a painfully exaggerated way, letting everyone know how irritated he is. It's clever, too, because the jury will think I'm petty and overly concerned with semantics.

'He was making no attempt to help the victim,' DCI Brady says, straight to the jury.

I get it. It's them against me. Against us.

'What state was the victim in?' Julian continues.

'He had blood coming out of his nostril. It looked like he'd been—'

I rise for the second time.

'Your Ladyship.'

'DCI Brady,' the judge bellows. 'Please do not speculate. We will hear from medical professionals in due course regarding Mr Smythe's injuries.'

He nods in compliance but is obviously furious. He looks at Julian, and they share a moment of irritation. DCI Brady strikes me as the kind of man who does not like being told what to do by a woman.

'Was he alive when you saw him?' Julian asks.

'Only just, but yes.'

Julian takes the jury through the gruesome part of looking at photos from the scene.

'DCI Brady, may I bring your attention to an item found at the scene which the jury can find at tab five in their bundles,' he goes on, confidently. 'Your Ladyship, permission to admit into evidence exhibit PB1. DCI Brady, can you please describe this for the jury?'

'It's a 10 kg kettlebell,' he confirms.

'My Lady, I am content for the statement produced by the defence to be admitted into evidence at this stage. It is a statement that confirms the kettlebell was permanently used as a doorstop in the defendant's apartment. The kettlebell is the weapon that caused the fatal blow to Mr Smythe, and the jury will hear expert evidence regarding this in due course.'

Great work from Davina, securing that statement.

'That's where you found the kettlebell when you arrived?' Julian goes on. 'As per these photographs, holding the door open?'

'It is.'

'What's the distance between the kettlebell in situ and the body?'

'It was about seven feet.'

'So, he would have used the weapon and then returned it to its original place?'

'An odd sequence of events, but yes.'

'And – this isn't in dispute, so I'm permitted to lead – can you confirm that no fingerprints have been recovered from this item?'

'That's correct. They'd been wiped.'

'What happened after you located the defendant?'

'He was arrested on suspicion of attempted murder.'

'How did he react?'

'Calmly. You wouldn't have thought he'd just been arrested for such a serious offence. He was compliant and polite. He made no comment to the caution and came willingly into custody.'

Julian takes the witness through the police procedure at the station; being checked in, having DNA samples and photos taken. The jury are directed to further exhibits in the jury bundle showing how Jack looked when he was arrested. You can see them thinking, Is this the face of a man who, only an hour earlier, killed another person?

'Were you able to secure his mobile telephone?'

'Unfortunately, no. In most cases, this offers us a window of insight, but we were unable to seize the defendant's mobile phone, and to this date, it has never been found.'

It sounds bad and it *is* bad. DCI Brady emphasizes the last part, so the jury can clock just how dodgy the whole thing is.

'Now, there was a significant development in this case after the defendant had been brought into custody, wasn't there?' Julian enquires, leaning against the back bench, arms folded. Occasionally, he strokes his chin while nodding his head. He's hit his stride now. The confidence of the man is staggering. I don't think I've ever leaned against that bench my entire legal career. It's very male behaviour.

'Yes. At 1.54 a.m., we received the news that the victim had died and, as a result, the attempted murder investigation became a murder investigation. The defendant was informed of this, and we interviewed him under caution. He requested a legal representative from Jessops.'

'Can you please recite the caution for the jury?'

'Certainly: "You do not have to say anything. But, it may harm your defence if you do not mention when questioned something which you later rely on in court. Anything you do say may be given in evidence."'

'And did he cooperate in the interview?'

'No, he did not,' DCI Brady confirms, shaking his head. 'He gave no-comment answers to everything asked of him.'

'What was the result of this?'

'We felt we had sufficient evidence to charge Jack Millman with the murder of Anton Smythe, so that's what happened.'

'Thank you, DCI Brady. I have no further questions.'

Julian sits back down on the creaky bench, struggling to hide that Cheshire Cat grin I know he wants me to see.

Now it's my turn.

45

Leila

R v Jack Millman
Day I
11.51 a.m.

Y͟O͟U͟'V͟E͟ G͟O͟T͟ T͟O͟ be careful with police officers. The basis of cross-examination is that you're disputing, or casting doubt, upon someone's evidence. At the very least, you're helping the jury explore beyond what was previously said. We are trained never to ask a question in cross-examination that we don't already know the answer to, and when you have as limited instructions as I do from my client, that's a very hard reach.

I rise. The jury stare at me, wondering, *Is she up to it? Is she any good? Why did the defendant pick her? Is she as good as the prosecution one? Who do we like and trust more?*

'DCI Brady, could I ask you to look again at the photos of Mr Millman which were taken when he was brought into police custody?'

He shuffles the photos around, and the jury too can be heard flicking pages to find the ones I'm talking about. He finds them, then faces me without saying anything. God, he looks pissed off.

'Mr Millman has a swelling to the right side of his face there, does he not?' I ask, leading everyone to look at the redness just to the side of Jack's right eye.

'I suppose.' He shrugs. This man doesn't take me seriously. 'That could have come from anywhere.'

'Do you remember if that swelling was there when you arrived on the scene at his flat?'

'I don't recall seeing it, no.'

'So, you're saying it wasn't there?'

'I didn't say that,' he answers back, defiantly, putting his hands on each side of the witness box.

'You made no mention of it in your evidence just now. Why not?'

'I didn't think it was important.'

'You didn't think it was important to mention that a man accused of murder had bruises beginning to form on his face potentially hours after the alleged murder had been committed, who now denies committing that act?'

'It wasn't immediately obvious.' He sighs.

'It's right, isn't it, that Mr Smythe was left-hand dominant?'

'So I'm told, yes.'

'If Mr Millman claimed he had been assaulted by someone who was left-hand dominant, his injuries would be consistent with that?'

'Is he saying that?'

'I'm asking you.'

DCI Brady directs a steely glare my way, and I can tell he does not like me.

'I suppose it would, but that wasn't immediately obvious when the defendant was arrested.'

The way he speaks is defensive.

'Was it immediately obvious what the murder weapon was when you arrived at the flat?'

'No,' he replies, 'it wasn't. It was difficult to understand what had happened at all because, outwardly, Mr Smythe didn't display many injuries. Just the bleeding from the nose, which made me think he'd been hit with something heavy.'

'You said in your evidence just now that it was an "odd" decision to place the kettlebell back to its doorstop position. Can you explain this, please?'

'I've worked in criminal investigations for twenty years, mostly murder scenes. Some of these crime scenes are well thought out. Others aren't. You can spot the rookie ones a mile off. The ones who panic and make stupid split-second decisions that end up getting them caught. The kettlebell is one of them.'

'How so?'

He glances at the jury, then directs his attention back to me.

'To use an object to kill someone, then return it to its place?' he says to me, slowly, as if I'm stupid. 'It had Anton's DNA all over it. We were obviously going to find it.'

'No one attempted to hide it, throw it out, remove it from the flat?'

'I'd argue that by returning it to the door, he was trying to get away with it, ignorant of how the scene would be scrutinized by a criminal court. An amateurish move.'

'To be clear, you're saying only someone who had no intimate knowledge of how crime scenes work would make such an un-sophisticated mistake?'

'Or someone who isn't very bright,' he points out, turning to face Jack in the dock at the back of the courtroom. 'A poor attempt at manipulating the crime scene, either way.'

I nod my head slowly, turning towards the jury for a moment before continuing.

'As you've just highlighted, the kettlebell had Mr Smythe's DNA on the rounded side of it. It's right, isn't it, that in murder cases, you normally make the connection between victim and killer with the weapon?'

'Of course, yes.'

'And you've struck gold when you have the victim's DNA on one end of the weapon and the alleged killer's DNA on the other end?'

'Where possible, yes.'

'You don't have that link here, do you?'

'We don't have that link in many cases.' He shrugs. 'It's not unusual.'

'Odd circumstances, though, yes? Reinstatement of the kettlebell. No attempt by Mr Millman to flee the scene. No-comment interview.'

'What exactly is odd about it, Miss Reynolds?' he asks me, abruptly, shifting his weight from one foot to the other. He's getting agitated.

'For somebody who doesn't have any DNA on a murder weapon, you appear to be very sure you have your killer. The evidence against Mr Millman in this case is purely circumstantial, isn't it?'

'The defendant was arrested under caution. You know the importance of those three sentences, Miss Reynolds. Mr Millman does, too. He was interviewed under caution. Twice. He gave "no comment" replies to both. He's had every single opportunity to say he's innocent of this offence, but not once has he done so. Does that sound like an innocent person to you?'

He directs the last line directly to the jury. This isn't going well.

'I'm the one asking the questions, DCI Brady, not you,' I say calmly, referring to my blue notebook to see where I'm going next with this. 'Did you think anything was odd about Mr Millman's appearance that night when you arrested him?'

'Odd? No . . .'

'May I take you to photo number two. It's a headshot of Mr

Millman in custody. You'll see he's wearing his T-shirt inside out and back to front. Can you see the label there? Just in front of his neck?'

DCI Brady holds the photo up to his face to get a better look.

'Did he put this T-shirt on in your presence?'

'No, he was already wearing it when we arrived.'

'What's that on the front of his T-shirt?' I ask, pointing to a large section of it which is a dark brown colour and looks wet.

'That turned out to be Coca-Cola.'

'And you recall seeing this when you arrived?'

'Yes.'

'Did any of this strike you as peculiar?'

'Within the context of a murder investigation?' He laughs. 'Not really.'

'You can't explain any of these things?'

'That's for your client to do, Miss Reynolds.'

'You maintain that Mr Millman was calm at the flat?'

'Yes.'

'Cooperative?'

'In the sense that he willingly came with us, yes. Beyond that, no.'

'One last thing, DCI Brady. You said in your statement – completed within twenty-four hours of the alleged offence – that you were hit by the very faint smell of women's perfume in Mr Millman's bedroom. Is this correct?'

'Yes.'

'But you didn't mention this in your evidence just now, did you?'

'It was more of a general observation of the crime scene, really. I didn't think it carried much significance.'

'Didn't you?' I ask. 'Why not?'

'The evidence against Mr Millman is sufficient.'

'Well, that's not for you to decide. That is a matter for this jury. Tell me, DCI Brady, was this an open-and-shut case for you?'

I'm pushing it, I know. My eyes flick towards the judge, and hers to mine. Julian shuffles out of the corner of my eye.

'I don't know what you mean.'

'It's a very high-profile case, isn't it? Cases such as these can't be left sizzling in the background for too long. People want progress and a conviction. It's almost too good to be true that the murderer was caught sitting right beside the victim as he lay dying.'

'Miss Reynolds,' the judge cautions. I need to be careful here.

'Did you investigate all lines of inquiry in this case?'

'Our methods are thorough, especially when a life has been taken. We want to ensure justice prevails for the victim and the victim's family.'

'Did it ever cross your mind that there may have been someone else there that night?'

Silence grips the courtroom.

'The defendant was at the scene when we arrived and refused to answer all questions put to him.'

'Let me phrase the question another way. Was there any evidence at the scene to suggest anyone else had been in the flat? Any at all?'

He pauses before answering, glaring at me from the box. The air is tense.

'It would be speculative, at best.'

'Could the jury please turn to tab two in the jury bundles?' I ask. After a few seconds of shuffling about, everyone is presented with photographs of a mixture of cocktail and beer glasses. Not ordinary ones, but the kind of fancy, ornate ones you get in Temptation for thirteen pounds a pop. Some are empty, but for a few dregs lounging in the bottom. Others contain unfinished drinks.

'DCI Brady, can you explain to the jury what these are?'

'Exhibits found at the scene of the murder. I really don't see . . .'

He's getting flustered. Shaking his head, he has no way to explain why this wasn't investigated.

'There are five in total. They have been photographed where they were found in the flat. Do you recall seeing them there?'

'I do, yes.'

'Where were they?'

'All except one were scattered around the living room. One was in the bedroom.'

'You'll see from the photographs that two of the glasses have lipstick marks on the rim. Do you see that?'

'Yes.'

'Do you also see that the lipsticks appear to be different shades?'

'I'm a man. I'm unable to differentiate between these things.'

'Are you colour blind?'

'Miss Reynolds,' the judge intervenes.

I need to be cautious. I'm starting to piss her off now; Julian will think he's got the upper hand.

'DCI Brady, that's potentially two other people who could have been in that flat on the night of the murder, yet you failed to follow that up.'

'Those glasses could have been there for days, weeks,' he says, holding the photo up and waving it around. He doesn't like being questioned in this way.

'Perhaps. But they also could have been placed there minutes before Anton Smythe was killed, couldn't they?'

'It's unlikely.'

'Is it? What about the strands of hair belonging to seven different individuals that were discovered in the same room where Mr Smythe's body was found? Or the lighter with unidentified prints on it?'

'There's no way of knowing when they were introduced to the room.'

'So, it could have been the night of the murder. In total, that's potentially thirteen other people whose DNA was present inside Mr Millman's flat. The fact is, you didn't even attempt to consider whether there might have been someone else responsible for this, did you?'

'We didn't need to,' he answers quickly, shaking his head.

'As far as you were concerned, you had your man, and you'd make it fit your narrative because it was easy. That's right, isn't it?'

'I've been a police officer for over twenty years. I've solved countless murders. We've got our man.'

He isn't budging. I've made my point and now I need to get out of here. Never push your luck.

'No further questions, Your Ladyship.'

First witness down and I've basically called a police officer incompetent.

This isn't going as well as I'd hoped.

46

Leila

R v Jack Millman
Day 1
12.19 p.m.

THE PATHOLOGIST IS next.
Always a vital witness in any murder trial because the prosecution must prove that the defendant's act caused the victim's death. The jury sit up as he walks into the witness box. After undertaking years of training and experience to get where they are, pathologists are aware that in situations such as these, people hang on to their every word. They're capable of ending a case with their opinion alone.

Dr Parker is the kind of man who looks as if he knows what he's doing. The sort of man who never makes bad choices but does make sound financial investments. Clean-shaven, with silver-rimmed glasses sitting perfectly on his face, his black hair marks him out as someone who's reached the professional level he's attained at such a young age through hard work and dedication.

Julian runs through his qualifications, before moving on to the post-mortem itself. It's written using clinical and medical terms – something juries often struggle with. It's a win for Julian, of course. Using these terms makes the offence more brutal, minimizing this father, husband, and friend into a series of stark facts: male, five foot nine, fourteen and a half stone. At the time of his death, he had 78 mg of alcohol per 100 millilitres of blood in his body. 80 mg is over the limit to drive.

'Mr Smythe suffered a dynamic head injury, or a blunt head trauma, in more common terms. This went on to cause a subdural haematoma and his eventual death.'

'Can you please explain to the jury what that is?'

'A collection of blood. There's a very small gap between the brain and the skull, and if the layer around the brain is torn as a result of trauma or impact, it can bleed into that subdural space.'

'And what happens if this occurs?'

'It exerts pressure on the brain stem, which controls breathing. Death is quick if medical assistance isn't sought rapidly.'

Julian pauses for a second, allowing the jury to process what they've just heard.

'Dr Parker, if I could ask about the impact itself,' he goes on. 'Where exactly was the victim struck?'

'On the right temple, just above his right eye. An incredibly vulnerable area.'

'What about the direction of impact?'

'It's unlikely it came from the front. I suspect it came from the side or behind the victim.'

'I really want the jury to be clear on this. You're saying it's very unlikely this blow was delivered from a place where the victim could see it coming?'

Smart. He's shutting off any opportunity to raise self-defence before we get started.

Setting up intent to kill.

'I would say so, yes.'

'How did the impact site present?' Julian goes on.

'Very slightly raised. The skin was not broken, which suggests he was struck with a heavy but smooth object.'

'If I could ask you to clarify for the jury,' he asks, in his patronizing voice, 'is it normal to be struck with such a heavy object and for there to be no swelling or bruising?'

'With trauma to the head, yes,' Dr Parker confirms. 'The impact is directed inwards, so the blood vessels that connect the brain to the skull are severed. All of the damage is internal.'

He is an extraordinarily calm witness, who speaks clinically but clearly. He's eloquent and takes care that the jury understand what he's saying. Dr Parker stands upright in the witness box, hands in front of him. He is an excellent professional witness, and that terrifies me.

'If I could take you to tab number five in your jury bundle, you'll see a photo of a 10 kg kettlebell. This was found at the scene. Could this have inflicted the injury you detail?'

'Kettlebells are designed to be swung. With enough momentum, someone could deliver a fatal impact with it, yes.'

'With an injury such as the one you've outlined, how much time would have elapsed between impact and death?'

'As I said, death is rapid with this kind of injury once the blow has been delivered. It entirely depends on each individual's circumstances and the medical situation of the person involved, whether they have any underlying conditions. But survival is possible if they get help quickly. A longer delay diminishes that chance.'

'To clarify for the jury, survival is possible if medical attention is sought quickly?'

Oh no. I know where he's going with this.

'Certainly.'

'It's impossible for you to comment upon how quickly the defendant called 999 after the fatal blow was delivered, of course.

But is it possible to say, in this case, how much time elapsed between Mr Smythe receiving the injury and receiving medical help?'

Dr Parker glances at the jury, and I watch as he delivers the subtlest smile. It's then that I realize he is very much hoping that Jack is convicted, despite his evidence supposedly being unbiased.

'Well, no. But Mr Smythe is dead, isn't he?'

Sometimes a witness delivers such a devastating blow, there's no need for them to elaborate on what they've just said. The impact of it sits quietly between the words. That's the true indicator of a professional witness – someone who understands how a jury works. He doesn't need to say anything else, and Julian, being as skilled as he is, doesn't push further. In a courtroom, silence is golden; a well-timed pause holds more power than a hundred careless words.

'Thank you, Dr Parker,' Julian says, after a few moments, once he's allowed the jury to swallow his last line. 'I don't have any further questions.'

Standing up, I'm reminded that going against a solid expert witness when defending is always difficult.

'Dr Parker, did Mr Smythe have any other injuries when you examined him?'

'Minor bruising to right cheek and light grazing to the knuckles on his left hand.'

'It's right to say he was left-hand dominant, isn't it?'

'That's correct.'

'These minor injuries are consistent with a physical altercation, or a struggle of some kind, aren't they?'

'Possibly, but I would generally expect more physical evidence on the body if such a struggle had occurred. It would be unusual to have only these two injuries. They're barely even injuries.'

I look down at my notebook for a second, taking a moment. This witness is incredibly dangerous for us.

'The kettlebell was ten kilos. As you can see, Mr Millman is a broad, strong man. He used to go to the gym every day. Wouldn't you expect more injuries if he had swung the weapon?'

'The victim is dead, Miss Reynolds. How much more injured could he be?'

Jesus. I need to shut this down.

'I mean superficially,' I go on, confidently, in an attempt to present this as anything other than the trainwreck it is. 'Around the trauma site?'

'As I have *already* said, with assaults of this type, you often don't see bruises or swelling. The damage is internal.'

I can almost hear Julian gloating from where he sits. I need to get this witness away from the jury quickly before he damages my case further.

'No further questions, Your Ladyship.'

'Thank you for attending court to give evidence, Dr Parker. I wonder whether this might be a good opportunity to pause for lunch?' the judge asks. 'Let's resume at 2.15 p.m.'

Two witnesses down, and the prosecution's case is definitely stronger.

I need to turn this around, fast.

47

Witness X

You

I WATCHED YOU IN court. The dignity and strength you showed just made me fall in love with you all over again. The bravery. The sacrifice. It reminded me of how different you are to the man I have to go home to every night.

I long for the time we used to spend together. I loved watching your face each time I brought you a silly little gift. They were always obscure, and you were always amazed I knew you so well.

The *Robin Hood: Prince of Thieves* poster was my favourite. After you told me it was the film your foster mother watched with you, I had to. It was just a joke, but you hung it up immediately.

After it happened – *the betrayal* – she told me that nobody would choose me if they knew the *real me*. It hurt, because that's what Dad used to say, too. That I didn't deserve love. That I wasn't good enough for it.

You've proved them wrong.

She always wanted what I had, right from the day I met her. She saw my power and she wanted a piece of it, too. I was better at the rules than her, back then.

Not any more. You changed that, Jack.

Loving you has made me lose focus. Made me more human.

She doesn't realize how close she is now. She will find it soon enough, the chink in my armour. And when she does, I'm finished.

The old me would never have made such a stupid, careless mistake. I question every day why we used your phone and not mine, Jack. It would have made much more sense. Not my real phone, obviously. I mean the burner phone I bought when the affair started. The one that was only used for you and nobody else. I made a rule from day one: no photos would be taken of us, no videos. And they certainly wouldn't be sent between us. If they ever got out, not only would my reputation be ruined, but they would also be ammunition for my husband.

You can imagine the narrative, can't you? *Look at what my slut of a wife did! Cheated on me with a nightclub doorman. A common criminal. Crazy psycho bitch.*

You see, men bounce back from acts of infidelity. With enough power and charisma, I've even seen men laugh them off. 'You are scandalous!' the lads smirk, secretly envious they weren't able to con an eighteen-year-old into allowing them to stick their dick into her for a few months before being unceremoniously found out (but ultimately forgiven) by their long-suffering wife. 'I'll never learn, will I?' they wink before doing it again months later.

Women are not afforded the same luxury if they commit a similar crime. A reality that's vastly unfair, given the fact that most often, men cheat because they're selfish and self-serving, and women also cheat because men are selfish and self-serving.

Women are treated more harshly. A life sentence with no chance of parole. You might as well pack up your life and move on.

If I could take it back, I would. But you changed me. Normally I'm good at saying no. At keeping control of the situation. But on that hot, sticky night, I found myself saying yes.

DISSECTION OF A MURDER

At the time it felt right, rebellious, sexy. For a few brief moments, we felt invincible.

Little did we know that by pressing the red circle and starting to record that video on your phone, you'd end up here, charged with murder.

And now, Leila Reynolds is responsible for keeping you out of jail.

Come to think of it, did you suggest the whole thing, or did I?

48

Leila

R v Jack Millman
Day 1
2.29 p.m.

'The Crown calls its next witness, Percy Wyndam,' Julian announces.

Everyone is feeling refreshed following lunch, and the jury watch a man in a sharp three-piece, pin-striped charcoal-grey suit walk up to the witness box. He's young, around early-thirties. His sandy-blond hair is neatly combed, with a quiff at the front. After taking the oath, he stands firm, eager to get started. It's useful to study witnesses before you cross-examine them, so you can assess how well they'll stand up to it. Some cave and some don't.

'Can you please tell the court what your job is?' Julian asks.

'I'm a mobile phone forensic expert.'

'And what exactly does that entail?'

'I analyse and examine data on mobile phones,' he explains, confidently. 'Occasionally, this data can be analysed and extracted even after it has been deleted.'

'And do you require the physical device of a particular individual in order to extract data from it?'

'Yes and no. Without the actual handset and SIM card, you're unable to retrieve a full picture of the data held on it. By using something called cell site analysis, however, we're still able to extract a significant amount of data in the absence of a handset.'

'If we could talk about the defendant's mobile phone first, please. Could you tell us what you know about it?'

'I was informed it was not found at the scene, nor has it been retrieved. In these cases, we go back to the mobile phone provider, which in this case is O2. Mr Millman was on a contract there, and we therefore have access to calls and text messages he made.'

'Do you have the content of those messages?'

'Without a handset, I'm afraid not. All we can access are the times and dates of messages and phone calls, and the numbers to whom they were sent. It wasn't backed up to the cloud, so this is all we have to work with.'

'What were your findings?'

'One number remains prominent throughout, from Tuesday, 6 February 2024 until 6 September 2024. Mr Millman texted this number 1,284 times in this period, and six times on the day of the murder.'

'Ladies and gentlemen of the jury, you'll see the phone log behind tab six of your bundle,' Julian directs.

Everyone flicks to tab six. They are engrossed in this now.

'This is not in dispute, Your Ladyship, so I'm permitted to lead,' Julian confirms. 'It's worth noting that no phone calls were ever made to this number. Only text messages?'

'That is correct.'

'Have you been able to locate the owner of this number?'

'No. It would appear to be a pay-as-you-go phone. No contact details are needed to set one up.'

'What else can you tell us about the defendant's phone?'

'Although we haven't been able to retrieve any data, we can trace movement with the assistance of cell site analysis.'

'Can you explain to the jury what this is?'

'Every time you use your mobile phone, that information is recorded by telephone masts. Cell site analysis places you at a specific location at a specific time.'

I'm grateful for the way this expert witness is explaining the technical content of his evidence. We need to keep the jury engaged and alert, and this could be a danger point for them to drift. He's concise, and all twelve members appear interested. I hope it lasts.

'Are there any circumstances in which it doesn't work?'

'Three. If the phone runs out of battery, is switched off, or is underwater.'

'What can you tell us about the defendant's phone activity?' Julian asks.

'The phone remained at the premises known as Temptation until 10.41 p.m., at which point the signal was lost. The last known activity previous to that was a text message sent to the pay-as-you-go phone at 6.47 p.m.'

'What conclusion can you draw from this?'

'In practical terms, the defendant's phone was likely switched off or ran out of battery. However, at 11.27 p.m., the signal reconnected, and the phone was located elsewhere.'

'Where was that location, exactly?'

'The phone had moved to the village of Pickford, twelve miles north of Durham, which is where I believe the victim lived.'

Julian pauses, very briefly, for the jury to take in what they're hearing.

'Thank you. Turning, then, to the phone of Anton Smythe. What can you tell us about this?'

'Thankfully, we did have his handset, so were able to retrieve everything by way of text message content. On 6 September, he went to work at Durham Crown Court in the morning, before going to Diamond Lounge at 6 p.m., where he texted his wife, "I'm just meeting Quinn for a drink". After that, he went home for a few hours before leaving again at 10.12 p.m., the data placing him at Temptation, from where he texted Quinn at 10.26 p.m. He wrote, "You don't need to worry about it".'

Julian explains to the jury that Quinn is Anton's eighteen-year-old son, and they will hear from him as a witness in due course.

'So, we're getting closer to the incident now,' my husband declares excitedly. 'What happened next?'

'At 10.39 p.m., the data suggests that Mr Smythe opened the FaceTime app on his mobile phone, and that it remained open for thirteen seconds. No contact was selected, and nobody was called. That was the last piece of activity before he died.'

'For the avoidance of any confusion, can you please explain what FaceTime is?'

'It's a function on an iPhone that enables you to video call a contact.'

I glance at the jury to see what they make of it all. It's a lot to take in.

'Mr Wyndam, thank you,' Julian says. 'My learned friend will no doubt have many questions for you.'

He knows I won't. Another tactical statement to make me look incompetent in the eyes of the jury. The problem with evidence of this type is that it's difficult to dispute. You can attempt to cast doubt on it, test its accuracy and minimize it, but ultimately, you can't argue with facts. And jurors love facts.

'Mr Wyndam, how accurate is the cell site analysis data?'

'Very accurate. Subjects can be located within a few metres.'

'Thank you.' I smile at him. 'No further questions.'

49

Leila

R v Jack Millman
Day 1
3.01 p.m.

Q**UINN SMYTHE STANDS** in the witness box, every inch the dutiful son. Well-fitted suit, shiny shoes, perfectly groomed hair. But he looks nervous; fidgeting with the buttons on his suit, subtly biting his bottom lip.

I cannot shake what I heard on the secret camera from Temptation.

'Mr Smythe, I understand this is tremendously difficult for you, but could you please tell the jury when you last saw your father?' Julian asks, going straight for the emotional drama.

Clearing his throat, he faces the twelve people who will decide if Jack killed his dad.

'He came to see me at work, the day he was killed, at about 6 p.m.'

'Where did you work?'

'Diamond Lounge, in Durham city centre.'

'He sent you a text message saying, "No, not there. Diamond Lounge 6 p.m. Don't panic. Nobody knows". Can you tell the jury what he wanted to speak to you about?'

'Jack Millman had been bothering me for a few weeks.'

He looks straight at Julian when he says it, almost fearful that if he makes eye contact with anyone else, they'll see through his lies. Every member of the jury turns to look at Jack, to see his reaction. As he's sitting behind me, I'm unable to watch, which is probably just as well.

'Bothering?'

'Yes.' He nods. 'He hates kids from private schools. He thinks we're all stuck up but hates me the most because my dad sent him to prison. We used to go to Innocence on a Friday night, but he'd always cause trouble for me.'

'How so?'

'Trying to get me kicked out of the bar, following me around, staring at me in a very intimidating manner. Everyone could see he had it in for me.'

Oh, this is new. And, cleverly, it's indisputable, because there aren't any CCTV cameras in Innocence or Temptation. Well, apart from the one that captured Quinn being involved in something dodgy as hell. But, unhelpfully, this is of course on a recording I can't use. If only the quality was better. If only Jack had led him a little further into the room so we could see his face. If only the audio was clearer. I know it's him, but a judge would never allow it into evidence. I sit, listening to Quinn, as the injustice of it all races through my body.

'Did the defendant ever say anything specific that would imply it was a personal vendetta during this time?'

'No. It was mainly just his demeanour. He's obviously intimidating. Look at him.'

There's an urgency in his evidence. It's rehearsed, unnatural. He's practised this. You can tell he's been told what to say. What eighteen-year-old uses words and phrases like 'demeanour' and 'intimidating manner'? He's been coached by Julian. I'm surprised he didn't describe Jack as a 'Caucasian male'.

'Did you tell anyone about this?'

'Yes, I eventually told my father about it.'

'And what did he do?'

'He said he would deal with it. That's why he went to Jack's flat that night. To tell him to stop.'

'What's the meaning of the "nobody knows" part of that text?'

Quinn's eyes dart quickly over to Jack, sitting in the dock at the back of the courtroom.

'I was worried that if Jack found out I'd told anyone about it, he'd hurt me. Dad knew I was terrified of him.'

'Whose idea was it for your father to go to see Jack?'

'It was his idea. I tried to stop him.'

'What was the purpose of the visit?'

'He was going to tell him to stop intimidating me.'

'Can you tell us anything else about that last meeting with your father?'

'No, just that I wish he hadn't gone,' he says, lowering his head.

Julian – King of the Well-Executed Pause – breaks for a few seconds, allowing the moment to ferment in the jurors' brains.

'Thank you, Mr Smythe. My learned friend will have some questions for you.'

Julian sits down as I rise.

People always ask me, 'How can you defend people you know to be guilty?' It's not my job to judge them – that belongs to the jury. It's my job to study the evidence and the facts, then advise accordingly. What I do find difficult, however, is dealing with the rest of them. The liars in the witness box. It's these people – not the defendants – who ought to be judged by society.

I pause for a moment before starting, just to unsettle him. He'll be expecting me to be hostile. I deliver a warm smile, catching him off guard.

'You're currently at Cambridge University, aren't you, Mr Smythe?'

'I am, yes.'

'What are you studying?'

'Law.'

Oh, the irony.

'Law?' I repeat. 'I'm sure your father would be very proud.'

'I hope he would.'

'You must have grown up in a household that promotes the importance of criminals answering for their offences.'

'Absolutely,' he confirms, leaning forward in the witness box to further his point.

'With a father as a criminal judge, this must have been instilled in you more so than others?'

'Yes.'

'He knew, more than anyone, the procedures involved when dealing with criminals. He dealt with them every day, didn't he?'

'Yes.'

'Bizarre, then, that when his son was being criminally harassed, he chose to deal with it himself rather than go to the police.'

'Your Ladyship.' Julian rises to object, as I knew he would. 'The witness is being asked to speculate upon the actions of his father.'

'My Lady, I am merely probing as to the discussions that were had that led to Anton Smythe visiting Jack Millman on the night he died. These are highly relevant.'

'I'll allow it,' she says. 'Be careful, Miss Reynolds.'

Julian sits down in a dramatic, slow manner, trying to let the jury know he still has authority. I know his games.

'He thought he could sort it out more quickly if he dealt with it,' Quinn says.

'Sort it out more quickly?'

'He didn't want to get anyone else involved.'

'Was he scared of confronting this man, who is – in your own words from a few moments ago – "intimidating"?'

'No, he was just trying to protect me.' Quinn frowns. I've rattled his cage.

'What was his "demeanour" like when you last saw him?'

'He wasn't happy about what Jack had been doing.'

'Is it right to say he was agitated?'

'I suppose so . . . he just wanted it to stop.'

'Upset? I mean, he must have been, if a "thug" had been harassing his son.'

'Yes.'

'Angry?'

'Yes . . .'

'Very angry?'

He realizes too late where I've taken him. I watch as his face changes. Confidence is replaced with panic.

'But my father wasn't a violent man,' he attempts to backtrack.

'Wasn't he?' I ask, without looking at him and turning to look at the jury.

'He'd never harm anyone or even attempt to harm anyone. If that's what *he's* saying, that's not what happened at all.'

'Well, you weren't there, Mr Smythe, so you are unable to comment. You've told this jury that your father was upset, angry, and agitated before going to confront a man who had been harassing you. They can decide what state of mind your father was in. This alleged intimidating behaviour – did it only take place at the club?'

'Yes.'

'Did Mr Millman ever approach you outside the club?'

His eyes drift off to the side, into the distance. It is, of course, a tactic many witnesses use to appear to be thinking about something before they outright lie to the court.

'Erm . . . no.'

'To be clear, and remember you are under oath, you're saying this harassment – this contact with Mr Millman – only ever happened within Innocence?'

'Yes.'

Liar.

I force a silence upon the courtroom, longer than necessary – perhaps ten seconds or so. Just to make him feel uncomfortable. He squirms and doesn't know where to look. His breath is uneven. I bet there's a film of sweat on his neck. He knows I'm onto him.

'Did a grievance of any other kind exist between you and Mr Millman?' I ask him, shattering the stillness.

He hesitates for a millisecond. His eyes flick towards Jack.

'No.'

Liar.

'Did you have conversations of any kind with, or did you know, Mr Millman outside the club?'

I speak the words slowly, hoping the jury will suspect there's something off here. I'm not doing anything wrong by asking the question, but my tone and delivery suggest otherwise.

He turns to the jury, confidently, before addressing them.

'Absolutely not.'

I want to tell this jury that he's a liar. I want to tell Quinn I know there's something else going on. I want to play the video of him talking to Jack in Temptation about murder. I want them to hear his cockiness and privilege first hand. Not this 'scared, vulnerable little boy' act he's performing now.

But I can't do any of this, because none of it is admissible in court.

I'm transported back to the last time I represented Jack, when the same thing happened. When the jury didn't have access to all the evidence and made the wrong decision. It's happening again. What kind of justice is this?

If he goes back to prison, I'll never forgive myself.

'I don't have any further questions for this witness, My Lady,' I spit out in sheer frustration.

Quinn is the last of the live prosecution witnesses. The rest of their case is undisputed evidence, agreed statements, exhibits, the police interview formally introduced into evidence, and a few other matters.

The judge closes court at 4.30 p.m. I watch the jurors leave the room and have no idea what they make of any of it. Usually, I can gauge what they're thinking, but for the first time, I really can't.

Tomorrow, at 10.30 a.m., Jack Millman will finally get his day in court. He will stand in the witness box and tell everyone what happened on the night he is accused of killing Anton Smythe. I don't think any of us are ready for what he's about to say.

What I do know is, so far, all we've been fed by the prosecution is lies.

50

Leila

R v Jack Millman
Day 2
10.34 a.m.

'Your Ladyship, the defence calls Jack Millman to give evidence.'

There's a slight quiver in my voice as I make this grand declaration; it's probably only detectable to Julian. And I hate that he will have noticed it. He understands the gravity of this moment. As a defence barrister, the second your client steps into the witness box is always tense. What will they do? Will they go completely rogue? Will they undo all your hard work and dig themselves into a hole?

Jack Millman has always wanted his day in court, and in about thirty seconds, he's going to get it.

Everything has led to this.

The security guard takes Jack from the dock at the back of the court and leads him to the witness box. Like a dangerous animal being released from his cage. The jury stare at him as if he could pounce at any moment. Except, Jack doesn't look like a criminal, or a killer. He looks presentable in the same suit he wore yesterday. A little more creased than it was then, but still, a million times better than what most defendants turn up in.

His hair is pushed back from his face, which has a day's worth of stubble on it.

As he steps into the witness box, he nods at the judge, who does not reciprocate the gesture.

He takes the oath and speaks clearly into the microphone. He swears to tell the truth, the whole truth, and nothing but the truth.

Facing me, with his hands placed confidently together in front of him, he takes a deep breath. The silence is deafening.

'Could you give your full name to the court, please?'

'Jack Millman. No middle name.'

'How old are you?'

'Thirty-two.'

'Mr Millman, this isn't in dispute, so I'm allowed to lead. Is it right to say that you live in the building that houses Innocence and Temptation?'

'Yes, that's right.'

'Explain to the jury where exactly your flat is located within the building.'

'It's an attic apartment on the second floor. The ground floor is the Innocence bar. The first floor is the club, Temptation.'

'And what – if any – is the connection between these premises?'

'They're owned by the same person: Eddie Sorrington.'

'What is your relationship to him?'

'He's my boss. But he's also been a friend for many years.'

'What do you do for him?'

'I'm head of security at both establishments. That's why I live upstairs.'

'How did you come to secure that position?'

'When I came out of prison four years ago, Eddie thought I'd be a good person to head up his security team.'

'At this point, Mr Millman, to clarify for the jury – you are content for them to know that in 2019, you were convicted of assault, and you spent two years in prison for that?'

'I am, yes.'

'And no application was made by your legal team to prevent the jury from knowing about it.'

'Correct. I have nothing to hide.'

'Very well. So, since then, you've been working the security at the clubs. What does that involve?'

'Temptation is an exclusive club with a particular clientele. It's my job to keep everything moving, ensuring there's no trouble while maintaining discretion. I work with a small but dedicated team.'

His voice is calm, not too loud. Soothing, almost. He's articulate. This is good for the jury to hear. So far, so good.

'Mr Millman, if we could turn to the day of the alleged offence. CCTV has placed you at the beauty salon of Daniella Sorrington, wife of Eddie Sorrington, at around 1.30 p.m.'

'That was me, yes.'

'What was the purpose of that visit?'

'There was something I needed to speak to Eddie about but wasn't able to. I left and went back home to chill out for a bit until work started.'

'Mr Millman, at some point, you ended up in your flat with Anton Smythe, who was assaulted. He is now dead, and you're charged with his murder. You've pleaded not guilty. If you have a defence, now is the time to give it.'

'Well, that's the thing,' he says. 'It wasn't me who killed him.'

51

Witness X

Rule #10
Life Isn't Fair

The thing I love about Jack is that he doesn't panic. He's cool in a crisis. We're both similar in that way.

'Always be prepared for things to go tits up,' Dad used to say. 'Especially when things are going well. That's the time to be on your guard. Life isn't fair. Get used to it.' I'm grateful for this rule. Because of it, I was ready to handle things when Anton died.

The air was gluey and warm that night. It always was in the attic apartment. It never seemed to matter what the weather was. The gentle boom of music circulated around the room and vibrated through the floor from the club below. It had become our defining soundtrack.

We never had long together. Our time was precious. Once a week, that's all we allowed ourselves, pretending it was just sex. The second I was in that apartment, our bodies were inseparable. His hands would be all over me; caressing, grabbing, pulling. His mouth needed to be on my skin, his tongue in every curve.

'Let me record us,' he said that night.

'No,' I replied, firmly.

'You know you can trust me.'

'It's just . . . phones can get lost. End up in the wrong hands.'

'It won't,' he whispered. 'I just need to see you when I *can't* see you.'

This is where it all went wrong.

In that second, I knew I had changed. I'd been relying on the rules less and less since I met Jack. I felt different. The old me – toxic, ruthless, cynical – had been replaced by a woman who had started to trust people. And the weird thing was I liked it. Jack made me feel safe enough to step outside the rules that had imprisoned me for so long. It was exhilarating, terrifying.

It made me feel normal.

I was like a different person when his body was against mine. I'd lose myself, forget my past, and just exist in the euphoric bliss of feeling something *real*. It was in one of these moments – one stupid fucking moment – that I said yes.

Grabbing his iPhone, he set it up so it was standing against the TV in the corner of the room. With the reverse angle camera on, the entire living room, kitchen, and front door of the apartment was onscreen, the large sofa taking centre stage.

'Thank you,' he said, kissing me hard on the lips before walking over to the phone and pressing the big, red circle.

RECORD.

I wasn't fazed by the camera. Our clothes came off, and we held nothing back.

And then someone was knocking loudly on the door. Three bangs.

We both froze, hoping whoever it was would just go away.

'Jack, let me in,' a very well-to-do male voice shouted. 'It's Anton Smythe. I know you've been expecting me.'

'He can't come in here!' I whispered, the panic rising in my gut. 'He can't see me.'

'Now isn't a good time,' Jack shouted back, grabbing his T-shirt and pulling it on over his head.

'If you don't open this door right now,' Smythe shouted in the angriest voice I've ever heard, 'I'll bloody break it down.'

52

Leila

R v Jack Millman
Day 2
10.38 a.m.

A COLLECTIVE GASP ECHOES throughout the courtroom when he says it, the kind of courtroom scene from an ITV drama I watch and say is unrealistic. And yet, here we are.

'Quiet, please!' the judge says.

'Mr Millman, for the court record, can you repeat what you said so there's no ambiguity and we are all absolutely clear?' I struggle to keep my voice steady. A veneer of sweat begins to collect on my chest.

'I didn't kill Anton Smythe. Someone else did. I told you, I'm not guilty.'

'Your Ladyship, I wonder if I might have a moment with my client?'

'I don't need a moment,' he interrupts. 'I'm not going to tell you anything different from what I'm saying here. I want people – the jury – to know the truth about what happened. So, I'm telling you. All of you. Now.'

Everyone looks at me because it's my job to steer this ship.

'Mr Millman, do you know who killed Mr Smythe?' I ask, slowly.

'I do, yes.'

I've never known a court be so quiet. It's as though everyone has stopped breathing.

'Can you please tell this court who it was?'

'I'm not prepared to do that.'

My heart races. I feel everyone's eyes on me. Whispers sprint around the courtroom. I see Julian in my peripheral vision frantically writing notes, preparing his cross-examination.

'Mr Millman, you're charged with murder – an offence that carries life imprisonment, if convicted,' I inform him. 'Are you prepared to risk that for someone else?'

'Yes,' he confirms. No hesitation. It sounds far-fetched and unbelievable.

'Is there any information you're willing to share with us about the night of 6 September?'

He takes a deep breath before turning towards the jury.

'For seven months before this incident I'd been having an affair with a married woman. I know how that makes me sound, but she was trapped in an abusive marriage and was very unhappy. We got together and would meet regularly at my apartment. She was there on the evening of 6 September.'

'What was the exact nature of your relationship with her?'

'I loved her. I *still* love her.'

Jack continues to gaze at the jury, but you can see the pain in his face. He looks awkward as he says it, having to reveal his most intimate feelings to an entire courtroom.

'What happened that night?' I ask him, pulling him back.

'She came around just after 9 p.m. We were . . . being intimate with each other when there was a knock at the door at about 10.30 p.m. I didn't answer it at first – I thought it was something to do with work and hoped they'd leave. Then there was more banging, and a voice shouted, "It's Anton Smythe, let me in."'

'What did you do?'

'I panicked. I didn't want him in my flat. But he shouted, "If you don't open this door, I'll break it down," or something like that.'

'Mr Millman, why was Mr Smythe coming to your flat in the first place?'

'It was regarding his son, Quinn.'

'What about him?'

Jack takes a moment. He peers down at his shoes for a second before facing me again.

'I told him to deal with it. I never wanted it to go on this long.'

'Deal with what?'

'I never wanted it to come out like this.'

'*What* to come out like this?' I ask, urgently.

Jack pauses for a brief moment and swallows hard, before turning to look in the public gallery. After a few seconds, his breathing becomes heavy, and he rubs his forehead; he looks like he's going to cry.

'I'm sorry, Eddie. I never wanted you to find out this way.'

Everyone in the courtroom is confused and looks between Jack and Eddie to see what he's going to say next.

'Mr Millman,' I say, firmly. 'What didn't you want Eddie to find out about like this?'

Turning to face me again, Jack takes a deep breath before settling his eyes on mine. 'Quinn is responsible for the death of Eddie Sorrington's son. I saw it happen.'

The court explodes into absolute uproar. Gasps race around the room, crashing against horrified cries coming from the public gallery. A glance at the jury reveals they don't know what to do with this news; each of their heads darts around the courtroom, not knowing where to look. Their mouths drop open; one juror at the front cranes her neck to look at Quinn, who is now sitting in the public gallery following his evidence yesterday.

Jack and I stare at each other among the chaos. I feel someone

– presumably Davina – tugging on the back of my robes, trying to get my attention.

Quinn is now centre stage. Everyone's eyes are on him. He sits in the second row of the public gallery, next to his mother. His face is white; he looks about to faint. Eddie Sorrington charges from the back of the public gallery down to the front in an attempt to reach Quinn. Daniella screams at him to stop. Security guards rush over and drag Eddie away as he shouts, 'Fucking murderer!' which echoes throughout the courtroom.

That's the video Jack told Quinn he had. Jack was forcing Quinn to confess about Eddie's son.

'Quiet, *now*!' booms the judge. 'I appreciate this is sensitive, but unless anyone wants to spend the night in the cells for contempt, we will allow the defendant to continue with his evidence. I will not tolerate outbursts of this nature in my court. This is a murder trial.'

Jack looks utterly broken in the witness box. He leans forward, head in his hands.

'My Lady.' Julian's voice belts through the courtroom as he stands to address the judge. I watch as his jaw flickers from the side. He is furious. 'I wonder if I might—'

'Mr Kesler, I think we need to hear what this witness has to say. You'll have your opportunity to cross-examine him in due course. Let's get on with it, Miss Reynolds.'

Julian sits down, slowly. I fear what's to come. I really hope Jack is prepared.

'Can you explain, Mr Millman?' I ask, my voice trembling.

'I never, ever wanted it to come out like this,' Jack says. The emotion in his eyes is clear to everyone in the room. 'His parents should never have found out here.'

He breaks off, unable to continue.

'Take your time, Mr Millman.' I think we all need a minute

to recalibrate. Jack takes a few deep breaths. The jury are bewitched. Their gazes are all focused on Jack right now. You could hear a pin drop in this courtroom.

Davina pokes my arm. I turn quickly to see what she wants, and she hands me a piece of paper with scribbled writing on it, none of which is legible. I acknowledge it but don't have time to read it.

Jack composes himself and stands upright. He's started this and has every intention of finishing it.

'About a month before the night Mr Smythe died, Quinn was in Innocence with his friends. They were full of private-school cockiness. Lewis Sorrington was in, and the two of them clashed over some girl they were both trying to crack on with. Lewis wasn't a bad lad. I've known him for years, but he wasn't one to mess with, either. He would defend himself if he needed to. Around 3 a.m., I was opening my bedroom windows – it gets hot in there, as it's an attic room – and I saw Lewis on his own round the back of the club. He'd parked his car down the alley. Quinn's boys jumped him and held him while Quinn punched him in the face. Thing is, I thought Lewis was going to absolutely smack the shit out of them all, so I got my phone out and started filming. Quinn was known for being cocky, and I was going to send the video to Eddie afterwards saying, "Look at your lad, sorting this posh boy out." Lewis went down and didn't get back up, then Quinn and his mates ran off.'

Everyone in court is stunned.

'What happened after that?'

'I think Lewis must have been giving some friends a ride home because suddenly, some girls were screaming and one of them was on the phone. I think she was calling an ambulance because it was there within minutes. I found out the next day that Lewis was dead. I met Quinn three weeks later and said if he didn't hand himself in to the police, I'd tell Eddie what he'd done, which would certainly be worse than anything the law could throw at him. It was for his own good.'

'Why didn't you just go to the police yourself?'

'I wanted to give him the chance to do it himself. I expected a man – a judge's son – to be morally responsible like that.'

Julian would have buried this if Jack had disclosed it earlier, and Quinn's family would have covered it up. Well played.

'What happened when Mr Smythe came to see you? Was that the first time you'd met him?'

'Yes, it was. Quinn must have told him where I lived. It was well known that my apartment was above the club. I opened the door, and he barged straight in, pushing past me.'

'Where was your female friend at this point?'

'She'd gone into the bedroom with all her clothes. There was no trace of her. He launched straight into a panicked rant about how his son can't go to prison because he has his whole life ahead of him, and how dare I blackmail him.'

'How did he appear, physically?'

'I could smell whisky on his breath. He kept saying his son was about to go to Cambridge to do law, and he wouldn't have me messing that up for him because of a mistake. That's what he called Lewis's murder – a mistake.'

I hear sighs and tuts from around the courtroom as the evidence is given. Jesus, this is risky. He's completely blackening Anton's character here.

'How did you respond?'

'I said it was hypocritical of him to come round here saying that, given he was a judge. I was disgusted, to be honest.'

'What happened next?'

'He kept saying, "How much do you want for the video?" He was offering me stupid amounts of money for it.'

'How much?'

'First, he said five thousand, but the offer kept going up each time I said no. Eight thousand. Ten thousand. Crazy amounts. His last offer was thirty thousand pounds. When I said no to that, he realized I wasn't playing. That's when he became really angry.'

'What made you think he was angry?'

'He started raising his voice and pacing around the kitchen. He just kept saying, "I can't have a criminal son. He can't go to prison." Then it escalated to the point where I got scared.'

'Can you describe exactly what you mean by escalated?'

'He picked up a kitchen knife, which was in one of those wooden knife blocks, you know, for really sharp knives, and pointed it at me. I was standing about four feet away at this point and he was, like, wild, in his eyes. It was as if he had just completely lost control. He said, "Do you know what this will do to his mother?"'

'How did you respond?'

'I held my hands up and said, "Look, I know you're upset, but he needs to do the right thing and go to the police. This isn't my fault. Put the knife down."'

'And did he?'

'Well, he didn't really get the chance.'

'Why not?'

'Because that's when she got involved.'

'Who?'

'I won't say her name. Let's call her, I don't know, let's call her . . . X.'

Taking my advice from all those years ago and saying nothing until trial is the smartest thing Jack has ever done. Everyone's attention is now diverted to *Witness* X. Let's hope she sounds credible to this jury, or Jack is going to prison for the rest of his life.

53

Witness X

Friday, 6 September 2024
10.32 p.m.

YOU COULDN'T MAKE this shit up. Even I couldn't, and I've lied my entire life. I found myself standing behind the bedroom door, wearing only my thong and a T-shirt of Jack's I'd found on the bed. I couldn't close the door properly because the stupid kettlebell – yes, that one – was holding it half open.

Which, of course, meant I heard everything they talked about through the crack where the door met the frame.

I knew nothing about Quinn before that night. I had received a message from Jack earlier in the day saying he really needed to talk to me about something – I now guessed that must have been it. That wasn't what concerned me, though.

The second Anton Smythe walked through that door, my defences shot up. I knew if he saw me, it was over. He would recognize me, yes, but it would go beyond that.

He had the connections to destroy my entire world.

I've been in some sticky situations in my life; hell, I'd put myself into most of them. But it was standing there, my affair so close to being exposed, that I felt true terror. My limbs were shaking uncontrollably.

He wouldn't leave. I watched as Anton got angrier and angrier.

He picked up a knife from the kitchen top and waved it towards Jack. I saw the man I love raise his hands above his head to communicate he wouldn't strike first, and my breath became heavy and fast.

I can't lose him.

What if he gets hurt?

Anton isn't going to stop.

And then, just as I'd feared, he lunged at Jack with the knife in his left hand.

It was instinct. I ran out from behind the door, out of the bedroom, and into the lounge. Yet more evidence of this new person I'd become. The old me would *never* have acted so impetuously. Everything *he* taught me had gone out of the window, and I was overcome by the ugly, messy, human emotions I'd never been allowed to experience before.

The problem with being human is that it leaves you vulnerable. And that is the one thing I was taught not to be.

This is why it's easier to never love anyone. You can't get hurt.

'Stop it!' I shouted. I don't think I'd ever heard my voice sound like that before. I wasn't playing a character. It was just me.

Jack knew I'd signed my death warrant as soon as he heard it. It was too late. I'd revealed myself. Anton looked genuinely shocked to see me. And then he smiled a kind of snarl as he looked me up and down, making sure I knew how much of a slut he thought I was.

For a moment, he seemed to have forgotten that only seconds ago, he was trying to kill someone.

'You know what?' he said, sneering. 'I always knew people couldn't trust you as far as they could throw you.'

And I was propelled back to being a nineteen-year-old girl, being treated like shit by Declan's dad. That time, at least, I was prepared for such an attack. The rules protected me. But in that moment with Anton, I was consumed by emotion. My thoughts were clouded by how I felt for another person.

It was in that moment I understood that abandoning the rules came with a cost, and that love was about to ruin my life.

54

Leila

R v Jack Millman
Day 2
11.05 a.m.

'She came out from the bedroom into the lounge,' Jack tells the court, everyone now gripped by his evidence.

'What was Anton's response to this?' I ask him.

'He was shocked. Panicked.'

'Can you describe what you mean by this?'

'He backed away from me with the knife and . . . stared at her. He realized someone else had heard the conversation about Quinn.'

'Did he recognize X? Were they known to each other?'

Jack pauses for a few seconds. I can see he's mulling something over.

'Not that I'm aware of,' he says firmly, shaking his head slightly. 'I don't think so.'

'What happened next?'

'It was as if he lost it. He started ranting and raving about how I'd set him up by hiding someone in the room. I pointed out he was the one who'd surprised me – that it was *his* son who had committed a crime – but he wouldn't listen. He was shouting, "Give me your phone, I want your phone!" In the moment, I told him I hadn't been able to find it for hours.'

'How did he react to that?'

'He lunged at me again, and we ended up fighting in the kitchen area. He pushed me onto the sideboard, knocking a bottle of Coke that had been on a shelf over me.'

'To confirm, this would account for the brown stain we saw on your T-shirt when you were arrested?'

'Yes,' he says. 'It was all down my T-shirt.'

'And can you tell the jury why your T-shirt was on inside out and back to front?'

'I was in a compromising position when Anton came round. I'd rushed to cover myself up.'

'Thank you for that, Mr Millman. Where was X when you were fighting in the kitchen?'

'She was behind him, screaming at him to stop.'

'At some point, around this time, Mr Smythe's phone records reveal he went into his FaceTime app for thirteen seconds. Can you account for this?'

'I don't know if that's what he did, but when he was ranting, he got his phone out. It might have been then. He didn't talk to anyone, though.'

'What happened next?'

'Mr Smythe carried quite a bit of weight and was able to pin me over the counter. The knife was inches away from my neck when, suddenly, he collapsed.'

'How did that happen?'

'She . . . X . . . hit him on the head with the kettlebell.'

I leave it for a few seconds before continuing.

'How did she react?'

'She was shaking. Scared. But she did it to protect me. She thought he was going to kill me. I knew it was bad straight away. He keeled over and started bleeding from his nose. Neither of us knew what to do.'

'What did you do?'

'I told her to leave. She'd never been in trouble before. Her whole world would collapse if she was found there. She protected me, now I'm protecting her.'

He aims the statement directly at the jury. It's powerful, but what they make of it is anyone's guess.

'And the kettlebell?'

'She'd grabbed the nearest thing she could. I think she put it back. You don't understand how quickly things happened. She's not like me. She doesn't deserve this.'

He's a genuine, caring person. None of this is an act.

'Mr Millman, Quinn Smythe has alleged that you have been harassing him. What do you have to say about this?'

'If by harassing he means urging him to come clean about causing the death of an innocent lad, then yes, I have.'

I momentarily turn to the jury to see how they're receiving this. As far as defendants go, he comes across as honest.

But this evidence sounds far-fetched and ludicrous.

'Earlier in the day on 6 September,' I continue, 'you visited Eddie Sorrington at the Electric Dreams salon. What was the purpose of that visit?'

'I told Quinn when I went to see him at Diamond Lounge that if he didn't go to the police by 12 p.m. the following Friday I'd tell Eddie myself. I'd given him enough time.'

'But you didn't tell him, going by what happened in court today, did you?'

'No. He was busy, and I didn't want to rush it. I needed to find the right time, and that wasn't it. The second I saw Daniella, Lewis's mum, I couldn't do it. They'd been through enough – I couldn't find the words. Quinn should have been the one to tell them, or the police.'

He's finding this painful. He takes a second to catch his

breath and rubs his eyes before straightening, ready for more questions.

'One last thing, Mr Millman. What happened to your phone? Everything you've said could be proved by the content on it.'

'I wish I knew. All I know is that I last had it around 7 p.m. on the night of 6 September and then it vanished. That phone would prove what I'm saying is true.'

'Mr Millman, why didn't you say anything about this in your interview?'

'I've always wanted to tell the truth, but feared I wouldn't get a fair trial because of the powerful people involved. I wanted the jury to hear the full story, not one with pieces of evidence conveniently going missing, like last time.'

'You're referring to the conviction in 2019 when you were convicted of Section 20 grievous bodily harm?'

'Yes. That case also involved high-profile prosecution witnesses.'

'You're also aware, are you not, that by not mentioning this defence before today, the jury will be entitled to draw an adverse inference against you while considering their verdict? They will be permitted to conclude that failure to disclose this defence before now is an indication of your guilt.'

His eyes glance down for a moment, to his hands. He lets out a deep breath.

'I'll take that risk. I'm not prepared to tell you who she is. I love her, and that night she saved my life. I'll do whatever I have to in order to save hers.'

I give his last words a moment to rest with the jury.

'Mr Millman, thank you for your evidence. My learned friend will have some questions for you.'

That's putting it lightly. Julian is going to love this.

55

Witness X

Friday 6 September 2024
10.37 p.m.

'I'd love to say I'm surprised, but that would be a lie,' Anton spat.

The three of us froze, as if we were in some kind of stand-off.

'Anton,' I said quietly, to calm a situation that was already completely out of control. 'Let's just all settle down. It's a bit out of hand, isn't it?'

'How much did you hear?' he interrupted.

'Nothing,' I said, quickly. 'I ran in there when you came in. I don't know what this is about and I don't care. I'd really love for us just to walk away from this and keep the whole thing to ourselves.'

We both knew I'd heard everything. But I was searching, grasping for a way out.

Looking at Jack, I wondered if Anton was also considering it. We could all agree to move on and say nothing. Anton would get what he came for and our secrets would remain safe.

That's when he saw it.

The phone resting against the TV, still recording.

'What's that?' he asked, pointing at it.

Jack and I glanced at each other, knowing exactly how it looked.

'Are you . . . ? Is this . . . ? Are you setting me up?' he growled. 'You're filming this?'

'No,' Jack said. 'That has nothing to do with you.'

'Planning on making a feature film? First, my son. Now, me?'

'It's not what it looks like,' Jack pleaded with him. 'How could it be? I didn't even know you were coming here!'

'I don't believe you,' Anton said, reaching into his jacket pocket, pulling out his own phone and fiddling with it. His words were calm, but his body spoke a different language. His rapid, loud breaths and shaking hands showed me all I needed to know: he had shot past the point of reason, and this was incredibly dangerous territory.

'What are you doing?' I asked.

'FaceTiming your husband,' he said casually.

An atomic bomb landed on my chest.

'What?' My breath was snatched away. I could barely force the word out. 'You don't have his number. You don't know him that well.'

I tried to sound unafraid and brave, but I knew he was capable of it. I was seconds away from being obliterated.

'You'd be surprised.' He snorted, his face contorted with anger.

'Put the phone down, Anton. Please. Look – you don't understand. It's hard to explain, but please don't. It'll ruin me, please don't do this,' I cried, as desperation stomped over my pathetic attempt to appeal to his better nature. 'Please, *please* . . . I'm begging you!'

The second the words left my mouth, *his* face flashed in front of my eyes. A look of disgust I had seen many times as a child. My father's.

Never beg. Always be the one in control.

Anton looked up from his phone for a second, considering it. His dark eyes landed on mine. He would have seen the fear, the terror I was unable to hide. What he did next changed all of our lives for ever.

'Fuck you. Both of you,' he said, tapping on his phone, placing us mere seconds away from my husband learning everything. Placing me in terrible danger.

Jack lunged at him, causing the phone to fall to the floor. Running to it, I noticed Anton had only got so far as his contacts in the FaceTime app.

I watched as they struggled in the kitchen. Before I even knew what was happening, I grabbed the kettlebell, the nearest heavy thing I could see. Swinging it with every ounce of strength I had, I carried it through the air until it connected with Anton's head.

It made the most disgusting sound, one I will never forget. He fell straight to the floor.

I knew, right then, that I had killed him.

Good girl, Dad whispered in my ear. *He deserved it.*

56

Leila

R v Jack Millman
Day 2
11.29 a.m.

'YOU'RE A LIAR, aren't you, Mr Millman?'
Julian goes straight in with an aggressive approach, just as I knew he would. It's something he's known for. We're told in law school 'cross-examine, don't examine crossly', but some advocates shine this way. That's why he was briefed in this case – it needed this approach.

This is going to be excruciating to witness.

'I'm not.'

'You're a liar *and* a fantasist.'

'No.'

'Do you honestly expect these twelve intelligent members of the jury to believe this ludicrous story you've told under oath?'

He stretches the question out, an octave higher than his normal speaking range, emphasizing every word. He signposts his arm out to the jury when he says it for maximum effect, as if Jack doesn't know who they are.

'It's the truth.'

'It's quite a story. Well thought out, I'll give you that,' Julian remarks. 'You had an opportunity to tell it to the police the second you were arrested, but you didn't, did you?'

'No.'

'You could have told them in interview, couldn't you?'

'I didn't have to say anything in interview, actually.'

'If you were innocent, that would have been the time to hold your hands up and say, "It wasn't me, I didn't do this, this is why I am innocent." But you didn't, did you?'

'No.'

'And the reason you haven't mentioned it is because you've made it up between then and now, haven't you?'

'No. Like I said, I wanted to have a fair trial. I didn't want evidence being tampered with. Things and people tend to go missing when you're dealing with powerful people.'

Jack stands firm in the witness box, hands together in front of him. Confident but not cocky.

'Oh, yes. Let's dive into this. You're talking about your previous conviction for s.20 GBH assault, which I have permission to bring into evidence. Members of the jury, in 2019, the defendant was convicted following a trial for a violent offence against a man that caused him severe injuries. In that trial, the defendant argued he was defending a woman from being sexually assaulted when the offence took place. You do like telling elaborate tales, don't you, Mr Millman?'

'No, just the truth. And you missed the part about how the "victim" I assaulted was one of the most dangerous criminals in the north-east,' Jack says, facing the jury.

'Can you tell this jury, Mr Millman, if the woman you were allegedly defending gave evidence in that trial?'

'She didn't. That's my point.'

'And were you convicted of that offence?'

'Yes.'

'After a trial, no less?'

'Yes, but—'

'So, the jury in that case heard all of the evidence, including your story, and they still convicted you?'

'Yes.'

'In other words, they decided you weren't worthy of belief in that case?'

'It wasn't a fair trial.'

'But this one is, presumably?'

'I hope so.'

Julian delivers one of his smug looks to the jury.

'Mr Millman, you do find yourself placed in sticky situations, don't you? Quite the knight in shining armour. Forever at the mercy of the law, saving young women. It's becoming quite a habit of yours, isn't it?'

'I don't know what you mean.'

'If convicted of this offence, you'll receive life imprisonment. Say you *were* completely innocent. You'd be prepared to risk that *for a woman*?'

'For the woman I love, yes.'

'That's a very bold and unrealistic claim to make, isn't it?' Julian sneers, directing the question to the jury.

'I don't know what the relationship with your wife is like, Mr Kesler, but I'd do anything to protect the woman I love.'

'Mr Millman,' the judge interrupts.

Sharp intakes of breath and a few sniggers bounce around the courtroom. A quick glance at the jury confirms it; they all know Julian is my husband. They would have seen the newspaper articles; it's common knowledge. Their eyes flick between the two of us to see our reactions.

But I know one thing: Julian does not like being laughed at. He will make Jack pay for that. Julian firmly places his hands on the sides of the lectern in front of him. His knuckles turn white. His blue notebook sits open for reference, but he doesn't need it.

'This story you've told us, casting allegations against the victim's son, Quinn. Do you understand how serious it is?' Julian asks.

'Yes.'

'You say that Mr Smythe initially came to your home to ask for the video, for which he offered to pay you a large sum of money?'

'Yes.'

'You claim that Quinn knew of the existence of this video, and that it caused him anxiety?'

'It did, yes.'

'This is the one thing that can prove you're telling the truth. Something tangible, something these jurors can physically see. The one piece of evidence that would exonerate you. Your phone. Where is it?'

'I don't know.' Jack shrugs.

Julian turns, slowly, to glance at the jury again. It's theatrically done, intended to convey his sheer disbelief. *I don't believe this man, and neither should you.* It's convincing.

What a fucking disaster.

'The one piece of evidence . . . no, I'll rephrase that. The *most important* piece of evidence in this trial, and you've, what? Mislaid it?'

'I last saw my phone around 7 p.m., about three hours before Anton came round.'

'Yes, you sent a text message to X at that time.'

'It went missing after that.'

'Where were you?'

'I was working, so I was in the club. Innocence, not Temptation. That doesn't open until 10 p.m.'

'What do you suppose happened to it? Because cell site places it at the premises where you live until 10.41 p.m.'

'I don't know. And the "premises where I live" is also a nightclub and bar. It was the last weekend before the kids went away to uni, so we were jam-packed. Maybe it fell out of my pocket, and someone took it.'

'It just happened to jump out of your pocket? This vital piece of evidence with a video on it that supposedly showed a man killing someone?'

'Yes.'

'Very convenient, isn't it? A bit too convenient, wouldn't you say?'

'Decidedly *inconvenient* for me, if I'm being honest,' Jack replies, directing his answer to the jury.

'You didn't like Quinn Smythe, did you?'

'I had no issue with him until what happened with Lewis.'

'Coincidence, is it, that his father sent you to prison in 2014?'

'It is, yes.'

'Quinn says you were threatening him.'

'Why would I do that? I had no reason to. If anything, he was aggressive towards me when I suggested he go to the police.'

'Another lie, isn't it, Mr Millman? All you've told this jury today is lies, haven't you?'

'No. Only truth.'

Julian takes a moment to pause. Everyone in court catches their breath.

'You were brought up in care, weren't you? Abandoned by your parents. It's fair to say you don't trust people, isn't it?'

Jack takes a long breath before answering. Where is Julian going with this?

'I suppose so.'

'You have a cynical view of the world. You're a bit of a lone wolf, aren't you?'

No, Julian. Please.

He's repeating what I said to him on his birthday weekend at Barkenfield Lodge. I remember it so clearly. Buttering me up beforehand, telling me how talented I was as a pupil, making me feel safe. Telling me it was normal to chat about cases, so long as you didn't cross a line.

The absolute bastard.

'I don't think that's unreasonable, given where I've come from,' Jack replies, with more grace and dignity than my rat of a husband will ever have.

'No,' Julian says, with the most patronizing tone in his voice, 'but it's made you resentful, hasn't it? Of people who have the life you don't. You wanted revenge against the man who stole your liberty, and you saw fit to execute that through his son, didn't you?'

'I'd never do that,' Jack replies, calmly.

'It was you who used that kettlebell to kill Mr Smythe, wasn't it?'

'No.'

'And you attempted to cover up the offence by placing it back as a doorstop, didn't you?'

'I've told you – it wasn't me.'

'Let's pretend for a moment that your version of events is true. I'll indulge it. Answer this, please. How long did you and your lover wait between striking this man with a kettlebell and calling the ambulance?'

He's going in for the kill.

'I don't know. I wasn't watching the clock. It was a very intense time,' he tells the court, rubbing the back of his neck with his hand. He's starting to feel the pressure now, and who can blame him? This is horrific.

'Was it, really? It sounds frightening, especially for Mr Smythe, who is now dead. Let me ask you this – did you check for any signs of life?'

'I can't remember,' he says, quietly.

'But you remember telling your lover to leave so she wouldn't get into trouble. What else did you talk about?'

'Nothing. There wasn't time. She got her stuff and left.'

'And then you called 999 from the club landline?'

'Yes.'

'Mr Smythe opened up FaceTime at 10.39 p.m. but you didn't call 999 until 11.07 p.m. What on earth were you – and your lover – doing for twenty-eight minutes?'

'As I said, I can't remember. We were in shock.'

'Isn't it right that the reason you didn't call an ambulance straight away is because you wanted Anton Smythe to die?'

'No,' he reaffirms.

'Something else happened in the room that night that doesn't add up here, and you needed to ensure that whatever it was didn't leave that room. Isn't that right?'

'No, I've told you everything.'

'There's no reason why you wouldn't call an ambulance straight away. The only reason would be that you wanted him dead.'

'That's not true.'

'And you needed him dead so he wouldn't be able to tell the police what happened, and that you attempted to kill him.'

'No,' he says, looking up at the ceiling. His tone is defensive now. His voice, louder. Careful, Jack.

'As for this lover of yours, she doesn't exist, does she? Or if she does, she wasn't there.'

'Yes, she was.' He nods, the faintest hint of irritation coming through.

'It's frankly absurd to suggest that you'd go through all of this for someone else. To put your liberty on the line without any guarantee it would work out in the end.'

'That's your opinion,' he tells Julian.

Please let this be over soon.

'Isn't it fair to say that you care more about protecting yourself or this *woman* of yours than carrying out justice for Anton Smythe's family?'

'True justice would be having Quinn Smythe take responsibility for what he's done. If he had, his father wouldn't be dead,' Jack snaps.

It's a bold statement, and I see why he made it, but it doesn't land well. It comes across as cold, uncaring, and, well, the kind of thing a killer would say. Julian got what he went in for. While Jack was calm and collected for the most part, all it takes is one sentence to throw the rest of the evidence off. One sentence the prosecution can hang their entire closing speech on. And that was it.

'No further questions, Your Ladyship,' Julian declares. He doesn't even bother trying to hide the smirk on his face.

'Re-examination, Miss Reynolds?'

No, thank you. I'm not making this worse than it is.

'None, My Lady,' I reply.

Jack is taken back into the dock as Julian sits quietly a few benches away. I refuse to look at him directly. He thinks he's decimated us.

Well, I'm not done yet.

'Who is your next defence witness, Miss Reynolds?'

'Your Ladyship, the defence asks for leave to recall Quinn Smythe to the witness box.'

Because, while Julian has been looking incredibly smug, sitting at the opposite end of the advocates' bench, what he didn't realize was that he just handed me a grenade.

And I'm about to pull the pin.

57

Leila

R v Jack Millman
Day 2
12.14 p.m.

I WATCH AS ALL twelve jurors shift to sit up straight as Quinn Smythe makes his way back into the witness box. They are intrigued. Eager to hear his side of the story. Good. At least I have their attention. He looks a lot less sure of himself than he did before.

'Mr Smythe, before we begin,' the judge speaks, 'I remind you that you are under oath. Do you understand what that means?'

'Yes.'

'That it is a criminal offence to lie to this court?'

'Yes,' he replies, quietly. He keeps his head down, refusing to look at anyone.

I need to approach this very carefully. Quinn Smythe has just become our most important witness.

'Mr Smythe, you've heard what Mr Millman said. After you gave your evidence, you listened to him make some very serious allegations against you, particularly in relation to the death of Lewis Sorrington.'

'My Lady,' Julian stands up and interrupts. 'This trial concerns the murder of Anton Smythe, this witness's father.

Tragic though it may be, the death of this other boy is not this court's concern.'

'Your Ladyship,' I respond, robustly, 'this issue is pivotal to the defendant's case. It sheds light on why Mr Smythe was at Mr Millman's home to begin with and illustrates his state of mind. Of establishing a threat to the defendant. It is relevant.'

'I'll allow it,' the judge says. 'Tread carefully, Miss Reynolds. I know where you're going with this. Mr Smythe, before you answer anything further, I must warn you that as a witness in these proceedings, you are entitled to avoid any self-incrimination and therefore may refuse to answer any questions that would put you at risk of criminal prosecution. Do you understand?'

'Yes,' he says. I watch his chest quickly rise and fall. He's trying to appear calm, but he knows I'm onto him.

I dive straight in.

'Quinn Smythe, are you responsible for the death of Lewis Sorrington?'

He grips the side of the witness box.

'No,' he says, immediately. 'There's no evidence of it. It's his word against mine.'

'Is it?' I ask.

'Yes. He has no proof.'

'Have you told the truth during this trial?'

'Yes,' he says, looking at the jury. He can't look at me.

'When you gave your evidence yesterday, I asked if you'd ever met Jack Millman outside of Innocence. Do you remember what your answer was?'

'I said I hadn't.'

'Can you confirm you had taken the oath before you gave your evidence?'

'I did.'

'My Lady, with permission, I'd like to play a short piece of CCTV to the jury.'

Julian shoots up from his seat. 'Your Ladyship, we have had no notice of this,' he barks.

'My Lady, this piece of film had no relevance until Mr Millman gave his evidence-in-chief and was so skilfully cross-examined by Mr Kesler. During Mr Millman's evidence, matters came to light that have necessitated the introduction of this CCTV into evidence.'

The judge's eyes flit between Julian and me.

'I'll allow it, in the interest of justice,' she says.

It's the CCTV footage from when Jack went to visit Quinn at Diamond Lounge a week before Anton was killed. Both figures can easily be identified in the recording. Quinn looks anxious and heightened, gesticulating in a way that comes across as wild. Aggressive, almost. Jack, in contrast, steps back and holds his hands up. Taking a glance at Julian as it plays, I recognize that he's livid he didn't catch this. There's no way he would have considered Quinn important enough to comb through his work CCTV. One thing that the footage makes clear is that Jack is in no way acting in a threatening manner.

'Can you tell the jury who the two men in that clip are?' I ask the witness, who is reluctant to answer.

'Me . . .'

'Yes, and who else?'

'Jack.'

'The man *you* said you'd never met before outside of the club. You said when you gave evidence to this court that *he* had been intimidating *you*. Your barrister called Mr Millman a liar when he put forward that it was *you* who had been behaving threateningly towards *him*. He's certainly not threatening you here, is he? In fact, if anyone looks angry in this video, it's you.'

Quinn doesn't say anything.

'Did you forget that you'd met him, or was it a lie?'

'It . . . you don't understand—'

'It was a deliberate lie, wasn't it? Everything Jack has told the court today is true, isn't it?'

'My dad has been killed and all you're bothered about is this?' he yells, swiping his arm towards Jack.

'Please tell the court where you were on the night your father died.'

'I was at work. My final shift before I left for uni.'

'And after that?'

'Innocence Bar. We always went on Friday nights. Everyone from school did, it was the place to be. But, also, why would I go to the place where I'd allegedly killed someone? Explain that to me!'

'Why would you want to go to a bar where one of the bouncers was intimidating you?'

It silences him. He knows his story doesn't add up.

'I'd have been the only one not going. I wasn't going to let *him* ruin my final night at home.'

'What time were you at Innocence until?'

'Not late. I was driving because I went there straight from work and I had to travel to Cambridge the next day. I didn't stay long.'

'Where did you go after you left?'

'I went home around 11 p.m. I was with Mum when she got the phone call about my father, and we went to the hospital. Look, you can't frame me for anything.'

'Tell me – how long were you in Innocence?'

'Why is this relevant? You can't do this to me! I'm one of the victims here. You have no evidence, except the word of a known criminal. Unless his phone turns up, which apparently has a video with me on it, you've got nothing. And even that won't show what he's claiming.'

'You're quite right, Quinn. That phone has been the one thing in this trial that none of us can pin down. I was hoping *you*, perhaps, saw something, given you were there the night it went missing.'

He doesn't even realize he's about to completely drop himself in it.

This is one of the reasons I became a barrister. The feeling I have now. Just before I land my biggest blow to this case, I wait, in silence, goading him into delivering the information himself. It has more impact with a jury than if I say it.

'Are you suggesting I stole it?'

And there it is. A quick glance at the jury tells me their suspicion is growing. Brows start to rise.

'What?' I ask him, surprised. 'Stole a phone, which happened to have a video incriminating you in a serious crime that, if seen by police, would send you to prison?'

Like most witnesses, he sees too late the path I've taken him down. Chester was right – I'm good at what I do. The colour drains from Quinn's face, and the jury see it, too. I turn to look at them, just to make the point. *Are you seeing this? Hearing these lies?*

'I didn't take it. I swear, I honestly didn't,' he says, flustered. His eyes jump between me and the jury, begging us to believe him. We don't.

'Just one final point, Quinn, then I'll let you go. Can you tell the jury which village you live in? Please don't give out the actual address.'

He doesn't want to say it. He knows where I've taken him now, and he's got no way out.

'Pickford,' he says quietly, staring at me, unable to hide his contempt.

'Could you speak up for the jury, please?'

'Pickford,' he repeats, louder.

'It's right to say, isn't it, that Pickford is a very small village, twelve miles north of Durham?'

'Yes,' he says in a tiny voice.

'Mr Millman's phone sent out a signal at 11.27 p.m. on the night your father died from Pickford before either being switched off or the battery died. In fact, the signal came a few metres away from your house. Are you sure you didn't take it? Is that a complete coincidence?'

His eyes dart between me and the jury. They plead with every juror to be on his side.

'It's a coincidence.'

I deliver a broad smile to him because I want him to know he's lost. I don't believe him and I'm certain the jury won't either.

'No further questions, My Lady.'

Quinn remains in the witness box for a few seconds, as if he wants to redo his evidence, but it's too late. The usher walks over and gently places her arm on Quinn's, indicating he needs to leave. Julian looks enraged.

'My Lady,' I say, loudly. 'That closes the defence case.'

'Very well,' she agrees. 'I am conscious both advocates have speeches to write, so I will adjourn for today. Be back at 10.30 a.m. in the morning.'

As soon as she leaves the bench, I almost collapse from the adrenalin. I'm beyond grateful for a slightly early finish. Cases have been won on closing speeches alone, so it's vital this one is exceptional. I need to start writing.

Walking out of the lift onto the ground floor of Crown Court, I pass the reception desk and hear someone call my name.

'This was left for you, Miss Reynolds,' the lady says, handing me a white envelope with my name and chambers written on the front in black ink.

Forcing my finger under the flap, I rip it open and pull out a card. It's an illustration of two cartoony matchsticks holding hands with cute faces and fire for hair. Above them it says: 'Twin Flames Forever!' I think I might throw up.

My hands shake as I open it.

> Saw this and thought of you. I bet I'm the only person who can say that. Pretty sure none of your lawyer chums know about your pyro skills. Really hope your husband doesn't find out. Sexy, isn't he? Ironic you're defending murderers these days when you are one yourself. I wonder what Jack would think of that.

Fuck.

Not now. Please not now. Although I recognize the delivery of the card is perfectly timed. Predictable, really, if I'd thought about it hard enough. But I've been so focused on this case, I've let things slip.

It's all part of her game, of course.

One I can't afford to lose.

58

Leila

5.27 p.m.

It makes sense she'd time her revenge so it'd coincide with the biggest case of my career. There's no way to stop it now. It's coming.

Soon. That's what she's telling me with this note. She's closing in on me.

I have to secure an acquittal for Jack first. Then I'll deal with her. I can't let him down.

When I arrive home, the house is cold. I feel sick but I'm starving. Everything in my body is telling me there's an imminent threat, but I'm also expected to save a man's life via an intelligent, well-crafted closing speech in the next seventeen hours.

Usually, when conducting a trial, you work backwards; figure out the main points you want to tell a jury in your closing speech, then work out how to get there by eliciting that evidence throughout the trial. You can prepare the bare bones of a closing submission before the trial even starts.

Usually.

This case has been monumentally difficult to prepare. The speech will keep me up all night and will have to be delivered perfectly in court against the backdrop of the timebomb ticking quietly in my ear, not knowing when – or where – she is going to strike.

One thing I can't work out is this: she's always had enough ammunition to destroy my life. Always. That's why the timing of everything now makes me nervous. She's clearly waited so the wound would be so crushing, so intimate, I'd never recover.

I get that.

But the recent messages also point towards Jack. They all seem to be connected to his case. How could that possibly be?

Then, a thought flashes through my head, so vile I physically have to close my eyes to get rid of it.

She wouldn't. Could she?

It can't be that. Please don't let it be that.

As hellish, unpalatable thoughts begin to consume my brain, my breathing becomes rapid and I stand, leaving my case papers and laptop on the dining-room table where I've set up to write my speech. It will have to wait.

Always be prepared for things to go tits up.

I need to check something.

As I'm about to leave the house, Julian arrives. He dumps his bag onto the floor in the hallway and walks into the dining room. He says nothing, just stands with his hands in his pockets, looking at me.

'What?' I ask, barely able to entertain whatever he has to say. I have bigger things to worry about.

'Very convenient you had the CCTV of Quinn to hand over after Millman's explosive revelations.'

'I don't know what you mean,' I say, putting my shoes on.

'You knew he'd met Jack before. You didn't raise it with him initially.'

'The CCTV only became relevant to my client's defence following his evidence.'

'And you found out about this mystery woman the same time as the rest of us.'

'What's your problem?' I snap at him.

'It all just ran a bit too . . .'

'What?'

'Smooth for my liking.'

I laugh, raising my eyebrows. He knows I've done something sneaky; it takes one to know one.

'Smooth? Yes, a bit like how Quinn worked out on his own that Jack had been harassing him, which suddenly gave Anton a motive for being there that night. As you say, smooth.'

God forbid I question *his* professional integrity.

'You know, Julian, one of the first things you taught me was how to use the opposition's own witnesses against them. I was always taught – *you* always taught me – it's much more powerful than using your own. You know what's even better than that? When you're the one who dictates whether they're used at all.'

The penny drops. He understands what's happened. It's not in his nature to show emotion on his face, but even he can't hide the anger that's swelling in his eyes right now.

'What did you call Quinn, Julian? A "smoking gun"? Only because I pulled the trigger and led you straight to him. I needed him in that witness box. You shouldn't have underestimated me.'

Julian is not used to getting played in trials. He's usually the one pulling the strings. But I've outsmarted him here. He will make me pay for it, but right now, I couldn't care less.

'One murder trial in and you think you're King's Counsel?' he says, mocking me. 'It takes more than flashy tricks to be good at this, darling.'

'Oh! But I thought it was all about the drama? Isn't that what you said?'

He's seeing a side of me he isn't used to, and he's unsure how to react. He stands, watching me, jaw muscle flickering.

'You know what I think?' I tell him. 'I think you don't like that your wife might actually win this trial. This *hopeless* trial.'

I don't believe I will, but I'm enjoying provoking him. What have I got to lose? It's all going to come crashing down soon enough because of her anyway.

'There's no way the jury will buy this nonsense,' he scoffs. 'This woman? I mean, who is she?'

'I know who she is,' I say, confidently, walking towards him.

'You do?' he asks, with a genuine air of intrigue in his voice. 'Who?'

I drag the silence out for a few seconds, allowing his face to rest fully so I can see his reaction when I say it.

'Demi Vernon.'

He seems taken aback at the suggestion but doesn't say anything. I think he's trying to work out if I'm serious or not. I watch his face; it stiffens slightly.

'Demi?' he repeats, his face now animated, as though he's recovered and is back to full function again. 'Having an affair with a criminal? Why on earth would you think that?'

'She fits the bill – married, and I can imagine she and Chester have a toxic relationship. You wouldn't want to mess with Chester, would you? The weekend Anton died, she was acting in the *strangest* way at his birthday drinks. Asking about the case and, I know this sounds bizarre, but she avoided you at the party. Actively moved away from you whenever you were near her. Isn't that *weird*?'

'That's what you're basing this on?'

'Not quite,' I shoot back. I don't take my eyes off him. 'Chester told me months ago he suspected she'd been having an affair.'

'He said that?'

'Yes. He didn't know who it was, but you know him – he doesn't let things go. He said he wouldn't be made a fool of. Said when he found out who it was, he'd make their life hell.'

'This is all coincidence, surely.' The mean tone in his voice moments ago has vanished. He's trying to steer me away from this, just as I knew he would.

'And now she's twenty weeks pregnant, which means the baby was conceived around the time of the murder. Took her months to tell him. I bet it's not even his . . . Chester has doubts, too. He's not stupid.'

'So, what are you saying? That Demi is carrying Jack Millman's child? Can you hear yourself?'

I shrug my shoulders and laugh.

'Well, it's either his . . . or *yours*.'

It doesn't happen often. In fact, I don't think it ever has before now, but Julian Kesler has nothing to say.

Nothing.

He takes a few seconds to recalibrate, aware he needs to talk his way out of this very carefully.

'Jesus Christ, Leila!' He fake-laughs. 'Your paranoia is something else! I'm sleeping with Chester's wife now?'

'It'd be easier if you just admitted it. Don't make me get the evidence out.'

'I don't know what you're—'

'OK.' I sigh. 'I'll show you.'

I get my phone from my bag and open the photos app. Scrolling through, I select the screenshots I airdropped from Demi's WhatsApp chat straight to mine, which had been safely in my handbag the whole night, not at Audrey's. Theatrically clearing my throat before I begin, I read them out, occasionally looking up at him – my husband – who is grasping for something, *anything*, to say in this moment.

I wasn't stupid enough to leave this up to chance; I took a screenshot of the number beside the messages he sent. He'd obviously removed her as a contact to communicate to her, rather brutally, that it was over. A common tactic he used to employ back when he was single, before we started dating.

'Did you think I wouldn't work it out?' I ask.

Even now, with his wife calling out his infidelity, I can tell Julian is thinking what a massive inconvenience this is, for me to accuse him the night he has to write the best closing speech of his career.

Let's be honest, neither of us has time for this bullshit.

'It was nothing,' he says, robotically.

'Nothing?' I parrot back to him, just to ensure I've heard correctly. 'Is that what you'd really call this? Nothing?'

'After six years, Leila? Really?' he asks, his tone aggressive. 'You're prepared to throw our marriage away over this? I don't want anything to do with her.'

My mind plays back to the time I came downstairs and heard him on the phone.

'That's who you were talking to that night, isn't it? I heard you, in the kitchen.'

'I've made it very clear to Demi that it's over. I don't love her. I feel nothing for her, and she can't prove the kid's mine anyway.'

'It's irrelevant whether you love her or not and, trust me, Julian, if she says it's yours, it will be,' I say, firmly. I'm not exactly Demi's biggest fan in this moment, but his insistence on simply discarding her – the woman carrying his child – makes me sick. 'Tell me, Julian, what was it I didn't do? Because I think I've been a pretty good wife.'

'Jesus, Leila!' he shouts, raising his arms into the air, exasperated. 'It had nothing to do with you! It was a mistake. *She* was a mistake.'

No sincere apology, no begging for forgiveness, no remorse. The entire thing is a chore for him. He's never taken accountability for anything in his life.

'And now you're going to pay for it. I wonder if your divorce solicitor will do you a "Buy One Get One Free" deal.'

My body reacts as I say it. My hands start shaking and a lead weight lands in my stomach. Adrenalin shoots through my veins at lightning speed.

Julian looks at me, confused. I know what he's doing, making me feel I'm overreacting. He's good at this.

'Why do we have to get divorced?' Julian asks in a quiet voice, frowning at me as if I've said the most nonsensical thing in the world.

I swallow hard. My heart races.

'You must be joking,' I reply, calmly.

'Nobody needs to know.'

This was always going to be his reaction. Be strong.

'I know. I'll never be able to trust you again.'

He slowly walks over to the dining table and pulls out one of the chairs. Taking a deep breath as he sits down, he locks his eyes onto mine and pauses. He knows I'm intimidated by him when he's like this.

He's always known.

'Maybe I won't give you a divorce,' he says, casually. 'Perhaps I'll just keep you around, like a pet.'

The blood in my body turns cold.

'What?'

My voice cracks. I use every ounce of strength I have to prevent tears gathering in my eyes. If he sees them, he's won.

'I'm in no rush for a divorce.' He shrugs. 'Sounds like you can't wait to get away from me. Yes, I think it might be better to keep you around.'

'You can't do that,' I say, shaking my head.

'Of course I can,' he says, a hint of amusement in his voice. 'If I wanted to, I could make it my life's mission to ensure you're not happy, Leila.'

The threat lingers in the ravine between us, along with everything else that remains unsaid. I have, of course, seen this side of Julian many times before, but never dared confront it.

'This is what you did to Sienna, isn't it?' I tell him. 'That's why she never spoke about you – she was just so relieved to get away from you. She didn't leave you for another man – she just wanted a life without you in it.'

'Sienna was a crazy bitch.' He laughs. It's the same line he's peddled for years.

'And you couldn't stand it, could you? It didn't make sense to you, a woman daring to leave you without a reason. So, you created one and made sure everyone knew it. All those times you begged me not to cheat on you like she did. Not only was it a lie but you were doing that very thing to me. That's top-tier hypocrisy, Julian.'

'I never told anyone she cheated on me,' he says, holding his hands up, feigning innocence.

'You heavily implied it. The truth is, you need women around so you can manipulate them to make you feel powerful.'

Audrey was right.

'I'm pretty sure everyone we know would disagree with that.'

'Yes, they would. Because outside these walls, you're a model husband. They don't see what I see. I used to idolize you.'

'Oh, give it a rest, would you?' he fires back. 'Spare me the victim speech. You haven't done too badly out of this. You think you'd be getting briefed in murders and high-profile cases if you weren't my wife? The fact is, Leila, you're an average barrister at best, and that's being kind. You only do well because you're attractive. Jurors like you, I'll give you that. But you wouldn't have achieved what you have without me, and you know it.'

Julian is the kind of man who chooses what comes out of his mouth very carefully, as all barristers do. He knows that saying this, right now, is going to throw me off. That's the intended consequence.

I want to scream. I want to cry, rage, and hurl abuse about betrayal, deceit, what a massive dick he is. But I don't.

'I need to go out,' I say, quietly. 'I don't know how long I'll be. Good luck with your speech.'

As I walk out of the door with my case papers and laptop, Chester's voice echoes in my head. *Trials aren't won on facts, it's all about likeability.*

I think this speech requires a change in direction.

59

Leila

6.26 p.m.

'Delilah? Is that you?'

I freeze in the dark hallway. Audrey's frail little voice carries through the air like a bird tweeting first thing in the morning. It's not that which scares me, but the name she calls out.

Opening the door to the lounge, I see she's sitting on the sofa with a pink blanket over her knees.

'I know you weren't expecting me tonight, Audrey. I've just come to collect something. I didn't mean to frighten you, but you left the door unlocked again. You promised me you were going to start locking it.'

'I thought you were Delilah.'

There it is again.

It's impossible to determine what's real and what's fantasy with Audrey. She flits so quickly from one to the other, often within the same sentence. But this feels real. I don't believe in coincidences.

'Who's Delilah, Audrey?'

'She's the girl you've been sending over to help me.'

Time stands still. All the life in my body is sucked out in a split second. I become a shell, a decimated, lifeless, walking corpse.

She *was* here.

'What?' I whisper, my breath staggered.

'We went to the park together. And she keeps playing Tom Jones!'

'What does she look like?' I ask Audrey, urgently.

'Black hair. One of those short bobs. I told her she wears too much lipstick.'

A tsunami of fear washes over my entire body. She's not just close, she's fucking here already.

'How long has she been coming?'

'Ooh, maybe a few weeks?'

'What has she been talking to you about, Audrey?'

'All sorts of things. She liked hearing all about you and Julian. I told her you got married in Italy. I showed her all your wedding photos.'

A chill runs down my spine when I think of her invading my life like this, having access to me after so many years. After everything that happened.

'But really, she spent a lot of time helping me tidy up the spare rooms.'

And suddenly it all becomes so obvious why she's doing this. Why hadn't I seen it before now? Her plan reveals itself to me with full clarity.

'The spare rooms?' I'm not sure how I manage to speak at all.

'Especially the small one at the front. She was in that one for a while.'

And *just like that. Game over.*

Keep calm.

Turning around, I leave the room and fumble for the light switch in the hallway. I flick it on and the huge chandelier bursts into illumination as I sprint up the stairs onto the landing.

The front bedroom door is unusually ajar.

My heart races at the possibility of what I will find.

The old mahogany wardrobe door is wide open. Audrey's dresses from years gone by are neatly lined up, displaying bright colours of swishy chiffon, peacock blue, hot pink, and canary yellow. My eyes are drawn to a corner of the wardrobe floor. Surrounded by old shoes sits a small metal box with a digital display on the front.

A safe.

I bought it on Saturday and had the locksmith attach it to the wardrobe.

I'm too late. She's been in here.

I walk over, defeated. When I place my finger on the side of the safe door, it swings open without any resistance whatsoever. It's empty, except for a piece of white paper with writing on in black ink.

Rule #1: Don't Get Caught

60

Witness X

Can anyone really change? That's the ultimate question, isn't it? Is anyone capable of becoming a better person?

What even *is* 'a better person'? Better than what?

I used to think I'd know it when I saw it, or sense when it happened – a warm glow on my skin indicating I was somehow healed, somehow better. But it didn't work like that. If anything, everything just became messier. I've lost count of the many versions of myself I've shown people over the years. Each one was a new attempt at survival.

A liar. A manipulator. A predator.

For so many years I've blamed the person who made me this way, but while I continue to do that, how can I become a better person? I've carried that shame and guilt and rage and terror for so long now, it's worn me down.

Yes, I've done terrible things, but I've also done good things. Does that make me a hero or a villain? Guilty or not guilty?

I think, perhaps, it just makes me human.

61

Leila

R v Jack Millman
Day 3
10.30 a.m.

The importance of today weighs heavily on every single person in this courtroom.

I've had, at most, three hours' sleep. Julian and I remained in separate rooms all night; even in the midst of what happened, neither of us can afford any drama before today. I am physically and emotionally wrecked. The bags under my eyes communicate as much. I didn't even use a brush this morning; I simply scraped my hair back into a ponytail (the wig will cover it anyway). My eyeliner looks as if it's been drawn on by a toddler. Never in a million years did I expect the last day of the trial to be like this.

I had an urgent breakfast meeting before court and then literally ran to court just in time to meet Davina, so we could head down to the cells to see Jack.

When they bring him in, I feel an overwhelming sense of emotion and I inhale deeply, while trying to be subtle about it. It will do no good for the others to see how nervous I am. How much this trial means to me, too. We can only work clinically for so long – I have this man's freedom in my hands.

'How are you, Jack?' I enquire. It's a stupid question, but I ask it anyway.

'I didn't sleep well.'

'Neither did I.' I smile. 'You set the court alight yesterday.'

'Yeah, sorry about that.'

'For what it's worth, I think we now have the best chance you'll ever have at being found not guilty. But you never know with a jury. At the end of the day, it all depends on their biases.'

'Whether they believe me or the judge's son?'

'Not technically,' Davina answers. 'It's a case of whether enough doubt has been cast on the prosecution's case. They've heard all the evidence they're going to hear now, so they have to go away and discuss it, then decide. We can only hope we've persuaded at least three of them to question the prosecution enough that they cannot, legally, find you guilty.'

'So, that's it?' he asks, eagerly, facing me. 'No more evidence? That's all the jury will hear?'

I swallow hard. I know he wants something more, but I can't give it to him.

'Yes, that's it.'

He is fidgeting again, scraping his hair back.

'I'm going to be found guilty, aren't I?' he whispers. His breathing has become heavy.

'Jack, it's OK,' I tell him. Placing my hand gently on his arm, I wait until his eyes are level with mine. 'It's going to be OK.'

He nods, quickly, anxious to believe me. To trust me.

'Whatever happens, we will deal with it.'

The truth is, I'm as terrified as he is.

I walk into court a different person from yesterday, as does Julian. The tension in the air feels impossibly thicker than it has over the last two days.

Everyone slots into their positions, making way to start at 10.30 a.m. sharp.

'Mr Kesler,' the judge says, inviting Julian to begin his speech. He looks dreadful, like a man who's been up all night, which he very likely has. Far from the slick pro who appeared on day one of this trial. He now stands before the jury as a tired, unshaven arsehole who requires notes to lead his speech.

The jury still hang on to Julian's words, though, as they always do. Even operating at 50 per cent, he's still a better advocate than most.

'Where is this mystery lover?' he asks during his closing submissions. 'Isn't it ludicrous to suggest that someone who professes to love you would rather risk you being sent to prison for life than admit to a crime they themselves committed? Does that sound like love to you?

'Jack Millman is a liar who commits heinous crimes and then spins elaborate stories in the hope that jurors fall for them. He is untrustworthy. He is a cold-blooded killer. And I invite you to find him guilty of murder.'

Julian emphasizes all the evidence that goes against us: no comment throughout the investigation, the length of time it took to call an ambulance, the bungled attempt to 'hide' the murder weapon, not to mention the sheer unbelievability of Jack's version of events.

Some of them nod along, but others remain stony-faced. Occasionally, some of them turn their heads to look at Jack in the dock, as if thinking, *Are you capable of what he's saying? Are you?*

When he finishes, Julian sits dramatically, swishing his robes out of the way before doing so. I always used to think it was cool. Now I just find it irritating.

Being the advocate closest to the jury box, I stand and turn towards it. I'm about five feet away. All twelve jurors stare at me, waiting for me to convince them my client isn't guilty of murder.

'What kind of man is Jack Millman?' I begin. 'He is the kind of man who has affairs with married women,' I say slowly, making eye contact with every single juror. 'That doesn't sit well with most of you, does it? It doesn't sit well with me, either.

'You may find his relationships unpalatable. You might consider his lifestyle unsettling. But you are not here to judge this man on where his moral compass lies. So, what is this case really about? At the heart of this case is the death of a man, a husband and father. You are tasked with deciding whether Jack Millman murdered Anton Smythe. His defence is simple – "It was someone else." It seems to me this case can be summarized by the following: good people do bad things. Conversely, bad people can also do good things.'

I've hooked them. Each one has locked eyes with me. They don't know where I'm going with this. There are various angles I could have taken. I decided to change tactics at the last minute. I hope it's enough.

'By all accounts, Jack Millman is a "bad" person. As soon as he was old enough to be in it, he entered the prison system. You, like anyone, would have him down as guilty from the off. But he's also the kind of man to be upfront about his past. I could have prevented you, the jury, from knowing all about his background. I could have made an application to stop the prosecution from telling you about his previous convictions, but Jack Millman stopped me. *That's* the kind of person Jack Millman is. Ask yourselves, are those the actions of a man who has anything to hide?

'Jack Millman is the kind of man who, by the Crown's own admission, had the opportunity to flee the scene of this murder, but didn't. He had a window of time to make a run for it but chose to face the police and go willingly to the station. It was he who called 999 to seek medical help.

'So, let me ask the question again. What kind of man is Jack Millman? I would say he is a man who would rather risk life imprisonment for an offence he didn't commit than destroy the life of someone else. He is a man who cares more about protecting a vulnerable, scared woman than his own welfare. And let's not forget the vital piece of evidence in this case – the murder weapon, the kettlebell. DCI Brady himself said it was used by someone who had "no knowledge of evidence or criminal law" and that replacing it by the door was a "poor attempt to manipulate a crime scene". Jack Millman has been in the justice system since he was ten years old. It is nonsensical to suggest he would have made such a rookie mistake.

'How easy it is to judge others from a distance,' I continue. 'It would be easy for me to stand here and paint Anton Smythe as a morally corrupt criminal judge who breached every ethical code by going to visit Jack Millman that night. It would be easy – given Jack Millman's evidence – for me to smear Anton Smythe as a nasty, vindictive, aggressive, privileged toff who deserved what happened to him. That is what the prosecution wants me to say.

'Unfortunately, life is not black and white. It is filled with a spectrum of grey. It is complex, layered, nuanced. And so is this trial. You are not here to cast the easiest judgement. You are here to make the correct one.

'I submit to you that Anton Smythe was a good man, a dedicated husband, and above all, a caring father – and it was this that led him to Jack's flat on that fatal night. No parent wants to see their child in trouble. But he got it wrong. His professional role in the criminal justice system skewed his perception of what action to take, and that was a mistake. Why?

'Because, sometimes, even good people do bad things. We are all flawed. Even Anton Smythe.

'Enter Jack Millman – always choosing the wrong path, always making the wrong decisions. He saw Anton's actions as wrong and refused to cooperate. Ironic, isn't it? Coming from a criminal. But, we have evidence of Jack speaking to Quinn a week before the murder. Something that, crucially, Quinn lied about under oath. The facts are there, ladies and gentlemen. Jack is the one who made the right decision on that night when he refused to take the money Anton Smythe offered him.

'Bad people do good things. Now, there may be some of you who have listened to all of this and thought it nonsense. Too ridiculous, too outrageous to believe. That this is an open-and-shut case.

'I'd say this to you. If someone took a snapshot of any moment in your life, can you guarantee it would be representative of the true situation? Or would it, perhaps, involve a more complicated story? Life is complex. There is a story behind everything.'

Jury speeches don't hinge on facts, they rely on connection. I speak to each and every one of the men and women on the jury and appeal to their human nature. Most people like to think they're nothing like the criminals we hear about, but the truth is we're all only a few steps away from ending up in the dock.

Having laid out my case, I then run through the forensics and evidence of each prosecution witness, pointing out inconsistencies and doubt where I can.

'It is for you to consider, ladies and gentlemen: is Jack a cold-blooded killer? One who struck Anton Smythe with a kettlebell and then sat on his sofa watching him die? Or is it more complicated than that? Was it, in fact, not Jack who killed him at all? The defence says you cannot be sure he is guilty, and I invite you to acquit.'

62

Leila

R v Jack Millman
Day 3
1.14 p.m.

THE JUDGE DIRECTS the jury to the law they must apply to the case and provides a summary of both the prosecution and defence evidence. She reminds them that the prosecution brings this case and must prove it beyond reasonable doubt. Jack Millman is innocent until proven guilty to that standard.

She sets out the elements of murder that must be proved, namely that Jack Millman intended to kill or cause serious harm to Anton Smythe and that harm caused his death.

She reminds the jury they may consider an adverse inference against Jack for failing to mention, before yesterday, the account he gave during the trial.

The judge tells them a unanimous verdict is the only verdict she will accept at this time and that they must elect a foreman or woman to represent the jury and deliver that verdict.

An usher leads them out of the courtroom. And that's it. I can't do anything more.

I can already feel the adrenalin slump kicking in. This is no way to live. This ridiculous job, with its high highs and low lows.

'Well done, Leila!' Davina says, walking over from her position in court.

'How do you think it's gone? Honestly?'

'I don't know, but that was a very impressive speech.'

'Can we grab some coffee? I feel I'm about to collapse,' I say, pulling my wig off. 'Actually, hold on a second.' I dash over to the dock before they take Jack downstairs.

'Are you OK?' I ask.

'Great speech,' he says. 'Got my vote.'

'We're not giving up yet.'

'Good to hear,' he says before being dragged away.

We get called back half an hour later so the judge can send the jury to lunch. But, make no mistake, we are now on red alert waiting for the loudspeaker to ring, announcing a verdict has been reached.

We all return at 2.10 p.m., and the clock starts ticking again. There is literally nothing to do but wait. Except there is something that needs dealing with before I do anything else.

'Can we speak in private?' I say quietly to Julian, who is sitting at one of the tables in the robing room surrounded by his cronies. He barely even registers I'm here. I am nothing to him now.

'When we get home,' he says, tapping away at his laptop.

'No,' I say firmly. 'Now.'

Julian senses the other barristers around him will pick up on the atmosphere if he doesn't come, so he pushes his chair back and follows me into one of the side rooms. It's raining outside and water streams down the floor-to-ceiling glass.

'What did you think of my speech?' I ask.

It irks him. He stands in front of me, puffing his chest out, hands behind his back.

'Leila, what is this?'

'I'm not allowed to ask my pupilmaster for feedback?'

He knows I'm being deliberately obtuse.

'What do you want to talk about?'

'You may have seen I was late into court this morning. I met a friend for a coffee.'

'What's that got to do with me?' He shrugs.

'It was someone you used to know. Sienna Fox.'

He does a sarcastic little laugh and looks out of the window but can't hide the fear that flashes across his face. I know him too well.

'I see. Best friends now, are you?'

'I wouldn't say that, but we did have a good chat. Although you probably should know I accidentally told her about your indiscretion with Demi.'

The smug mask Julian wears most of the time completely drops.

'You what?' he sputters.

'Just slipped out.'

He quickly turns away from me and runs his hands through his hair.

'Jesus Christ, Leila!' he barks. 'Of all people, you told *her*? Do you know how close she is to Chester?'

'I do,' I confirm, calmly. 'That's why I told her.'

He looks at me as if I'm insane.

'What the . . . Leila . . . she's going to fucking ruin me.'

'Yes, she will . . . unless you give me a divorce.'

'What?' he asks, clearly scrambling to find a way out of this unscathed.

'That's all I want. A painless, quick divorce, and neither of us will ever say anything about it. You have my word.'

He walks to the other side of the small room, away from me, and leans against the wall. Julian isn't used to people – especially me – so openly calling the shots. He is accustomed to being in control.

'Why are you doing this?' he asks, seemingly forgetting that less than twenty-four hours ago, he threatened to destroy my life after I discovered he had impregnated another woman.

'Because she's the one person in the world you can't stand, and your fate now rests in her hands. She could destroy you with one phone call. Your reputation would be ruined, and you'd have to leave chambers, probably Durham, and practise in a different part of the country. There's a poetic justice to her having that power, given what you've done to her.'

He knows he's fucked. Defeated. He sighs, loudly.

Checkmate.

'Fine,' he says, quietly.

'Was that a "yes"?' I can't resist.

'For god's sake, Leila! Yes. Let's just be done with it.'

I nod and walk towards the door.

'How did you know?' he asks as I reach for the handle.

'What?'

'How did you find out? About Demi?'

I smile. That's what's bothering him. He can't stand that I figured it out.

'Let's just call it a tip-off. You weren't as discreet as you thought you were,' I tell him. 'You knew she was at our house that night when I thought we were being burgled. You let me believe we were in danger.'

'I wanted nothing to do with her by then. Earlier that evening, she'd told me she was pregnant. Things were left on a bad note. She tried to call me several times about it, but I ignored her. I think she came to the house to scare me, threaten me, get me to talk to her. It backfired because you woke up. She should never have come to our house. I don't know what she was thinking.'

As I turn the door handle, he asks, 'How do I know you'll keep your end of the bargain? That Sienna won't use this opportunity to ruin me, regardless?'

'Because Sienna and I have more integrity than you do,' I tell him, in the way a mother scolds her teenage son. 'And that's enough.'

A smile creeps onto my face as I walk out.

I remember the day Julian signed me off as his pupil. It was the proudest, most satisfying day of my life. That action told the world, 'She's good enough', and his opinion meant more to me than anything.

I walk away from him today – no longer his pupil or his wife – not caring one bit what he thinks of me.

Whatever happens in this trial, I won.

By 4.15 p.m., people are starting to pack their stuff away. The judge will send the jury home at 4.30 p.m. Most of the other courts have closed for the day, and it's only the people involved in Jack's case hanging around.

I hear the click of the loudspeaker amplify through the robing room and my stomach lurches.

'Could all parties in the case of *R v Millman* please report to Court 1 immediately?'

Davina and I look at each other, alarmed.

'A verdict already?' she says.

'Bad news, if so. They'd never acquit this quickly.'

We pick up our bags and rush down, the prosecution team in front of us. We all try to look calm and collected, but we aren't. You can practically hear our unsynchronized hearts beating like drums.

The press are already in, like vultures, ready to dine on whatever is happening. There's an audible buzz in the courtroom.

'Is it a jury question or a verdict?' I ask the usher.

'It's a verdict.'

My heart jolts. They've only been deliberating three hours. At this stage, it has to be unanimous, so they either all think he's guilty or they all think he's not guilty.

'Leila?' Davina calls, gesturing for me to get into place. I can hear her, but I'm not really in the same room. The enormity of what's happening is only just registering. Slowly walking to the same seat I've been sitting in for the past three days, I look around the courtroom as people pile in to view the spectacle that's about to occur. I see people from chambers, including Chester, all of whom will be judging my ability as an advocate based on this verdict.

But none of them matters as much as Jack.

Have I worked hard enough? Have I done the absolute best I could have, in the circumstances? Could I have done anything else? For so long, I've wanted to prove myself in this job, prove I have what it takes to do this kind of case, and now I've had my shot.

In he comes, to the dock. Gone is the self-assured, almost-confident man we've seen throughout this process. Jack looks like a man about to lose everything. I see the fear in his eyes from four benches away. I say nothing to him, only nod, which I hope expresses that whatever happens, I'm here. It will be OK.

The jury bailiff brings the jurors in through a door at the side of the dock. I do not turn to look at them. If I do, I'll make all kinds of assumptions about what their verdict is. I concentrate on looking straight ahead, as a barrister should. My heart feels about to burst, but I maintain a cool exterior.

'All rise!' the usher yells, at which point the judge walks onto the bench.

Court is silent.

'Before we begin, I would like to say now that any outbursts from anyone in the next few minutes will not be tolerated. Those causing trouble will be removed immediately.'

The court clerk asks the jury foreman to stand. A man wearing black-rimmed glasses rises. He clasps his hands together and clears his throat.

He's about to change all of our lives.

63

Leila

R v Jack Millman
Day 3
4.28 p.m.

'Have you reached a verdict upon which you're all agreed?'
'Yes.'
'On count one, a charge of murder, what is your verdict?'
Time stops. The longest eternity, packed into a single moment.
'Not guilty.'
I feel as if I black out for a few seconds.
I come round quickly to Davina shaking my shoulders and whispering, 'Well done!' into my ear. Turning to see Jack, he is as shocked as I am. He stares back at me in sheer disbelief.
People mutter and whisper, filling the courtroom with sounds I'm not sure how to interpret. Out of the corner of my eye I see Julian throw a pen down onto the bench, which bounces onto the floor. His left leg taps repeatedly on the floor, something he does when he's highly agitated.
The judge addresses the jury and thanks them for their consideration on what has been a difficult case.
They returned a verdict within hours. A unanimous verdict. I placed enough doubt about the prosecution's case in *all of their heads*. How on earth did that happen?

'Mr Millman, please stand,' the judge says. 'You've been found not guilty of murder. You are free to leave.'

Just like that. All the months Jack has been held without bail, suddenly cast aside. He is a free man.

Leaving court, I'm swarmed by colleagues who offer their congratulations on a stunning win. It feels surreal.

This time, we meet Jack not in the cells, but in a conference room. No handcuffs, no security guard. We sit beside him, and I can see he's shaking.

'It's over,' I tell him, aware he likely needs to hear it again. That it hasn't sunk in yet. 'You can move on with your life.'

'Thank you,' he says. 'I know it wasn't the way you usually run things.'

'It worked out well in the end.'

'You too, Davina – thank you.'

'No problem, Jack, and don't worry about anything – I'll ensure everyone knows you didn't mention any names, and were utterly loyal to whoever it was you were protecting. I assume that's why you instructed me in the first place,' she says, winking. 'You've conducted yourself impeccably.'

'Thanks.' He grins.

'So, what now?' I ask him. I really hope he's going to do something positive – that he'll never end back here again.

'I don't know. I might go travelling. I've been locked up here long enough.'

'All I'd say is, be careful who you associate with,' I warn him, cautiously. 'They'll be watching you to find out who this woman is.'

'I know.'

'Might be good to lay low for a while.' I smile. 'It's been a pleasure, Mr Millman.'

He stands up and offers his hand for me to shake, but it feels too impersonal, too flippant after what we've been through. Instead, I wrap my arms around his shoulders. He tightly grips my waist in a way that suggests it's the most important hug he's ever had.

'Well, if we're doing hugs!' Davina interrupts, before breaking us up and going in for one herself. We all laugh, not quite believing that, after everything, we really won.

As I drag my exhausted body up the stairs to the robing room, I wish, more than anything, I could go home and quietly congratulate myself on this win. For me, for Jack. For what we've managed to pull off. But I can't.

It's a peculiar concept to grasp: achieving the biggest win of your professional life, yet feeling flat afterwards. The reason is that I know this isn't the end. I have not yet won all my battles.

Sure enough, it comes about half an hour later. A new message from @JustAnotherDumbBlonde.

> The girl who always thinks of everything seems to have misplaced a vital piece of evidence from her trial. Slippy fingers! Don't worry. I can hand it in at the local cop shop or you can come get it from me yourself.

This is the problem when you leave toxic people behind in life – they never really go away. If you dig shallow graves, you can't be surprised when the bodies emerge. I need to put an end to this, once and for all.

Tonight.

I compose a reply.

> I'll meet you 6 p.m. Not in public. Nightingale Dene, on the bridge overlooking the river.

64

Elise Vernon

Friday, 26 July 2024
10.04 p.m.

They all look so young nowadays. I know that's what all people my age say, but they do. I used to sneak out of the house when I was fifteen, wearing a long coat so my father wouldn't be able to see the obscenely short dress underneath, much like the ones the girls wear now. Back then, in the noughties, our hair was poker straight, ironed with wide-plate BaByliss straighteners. That's all changed now; the girls these days look like hair models, with long, bouncy waves shimmying around their waists.

Durham city centre was my stomping ground in my mid-to-late teenage years. I barely recognize it now. Bar names have changed, some have shut down. Music I've never heard before blasts from buildings; it's barely even music. But nothing makes you feel older than being sober, rocking up on a Friday night to collect your eighteen-year-old godson from a bar.

It's a favour to one of my friends, Tally. Kit has this little job in town he's doing alongside his A-levels. Collecting glasses, that sort of thing.

It's at one of those pretentious bars, the kind that plays dreadful music, where drinks cost a fortune. Even from the outside, it looks utterly dire; lilac uplighters attempt to suggest a classy ambience but fall drastically short. What kind of name is 'Innocence' for a bar, anyway? I wouldn't be surprised to see my twat of a father inside, to be honest. It looks the kind of place he'd frequent, given that the clientele appears to be gaggles of impressionable women in their twenties. Although, I hear he keeps one at home now. Younger than me, apparently. Some kind of Instagram influencer named Demi, who is no doubt fleecing him for all she can get. He never learns.

Incredibly, I've managed to park just opposite the entrance. It's busy. Kit finishes at 10 p.m., and I'm hoping he gets off on time.

After a few minutes, Kit scurries out, dressed in a tight black T-shirt and trousers. A few months ago, Kit was a tall, weedy little thing (takes after his mother), but since he's got this job, he's been working out. As a result, he's developed biceps and abs and likes to show them off at every opportunity. As usual, he has his head buried in his phone, looking up only briefly to locate the car.

'Well, lovely to see you, too!' I laugh as he opens the door and shuffles in without so much as a hello.

'Hiya,' he grunts back resentfully, in that way teenagers do.

Putting the car into reverse, I start pulling away. And that's when I see her.

Clear as day. Walking out of Innocence. She's alone.

I brake hard, and we both jolt forward.

'Jesus!' Kit shouts.

'I know her,' I say out loud, god knows why. I don't know what I expect Kit to do about it or why he should care. But I can't drag my eyes away from her. She sashays down the street in that carefree, confident way she's always had about her. But there's something different tonight, something only I would notice because I know her so well. Better than anyone, really. Her walk is quicker than usual, her head lowered slightly. She's trying not to stand out, but in doing so, she does, at least to me.

I know she doesn't want to be seen.

Her long, honey-blonde hair looks dishevelled. She wears a red, midi-length, floaty summer dress, the kind of thing you'd wear to the shops, not a trendy bar on a Friday night.

'Have you seen her before, Kit?' I ask, pointing at her before she goes out of view.

'Yeah,' he says casually, not understanding the gravity of my question. 'She comes every Friday. Never see her in the bar having a drink or with anyone, though. Always meets up with Jack. I think she's a manager or something.'

'Jack? Who's Jack?' I ask, urgently.

'Head of security. He's the one who's been training me.'

'Weight training?'

'Yeah! I usually go into work an hour early and we lift stuff in his apartment. He lives above the club. Dumbbells, kettlebells, all that . . .'

And with that, he goes back to burying his head in his phone. Only, he's wrong. Very wrong. She's certainly not a manager at Innocence.

I smile as she hurries into the shadows.

Rule #8.

Looks like patience really is everything.

65

Witness X

Delilah

MY FATHER LOVED Tom Jones. Played him all day long. It used to drive me mad.

His songs were the soundtrack to my childhood. Sounds innocent when you say it like that, doesn't it? But mine was no ordinary childhood. Even now, when I hear his voice, I can still smell the overbearing scent of cheap corner shop-bought lager and cigarettes. I continue to hear the muffled sounds of raised voices screaming at each other through the bedroom wall, occasionally interrupted by a thump on soft flesh or the sound of breaking glass.

I will forever hate that man's music. Even when no song was playing, my name served as a constant reminder of the past I'd left behind. *Delilah*.

But I had to honour *Rule #5: Be a Good Liar*.

And always base your lies on truth.

I knew I couldn't stray too far from my real name. I needed to make sure that, if I ever did slip, it was easy enough to cover up with the truth. It was just a matter of finding the perfect variation. Something that sounded classier, more elegant.

Delilah.

Lilah.

Leila.
That was it. I knew it was perfect the moment I wrote it down. The day Leila Reynolds was born, I'd never felt so free.

66

Leila

Friday, 6 September 2024
10.41 p.m.

THE STILLNESS. THAT'S the most chilling thing about it. It sounds ridiculous, but after being hit so hard with something so heavy, I expected him to be in a different state, gushing blood, gurgling and writhing around on the floor or something, begging for help.

His skin has turned white. He looks dead.

'Fuck, Leila! What have you done?'

Jack's voice is overcome with panic and fear. We both stare at Anton, lying on the floor. I watch as a thick trickle of dark blood starts to run out of his right nostril while the sound of loud house music vibrates through the floor.

'I . . . I just panicked.'

Jack leans over him to see if he's breathing. I remain standing, not daring to move. My lawyer instinct is already screaming, 'Don't get closer than you need to.' I gently place the kettlebell down on the floor. As I do, I catch myself being filmed by Jack's phone, which is leaning up against the TV.

'It's still recording,' I whisper, running over and pressing the red button to stop it.

'He's barely breathing. We need to call an ambulance!' Jack says, urgently.

I don't move. I stare at Anton, lying motionless on the floor. He's going to die.

'Leila!'

My breathing is fast and shallow. In a split second, my life has changed. All of our lives have changed.

'I'll be prosecuted for murder,' I say, calmly. 'I'll get life imprisonment. I won't get out.'

'You won't, you won't . . . you were defending me. Shit!' Jack cries. 'He might not die. It'll be OK. We just need to keep him alive. Call an ambulance!'

He doesn't understand. Why would he? All I can think about is my past, who I really am. There's no way it would stay out of court. Even if the childhood abuse was used to try to justify my actions, my career, my life as I know it, would be over. Having my past raked over like that, even with the best intention from a defence barrister, is a risky move. Something I'll fight tooth and nail to stop from happening.

Jack looks at me like a scared little boy. I'm the responsible one, the lawyer, the one with the answers. And yet, I have nothing. His head keeps turning towards Anton, who is edging closer to death by the second.

'What are we going to do? We can't just do nothing!'

'Let me think,' I tell him, calmly.

Patience.

My mind moves at speed. What's the best way out of this? How does this look to the police? How would it look to a jury?

How can we play this?

After a few minutes it becomes brutally clear.

'He can't leave this room alive,' I say, bluntly.

'What?' Jack looks at me, incredulous.

'If he leaves this room alive, my life is over.'

The colour drains from Jack's face. I need to be the authority here or he will crumble.

'But . . . it's a man's life!'

'It's his or mine,' I interrupt, standing in front of him in nothing but a pair of knickers and an oversized T-shirt. I'm shaking so much, my legs are knocking together.

'There must be another way. We could both leave. Claim to have nothing to do with it.'

'There's far too much evidence linking us here. Besides, it's your flat. Our best way out is for one of us to be arrested and then get the best defence team there is. Juries are unpredictable. There's always a chance of a win. No matter how cut and dried it might first appear. We need a jury to find one of us not guilty. That's our only option.'

The words leave my mouth, but they don't feel real. *How is this real?*

'You could do it,' he suggests, after a few seconds.

'What?' I ask, as though I'm not already ten steps ahead of him.

'I'll let them arrest me for it. You can defend me. No one can understand this case better than you.'

Still, I hesitate. 'I can't let you do that for me.' And I mean it. I know it's our best chance but the thought of losing him is too much to bear. Then again, I can't destroy everything I have, everything I've built.

I would rather die.

'Yes, you can.'

'I'm not guaranteed to win,' I remind him. 'I've never led a murder trial before. I might not even be allowed. You'd have to insist I be your barrister.'

'I will. I'll make them let you do it. I believe in you, Leila.

You'll win because it's me. And because you were here. I didn't kill him and that's the truth.'

Can I pull it off?

The person I am now can't. But I know someone who can. *Delilah*.

I need to bring her back. The most dangerous, destructive, toxic, ruthless parts of me. The person I'd finally managed to escape. She's my only hope of getting out of this mess.

From now on, no more of this emotionally driven, weak Leila crap. She's the reason I've ended up here to begin with. My dad was right. The rules protected me all those years, and they'll protect me again. Until after Jack is acquitted, I need to be that girl again.

Well, I say *girl*. I don't think that part of me is even human any more.

It's just temporary. As long as I don't allow her to consume me, I'll be fine.

'The first thing we need to do is get rid of *that*,' I tell him, pointing at Jack's phone.

We sit down and I go through *exactly* how I'll run the trial with him. There is no room for error — every step must be meticulously planned. Jack fills me in on what happened between Lewis and Quinn, why Anton was at Jack's apartment in the first place. I can't believe he didn't tell me before now. Yet more information to process on top of everything else.

Breathe.

I tell Jack that the second I receive the brief, I need to prepare it as if I know *nothing* about the case. I'll need hard evidence to present to a jury and will need to go through the motions of collecting it, so as not to arouse suspicion.

Suspicion, however, will be raised around why Anton was here to begin with. Suddenly, I know exactly what to do. The phone will be vital evidence because it has the video of Quinn killing Lewis on it. But we can't let the device itself be found, since the recording of everything that just happened now is on it as well. Even if deleted, it could be retrieved by a digital expert. *How do I fix this?*

I stand up, start pacing. Quinn killed someone. He can be our linchpin here. I'll take the phone to just outside Anton's house as soon as I leave and switch it on when I'm there. I know where he lives – I remember going there years ago when I first started dating Julian for some awful garden party. Cell site analysis will pick it up, and I'll plant in the jurors' heads that Quinn stole it to get rid of it.

I'll then store it safely at Audrey's house, the place that has become my alibi for the affair for the past seven months. It's been a godsend, being able to nip off to my mother-in-law's house on a Friday night, go in for five minutes and then leave. The best part about it is she doesn't even remember if you've been or gone.

We need to plant more female DNA around the flat to muddy the prosecution evidence. I run downstairs to Innocence, picking up a few used glasses on the way. Thank god they don't have CCTV here. Nipping into the girls' loos, I compliment some random girls on their hair, running my hands through their locks to collect some strands, before running back upstairs and placing them around Jack's flat. I swipe a lighter that has fallen on the floor to take up, too.

If we raise self-defence at trial, there has to appear to have been a struggle, so I tell Jack to pick up Anton's left hand and bang his knuckles on the floor. I hit Jack in the face a few times as well, to corroborate evidence of a confrontation. I do it quickly and devoid of emotion.

Delilah is in charge now.

We turn Jack's shirt inside out and back to front to corroborate the story he was having sex when Anton knocked on the door. We also need to locate a struggle in the kitchen, so I pour Coca-Cola down his T-shirt and leave the remainder of the bottle spilling onto the floor.

I'm on autopilot now. I've crossed a line and there's no going back.

One thing that works well in serious trials is intrigue. So, I wipe my prints off the kettlebell and place it back in its doorstop position. It'll look as if I was trying to hide it, and in doing so, slipped up; a seasoned criminal like Jack would never make that mistake. But a poor, panicked woman would. Jurors love trying to figure out these kinds of things. This theory will be corroborated by Jack presenting as an 'honest criminal' at trial; we'll agree to the jury knowing about his previous convictions under the guise of having nothing to hide.

I spray some perfume in Jack's bedroom. It's vital that a woman's presence is hinted at, but not enough that the prosecution investigates it. It needs to be appropriately pitched so when Jack does the big reveal at trial, it makes the prosecution look incompetent and Jack's story 100 per cent plausible.

Jack tells me Quinn came to see him at Temptation the day of the murder and that he led him into the only room with CCTV. Incredibly, I made reference to this room in my conference notes at the last trial. I will use this as a vehicle to make our knowledge of it believable to the solicitor. He also tells me there will be CCTV footage of Quinn being aggressive with him the week prior from Diamond Lounge. I'll admit this to evidence, but it'll have to be done after Jack's evidence, for maximum impact. Jack must hint at this incident when he's being cross-examined, which will allow me to introduce it in re-examination.

The prosecution must not be told the truth about Lewis until trial. It is *vital* that this be the first time Eddie hears about Quinn killing his son. I'm hoping he has an explosive reaction and will attempt to assault Quinn in court. Chaos recalibrates a jury, and it becomes more about them and less about you.

Taking Quinn down will be the key to winning this trial.

Just before the jury retire to consider their verdict, I'll collect the phone from Audrey's house and anonymously send the police the video of Quinn killing Lewis. It'll be admitted as last-minute evidence and corroborate everything Jack has said. I change the PIN of his phone to something only I would know.

After what feels like seconds but also hours, I look down at Anton on the floor. Planning how to get away with the murder of a man – a judge – who isn't even dead yet is a new low, even for me. There's one aspect I daren't bring myself to think about.

The CPS will probably instruct Julian to prosecute. Going up against him in a murder trial frightens me more than anything, but the alternative is unimaginable.

I will do whatever it takes to win.

After thirty minutes, Anton's breathing becomes shallow. He starts gurgling. It sounds like he has blood in his airway.

'I don't think he's got long left,' Jack says, handing me his mobile phone.

'No,' I reply. 'I should get going. Give it five minutes, then use the main landline to call 999.'

'It's going to be hard seeing you but not . . . you know.'

'I know,' I whisper, placing my hands gently on either side of his face.

He kisses me softly, but passionately. We don't have long. It'll be the last time we do this for a long, long time. Possibly for ever.

Reluctantly dragging his mouth away from my lips, his eyes meet mine.

'I love—'

'Don't,' I interrupt him, placing my finger on his lips. 'Please don't make this harder than it already is.'

I can't hear that. If I do, I'll crumble. I can't be Leila right now.

Taking a deep breath, I look at the almost dead man by my feet.

Just stick to the rules one more time. You can do it.

For Jack.

67

Leila

Wednesday, 15 January 2025
6 p.m.

I HAVEN'T SEEN OR spoken to Elise Vernon in fourteen years. I can tell by the steely look on her face as she walks towards me that she has very much not forgiven me for what happened. What I did to her.

We used to come here, to Nightingale Dene. It was beautiful in the summer. The trees were rich with lime-green leaves, and we'd lie on the grass, take turns buying ice-cold drinks from the cafe.

'Well,' she says, approaching me on the wide, ornate bridge we've walked over more times than I can count. The sound of the river rushing underneath is amplified around the park. 'I hear congratulations are in order.'

She looks the same as she always did. Well, before she changed to look more like me. A blunt-cut black bob rests just above her shoulders, not quite skimming the fitted dark green coat she's wearing.

'Cut the crap, Elise. Just tell me what you want.'

Her eyes widen, and a tiny smile appears on her face.

'I don't think you're in a position to be making demands,' she says. 'You know why I've contacted you.'

'I know you have it,' I interrupt. 'What's the plan? Bribe me? Take the phone to the police?'

'Don't you want to know how I got it? How I knew it was there?'

She's playing with me. She's waited a long time for this moment. *Rule #8: Be Patient*. Now she has her time for revenge, she wants to enjoy it.

'I can see you're dying to tell me.'

'You see, *this* is your problem, Delilah. You're very clever – astoundingly so – but you get so wrapped up in your own *cleverness* that you miss things.' I watch the white, cold air leave her mouth and dance into the sky. 'You didn't see me the night you ran out of Innocence, did you?'

I'm taken aback.

'What?'

'This is the bit you'll struggle with. It's difficult to admit you made mistakes – you thought you'd been so discreet, didn't you?'

There's no point in denying any of it. Not with her.

'I saw you leaving one Friday night when I came to pick up my godson. He works at Innocence, too. Told me you went there every week at the same time and left at the same time, and I thought, "Hmm, why would a married woman be doing that?" No. Why would *you* be doing that?'

She performs every word with delight. She's building up to something.

'I simply had to find out what you were up to, so I kept going every Friday to watch, and, sure enough, there you were. Bang on time. Just as Kit had said. Having an affair with the doorman.'

Anyone else would think this was mad, stalking someone week after week. Obsessive. But I understand. After everything that happened, I would have done the same. She'd found her opportunity, and she was going to take it.

'You always looked different leaving that place. Lighter.

Actually *happy*. I noticed it that very first Friday. But that night, you looked terrible. Panicked. Naturally, I was intrigued. Delilah? Scared of something?

'I followed you to Pickford and watched you park just outside that house, fiddling with a phone. You didn't get out of the car, you just sat there. And then you went straight to little old Audrey's house, which I knew by then was very late for your usual visit. You went straight into the front bedroom. I watched from the road as you turned the light on.'

She's right. I had missed all of this. *How could I have been so fucking stupid?* I'd been so wrapped up in dealing with Jack's phone that I never even stopped to check if anyone was following me.

'None of it made sense until I saw the news the next day, when I saw that the doorman had been arrested for murder. I knew immediately you'd been involved. Not only that – my instincts told me you were the one who killed him. Getting someone else to confess to a crime you committed? Well, that's exactly the kind of thing I knew you'd do. Because you can't be trusted, can you, Delilah?'

'Stop calling me that,' I snap. 'It's not my name any more. It's not who I am.'

'You think a different name changes who you are?' She laughs, but it is callous. 'I mean, bravo to you for fooling everyone. I was almost impressed, watching you play the humble, nice girl at that lecture you did at the school.'

I hate that she can see right through me.

'You've changed your hair, I see. Not too drastic. Again, clever. Let me guess – you couldn't remain blonde, in case anyone saw you leave the club, but couldn't go full-on brunette, as it'd be too obvious a transformation. What did we say? If you do something subtly over time, nobody realizes anything has changed.' She looks wild now, euphoric.

'What do you think your colleagues or followers would do if they knew the truth? About who you really are? The things you've done.'

'Enough! Stop this, please!' I plead. 'What do you want from me? Money? Is that what it'll take to get you to leave me alone?'

'Are you kidding? You've got to be. After what you did to us?'

And there it is. Elise's wound. The one she's been waiting to make me pay for.

When I met Elise, it was off the back of sixteen years of emotional, physical, and sexual abuse. I was out of control, and I liked destroying things as much as I hated it. I despised myself for the behaviour but relished the power I finally felt. Elise was determined, headstrong and ambitious, with aspirations to set the corporate world alight. She wanted respect, and like me, craved power – and was prepared to do anything to get it.

We both hated our fathers and had been made to feel worthless and undeserving of love. The shame we felt as a result manifested as destructive behaviour towards ourselves and others. We had suffered for so long, we pretended we enjoyed it. We dressed it up as a sport, as fun. It was nothing but a cry for help.

It's no coincidence we both ended up desperate to be professionally successful. In the absence of paternal validation, it was the next best thing and would surely prove to everyone – including ourselves – that we were, indeed, worth something.

But, as I have come to find out, it doesn't work like that. Self-worth is an inside job.

Elise's father had always made it impossible for anyone else in their family to rise to the top. He enjoyed making the rest of them feel small. She'd had enough of that life by the time I met her.

And so had I.

We both wanted more.

Her father was Queen's Counsel and head of a set of chambers in Durham. I knew from the moment I met him when I was sixteen that I wanted what he had. Chester Vernon commanded respect, people listened to him, and so I became set on training to be a barrister. I wanted a taste of that deference.

She'd invite me to spend school holidays at her house. It was like nothing I'd seen before. They had acres of land. *Staff*. Chester gave me advice about what I needed to do to increase my chances of gaining pupillage. I made it clear I'd do anything to succeed. Anything.

He saw me as a tragic case; a poor, working-class orphan girl who was just trying to do well for herself against the odds.

Even intelligent men don't know poison when they taste it.

It was in my final year at Cambridge that I suspected Chester wanted me. By law school, I was sure. It was an arduous task, titillating him for that long. But it was necessary. I had to make sure I succeeded. And so, for six months, I gave it to him in every filthy way he wanted. *Rule #2*. I became his fantasy, his addiction. I intoxicated him to the point where he would have done anything to get me into his chambers.

I never intended for Elise to find out, but Chester slipped up.

The ultimate betrayal. Not only did her best friend fuck her father, but Elise had to live with the fact that I received more love and validation from him than she ever had.

'I wasn't the only person involved, Elise,' I tell her now.

'I haven't spoken to my father since it happened. Too busy looking after my mother, who you destroyed. How is good old Chester, by the way? I hear his new child bride is pregnant?'

'It was fourteen years ago, Elise. And sometimes . . .'

'Oh, go on.'

'Sometimes, these things just happen,' I say, cringing once the words have left my mouth.

'Do you think I'm stupid? This was all part of your game. I was just a pawn to you. Right from the very beginning. You befriended me to get to my dad, to sleep your way into his chambers. And it worked. The only person you care about is yourself.'

Her words punch me in the chest. They aren't true, either. Elise was my best friend. Yes, Chester became part of my plan, but that came later. It was never about him at the beginning, but there's no point denying it. She knows too much of the bad parts of me for it to be worth trying to convince her of the good.

'You knew the rules. You used them just the same as I did,' I say, trying to stay calm. Yes, I've done terrible things. But Elise has, too. We did them together.

'My father!' she spits at me. 'Because of you my family broke up!'

'Sorry, Elise, but knowing Chester the way I do – if it wasn't me, it would have been someone else. It probably already had been.'

'Who the hell do you think you are? You think you're cleverer than everyone else, don't you?'

'Trust me, I don't. And I am sorry. I am. I'm a different person now. I'm trying to be better.'

She laughs so hard, she has to turn away from me. It echoes around us in the darkness. The sound of it hurts my ears.

'You really believe that, don't you? That you're different?' She snorts.

'Who are you to decide whether I've changed or not? You know what your problem is, Elise?' I lean in towards her and, my voice almost a whisper, I say, 'You just need to get over it.'

She's caught off guard. Of all the things I could say in this moment, she didn't expect those words.

'I can guess how this has played out over the years,' I continue, folding my arms. 'You hate men because of what Daddy did, and you hate women because of what I did. It's you against the world. I'm right, aren't I?'

She says nothing, continuing to stare at me.

'Still masquerading as the working-class hero, Elise?' I ask, quietly. 'Still pretending to be me because it makes you more interesting? *More edgy?* Do all your corporate work buddies know about your privileged childhood? The ski holidays? The second home in France? The boarding school?'

'Shut up,' she whispers.

'You're a hypocrite, Elise. Neither of us is who we say we are. You want to expose me? Go ahead. I'll do the same to you.'

When Elise found out about Chester and me, the only thing that prevented her from telling everyone was her own vanity. By that time, she'd created a persona for herself where she'd become some kind of token 'poor girl' and gained popularity with it within her corporate gang in London. It made her seem special, interesting. She stood out. Before me, she'd been just another rich girl in a sea full of them.

'You forget I have Jack's phone,' she says, her mask back in place.

'You haven't seen anything. It's PIN protected.'

'Yes, it is, just like the safe was.' She frowns almost comically. 'And I thought to myself, "I know Delilah, she will have changed the code on the safe and the phone to something only she remembers. Now, what number is so important to her that nobody else knows?" Easy to remember but hard for anyone to guess. Except for me.'

My heart sinks.

'140505. That was the day of your first murder, wasn't it? Nice touch to use it to hide your second.'

As an advocate, words are my weapon. Carefully selected words, in the right circumstances, can knock you breathless. But this time, it's not me delivering the blows. It's her. That date will be burned into my memory for ever as the most significant of my life. I should never have told her my biggest secret.

'Honestly, the whole thing is quite scandalous,' she continues, revelling in the power she's now wielding against me.

She pulls the phone out and leans forward on the low stone wall of the bridge, tapping away at the screen as she inputs the code. The video begins to play. It's the part where Anton has just come in and is arguing with Jack. He doesn't yet know I'm there.

'Not only are you having sex with a former client, but then you kill a judge. From this angle, if I'm being honest, it doesn't look like self-defence. In fact, you seem to be quite enjoying it.'

'Elise,' I beg her. I hate myself for it, but there's too much at stake. 'If you do this, you'll ruin not only my life but Jack's, too. He's done nothing wrong. He went through this for me. You hate me – fine. I get that. Don't take this out on him.'

Although the video proves Jack's innocence, it would also expose that he's lied under oath; that he knew his phone hadn't been stolen and that I was, in fact, known to Anton. I won't have him dragged back into this again. I look around to check we're totally on our own. The only light in the park at this time of night comes from lamp-posts intermittently placed along the bridge.

She glances away from the screen for a moment and looks at my face.

'You love him, don't you? I can tell. Jesus, what the hell happened to you? It makes this all the sweeter.'

I've been through too much to let this happen.

'He's the best thing that ever happened to me,' I whisper, as she watches the video again. 'Which is why I can't allow you to take that video to the police.'

I lunge for her and attempt to snatch the phone from her hand. Clinging to it, she smashes her other hand into my face. Undeterred, I grab at her hair as hard as I can, but then she pins my body over the side of the low stone wall. The sound of the river rushes through my ears as my head hangs over the edge.

'Nice try, *bitch!*' she spits out, before repeatedly punching me in the face so hard, my cheekbone feels about to crack.

Elise starts trying to push my body up the wall and I'm so disoriented it takes me a second to work out why. She's trying to throw me over the side. This is the result of fourteen years' worth of hate and revenge. She won't stop until I'm finished.

An animalistic instinct kicks in.

Using every iota of strength I have, I swing my right leg out from underneath her and aim the stiletto heel of my boot at her body. Jabbing sharply, it connects with her lower leg on the third attempt, and she screams. As she slightly releases her grip on me, I push her off me and turn her around so she's now backed against the wall. She struggles and kicks, each blow landing forcefully on my body.

Raising my hands, I place them around her neck and squeeze. She pushes at me, gasping for breath, looks at me with wild eyes. She knows I'm capable of this. She knows I'll do it.

I must protect myself. Nobody else will.

She's losing strength. Quickly, I reach for the phone still in her hand and grab it from her. In an act of desperation, she reaches for my hair with both hands and screams. In one quick move, gathering all the strength I have, I push her up and over the wall.

I didn't technically push her. She lost her balance.

A large splash signals her entry into the water. It's a deep river. Cold. I place the phone in my coat pocket.

Rule #1.

Don't Get Caught.

68

Delilah

Friday, 13 May 2005

'Boarding school?' he frowned. 'What are you on about, DeeDee? Who do you think you are? The Queen of Sheba?'

My heart pounded. His reaction wasn't surprising, which is why I came prepared.

'It's not what you think,' I said, my mouth dry. 'You wouldn't have to pay anything. They do these fully funded scholarships, you see. For people like me.'

'People like you?'

'You know, disadvantaged . . .'

'Oh!' he said, in mock surprise. 'Poor little Delilah. Always the victim. What's wrong with your normal school?'

'I'm better than that. Better than this.'

It slipped out. I knew he'd see it as arrogance, but in that moment, I didn't care. It was true. I'd had enough of hearing him say he couldn't afford to buy food or clothes that actually fitted me because he had no money, only to blow what he did have on booze and fags. It was no way for a child to live.

'What? You want to go and live in a stately home and hang around with lords and princesses while I fester here alone?'

'Yes,' I said firmly. 'I do.'

His eyes burned into me, but I didn't look away. He was

sitting on the sofa drinking a can of lager. I stood above him; it was important in this moment to feel bigger.

'You're not leaving here,' he said, quietly.

'Why not?'

He thought about it for a moment, standing up to face me, hoping I'd back down. I didn't.

'It'll be full of lads, being all over you.'

'As opposed to *you* being all over me, you mean?'

It shocked him, my saying it out loud. Of all the rules he taught me, that was the most important one, the one that remains unspoken for ever.

For abuse to thrive in a dysfunctional and toxic family, it must never, ever be mentioned.

I made it real. The silence was broken. I couldn't – and wouldn't – take it back. If it resulted in a beating, I didn't care.

He looked me up and down, trying to make me feel small and dirty and insignificant.

'You're not going,' he snarled, ignoring what I said. He would make me pay for it later.

'It's girls only.'

Glaring, he stepped away, reassessing me. He sensed I'd grown a backbone, and that was not allowed in our house.

'No,' he said, casually.

'I'm going,' I said, firmly. I swallowed hard to centre myself. I knew I mustn't back down now.

'You're sixteen.'

'I don't want to stay here.'

My voice trembled. Forcing myself to look him in the face went against all my instincts, but this was it: my escape. I was getting out and he needed to know I was strong enough to do it.

'Oh, we're not good enough for you here any more?' It was

little more than a whisper; it didn't need to be louder than that to have the intended effect.

'You're not,' I shot back without thinking. 'You know you're not.'

I knew immediately it would escalate, but adrenalin was coursing through my body, and I understood that if I wanted this, I'd have to fight with everything I had.

'You think you're better than me?'

'I know I am.'

He said nothing, initially. But he looked at me in a way he never had before, in that moment. It was a look of sheer hatred. He moved closer so that his nose was inches away from mine. I could feel his hot breath on my face, as I had on so many occasions before.

'You're *mine*,' he spat. 'You think you can get away from me? You even *think* like me now, you stupid, stuck-up, ungrateful bitch.'

'This isn't the life I want. It's not normal – I know that now. I don't want to be like you.'

'You already are. And you know it.'

'No.'

'And the best part is, you *like* being like that, don't you?'

'No.'

'You love everything I taught you.'

'No, I don't.'

'You just don't want to admit it,' he said, softly, delicately placing his hands on the sides of my face. 'Just like you don't want to admit you love me. You don't want to leave. Not really.'

He put his arms around me.

Having Stockholm syndrome with your own father is very complex. How does a child make sense of that? He had imprisoned me with a set a rules. Coached me to be just like him. To rely on him. But the rules had given me more than he'd bargained for. They'd made me cunning.

Rule # 7: Beware the Talented Student.

I knew he'd never allow me to leave, but this truly felt like my last chance to escape. And so, after promising him I'd reject the offer, I went upstairs and waited.

Rule # 8: Be Patient.

He used to settle on the sofa and watch films on Friday nights, drinking and smoking until late. He never used to open the windows. A thick fog of smoke would sit in the room, blurring everything in sight. He'd usually fall asleep, and I'd find him in the morning, passed out with the TV still on.

I stayed awake all night, watching the digital clock in my bedroom as it passed midnight. At 1.40 a.m. I crept downstairs in the freezing cold, tiptoeing to avoid the creaks on the third and seventh steps, until finally, I reached the bottom. I held my breath the entire time.

He was snoring, heavily. One arm was hanging off the sofa. His mouth gaped open. A glass ashtray on the floor housed cigarette butts surrounded by eight empty lager cans. This man – this monster – had ruined my life for long enough. I knew I'd never be free until he was gone.

Walking over to one of the armchairs, I quietly removed a single match from the box I'd bought earlier that day. I felt no remorse, no emotion, no regret for what I was about to do.

As I dragged the match down the strip on the side of the box, it burst into a single flame. I took one final look at him before dropping it on the cheap fabric.

I calmly walked out of the back door, locking it as I went. The living room was engulfed in flames by the time I was across the street.

Nobody questioned it. Everyone knew Dad smoked like a chimney.

From that day on, I stuck to the rules as best I could. They were, after all, what had allowed me to get away from that place. I knew they made me the same as him, but for some time after his death, I had nothing but the rules to guide me in the world. I did not have my shit together, even though I pretended I did at that posh school. But who could blame me? I'd just murdered my dad.

The grief knocked me out. I expected to feel relieved, free, but I didn't. It was messy, complicated and multilayered. I hated him, but I also felt angry with myself for loving him. Why did I love someone who abused me? Why was I sad he was dead? He'd be so mad at me for killing him.

He was the only person in the world who loved me, and I murdered him. I carried that shame and guilt for years, unable to see I was still under his spell.

How do you begin to unpack all that childhood trauma? At the time, I couldn't. I pushed it away, made very bad choices, formed toxic relationships. Elise was a part of that. I stuck to the rules, too afraid to have nothing.

Then I met Jack.

And everything changed. *I changed.* I finally felt brave enough to cast aside Dad's legacy. I discovered my own capacity to love and be loved, something I'd never imagined would be possible. I wanted to be a better person around him. No longer was I interested in obtaining power or influence; I wanted to be a decent person with integrity. No longer did I want to seek external validation to feel complete; I wanted to create that myself.

While my father taught me things that gave me the illusion of control, living by his teachings, his rules, kept me under his thumb, unable to think freely and be who I could have been without his influence. Becoming Leila – deliberately exorcising my past and embodying the characteristics of someone good and caring and honourable – is what finally set me free, giving me the *real* power I needed to let go, to start again.

So when I say I'm not having anyone threaten what I've worked for, what I've endured, I mean it.

Don't talk to me about real justice. I've seen it all. Sometimes, justice isn't served in a courtroom. It's served at 1.46 a.m. in a living room with a box of matches.

69

Leila

Friday, 19 July 2024
Two months before the murder

I BOTH LOVE AND hate summer nights. On the one hand, I adore the hazy, hot, sticky vibe that comes with them. On the other, they create more risk.

By the time I leave Audrey's house on Fridays, I usually arrive at the club between 7.30 p.m. and 8 p.m. In the winter months, I could hide under my winter coat without being seen. But now, it's still light at that time, which makes me nervous; anyone could see me. I worry it's only a matter of time before I'm found out.

I barely recognize myself lately. Fantasizing about doing things with Jack – merely existing outside his apartment, especially now it's so bright out – is my new hobby. I catch myself in court, sometimes, daydreaming about us walking on the beach hand in hand, drinking cocktails at sunset, even just walking down the street together. Things we'll never be able to do in real life. I'm aware our relationship can never escape the four walls it's been consigned to. We're trapped.

It was never supposed to be more than a one-night thing. A few hours of filth, lust, passion, whatever you want to call it – and it *was* all of those things, ramped up to the hilt. But those things are addictive, aren't they? So, we did it again. And again. The weird thing was, not once did it feel like we shouldn't be doing it. I never felt a sense of taboo, that we were abusing the barrister–client power dynamic, because we're both so similar it doesn't matter.

We are equals.

That's why it didn't take long for things to shift. We never spoke about it but we both felt it. The sex became slower, more intimate. His eyes would latch on to mine and I'd want them never to leave. I started staying afterwards, my naked body pressed tightly to his beneath the covers, and right there, in that tiny bedroom, with his arms wrapped around me, I felt more protected and loved than I had in my entire life. Sometimes we'd talk; other times, we'd lie there in silence. But his touch never left mine. He made my body feel it was my own again. It no longer belonged to Dad or to any of the other men who had used it. Jack is the only man I've ever felt comfortable enough with to tell what happened to me. The relief when he didn't turn away was overwhelming.

Our meeting became the highlight of our week. We had two – maybe three – hours together, at the absolute most.

I didn't like talking about Julian; his moods, his ego, the fact I suspected he was having an affair. I couldn't care less, and it would make my life easier if he was. At least, then, I'd have something to use against him, especially if I could prove it.

I was tired of pretending I had the perfect life.

It's one of the hottest days of the year, according to the forecast, and it's always boiling hot in Jack's apartment. The film of sweat that covers our bare bodies acts like glue. Even with the covers thrown off, we melt in the heat. The Velux window is wide open, but there's still not enough oxygen.

'My life is better because of you,' Jack says to me now, as my head nestles in the crease of his shoulder. A fissure of fear runs through me when he says this; Elise said something similar to me years ago.

'How can you say that, Jack?' I whisper. My body radiates with guilt when I think about it. 'I got you sent to prison.'

'I don't blame you for that. You know I don't.'

'I'll always blame myself. I should have trusted my gut.'

'No,' he says, giving me a squeeze. 'Everything happens for a reason. It all ended up OK. I'm happy where I am now. More than happy.'

Jack is so forgiving, so balanced. I found it difficult at first. I was brought up to be cynical, to always see the worst in people. He's the exact opposite.

'Me too.' I smile, tracing my finger up his torso and onto his chest. 'It's just . . . messy.'

'We could make it simpler.'

I wish I was as laidback as him. I wish I didn't have the constraints I do.

'You know it's . . . difficult,' I tell him, again. It's what I always tell him in a bid to convince myself, because considering doing anything about it is too terrifying.

'Just leave him and we can go somewhere. Anywhere. Away from here.'

'Jack . . .'

'I know it's only been five months, but I'm sure about this. I'm sure about you.'

And the stupid thing is, I'm sure, too. Is that crazy? I've never felt anything like this before. We can heal each other, I'm sure of it.

'I want to. You know I do. But I can't just leave. I've got my job – a job I've worked so hard for – and he wouldn't make it easy for me.'

Jack kisses the top of my head and strokes my hair, letting me know it's OK. He gets it, how conflicted I am. He's the only person who understands.

'I can't stand the thought of you going back there to him.'

Neither can I.

'He would destroy me. Julian Kesler KC can't have two women divorcing him. I need time to figure out the right way to do it.'

I've become used to it now, the sense of dread gathering around me as I approach the house. Not knowing what I'll be hit with first – the parade of subtle put-downs or the sneaky, controlling behaviour. There exists now a familiarity to his quiet nastiness, and I feel like that little girl again – trapped – living at home with my father. I promised her I'd get her out, but I dropped her straight back into an environment just as harmful, and now she's too frightened to leave. Again.

'I just wish I could take you somewhere, protect you.'

I'm not the kind of woman who cries. I don't get emotional; I never have. Crying was only ever used to manipulate a man or get something I needed. But, right now, here, I have to try hard to stop myself.

'I'd like that, too,' I tell him. He has no idea how much.

We lie in the heat for a few more minutes, just taking in the time we have together. The bright blue sky and cottonwool clouds through the skylight, our rhythmic breaths that always sync when we lie beside each other, the atmospheric notes of 'You'll Never Walk Alone' by Gerry and the Pacemakers. I like to have music on when I'm here so I can listen to it later and think of him.

'What did you think of me when you first met me, that day I first represented you?' I ask him, out of nowhere.

A broad smile spreads across his face. It's the kind I love, the one that shows off his dimples. He hasn't shaved for a few days, so he looks rugged and wild. His black hair frames his beautiful face and makes his blue eyes pop.

'Honestly? I thought you were just like me, which was weird for a lawyer. And down to earth. Smart. Beautiful.'

Hearing him say that makes me light up inside.

'Say we did run away.' I sigh. 'Where would we go?'

'I've always wanted to visit Australia.'

'That's the goal, then. Even if it's in five, ten years' time. We'll walk down the street in Sydney, holding hands, no sneaking around. Nobody will know us or care who we are. How does that sound?'

'I thought you told me not to trust lawyers?' he says, frowning at me jokingly.

'Don't use my own words against me!'

He pulls me closer to him and places his hand on the side of my face, kissing me slowly, softly, sensually. He's so close I can feel his heart beating against mine.

'I love you,' he says. It's the first time either of us has said it. I'm glad he said it first.

'I love you, too. So much.'

I was always led to believe this wouldn't happen. That no man but my father would ever love me. That I wasn't truly worthy of it.

It's not going to be easy, but I will make this happen. I'll find a way to leave Julian. Never did I ever believe that people could change – that I could change – but they can, and I like the person I've become.

I never thought I'd be able to say that.

70

Leila

Rule #11
Never Push Your Luck

One of the fundamental rules of cross-examination is 'know when to stop'. You can ruin an exceptional piece of oratorical art by asking one question at the end that derails your entire case.

Never push your luck.

Dad said it was one of the most difficult rules to master. I think, mainly, because you can't quite grasp it as a concept until you're older. In fact, it may be the one rule Dad never quite followed himself.

It's been two weeks since the trial. By sheer chance, a colleague from chambers had a rental that became available just outside Durham. It's a small, semi-detached new-build, everything Julian despises. I love it.

My victory in the Millman trial has sent my career skywards. Jim has had solicitors calling him and booking me in for trials for the next year solid, and they ask for me personally. He sat me down a few days ago and said chambers had met and decided they would support me applying for silk in the next round of applications. Me, applying to be King's Counsel. They think I'm good enough.

Shame my own pupilmaster never did.

That stings more than anything else. I can handle the marital betrayal – I'm hardly in a position to be upset about that. But my mentor and professional guardian? I would have expected Julian to screw his wife over, not his pupil.

That genuinely hurts.

So, I took everything he taught me and used it to defeat him – much as I did with my own dad. *Rule #7: Beware the Talented Student.*

Looking back on it, I can see that Julian was always a means to an end. A fast-track to better cases. He elevated my career in ways I never deserved – much as Chester did – but I despised how it made me feel. At least with Chester, nobody knew how I used him to get where I was.

Julian was an unbelievably easy target; not long after his divorce, it became painful listening to his 'date disasters', but I went along with it, pretending to care, offering 'advice'. It formed an excellent blueprint for what Julian wanted in a woman and who I needed to be to land him.

Don't complain, don't be needy, be subservient, be sexual, be compliant, don't question anything, and don't ever cheat, or you will be punished for it.

It worked for as long as I needed it to. And I had wanted him, to a certain extent, at least in the beginning. I was not immune to his confidence, his swagger, his power. But I hadn't counted on him being as nasty as he was. He ended up being a hot poker that plunged into the gaping wound that hadn't yet healed inside me, the hurt of the little girl who hadn't yet processed what had happened to her.

Serves me right, I suppose.

He wore a mask at work, just like I did. Only Sienna knew

what lay beneath it. I knew he'd cheat on me eventually. It was just a case of when.

Now, I've personally earned the reputation I always craved, but something about it leaves me cold. I should be elated. I've finally got what I wanted. I am no longer relegated to the 'stupid blonde' ranks, having to play puerile mind games with misogynistic arseholes like DCI Brady.

Yet, I'm disgusted by my relapse to Delilah, for how I manipulated those jurors and everyone in that courtroom.

The nightmares have started again. Every night, I see *him*, pinning me to the wall, so close I can smell the sweat on his skin, gloating that I am no better than him, that he might have been a bad father but at least he never killed anyone.

Not just once but three times.

That's a heavy load to carry.

It's a stupid thing to do. Even as I pick up the phone, I fully understand the risk I'm taking by doing it. But it's a risk I'm willing to take.

'Davina? It's Leila Reynolds. Listen, I need a favour.'

71

Leila

Two weeks after trial

WE COULDN'T MEET anywhere locally so I booked an Airbnb – a little cottage deep in Northumberland, miles from anywhere. I arrive first, shaking with excitement, barely able to believe it was happening. I get the fire going and put some food out for us. It's a wild and windy night, perfect for locking ourselves away.

Just after 7 p.m., I see headlights moving down the lone road towards the house and my heart races. I take a second to compose myself.

A few minutes later, there's a knock at the door. I open it.

'Hey there,' he says, smiling in the way he does when he's with me. In the way I haven't seen in the longest time. He immediately wraps his arms around me as I burst into tears. Sinking his face into my hair, he rubs his hand gently over my back and says, 'It's OK, it's all going to be OK. I'm here now. I love you.'

He is 'home' to me, not like the home I grew up in, but the home I want to be in for ever.

I'm not exactly sure what Davina thought when I asked her for Jack's new number; barristers aren't supposed to have direct contact with clients, but she gave it to me. I said I wanted to check on him. I don't think she believed me, but Davina is used to turning a blind eye. She was always going to be our best bet.

It's the most surreal feeling, to be with him again. Only a few weeks ago I thought I'd lose him for ever. For the next few hours, I barely let go of him. We sit in front of the fire, drinking wine, eating food, acting like a normal couple. Yet again, we exist only within four walls, but this time, it feels different. There is a glimmer of hope for us now. It is professionally inappropriate, but not seedy or illicit. We have to take the small wins.

I tell Jack about Julian and how I am now free of him. He struggles to hide how happy he is about the news and sweeps me up in his arms, whispering into my ear, 'I'm so proud of you.'

We don't talk about the trial. It feels like something we endured and were lucky to survive. There's no need to rake over it. It's in the past. We're only looking forward now.

In bed that night, I lie in his arms as the wind whips around outside and the radio plays on low. A vanilla-scented candle burns on his bedside table. There's something about being in a dark room with just music and the sounds of nature.

'I don't want to do this any more,' I say to him, breaking the silence. It feels a brave statement but one I am absolutely sure about.

'What?' he asks, confused. 'Us?'

'No, not that,' I reassure him. 'I want that. I want all that. I mean everything else. Law. The Bar . . .'

He looks at me with concern in his eyes. The gentle glow from the candle makes him look even more beautiful – can a man be beautiful?

'But that's your life.'

'I'm not sure I want to be that person any more.'

'What exactly *do* you want?'

'You said last year you wanted to go to Australia. Now I'm free of Julian, there's no reason we can't.'

It feels scary and brave but very right.

'Are you absolutely sure about this?' he asks, looking at me intently.

'Yes.' I nod. 'I want to disappear with you, start again.'

He sweeps a piece of hair off my cheek.

'Then let's do it,' he says. 'If you want me to run away with you, I'm all for it.'

His eyes lock with mine and I know he means it. This is all we've wanted, to be together, away from everyone and everything. We kiss each other harder than we ever have. Although we've been through a lot to get here, this is exactly where we were supposed to end up.

I sink into him, knowing the girl I was is not the girl I am now. Delilah. Leila. I can put everything behind me and start again with Jack. Live on my own terms. Maybe even take on a new name. Be who I am and get it right this time.

Because everyone can change, even me.

72

Leila

Four weeks after trial

'Could the remaining passengers for Qantas flight QA13 please make their way to the boarding gate immediately?'

It's happening. It's really happening.

Usually, on a Wednesday morning at 6 a.m., I'm dashing around trying to get ready for whatever case I have that day.

Instead, I'm at Manchester Airport with Jack, holding an oversized Toblerone. In twenty-four hours, I'll be in Sydney. It's currently summer in Australia, and we've booked an apartment for a month not far from the beach.

My professional qualifications should expediate any visa application, and Jack just wants to get as far away from the UK as possible.

I brought Jack's old phone with me on this trip, and I intend to dispose of it in Australia. It's the one thing that still links me to the case. It didn't take much for Quinn to crack, and I hear he confessed to his part in Lewis's death shortly after Jack's trial. Obviously, he painted it as an act of bravado gone wrong, and the prosecution accepted a plea of manslaughter. He'll have glittering mitigation and be out of prison in a few years.

It's not justice in the way Eddie and Daniella know – is it ever, for parents who lose a child in such a cruel and senseless way?

Quinn also admitted to placing a tracker on my car, which surprised me. I'd assumed it was Elise. He'd been keeping tabs on me so he could scare me away from delving into his involvement with Jack. He obviously didn't understand who he was dealing with.

'You ready, then?' Jack says, towering above me wearing a black T-shirt and shorts. He's already dressing for Aussie weather, it seems. I like it.

'No turning back now!'

He takes my hand (the one not occupied by said enormous Toblerone) and we walk to the gate. There are a few passengers ahead of us getting their documents checked before walking down the tunnel towards the plane.

'Look, I need to tell you something,' Jack says, turning to me.

'What is it?' I ask, immediately searching for a threat. Even now, I can't stop being on high alert. I know Elise is dead, but the feeling of her closing in lingers. Her body still hasn't been found, but I'm certain there's nothing linking her to me that the river wouldn't have washed away.

He pauses before squeezing my hand.

'I've never been on a plane this big before,' he says, looking embarrassed. 'Can I have the window seat?'

Laughing, I lean up and kiss his cheek. Tell myself to relax.

'Of course! But you're not allowed to fall asleep the entire flight. I need someone to talk to.'

The people in front of us take ages, so I start to look around the airport lounge.

In the distance, I see a police officer walking quickly, talking into his radio. People move out of the way for him, watching as he passes. I continue to stand in line and turn to face forward, gripping Jack's hand a little tighter. Remind myself that I tied up all loose ends. That they have not come for me.

After a few seconds, I look back, and the police officer is nearer now. Behind him are another three – all running. Turning the other way, I see more officers and men in suits heading towards our gate.

Except they're not just normal men in suits. They're detectives.

The flurry of activity is too obvious to ignore now. People around us are craning their heads, asking what's going on.

They're here for someone else. You need to relax.

They get closer and closer on both sides, and Jack eventually spots what's happening. He turns to me with fear in his eyes, the same fear I saw every day at court. I realize, then, that my first instinct was right.

They have come for me.

I know I only have seconds now. I take Jack's face in my hands and look directly into his eyes.

'Tell them everything,' I demand. 'The whole truth, and nothing but the truth. I love you.'

By the time I drop my hands, we are surrounded by police officers. They shove Jack out of the way. He is grabbing for me, shouting, but I remain still. I know what's to come.

The detective sergeant stands in front of me. We don't know each other – our paths have not crossed professionally – but I can see how much he's relishing this. His big moment.

'Leila Kesler, I'm arresting you on suspicion of murdering Anton Smythe. You do not have to say anything. But it may harm your defence if you do not mention, when questioned, something which you later rely on in court. Anything you do say may be given in evidence. Do you understand?'

I know how important this is. Most defendants don't really listen to the words in the criminal caution, but the response to it can make or break your defence. The words you say in the seconds following arrest are pored over in a trial.

I've often wondered what I'd say if my past caught up with me. A million thoughts rush through my head. I think about what Delilah would say and what Leila would say. Two ends of the spectrum. A choice.

Who am I now?

Here, with the man I love more than anything, after what I've already put him through, there's only one thing I can say. I know the weight it will hold, its significance, its consequences.

'Jack had nothing to do with it. This was all me.'

And in that moment, Leila Reynolds transforms into the person I never thought she'd be brave enough to become. Dad would be utterly disgusted.

Just the way I like it.

Epilogue

Delilah

R v Delilah Reynolds
Rule #12
Always Have a Backup Plan

'IF THIS TRIAL has taught you anything, ladies and gentlemen, it's that not everything is as it seems. One thing you *can* be sure of, however, is that this defendant is not trustworthy. The Crown rejects the preposterous tale offered by the accused. It is one of a fantasist. One of a liar. One of a killer. And in due course, I will invite you to return a guilty verdict.'

John Henley-Bow KC prosecutes my murder trial. He is quite the savage beast. Aggressive – he reminds me of Julian. I'd never heard of him before – he was instructed from London (very fancy), given the high-profile nature of the case. He kept me in the witness box for a whole day. It was a relentless attack, in which he called me a liar, a manipulator, and a delusional woman who lived by a set of 'harmful rules' that made me 'a danger to everyone I came into contact with'.

A bit overdramatic, if you ask me.

He forced Jack to give evidence against me, of course, which he did, reluctantly, as per my instructions. I watched and listened as the details of our affair were laid bare in court for the world to hear. Printed in newspapers for people to ridicule.

My downfall was the phone.

Fury surges through my body, even now, when I think about it. A monumental mistake. I should have known better. Watching the video play out in court was the lowest moment of my life. A final fuck-you from Elise beyond the grave, whose body remains missing. I thankfully haven't been charged with her murder. Yet. She'd sent the video to her mother, Lynette, the day we met on the bridge, with instructions to send it to the police if she suddenly went missing. I never stood a chance.

Life's not fair.

Quite.

There it was, for all to see – a murder filmed on camera. The question was, was I acting in defence of another? If the jury decided that I was, then I'm not guilty and free to go. If they think I wasn't, I face life imprisonment.

And everything came out in this trial.

Everything.

The press has had a field day with it. They've heard it all. Well, they think they have. No one suspects the house fire was me. They still refer to it in court as an 'accident'. At least I still have that. My revenge against Dad is mine to keep.

Maxine Connor KC defends me. I wanted a woman to do it. She's very good. Her closing speech is persuasive. Not quite how I'd have executed it, but probably the best anyone else could do. Obviously, I thought of representing myself, but you must consider how everything looks to a jury. There's an arrogance to doing that, and the last thing I want them to think is that I'm some kind of narcissist.

They've been considering their verdict now for two and a half days and were given a majority direction this morning, as they weren't able to reach a unanimous decision. I've rattled them.

But now they have reached a verdict, so here we are.

I stand, ready to face my fate. I know the drill. Sticking with tradition, I wore the slick trouser suit I always wear for important trials. My hair, now fully blonde again, is tied back into a sleek ponytail. And, of course, I wouldn't go near a courtroom without my red lipstick. If I'm going down, I'm going down in style. The jury foreman stands up.

'Have you reached a verdict upon which at least ten are all agreed?'

'Yes.'

'On count one, a charge of murder, do you find the defendant guilty or not guilty?'

It's true what they say about time slowing down in these moments.

Just like it did on that night.

I've spent the last six months going over and over it. *If only I hadn't let him film us. If only I hadn't picked up that kettlebell.*

I'd love to say it was an accident, but it wasn't. In that split second, I meant Anton Smythe real harm. I wanted him to die, because *fuck him*. I hope, in those final moments, he really suffered. I hope the pain was unimaginable. That in the half-hour before the ambulance arrived, he knew we were plotting to get away with it.

'Let's FaceTime your husband, shall we? See if he knows you're here,' he'd said. 'Not that he'll care. Rumour has it he's been knocking off your head of chambers' wife anyway. Younger, prettier, and better tits by the looks of things.'

Why must men be like this?

The only good to come from it is that he told me about Demi, and I found a way finally to get Julian out of my life. Seeing the panic wash over his face when I had that wine sent to our cabin was priceless. Or catching him in his late-night phone call with

Demi and watching him try to lie his way out of it. I thank Anton for that.

But how *dare* he threaten everything else, everything I'd worked so hard for?

All my life, I've been tested by toxic men who have underestimated me and tried to drag me down – my dad, Julian, and now Anton. A triad of males who controlled, abused, and threatened to derail me and my achievements. I couldn't let it happen again.

I didn't tell the jury that, though, of course. They wouldn't understand. They needed a version that made me more tolerable, less murderous, more . . . relatable.

Likeable.

The tragic childhood. The abuse. Dad's obsession with power that he transferred to me. The rules, scrutinized one by one. How I managed not only to survive, but to thrive, by becoming a barrister. Ending up in an emotionally abusive marriage, only to be saved by a criminal who helped me find redemption. Ironically, honesty might be the thing that saves me in the end.

A jury loves nothing better than an unbelievable story. And nobody has a more unbelievable story than I do. If I've learned anything from watching jurors for thirteen years it's that they don't want facts, they want to be entertained. They want a show. And I'm the best actress there is.

Rule #12: Always Have a Backup Plan.

So, I return to my original question. What is real justice?

Now you know my story and every nuanced crevice of this case. Am I the hero or the villain?

Nothing is ever black and white, especially when it comes to the law.

But it's out of my hands now.

Guilty or not guilty?

You decide.

Acknowledgements

There isn't a thank-you in the world big enough for my agent, Sarah Hornsley. It's been quite the journey, but one I'm glad you held my hand on. When the call eventually came, it was worth every second of disappointment that preceded it. Thank you for believing in me.

This book would not be the version you have read today without the vision of my editorial team. I knew from the moment I met my UK editor, Francesca Pathak, that I was in expert hands. Her support and enthusiasm for this novel has only increased since day one. Thank you, Francesca, for everything.

Thank you to Rachael Kelly, my razor-sharp US editor. As soon as I read that letter, I knew you were the right person to take this novel to North America, alongside Caroline Payne and the rest of the magnificent Dutton team.

Enormous thanks to Lucy Hale, Laura Carr, Jon Mitchell, Anna Shora, Laura Sherlock, Emily Sumner, Rosie Friis, Claire Bush and the rest of the phenomenal team at Pan Macmillan, who have publicized this book and sold rights across the world. To the art teams who designed the outstanding covers for this novel – you took this brief and smashed it out of the park. Thank you to all my foreign publishers: because of you, this story will reach readers across the globe. I can't believe I just said that.

Thank you to my film and TV agent, Rosie Gurtovoy, for creating some of the most exciting opportunities, and for introducing me to a world I didn't know I could be a part of.

Thank you to Isabelle Broom, Cesca Major, Kate Gray, Steph McGovern and Nicola Sturgeon for championing my book all weekend at the Theakston Old Peculier Crime Writing Festival 2025 in Harrogate, even when I wasn't in the room and they had nothing to gain from it. Women supporting women at its finest.

To the authors, booksellers, librarians, book reviewers and readers – thank you for your passion for books and unwavering kindness. I've never known a community like it. You really are the reason we do this.

I have always been fascinated by dark psychology. When you cross-examine criminals for a living, it offers an insight into how the darkest minds work. The amateur psychologist in me had a desire to understand the origin of this mindset, which is often rooted in trauma. When a child feels unsafe, they develop coping mechanisms which are effective when they're little, but cause chaos as adults. Growing up in that kind of environment can make you cynical; it can also make you cold and ruthless, the only way you know how to survive. You become a prisoner within your own trauma – the unspoken rules set for you in childhood – and it feels impossible to escape. I broke those rules, I made it out, and I took Leila with me. Thank God for therapists.

Forgive me (and Leila) for tweaking legal procedure slightly. You got the good, dramatic bits.

My circle is small, but I couldn't have written this without the people in it. Specific thanks to my medical advisor/kettlebell expert, and the woman who keeps my chimp in check, Dr Lynette Ewart. Caroline Wilkinson, thank you for your fabulousness and wild voice notes. Chelsea Walker, I will always need our walks in the rain.

Finally, to my kids. Thank you for never complaining when I had a deadline, or especially that time in the summer holidays when I said to you, 'We won't be able to go many places over the next few weeks because I have an important thing I need to finish.' It was just before this book went out on submission. A month later, I sat you down and told you the news. Our lives had changed, and it was one of the proudest moments of my life. This is all for you.

Jo Murray grew up in Teesside during the 1990s when working-class girls were told they probably shouldn't try to become barristers. Thankfully, she ignored everyone. After studying Classics at Newcastle University, she went to law school and was a criminal barrister before leaving the profession to look after her two children. *Dissection of a Murder* is her debut thriller.